The Christmas Spirits

Whitley Strieber

CORONET

First published in Great Britain in 2011 by Coronet
An imprint of Hodder & Stoughton
An Hachette UK company

1

A CIP catalogue record for this title is available from the British Library

HB ISBN 978 1 444 73260 3
TPB ISBN 978 1 444 75537 4

Typeset by Hewer Text UK Ltd, Edinburgh
Printed and bound by CPI Group (UK) Ltd, Croydon, CR0 4YY

Hodder & Stoughton policy is to use papers that are natural, renewable
and recyclable products and made from wood grown in sustainable
forests. The logging and manufacturing processes are expected to
conform to the environmental regulations of the country of origin.

Hodder & Stoughton Ltd
338 Euston Road
London NW1 3BH

www.hodder.co.uk

This book is dedicated to Charles Dickens
and the spirits of Christmas.

I

A faint music of bells from the great carillon at St. Mary Magdalene, the old church two blocks away, drifted into George Moore's office. Megan came in, stopped and listened.

'So beautiful,' she said. 'Don't you just love Christmas?'

'Money is spent, that's for sure.'

'I mean the feeling of the season, the celebration of life.'

'I don't get it, frankly. All those presents. What's the point?'

She laughed. 'George Moore, at least nobody could call you sentimental. Presents are an important part of it. I love to sit and think about Charlie and Michael and what they'd enjoy.'

George hardly heard her. He was working, analyzing the market action in sugar futures.

'Why not try getting out into the streets? Enjoy the spirit of it! Or hop over to the Mag and leave a few gifts for the poor kiddies. Or the bus depot on Charles, it's closer, and they're collecting there, too.'

'Sentimental rubbish.'

'You're muttering.'

He got up and went to the door of his office. The trading floor was three-quarters empty. 'Great,' he said to himself. 'All I need.'

George had forbidden early departure. You didn't leave before your markets closed, not ever. There was always money to be made, every day, even in these slow, stifled days before Christmas.

His memo had been very clear: We are open when the markets are open and employees are expected at their desks at eight.

As far as the futures trading business was concerned, Christmas just got in the way.

When he'd started out, he'd traded for the legendary Bill Hill, whose philosophy was simple: you worked until you lost consciousness. There had been a sign in the office which read, 'If you don't come in on Sunday, don't come in on Monday.' In Bill's operation, it was not a joke. He kept records.

The carillon stopped at last, only to be replaced by the racket from the Salvation Army guy's boom box on the sidewalk just below.

He worked on, blocking the distractions as best he could.

By four, the snow was hissing against the windows and muffling the traffic noises from the street below – but not, unfortunately, the tinny carols emanating from the boom box. They used to have bands, those people, fools with blaring horns and tambourines. But at least it didn't go on and on and on. People have to stop and rest; boom boxes do not.

Megan appeared again. The glance he fired at her should have been enough to communicate his annoyance, but she kept coming. Her lips drew back into that simpering smile of hers. Yet again, he reflected that he needed a new assistant. But Megan was wonderfully cheap.

'Mr. Moore,' she said, the smile spreading into an astonishing fissure, 'Mr. Moore, I need to leave a little early today—'

'Please don't.'

'Michael isn't able to pick up Charlie—'

She'd often defeated him with that damned little boy. 'What's the problem with Charlie now?'

'He's coughing and his father can't get away.'

'You might not realize it, but this is a work day here, too.'

'Of course, I understand that, but – well, they've all left.'

'Not me.' He gestured toward the desk outside where his secretary sat. 'Not Miss Jefferson.'

'She—'

'What?'

'Nothing.'

Behind him, one of his array of monitors bleated a signal of the kind he liked to hear. Wheeling around in his chair, he saw that the position he'd set up in sugar futures that had looked so dismal all week had moved nicely into the money. He could take the profit off the table right now or wait for more the day after Christmas. He checked the technical indicators on the market. There were buyers still coming in. Should he wait, or take home a nice Christmas bonus right now? The price kept ticking up.

Then the monitor flickered. The lights flickered. The system crashed and began its reboot sequence.

There was nothing to do but wait, and he could be losing money. Damn the power company; they must surely have noticed by now that it snows in Chicago, so why weren't they prepared?

'Mr. Moore?'

He turned on her. 'Yes, Megan!'

'Can I?'

What was she about now? 'Can you what?'

'Go? For Charlie?'

He just couldn't stand it. His staff might be a gaggle of disloyal pricks, but *he* was working, couldn't she see that? 'No!'

'They can't wait with him, they don't do that.'

'Please make other arrangements. Thank you.'

'Mr. Moore—'

'Thank you, Megan.'

As she turned and hurried out, his system came back up. A moment later, he could hear her speaking into her phone, her voice urgent, but he couldn't care less. The system could go out again at any moment. He transmitted the orders that would take his profits, and none too soon. The close was less than a minute away.

He sat back, waiting for his fills. Outside, Megan was still jabbering away on the phone. He punched the intercom. 'Keep personal calls to a minimum, please. You know the rules.'

She started to respond, but he clicked her off.

That little boy, autistic – whatever that actually meant – or not, would no longer be allowed as an excuse. This was a workplace and she needed to respect that.

Which reminded him that she'd been late this morning for the fourth time this week, and he'd devised a little surprise for her. Now was the perfect time to spring it. He said into the intercom, 'Megan, how are you doing on those trading reports?' Annual evaluations of his traders were done every December. They told him whom he had to bonus, whom he could terrorize into taking a lower draw, and who needed to be sacked.

She appeared in the doorway. Her face was gleaming with tears. Fighting down his disgust, he looked up at her in silent question.

'That'll take through Christmas.'

'You haven't started them yet?'

'You didn't ask.'

'I did. At eight sharp. Over the intercom.'

'I'm sorry,' she said in a constricted voice, 'I was a little late coming in. I didn't hear.'

'And I didn't know you weren't there. So please get started. I'll expect them as soon as possible.'

'Right after Christmas.'

'Christmas is fine.'

'You don't mean Christmas day?'

'I'll be here at eight sharp.'

Megan flounced out. He listened to her heels clicking away across the tile floor of the outer office. He would make certain that her replacement, when she was found, would be childless.

Pressing the intercom button again, he said to Linda, 'Miss Jefferson, I'm leaving early today. I'll be going straight home, reachable on my cell if anything important comes in.'

'Yes, sir. Sir? Mr. Moore?'

'What?'

'I just want to let you know that I've accepted a position at Goldman Sachs.'

He took a deep breath. He was tempted to tell her to get out right now, but he couldn't afford to be without her. 'When?'

'January 2. Right after the holidays.' Her voice was flatly indifferent. She'd given him the absolute minimum amount of notice required by her employment contract.

'Nice,' he said. He clicked off the intercom.

His fills were back. He had made a hundred and twenty thousand dollars on the trade. A fair profit for the days he'd endured sweating it out. Fair enough.

The hell it was. If he'd stayed in he would have managed a half million by the middle of next week, maybe more. He was a damn coward, was what he was.

Well, the hell with it. Day before yesterday the position had been three hundred grand in the red, so who knew what would happen next week? No looking back, anyway, was there? Nobody evaluated the boss.

He shuffled on his overcoat, which was just beginning to fray but was still perfectly wearable. Then he tied his wool muffler snugly around his neck. He jammed on the winter hat he'd been wearing for ten years.

As he picked his way through the jammed desks of his traders, he had a shock. There was a huge food basket on Megan's desk. He saw canned duck terrine, a bottle of Pol Roger, luscious strawberries, dark, gleaming chocolates, *foie gras*, fat, juicy-looking dates and figs – the variety was extraordinary.

'What's this?'

She looked up at him, a frown of confusion crossing her face. 'We all got them. From you.'

'Not from me!'

'But – look.' She held out a card. On it was typed, 'Joy of the Season, George.'

'This is absolutely ridiculous. You say *everybody* got them?'

'Even Tuffy.'

'This is three hundred dollars' worth of food! Who gives a gift like that to a janitor? Let alone a roomful of hostile ingrates like my excuses for traders.'

'You do.'

He turned. Miss Jefferson stood beside her desk. 'I did it on your behalf. And they cost $349.50 each.'

'*WHAT?*'

'You have got to be the nastiest, meanest, most ungenerous man I've ever known, Mr. Moore.'

'How dare you do this to me! This is thousands of dollars' worth of gifts! You're a damn thief, is what you are, and I'm gonna wreck you over at Goldman.'

'You can't. Nobody cares what you say. You're the Scrooge of the commodities business, Mr. Moore. Everybody knows about you. Do you understand that? How despised you are?'

He didn't have to listen to this drivel. He'd make a few calls and put this bitch out on the street for the rest of her life. 'You're done here, Miss Jefferson. Gather up your personals and get out.'

'I'm done? I don't have to work out the notice weeks?'

'Get out of my office!'

She grinned from ear to ear. 'Well, merry Christmas to you, too, you old miser. Deck the halls with boughs of holly, I am outta here!'

Leaving her to box up her belongings, he strode across the trading floor and out to the elevator bank.

'Goodnight, Mr. Moore,' Megan said behind him, her voice dull. 'Merry Christmas.'

He kept going. But then he stopped. 'Happy Saturnalia,' he said back to her.

'Excuse me?' Her eyes were moist. Still crying. Stupid cow.

'Saturnalia,' he said. 'It was the Roman winter festival. The Christians took it over. Nobody knows when Christ was born. Or if.'

Julie Jefferson said, 'It's a time of the heart. That's why you hate it. You haven't got one.'

'A pagan festival became a Christian festival. It's still a lot of magical thinking and sentimental rubbish.'

'No heart, no life. You ought to think about that.'

Why bother to reply? He didn't give a damn what she or anybody else thought of him. He was one of the world's most successful traders. That's what he gave a damn about.

He waited in the dim corridor for the elevator. The lights flickered again. What the hell was going on?

Slowly, the car came clanking up. Slower than ever, he thought. His time was extremely valuable and Ed Cogner needed to get that through his thick skull, because who else was going to rent this rat-hole? If Moore Futures left, Cogner would end up with a couple more starving detectives and fly-by-night phone sex operations like he had on his other floors. Or, more likely, with empty space.

As it dropped, the elevator clanked even more. The last time he'd been trapped in it, he'd assured Cogner that there would be a lawsuit if it happened again.

Once, the building had been pretty grand. You could see that by the marble columns that disappeared into the lobby's dropped ceiling.

There was no doorman, which was fine by him. Who needed some old man sitting down here blowing his nose and farting all day long? Just another mouth to feed, part of the vast and worthless human mass. That was the basic truth of this world, a truth that he had realized as a boy. He'd watched his father defeated in business by his own inability to deal with the reality of buying and selling, which is that the process has victims.

What you get, somebody else loses. Today he'd taken a hundred and twenty grand from somebody who'd bet wrong in the sugar market. Right now, somewhere on planet Earth, that guy was going home without his damn money, and happy Saturnalia to you, sir.

He stepped out into the weather, the infamous Chicago wind already driving great gusts of snow in off Lake Michigan.

An odd figure came toward him, a small woman draped in the black of a nun's habit. Her head down, she pushed against the wind.

He did not care for nuns. Among his earliest memories was the moment that Sister Euphrasia had said that everybody was to wave a last time to their mothers standing in the hall, and had then closed the door to the first grade classroom. He had not cried, because his mother had not been there. She'd dropped him off and gone on to work. While the other children cried and tried to escape, he'd taken out his colored pencils and drawn.

His mother had not cared much for him. She'd made that plain enough. She'd often said that she'd wanted a daughter. She'd only been able to bear the one child.

The nun in her old-fashioned habit came like a shadow from the past, her hands clutching a black can

The Christmas Spirits

with a white cross painted on it. The hands were narrow and blue. Spider-like skin wrapped the bones. She shook the can, making the change in it clink.

Revolted, even a little frightened, he hurried past her.

The snow was pouring out of the sky now, but even so the street was full of happy people, jerks humping along lugging bags of presents, people grinning, ruddy faced in the biting cold. On the corner, 'White Christmas' blared out of the Salvation Army boom box.

A ragged family appeared, gypsies or Muslims or whatever, the father puffing along with snowflakes in his moustache, grinning. The mother wore a black veil. Her face was visible, her eyes dark and wide with pleasure, reflecting the glitter of the Christmas lights that overhung the street. She was delicately beautiful, fragile in the snow.

Two rosy-cheeked boys clutched her hands. Their clothes were thin, the children shivering.

'Merry Christmas,' the man said, his voice aggressively cheerful.

George moved faster, trying to get around them. But then the wife was in front of him, and then she was tripping. As she fell, she thrust her baby toward him.

13

He was a man with a temper, always had been, and as he dodged her, he couldn't resist colliding with her shoulder, just to feel the blow, just to feel his outrage satisfied, and most especially to knock the cardboard baby to the street.

The cardboard baby scam was the latest pickpocket dodge. He'd read about it in the *Tribune*. While the victim fumbled with the fake infant, the rag-tag children picked his pockets.

Reeling, she cried out. The baby went tumbling from her arms and fell onto the snowy sidewalk. Struggling for balance, she fell hard against the side of a parked car and ended up in a heap of black cloth in the snow, her limbs flailing like the legs of a spider as she groped for the infant.

It was a real baby. Her slip had been a genuine accident. As the father and the boys sprang to help her, George, fearing a lawsuit, pushed past them.

In the distance the carillon began playing again, its bell tones cascading through the wintry evening.

He got to the street corner and started to cross against the 'Don't Walk' sign.

An unexpected sight froze him where he stood.

Somehow, the nun had come to be there. She'd been behind him, and she hadn't passed him, but here she was. She seemed to be watching him. Staring at him. *Was* it Sister Euphrasia, grown incredibly old?

No, that could not be. Forty years ago, she'd already been old.

In any case, the closer he looked, the more it came to seem that this was not actually an old face, but rather one that was young but wizened, as if she'd reached the age of eleven or twelve and matured no further, only dried up.

He couldn't take his eyes off her, which she clearly knew. When she smiled he saw blackened teeth. Her eyes were sunken pits. But there was a girlishness that shone in the grin. She shook her tin, grinning and nodding.

The snow swirled around him as the bells resounded with 'Adeste Fideles'.

He turned to get away from the weird nun, but his way was blocked.

The beggar, his face dark in the driving snow, was standing in his way.

2

The beggar's eyes were twinkling. He said, 'You dropped this.' George looked down and there was the one object of any value that he possessed, the Montblanc pen he'd won as Bill Hill's most profitable trader of 1994.

George took the pen from the jerk and slipped it back into his inner pocket. How had it ever fallen out?

'Are you having merry Christmastime?' the man asked in his thick accent. 'We are having happy time, our first America Christmas. We are from Lebanon.' He smiled again. 'So happy. So happy in my soul.' He spread his arms. 'The Christmas of Jesus, everywhere here!'

'Yeah, yeah,' George muttered. Wasn't the guy Muslim, though? Or were there Lebanese Christians? Whatever, George was trapped between the nun and the Lebanese family. He was about to thread his way out into the street traffic to escape them when he realized that the nun had gone.

He crossed as fast as he could without actually running. He feared that the man would be staring after him with hurt dog eyes and he just didn't care to deal with that. No reward had been on offer. He hadn't even realized he'd lost the pen.

As he moved through the driving snow and the falling dark, he watched for the nun. He did not want her and her jingling can anywhere near him. He might have given her a dime but he had no change. He'd have to offer a dollar and who knew if she was even a real nun? From the looks of her, she was probably some sort of addict in costume.

In any case, he was ready for dinner at Bickford's, some market analysis at his home workstation and then bed. Markets rise early and information flows twenty-four hours a day. Unless you're plugged in, you're a waste of space. The best were not just the smartest, but the smartest who worked hardest.

He ate his dinners at a cafeteria because if you added the shopping and cooking time and transportation charges to the cost of staples at Costco or Wal-Mart, the cafeteria won easily – as long as he didn't indulge in expensive entrees. Six dollars could make a meal at Bickford's, from salad to a small dessert.

As he passed along the line, Hosie – at least, that's what his name tag said – offered a smiling 'Merry Christmas.' George managed to drag his lips into a smile in return. Lupe at the checkout, thank God, was her usual self, comfortably sour.

He'd gotten a piece of fried fish, some spinach, some rice and lime Jello, and a glass of water. Tonight was going to be a good night: five dollars, fifty-three cents. There was a turkey plate on special for nine ninety-five. But he knew that it would be there tomorrow for three dollars less. A day older, but what difference did that make?

His usual table was occupied by a young couple giggling over glasses of Bickford's rotgut wine. Another annoyance. He liked being a creature of habit, and that was *his* table. No choice but to find another, which he did, in a spot as out-of-the-way as possible.

He ate methodically, chewing carefully. In his business, digestion was always an issue, and he certainly didn't want to spend money on a doctor. He stared out the big picture window, watching the flow of people. Across the street, the windows of Taylor Brothers were aglow with Christmas lights. In some of them, live models moved slowly around in seasonal cocktail dresses. How much did they have to pay those beauties to do that? Ridiculous.

There was also the obligatory Santa Claus. He sat in a little sort of an igloo. Plaster reindeer danced across the top of his window, and a sign urged children to come in and meet him. Just the sort of place Megan would take her little cripple.

But what in the world was wrong with the Santa, lurching like that? Was the man drunk? And those elves – God, who'd dreamed up those dark blue costumes? They looked more like trolls.

A drunk Santa, trolls instead of elves. No wonder Taylors' was having trouble. Actually, it was having the same trouble that beset downtown department stores all over the world. Big box chains and the internet were killing them. In another year or so, the place would be as empty as Adler's.

In fact, now that he thought of it, Taylors' stock might be a decent medium-term negative play. Short a few hundred thousand shares in anticipation of a bankruptcy, then blog negative rumors to speed matters along. He made a mental note of it.

But wait a minute. *What* was going on in the Santa window?

The elves were actually dragging the looped Santa away. Very funny: the man struggled to retain his seat of honor but they pulled him toward the rear of the display . . . and there he went, back behind the curtain.

It shook and waved. Santa was putting up a fight. Then his head reappeared. The beard was off and the man seemed to be screaming.

He was whipped out of sight, and this time the curtain remained closed.

A moment later, the entire store went dark. Another power failure, apparently.

Bickford's was fine, at least for now.

The crowd continued to pass Taylors' windows, indifferent to the disappearance of the Santa.

And here was the damn nun again, creeping along, shaking her can. Merciful heavens, what would make that creature go away?

Behind her, the lights came on again and Taylors' returned to normal – absent its Santa, of course. In the other windows, the parading models pranced in their cocktail dresses.

He was reminded of Christmas cocktail parties with that god-awful eggnog they always served. As always, he'd been invited to the Chicago Mercantile Exchange's party. No thank you. He'd been once. They'd sung 'O Holy Night'. Imagine, that crowd singing about anything holy. Hilarious.

The lights in the cafeteria flickered. Damned incompetent fools at ComEd.

And then George noticed that the table opposite him was occupied. A moment ago, it had been empty. He'd been looking right at it. So where had the old man now sitting there come from?

He caught George's eye. It was just the briefest connection, but it communicated what George feared was a desire for contact. The old waste of space saw another singleton and was hoping for some conversation.

George loathed social conversation, and with strangers – never.

The old man looked somewhat like Bill Hill; but Bill, of course, was dead. He hadn't been a conversationalist, either. 'Work, don't talk,' was another of Bill's very smart sayings. Talk wastes time and time is money. Therefore, talk wastes money.

Eating methodically, he kept his eyes on his plate.

'Hey, fella, you alone during Christmas? Me, too.'

He even sounded like Bill. Bill had dropped dead at fifty-six, right in the middle of his trading room.

The fool was still peering at him, so George finished his meal, gobbling down the last morsels and draining his water glass. Then he got out of there.

It was very windy now, causing the snow to blow in great gusts that drove the greasy gray flakes down George's neck and under his hat. He hurried through the crowds that still surged beneath the wind-whipped Christmas lights.

When he turned onto the old industrial block where he lived, there were no more crowds and – thankfully – no more of those red and green lights, grinning Santas and reindeer cutouts that filled the main thoroughfares.

In times past, this part of the city had been a thriving manufacturing center. No more, though, thanks to all the jobs being shipped off to Asia. And why the hell not? You could manufacture a pair of sneakers in Bangladesh for under a dollar and sell it here for eighty. Plus there were no unions, no damn safety restrictions, and never a labor issue or tax problem that a little *bakshish* couldn't fix.

People in the West whined about being out of work. Then they went out and bought sneakers made in Asia with their fat unemployment checks.

There was still some light manufacturing in several of the buildings. A bag manufacturer was here taking advantage of the pool of illegal immigrants in the neighborhood. A machine shop survived because it was faster to get things repaired locally than send them to Vietnam or wherever. A couple of printers eked out a living somehow. But mostly, the neighborhood was abandoned, so his rent was pleasantly cheap.

Halfway down the block stood his building, a relic from another era, small and dark, crowded between a nameless structure where they precooked food for Chinese restaurants and an empty warehouse which George knew to be full of rats – slow, imperturbable giants he always feared might get into his place.

The snow was really coming down, so he was glad to be getting home. The decision to leave early had been the right one.

He'd fix himself a cup of tea and watch the Asian markets open. The smart bastards didn't do Christmas.

Behind him, as he unlocked the heavy front door, he heard a scraping sound. A shadow loomed at the end of the block, a bum pushing a rickety shopping cart.

Goddamnit, it was the guy from Bickford's. The worthless old creature had followed him here.

George got the door opened fast and hopped into the building before the man had come another twenty feet. Slamming it hard, he twisted all three locks.

The scraping sound got closer. Was the old fart considering ringing his buzzer? Let him try. George had disconnected it years ago.

There was a walk-in tax accountant on the ground floor and a psychic above him. Neither was here at this time of day. George mounted the creaking stairs two at a time. He kept himself in good shape, and these stairs were one of the reasons. Stairs meant cheaper rent and better health, a double win as far as he was concerned. No need for gym membership, not with these babies waiting for him when he got home every night. He had no intention of following Bill Hill to an early grave.

He reached his apartment, opened the door, and entered its gloom. You never left lights on, that was stupid. The air was cold, freezing, in fact. You never left heat on, either, or just enough to keep the pipes from freezing.

Carefully, he closed the door and locked all four locks, then he tried it to make sure.

So he was home, and another day had ended – at least, on this side of the world. He looked over toward his home workstation. Asia was opening shortly. Time enough, though, for a cup of tea first. Time, even, to admit that he was a bit tired.

He'd close his eyes for half an hour. Then back to work.

3

His apartment consisted of a front room used for living and dining, with an open kitchen against the back wall. Behind it was a short hallway lined with bookshelves, and behind that the bedroom and bathroom with its ancient claw-foot bathtub. The bathroom was original to the structure, the kitchen appliances maybe fifty years old. But they worked, and he generally only ate breakfast here, so they were more than adequate.

He lit the gas under the kettle and turned on his workstation. It was the one thing in the apartment that was new, and it was a state-of-the-art system, identical to the one in his office. Twenty thousand dollars' worth of computer equipment connected to his own servers via a T-1 line. He could trade as quickly from here as he could from the office, and often sat through the night scalping the S&P 500 electronic futures or trading Asia. He was an efficient scalper, and could make twenty grand between midnight and dawn. His record was a hundred and fifty-three thousand dollars in the overnight session, on the night in 2008 that the market fell apart.

The lights flickered. What in *hell* was going on? There was a beep from across the room. His system was rebooting. Fine, more time wasted. He should bill ComEd for it.

As the tea kettle whistled, he also heard – or thought he heard – another noise.

He pulled the kettle off the gas ring and listened. There it was again, a scrape, very distinct. It was followed by a thud.

Could it be the rats?

No, there was something being dragged. Or no, now it sounded like wheels. So it must surely be outside. Was it the bum, still out there pushing his grocery cart up and down, waiting for George to reappear?

Shit! Bickford's was wonderfully cheap, but if this kind of thing kept happening, he was going to find another cafeteria.

The lights flickered. Enough, already!

He listened. Another scrape, then a thud, deep, then more scraping. There was a rhythm to it and it was getting louder.

It was not outside, it was *coming up the stairs.*

He grabbed the phone, pressed it to his ear, hammered out an emergency call. But the line was dead. Worse, the lights were now going out for seconds at a time.

Another scrape, another thud. Very loud now. Whatever this was, it was now on the third landing.

A long scrape and then silence, then a distinct groan and another thud.

Thinking to call the police, he fumbled his cellphone out of his pocket – and was shocked to discover that the signal was gone.

The doorknob rattled. He had a pepper spray in his workstation desk. He fumbled toward it – and proceeded to knock one of his monitors to the floor with a terrific crash.

There went two grand.

The door rattled hard and unnaturally, as if it was being shaken by some kind of machine.

Please don't let this be a kidnap. If they weren't professionals, you could be killed.

Through the door he heard a low sound, almost a rumble. For a moment, he couldn't tell what it was, but when he pressed his ear against it, he began to discern a word, repeated again and again.

'George . . . George . . . George . . .'

No, it could not be.

Then he heard something else . . . slow, deliberate, and precise.

Something was breathing. It was in the room. It was behind him.

This was impossible. The door was locked.

'George . . .'

Panic frothed within him. He wanted to run, but the front door was still clearly locked. Slowly, he turned around.

He found himself face to face with something so incredible that, had he not been wide awake, he would have been convinced was the worst nightmare of his life.

Standing before him was a shadowy form, its eyes dull, its face covered by dirty gray stubble. The hair, what there was of it, was lank and greasy.

It was the bum.

'Get out of here!'

The reply was a rasping chuckle.

'Get *OUT*!'

The apparition shook his cadaverous head.

With him he had brought two things: a grocery cart full of rotted clothes, old newspapers, electronic debris and black plastic bags; and the cloying odor of death.

There issued from him a long, rattling cough that seemed to echo off into some deep, unseen cavern. He gestured toward George's one dining chair. 'I'm tired,' he said. 'So tired.'

Surprise was not enough of a word to describe what George was feeling, because this was Bill Hill. Unmistakably. But Bill was dead and buried. He slumped heavily into the chair.

'Everything you've been led to believe about death is a lie.'

'But I was at your funeral. I was at the viewing, I saw you dead!'

Slowly, gravely, he shook his head.

'So you—' George stopped. He couldn't think how even to finish the question. 'You were embalmed. I saw you at the viewing. Dead and full of formaldehyde, Bill. I saw you!'

'You're missing your life, George,' Bill Hill said. 'Look at me; I never really lived, either.'

'You were rich!'

He gestured toward the shopping cart. 'It's all in there. We walk the streets of Chicago together, me and my wealth.'

'The dead don't walk the streets.'

Bill's laughter ground through the silence.

With an uneasy hand, George reached out. He had to touch this man. He had to feel if he was real or if he was some sort of bizarre illusion.

Bill's hand was as dry as a dead leaf, and ice cold. But it was definitely real.

George was at a loss. 'Who the hell are you?'

The man groaned again, uttering a sound that seemed to contain all the cold of the night. As if in sympathy, the wind wailed in the eaves of the old house and the structure shook with a great gust as if from the beyond.

George then found himself looking directly into the saddest eyes he had ever seen. A horrible chill shuddered through him, the kind of chill that announces a heart attack or a stroke, and he thought, 'Maybe I'm dying, maybe that's what this crazy hallucination is all about.'

Bill Hill now uttered a harsh, bitter growl. It was a moment before George realized that he was laughing. 'You're not dying yet,' he said. 'But when you do, you'll be like me, George, pushing your cart on the same route from Jefferson Park to East Chicago, back and forth, back and forth.'

'But what – Bill – you're saying that you're dead, but you're here?'

Still Bill did not look away. 'Hell isn't underground—'

'That's crap. There is no hell. I don't know what's going on here but hell and heaven – that's grade school blather. Whatever you are, you're obviously not burning in hell.'

'The world of the dead is all around you.'

'Street people are actually the dead? Come on!'

'We're hidden among the street people. We rub shoulders with you all the time.'

'Whoever you are, you're here because you're alive. End of story.'

'Love is the only thing worth taking with you into death.' He gestured toward the cart. 'Nothing in there matters – not the money—'

'Money? You've got money in that cart?'

Again laughter came, but this time it was high and full of howl and anguish. 'George, there are millions in that cart, but I am poorer than the poorest beggar on the poorest street on earth.' Another groan escaped him. 'I kept putting off doing something with my money – endowing some charity or whatever. I dropped dead. No warning.' He leaned forward. 'I felt a crushing weight on my shoulders and an emptiness within that was the worst thing I have ever known.' His whole body shook as if with a seizure, and once again his eyes locked onto George's.

What George saw there was a vast, stinking, rotting ocean of garbage that heaved like the tormented flanks of a beached sea monster. It was like an immense discard of greed.

'What you see is my soul,' said Bill. 'I am sorry to tell you that yours is worse.'

'*Worse*? How could it be worse?'

Bill stood up. Before George's horrified eyes, he began shuffling toward the door.

George ran to him and grabbed at him. 'No!'

To George's touch, Bill seemed as insubstantial, almost, as the air itself. But when he turned back toward George, his movements were slowed by what appeared to be a great burden. 'My memories weigh me down,' he said. 'They're chains draping me.' He sighed. 'With my money, I could have given hundreds of thousands of children educations. Each ignorant mind, each failed life, is another link in my chain. When you're dead, you remember not only what you did, and that's bad enough. But you also remember what you didn't do, and that is agonizing.'

Now George saw a chance to assert himself. As terrible as this situation was, as pitiful as Bill seemed, it still had to be true that he was here for a reason. He uttered the words that he had dared not speak, for fear that the answer would be 'no'. 'Bill, do you have any advice for me?'

Bill was heading toward the door, and as he went, he was becoming a hazy sort of a blur, as if he was moving down the corridors of another reality altogether. 'You will be visited three times,' he said, his voice now fading. 'Notice them, George. That's what I've come here to tell you. *Notice them.*'

'But how? What should I look for?'

'They will walk out of your dreams, out of the air, out of the sky. Remember, George. They're your only chance. So *remember*!'

Then Bill Hill was gone. The apartment was entirely normal, the only trace of what had happened the smashed monitor on the floor.

The air filled with a wild, piercing whistle, so loud

that George screamed, so sharp that he clapped his hands over his ears.

It was the kettle. With shaking hands, he took it off the gas, and made his tea.

4

He huddled on the couch, cradling the cup in uneasy hands. 'No matter what you think, *it did not happen.*'

His words shuddered in the air. But no, he was right, Bill Hill had not been here. There had been no conversation. Could not be. He was overtired, that was all. It had been a rough week.

Best to shove it aside and keep going. 'A nightmare,' he muttered. Then, 'Talking to yourself now.' He laughed a little. It was ironic that a mind such as his, as rock-solid and stable as it was, would suddenly generate a hallucination as bizarre as that.

He did have, tucked away in the back of the pantry, a bottle of fine Scotch, Johnnie Walker Blue Label. Not the liter, of course, just the small bottle. It had been there for five years, receiving only the absolute minimum of use. A celebration, every so often, would justify a finger to be poured into the bottom of a glass. It had been bought the afternoon Bill died. He'd drunk a full shot from it, at least ten dollars' worth of whisky in a single, soft, soul-warming swallow.

Turning on lights as he went, he crossed to the tiny pantry, opened it, and felt for the bottle. Grasping it carefully, he took it out and put it on the kitchen counter. He looked at the Scotch inside, already half gone.

He picked up the bottle and put it to his lips, and drank and drank, and then gagged and coughed and slammed the bottle down. His head was blazing. A long, wet cough heaved through him.

Again he took the bottle and threw his head back and drank long and deep. Again, he slammed it down.

'Bill, my God, what happened to you? What the hell happened?'

The Scotch hit – a wonderful, reassuring anesthesia. Bill Hill didn't matter. Bill Hill hadn't been here. ''Course not,' muttered George. He laughed again. He looked out into the night, watched snow swirling past the living-room window, listened to the wind wailing in the eaves and rattling the gutters.

Dragging the bottle, he reeled back to his couch and threw himself down on it. Thing was, he could still smell Bill Hill. His garbage had stunk. He had stunk. That once fastidious man now didn't bathe, not since he'd become a street person.

But he'd been embalmed. George had seen him in his coffin, his face painted like a wooden doll's.

That bum was real. Damn right he was. Absolutely real. No matter what had seemed to happen in the past, it had not happened that way because Bill was alive. So he had not dropped dead, he had not been embalmed, he had not been buried.

Something else had happened. But what in holy hell was it?

He hit the bottle again, but a quivering wave of nausea caused him to leap up and run across the living room, down the narrow hall and through the bedroom with its carefully made bed, into the bathroom.

Great heaves wracked him as he bent over the toilet, clutching the bowl. Again and again they came, until he feared that he was going to faint and hit his head on the floor.

Bill Hill had been the dirtiest human being he'd ever seen. Ugly, ugly, ugly.

The heaves slowed, then stopped. He sat back on his heels, holding on to the rim of the toilet.

What the hell was going on?

The menacing elves were scary, the nun even more so. But this – this was unthinkable. Bill Hill was *dead*.

Oh, shit, I'm drunk . . . goddamn stupid ass, you can't trade drunk and Asia is open.

His gut stopped pitching.

Better – a little.

On trembling legs, he stood up from the toilet. Flushed the damn thing down. His filth, his weakness.

He went into the living room and sat down at his workstation, turning on the monitors that still functioned. Yes, this was his world, this was reality: the dancing numbers, the indicators snaking slowly across the charts, revealing to him where the minds of others were going, showing him how to beat them all right into the ground.

There, look at the yen, touching the lower line of its trading channel. Stupid people, they were shorting it. So he went long. And it continued down, sinking quickly through its ten-day moving average. He was down six thousand dollars. Through the twenty-day moving average. He was down fifty-three thousand. Had to hang on now, must get that money back. Through the fifty-day, down eight hundred and seventeen thousand.

No. NO!

Down one million and sixty-one thousand four hundred and six. Ten. Seventy-seven thousand. One million two hundred and six thousand.

He pulled the plug and watched what was left of his money come back into his cash account.

Now, that was a loss, that was. One million two hundred and fifty-three thousand six hundred and one dollars and fourteen cents. That was what the whisky had really cost.

It was his largest loss in years. He stared at the screen. Went to his foreign exchange account. Down from seventy-two million dollars to UNDER seventy-one! Just like that. That was money thrown away.

Drunk. Room reeling. Filthy smell still choking the air, Bill Hill's garbage, his filthy clothes, his body stink.

George heaved again, all over the couch. So there was a cleanup job, hours of work, quarts of cleaning fluid, the need to rent a steam-cleaner.

'Merry Christmas,' he shouted. The hell with this pigsty, he couldn't stand another minute in this hell-hole. He threw on his overcoat and hat, wrapped his scarf around his neck and unlocked the top lock.

What if – but no, Bill was long gone. Or was he? How could he know?

In quick succession, he threw back the center and bottom locks. He wanted to walk the lake front, breathe the icy air, get the alcohol and the feeling of dirtiness out of his system. He had to be where everything was clean and cold and he could be away from this crazy apartment and above all away from the memory of Bill Hill.

When he opened the door into what he expected would be the usual black pit that presented itself to him at night, he was surprised to find the narrow stairs visible in softly glowing light. But from where? How? The lights weren't on.

When he looked up at the skylight, he had a surprise. Morning had come. He looked at his watch. Six forty. But how could that be? Where had all the time gone?

Then he knew, of course. Obviously, the booze had knocked him out and he'd spent the night on the bathroom floor. That would also explain why his mouth was so dry and why he was so shaky. He needed strong tea and a good breakfast. Normally he made his own, but he wasn't going back into that apartment, not until he'd had it professionally cleaned from top to bottom. He refused even to think about what he'd seen. The hell with it.

He pounded down the stairs, moving as fast as he could without losing his footing, threw back the locks on the front door – and stopped.

What if he was still out there, still pushing his grocery cart up and down?

George surveyed the street. Snow had transformed the cityscape of grimy buildings and dark windows into something like childhood.

He'd made snow angels on days like this, with those boys from the old neighborhood, David and Franklin and Al, oh, and Larry Blair who'd bought it in Iraq. Funny thing to go so young, your life thrown away.

He took a deep breath of the smoke-shriveled air, tasting the tang of chimneys and the cutting freshness of the winter ice that covered Lake Michigan. They'd dared each other to walk out on that lake. Deadly game, for sure. How had they ever survived, any of them?

The city was more silent than memories of stillness, all detail softened into dream by the snow, which fell gently upon itself in the limitless streets, and upon the trudging, shaken man.

All he wanted was his breakfast, but the Dot Diner on the corner was closed, and because it was a holiday – Christmas Eve – Bickford's didn't open until eleven. There used to be a lunch counter in the drugstore, but it was a Rite Aid now. Open for business, but what kind of a breakfast could he get in there, a bag of corn chips and some canned chicken?

Please let Christmas be over. He'd lost a million dollars because of Christmas. Gotten sick drunk because of Christmas. Experienced terror.

'How about it, Santa, damn you, how about a poached egg?'

'Santa's gonna bring me new toe shoes.'

He stopped. The voice was as pure as sea foam, delicate but somehow powerful. It was happiness he was hearing, he realized, and that startled him. He'd never really noticed happiness in a voice before.

He turned toward the sound, and standing there in the entrance to a row house was a girl as tiny and exquisite as a firefly, wearing pink pajamas and scuffed old toe shoes. She tossed him a complicated, hesitant smile.

She did a solemn *plié*, deep and very grand, and he saw how small she was, and that she was shivering slightly.

The door behind her opened, and for the briefest moment there was music, 'The March of the Wooden Soliders' from the *Nutcracker*. The little girl laughed and turned around and said to a tall man standing in the doorway, 'It's my *stage*, Daddy!'

He picked her up and she threw her arms around him and the door closed.

George stood staring at the spot where the scene had unfolded. This was a slum, the house rickety, the steps crooked, the whole block, in fact, afflicted by the vast tiredness of old cities, the long lines of gray front walls, punctuated by windows that went nowhere.

He walked on, trudging toward the lake and more prosperous areas. He'd have to pay a damn fortune, but somebody somewhere had to be frying eggs. That was the marketplace, that was the way it worked. Close all the diners and restaurants, it would cross some guy's mind that there was an opportunity there.

Far ahead, in fact, he could see a familiar sign, a Denny's café. Well, hallelujah. Merry damn Christmas after all. He'd have tea, or even coffee, they cost the same at Denny's. He'd get eggs, sausages and toast, the whole deal. Oh, yes.

As he walked, he heard Mary Magdalene's bells again, this time rolling *Angels We Have Heard on High* across the quiet of the morning in a cascade of bell notes.

There was someone ahead at the end of the block, a man standing very still, his head down, staring at the snow-covered sidewalk.

Was he looking for something? Or frozen, perhaps, a street person who'd been overcome by the cold?

The snow drifted down. Shadows darted in the air, chimney swifts, he thought, disturbed by winter fires. The bells stopped, leaving a silence so deep that he could hear the whisper of the snow.

The figure moved. George remembered Bill Hill's words: 'Notice them!'

The figure made a beckoning gesture toward him.

This was crazy. It was part of the Bill Hill thing, some kind of out-of-control fantasy.

The figure gestured again, this time more forcefully.

George didn't have any intention of going closer. In fact, what he wanted to do was run in the opposite direction. But the next thing he knew, he had indeed taken a step toward the figure. He did not want to, but he could not seem to prevent himself. Another step followed, then another.

Still he struggled, still he attempted to turn and run, but every move he made had the same result: another step forward.

As he drew inexorably closer, his movements made stiff by the effort to resist, the man's face increased in definition.

George saw the smile there, as gentle as it was terrible, the smile at once of a lover greeting his beloved, and of a predator luring its prey.

As he drew closer yet, he realized that the unholy face was familiar.

'Who are you?' he shouted. 'What do you want from me?'

The nun's lips crinkled into an odd, slurping smile.

She opened her arms to him, and he was swept helplessly into her embrace.

5

When she touched him, it was as if the life-force of his body was removed into her long finger. He tried to shout for help but all that came out was a soundless puff of air.

Bright light shone down from above, as if a huge searchlight had been turned on.

George's feet lifted off the ground. He could not kick, he could not struggle, but instead watched helplessly as the sidewalk slipped away below him. Then he was looking down at the top of a streetlight gleaming with ice, and then into the canyon of the street.

Higher he went, until he could see the whole block spread beneath his feet, and then the neighborhood, even his own street, a gnarled scar off to his left. Finally he could see the lake, its quick, gray waves arrayed in military rows.

He was drawn into a tight room with an arched ceiling. The walls were woven of a fabric that reminded him of canvas. His mind, dulled by fear and helplessness, could not make sense of his situation. Unable to move, he lay on his side staring across a gleaming gray floor at dark brown ribs that arched upward to a peak. A round room, then. But where was it, on a roof, and how had he come to be up here? He knew that he'd gone up in the air, but how? Had he been on an elevator? No, he'd been outside. Pulled up by a crane, then? No, again, there was no crane on the street.

He'd just . . . risen.

It was impossible, of course, but he was beyond rejecting the impossible. He lay there, every muscle in his body screaming to move.

There was a sound, then a brief buzzing roar, as if an enormous insect just outside of his field of vision had sped its wings for an instant, then become still. As hard as he strained to see what was there, he could not.

The sound came again, and now he could detect movement at the edge of his field of vision. He lay there helplessly, watching as first one and then two and finally three of the most dreadful apparitions slid into his view, buzzing as they came.

He had seen them before but not this close. They had dragged the department store Santa away.

They wore dark blue overalls covered with many pockets. But it was not the uniforms which were disturbing, it was the broad faces of their wearers, frog-like, and their immense compound eyes, in which he could see thousands of glittering reflections of himself, a man lying still, his mouth opened wide, his eyes glaring insanely.

Now a voice started to speak, soft enough to seem female, but entirely lifeless. It kept repeating the phrase, 'What can we do to help you stop screaming?'

He hadn't realized that he was doing that, but now that he did, he couldn't stop.

Fear this deep unleashes an array of physical changes. Adrenaline runs out, blood pressure drops, the body is enveloped in catatonic plasticity, and the mind retreats into wintry silence.

It feels like peace, and perhaps to some extent the fact that his heart ceased to pound and his breath ceased to surge in his throat did bring a certain calm.

He felt them removing his clothes, their fingers fast with the buttons and the belt, their buzzing low now, as if it was their speech among themselves, and they were muttering to one another as they worked.

Then, very suddenly, he was naked. Very suddenly, also, he was alone. He lived a solitary life and part of the reason was that he was extremely private about his body. He wasn't ashamed of himself; it wasn't fat or malformed, but it was his private business. Almost by reflex, he moved his hand to cover himself – and found that he was no longer paralyzed.

The room was cool but not cold, and he could hear snow hissing against its thin walls. Seeing what might be a door, he went carefully toward it. Crouching and hunched, he protected himself as best he could. He felt along the door's arched seam, but the join was too fine for him to gain purchase. There was no handle, only a gleaming black half-orb in the center.

To his touch, it felt like glass, faintly warm. In it, he could see his own distorted reflection, his face warped as if by a funhouse mirror.

He went to one of the walls, which looked and felt like canvas or something like it, but had absolutely no give. It might as well have been steel. Finally, he went to the center of the room and jumped. The floor gave slightly, but there was nothing else.

'I'm going to give you an injection. Do not be alarmed.'

He threw himself away from the sound of the voice, falling against the wall in the process. He looked up to see a figure in a tattered gray robe, with arms like pipes and long claws. It had a narrow face, with complex lips, thin but human in their appearance, lips that communicated both laughter and sadness. Sad mirth. The eyes swam in darkness, like pools of night. He thought, 'That was once human, but it is not human now.'

Was it an alien or was it the nun transfigured? Is the truth, perhaps, that human beings are like caterpillars to such butterflies? But butterflies are beautiful, and this thing was certainly not that.

Of course, the caterpillar, on coming face to face with his own destiny, might find the butterfly hideous.

Then he saw, carried delicately in one of the claws, a syringe with a golden needle. From its tip there dripped yellow fluid.

'This will help you see,' the apparition said.

There was kindness in the tone, and feminine gentleness, too, despite its rumbling depth.

As the creature came closer and he could see it in more detail, George became aware of something unexpected. He had seen this thing before.

'I know you,' he whispered. 'But who are you?'

It stopped. Something changed in its face. Was it smiling? He could not be sure.

It said, 'Remember.'

The word entered his mind in a way that was at once unique and also completely familiar. The tone itself had power; he could feel it like an echo filling a great silence within him.

He felt a rush of love, respect, and awe not because he was in the presence of some alien being, but rather because this spirit, he knew, was part of the mystery and dignity of man.

'Teacher,' he heard himself say. 'Why have you brought me here?'

His own words dumbfounded him. Where had they come from? What did they mean?

The apparition replied, 'Not because you're doing well.'

Then it leaped at him, for all the world like a gigantic insect and with an insect's speed, and he felt fire in his head and heard a terrific crack, and he knew that the needle had penetrated through his right temple and deep into his brain.

He grew helpless again, his legs buckling. As he fell, the creature caught him. Cradling him, it lowered him to the floor. When he was close in its arms, he smelled a sour humanity, the thick, sharp odor of an unwashed body.

As if from somewhere inside his consciousness, George sensed a growing blackness, and he cried out in anguish, 'You've ruined a beautiful mind.'

There was laughter in response, deep and ominous and touched with irony. Without a word, the thought was communicated, 'I do not find your mind beautiful.'

He was seared, stripped bare, by this comment. A dreadful shame filled him. He strove to conceal the blazing red of his face. He was feeling more naked than naked, and wanted something to cover himself with. More than he had imagined he would ever want anything, he wanted to escape the cold of those eyes.

A hand touched his forehead, as soft as a cloud but tipped by claws which, even so gently placed against his skin, felt disturbingly sharp.

He managed a bare whisper, 'Are you aliens?'

'There are no aliens here,' the apparition said in its rumble of a voice, oddly complicated by a paradoxical sense of the female, even a girl. An ancient girl, filled with knowledge. 'There is only man, and the mysteries that surround us all.'

For a moment, the touch was gentle, but then it became more firm, then unpleasant. He could not move away, though, not even when it began to hurt, or when the pressure rose to the point that he thought it would crack his skull. When he tried to cry out, all that emerged were the little puffs of air that he had experienced earlier.

Then the pain ended. The creature rose to its feet and stood looming over him, tall and spindly, peering down at him with its awful eyes.

'Take him,' it said, then went slowly off toward the far side of the room, its head bowed, its shoulders slumped. It seemed very old to him, but there was also that startling, inexplicable sense of innocence. It was his teacher in a school he had entirely forgotten, but which was the center of his being, as it is of all being – the school where we learn how to live, or do not.

He felt himself being carried again, this time down a dark corridor. He did not try to struggle. He was beyond that. He simply lay in the arms of the blue creatures, the elves, actually, from the department store window.

The Santa hadn't been drunk at all, then. He'd been captured and taken wherever George was going.

Hell? Could such a place actually exist?

Then they were in light again, but there was nothing mysterious about this place. He had been here before. Only twice, it was true, but he remembered it vividly. His first visit had taken place when his father died, the second at his mother's funeral.

He had been brought to the graves of his parents.

After Dad died, George had had to work hard to find a graveyard that offered perpetual care at a reasonable price. He'd bargained effectively, though, and gotten this little corner for a discount. It was really intended to be one grave, but the shape of the graveyard made it just large enough for two, if they were close together.

He'd wanted to cremate them and dispose of the ashes, but his mother had insisted on a burial.

The graveyard was choked with snow, the stones barely visible. He wasn't cold, though. He also wasn't able to move his head even enough to look down at his own body. He was rigid, forced to stare only at the gravestone. As he did, he saw into the graves, and saw their decaying corpses, the tangled hair, the teeth, the gaping eyes.

'No,' he said, choking out the word, trying to turn his head. Because he now also saw himself dead, lying gray in an aluminum tray, his body sunken, on his face a frozen expression of agony. He knew the means of his death. It would be cancer. And it was already growing in him, a cell here, a cell there, still well beyond the ability of medical science to detect.

The hell, he'd get chemotherapy, he'd do it right now, today. Somebody would be willing to do it. Money always talked.

Light changed to darkness, then to light again. The snow disappeared. Darkness and light followed one another backward, autumn came, then summer, then spring and another winter, faster and faster. Now the grave itself was no longer there. Now the graveyard had not yet been built, and wheat waved in the moonlight, and now it was winter again, and a car was passing, and in it a child was singing.

It was a little boy, and he was singing 'The Holly and the Ivy' in a high, happy voice, and then George was that little boy, sitting in the back seat of the Pontiac on their way home from midnight mass.

He heard his childish thoughts and felt himself in his deliciously light child's body, full of brimming energy and excitement.

It was late, but he was trying not to be sleepy. He wanted to stay up all night so that he could catch a glimpse of Santa. As they drove through the streets of Galesburg, he watched the sky, looking for the sleigh.

He heard his boy's voice say, 'You've gotta be able to see the reindeer, they're big.'

Then his mother's voice replied, and it was as if his own heart had awoken from a long winter's sleep, and was speaking to him. 'Eight tiny reindeer, Georgie. They're tiny.'

He wondered about that. 'How tiny can they be if they're gonna pull a sleigh full of presents and a fat man?'

His parents laughed, and so he laughed, too. Why not? Santa had always come before, and Santa would come this time, too.

The sky held only stars, though. 'It's too big,' he said, 'I'll never see him.'

'Maybe we're not meant to,' his dad said. 'Santa is a magic elf. They don't like us looking at them.'

'How does he pay for the toys?'

'He has his own workshop. He makes them.'

George was watching this through his adult eyes, but living it in his child's body. He knew that it must be some sort of an illusion, but the realism was impeccable.

'Last year a lot of mine came from Toys-R-Us. My G.I. Joe did. So he had to pay for them somehow. Does he shop at Toys-R-Us?'

'Santa is magic, Son,' his dad said. 'We have to respect his magic.'

Georgie knew that Santa bought millions upon millions of toys, he had to. If he didn't, his workshop would cover the entire North Pole and it didn't. He had seen pictures and there was nothing there but snow. He wondered what Santa's day job was, but kept the question to himself.

As they passed a late-night McDonald's, Dad said, 'I'm hungry.'

Mom said, 'Four bucks and the credit cards are all full.'

Little Georgie didn't understand. 'I want Chicken McNuggets,' he called out. The adult George remembered how his parents had struggled. His father was an outdoor salesman for a construction firm. Hard work, not very rewarding. Mom worked at Target – when there was work.

As they passed the hamburger stand, Georgie was disappointed. George now saw the nobility of his parents, and realized for the first time just how much they had sacrificed for him. The Christmas toys he would get, for example – what had they given up for them?

He watched them sitting side by side in silence, Christmas carols playing softly over the radio. They had been faithful to one another all of their lives, and to him, and there they lay, jammed into a single grave so an immensely wealthy man could save a couple of grand.

George wanted out. He didn't want to experience this anymore. He tried to somehow pull himself out of himself, but the ride went on.

They arrived home and he went to wash up and put his pajamas on. While he was dawdling in the bathroom, there came a tinkle of little bells outside in the dark.

His mother came in and said, 'Did you hear that?'

He had heard it.

'We need to get to bed right now,' she said. 'If we're not asleep when he comes, he might leave without giving us any presents.'

'Santa wouldn't do that!'

'Georgie, Santa is *very* shy.'

He rushed into his room, threw himself in his bed and pulled the covers up over his face. His mother came behind him, and sat in her place on the bed, and laid her hand on his forehead. His boyhood self enjoyed the love in her touch, and his adult self was reminded of the touch of his teacher. She said, 'Life is a voyage, but you can't sail its seas without sleep.' Her gentle fingers closed his eyes.

She sang, then, 'Silent Night', and he sang with her. Dad came to the door and added his voice to theirs, and for a moment the three of them were sailing the waves of Christmas together.

Dawn was red against the black skeletons of the trees when George awoke. Hanging on his doorknob was his stocking. For a horrified second he thought that it was empty, but then saw different. It was bulging.

The rule was that he couldn't go to the tree until seven, but he could get into his stocking whenever he woke up. So he threw back his covers and, braving the cold of the early morning house, went across and took it down. It had been his dad's stocking. His grandmother had made it, with its snow scene and its Santa flying in his sleigh.

There was a tiny wooden train set in it, a Snickers bar, and a miniature ship in a bottle. He made waves with his bed sheets and sailed the ship on them, whispering to himself, 'The ship of life, the ship of life . . .'

Morning came, and the tree, and the purest happiness that can be, of a child who is cherished.

He awoke again, and once again it was dawn. But he was not a child anymore. He was a man who had spent the night drunk and passed out on a cold floor.

For a long moment, he stared across the room, unable to believe that he could be back in his apartment. Tears of frustration sprang into his eyes. He'd been a boy. He'd been so happy.

But no, he was here and this was what was real. He hadn't gone out, hadn't had that strange experience, hadn't visited his parents' graves and certainly hadn't returned to his boyhood.

No, and in the real world he had a workday to face, and it would be a busy one, as they all were.

Getting himself up, though, he heard, faint on the still air of the morning, the Salvation Army Santa's boom box playing 'The Holly and the Ivy'.

When he was eight, it had been his favorite piece of Christmas music.

As he shaved, he reflected on what had happened to him. He'd started out for breakfast, and then – but good Lord, what *had* happened?

The apparitions of Bill Hill, of course! He'd just met the first one.

How could that be true, though? No, it couldn't be.

And yet, he was disquieted. Should he not acknowledge the season a bit, perhaps stroll a bit, exchange Christmas greetings with passersby?

What if he arrived at ten instead of nine? Who would chastise him, Megan?

He shrugged on his overcoat and stepped out to make an attempt to enjoy the spirit of the season.

6

The streets were far from quiet now, and it was only just nine in the morning.

The music was also louder, still 'The Holly and the Ivy'. The tune slipped through his mind like sweet smoke, reminding him of how it had felt to be a boy. In all these years, he had hardly thought of Mom and Dad. He'd have to give them a better resting place. Of course, there'd be the cost of disinterring them and moving them, of finding a better plot, on and on. He was probably looking at fifteen grand if he was looking at a penny.

Right there in the street, he stopped. He said aloud, 'No. Don't think like that.'

People passing glanced at him. A man smiled, raised an eyebrow. 'Merry Christmas,' he said.

George looked at him. The music changed to 'God Rest Ye Merry Gentlemen'. He felt a little unaccustomed stab in his heart. 'Merry Christmas,' he muttered.

The man was gone, though, disappearing into a snow flurry with two children in hand.

Earlier, George had set out to get a meal, and he was now far hungrier. He wanted eggs and bacon and toast and coffee, but everything, absolutely everything, was closed.

He turned the corner, hoping against hope that Bickford's had changed its policy – and almost tripped over the Salvation Army sergeant's boom box, which was set in the snow beside the cardboard chimney where you were supposed to toss your money.

'Sir! Sorry! Oh, my are you hurt?'

'Of course I'm not hurt. But you'd better get that damn thing—' He stopped. How incredibly harsh his voice sounded.

The Salvation Army guy looked at him. He blew on his hands. 'Let me get that thing moved,' he said, pulling the boom box closer to the chimney.

'Didn't you people have bands?'

'We're getting old. Not that many of us now. Who wants to stand out here blowing on a trumpet all Christmas? The young people have other interests.'

George started to move on, but then found himself reaching into his pocket. There was some small change there, a quarter and a couple of nickels. He felt the quarter, rejected it, then drew out the nickels. He tossed them into the chimney.

'Thank you, thank you,' the Salvation Army man said.

George went on. But there came a voice from behind him. 'Hey, fella.'

He turned back to the Salvation Army man. 'Yes?'

'You look like you're hungry.'

'I am.'

'Why don't you go on over to the shelter? They got eggs and toast and coffee till ten. Bacon, too, for Christmas. Go on, fella, there's no shame. You gave, for pity's sake, a guy in a world of hurt.'

He thought George was a panhandler.

He came closer. 'How much did you drink last night? 'Cause I know a morning-after when I see one.' He clapped George on the shoulder. 'Go on over, you get yourself somethin' to eat, and don't give away money, no-sir, that pot's for rich folks what can afford it.'

Of course it had never occurred to George to eat at the Salvation Army shelter, but in his present condition he could obviously get away with it. It was open and so why not save a little money?

He turned toward the shelter, which was just four quick blocks from where he was. Eggs, toast, coffee, even bacon and all as free as the wind. Nice.

He quickened his pace, slogging along a side street with an unswept sidewalk.

He was passing the bus depot when his life changed again. A family laden with Christmas packages was coming toward him, a woman, a man and two little kids. As they came closer, the woman began to seem more and more familiar.

He slowed down, trying to figure out who she was. Then he stopped. 'Mary,' he said. 'Mary Reed.'

She'd been speaking to one of the children. Now she glanced up, a smile beginning in her face. When she saw him, though, the smile froze. Then it became a questioning expression. 'Yes?'

'It's a bum, Mommy.'

'Uh, Mary, Mary—'

'Oh my God.' She turned to her husband. 'Jake, it's George Moore. You know.' Then back to George, the smile becoming uncertain. 'George, are you okay?'

'Mary Reed . . .' He had dated her in high school. She had been in love with him, so she'd said in the moonlight in Galesburg, on the sidewalk in front of her big old house. He had kissed her and in her arms felt the comfort of women.

They had walked beneath the tossing trees of summer, and counted lightning bugs and stars, and imagined a future life. How shyly she had asked him, her fingers touching the back of his hand as if for gentle emphasis, how big a family he wanted.

He had not been able to answer. At home, as was more and more often true, he lay in bed listening to his parents arguing in their suppressed, angry whispers. Arguing money.

Women and the children that followed after were expensive. He had made a decision: no children. None. The world was overpopulated anyway.

Mary had said she didn't mind. She'd even pretended to embrace it as a cause. Childless couples, sacrificing to slow down the population explosion. He had seen the shadows in her eyes, though, and tasted the new emptiness in her kisses.

He had decided to test her. One night on her porch, sitting in the swing while the south wind filled the air with the perfume of the tasseling corn that filled the fields, he had made a false confession.

'Mary,' he had said, 'I've changed my mind about

71

something.' Her hand had slipped into his. 'Mary, I can't face a childless marriage. I want kids.' She had burst into tears and thrown her arms around him. She had covered him with kisses and talked of boys and girls, which one might come first, and names and the best seasons to give birth . . . and had revealed herself in her truth.

He had walked down off of that porch in a shower of kisses and smiles, and had not seen Mary Reed again until ten years ago, when, very suddenly, he had found himself face to face with her on State Street.

A thousand reasons to say nothing had raced one another through his mind, but then she had smiled, and in her smile he had seen all that he had sweated for in his youth. The years meant nothing, she glowed still.

The moment so threw him off balance that he had taken her to lunch. He still remembered the restaurant, a seafood place where he'd had a tuna salad and she a trout. They'd shared a bottle of wine and when she had invited him up to her hotel room to revisit old times, he had taken off the afternoon, the only time he had done this in his career.

'He's the millionaire,' the little boy cried excitedly. 'He's the millionaire mommy almost married!'

Mary laughed. 'George, this is my husband, Jake.

And that's Kimberly, and this little mouthpiece is . . . George. George, say hello to George.'

This was impossible. But, the boy had the same dark flounce of hair, the same brown eyes, the same . . . configuration.

Reading George's face, Jake said quickly, 'He's named after my dad.'

But Mary smiled as he said it, and threw George a glance that he'd always called her secret look, which said, 'There's another story.'

He thought that she might be going to hit him up for money, and made as if to move on.

'Come with us to the party,' Kimberly said. 'There's all kinds of presents if you're poor.'

'George is not poor,' her mother said.

'Well, he looks poor.'

'Yeah,' little George agreed.

They went on, slowly passing the bus yard. To his surprise, Jake opened a small door in the brick wall of the depot itself. Light and music and wonderful smells escaped. He hesitated. 'Come on, you'll get a present, too,' said Jake.

'He needs a razor,' the boy said.

George hadn't shaved since day before yesterday, and should have done so this morning.

'Don't make personal remarks.'

Georgie whispered, 'He *smells*, Mommy!'

'I'm sorry,' George said. He hung back. Obviously, he needed to get out of here.

Mary knelt down to her son's level. 'Now you've hurt his feelings and on Christmas Eve, Georgie. How do you feel about that?

'I'm sorry, Mommy.'

Smiling at George, she rose to her feet. 'You do look like you've had a hard night.'

He nodded. 'Not as hard as the nights I had with you.'

Throwing her head back, she laughed, and he heard the golden notes of her youth. The sound evoked memories of her kisses, and he thought how it was that he had not had a woman in years. And yet, until this moment he had not felt the loss, only the freedom. He felt it keenly now, though, and found that he wanted Mary as much as he had when they were seventeen.

The children drew him through the door.

The color, the lights, the music, for a moment it was overwhelming, even confusing.

'Come *on*, Mister Bum, you need somethin' to eat!'

Pulling him by the wrist, Georgie drew him toward a table at least fifty feet long, that was laden with fat roasted turkeys, hams knotted with cloves, heaped bowls of candied yams, mashed potatoes, runner beans, peas and steaming mounds of stuffing, macerated grapes and peaches and apples, chocolate cakes and strawberry cakes and lemon cakes, mince and apple and cherry pies, a truly vast array of foodstuffs.

The music, 'The Wassail Carol', the glorious, colorful and delicious spread, made a man who ate his meals at a dreary cafeteria smile openly.

Georgie looked up at him. 'My mommy made the rhubarb pies and the chocolate putting.'

'*Pudding*, dear,' Mary said. 'The wives' club puts this on,' she said to George. 'It's a project, you can be sure.'

'George, c'mere,' Jake said. 'Let me introduce you to our chairman. This is Mister Rose. No better man ever drove a bus. Louis, meet George Moore. George is a big boy in the markets.'

Mr. Rose's color matched his name. To play a jolly old elf like Santa Claus, all he would need would be a red stocking cap.

A smile glowed behind his white handlebar mustache. 'You a floor trader?' he asked. All of Chicago knew the commodities business.

'Upstairs,' George said. 'I did my time in the pits a while ago.'

'Well, anyway, welcome and merry Christmas.' He gave George a long, appraising look. 'I gotta ask, what are you doing on Christmas Eve with a bunch of bus drivers?'

George smiled, and it was quite genuine. 'To tell you the truth, I have no idea.'

Jake's eyes twinkled. 'I think Mary has a follower,' he said to Mr. Rose. He laughed. 'From long ago.'

Now they both laughed. 'Hey, folks, Mary's got an old flame tagging along! Let's hear it for the old flame!'

There was a ragged chorus of hellos. George waved weakly. How could this get more embarrassing, and how could he get through this party with a gaggle of poor bus drivers and their children without parting with a good deal of money? And here he'd been on his way to a free meal.

But it was nice, even so. There was happiness in this room, with the running children and careening dogs, and the music and the laughter.

Dominating the space even more impressively than the laden board was a Christmas tree at least twenty-five feet tall. It was glittering with tinsel and ornaments of every description, glass Santas and reindeer, balls and stars and long strings of candied popcorn and hooked peppermint sticks.

Around it piled to an amazing height were great heaps of gifts, and he saw Mary and her kids add the ones they had brought in.

'So you give each other gifts, here, is that how it works?' he asked Mary.

She smiled at him. 'Just watch.'

One of the other wives got up on a chair. She clapped her hands until the only movement left in the room came from tussling dogs. 'All right, now, it's time. We're going to let them in. Make them feel welcome, kids, this is the nicest thing that happens to them all year, and maybe the only nice thing.' She called out, 'Open it, guys!'

Two of the drivers pushed back the large sliding doors that separated the repair facility from the bus yard. At the same moment, the tree lit up in a blaze of color and 'Joy to the World' blared out of a set of speakers.

A sea of small faces peered into the glory and the lights.

'They're orphans,' Mary said. 'We give them Christmas.'

They came forward, eyes wide, uneasy smiles playing on their faces, and were taken in hand by the children of the drivers and mechanics and maintenance workers, and drawn close to the tree.

'They save all year for this,' Mary said.

'The orphans? What do they save?

'Our children save. To buy the gifts.'

George felt a pull and looked down. A tiny boy was there. His lips moved but he made no sound. Thinking that he couldn't make himself heard above the din of giving and receiving, George leaned down to him.

He spoke again, but made no sound.

A great, grinning woman in a red velvet dress came rolling over.

'I'm Flo Pierce from Stafford,' she said. 'This here is Eugene. Both his parents got did in a drive-by. He think he need to be real quiet, or they gonna get him, too. So he cut the sound outta his talkin'.'

George looked up at her helplessly. He had no idea what to do with this child.

'He askin' you to give him somethin'. Eugene got a lotta manners. He too polite just to take one on his own.'

In confusion, George pulled out his wallet. He liked the feel of money, cash between his fingers. He pulled out a bill. It was a hundred. But what could he do? He couldn't ask the little creature for change.

He handed Eugene the money. Eugene looked at it. Then at George. Tears rolled down his cheeks.

Flo Pierce laughed. 'You ain't from around here, are you?'

'No. No, I'm not.'

'That bill don't mean nothin' to Eugene. He got a dump truck on his mind.'

George looked over the sea of gifts. Not all of them were wrapped, and there was a big red dump truck near at hand.

He reached over and picked it up. He handed it to Eugene.

The smile that burst across Eugene's face finally opened a door – a small one – in a heart that was so tightly closed that not even an angel had succeeded in opening it.

'You givin' away C-notes, I could use that,' Flo Pierce said.

George returned his money to his wallet.

7

Mary came and put her hand on George's elbow. 'That's hard for Flo. They've got a lot of needs at the shelter.'

'There are foundations. Plus state and federal—'

'They need everything all the time. It never stops.'

Flo had turned her back and busied herself with helping children who were tearing eagerly at the wrapped gifts.

Gently, Mary spoke again. 'George, you could change things for them. The lights are almost out over there. These are hard, hard times.'

Now, here it came, the inevitable touch. He should never have walked through these doors. 'I'll give her the hundred.' He opened his wallet and went over to Flo.

'Well, a change of heart.' She took it. 'Thank you. We'll put this in the food fund. End of the month, our meals get pretty simple, what with all the cutbacks.'

George gestured toward the dinner, still waiting on its table. 'What happens when they go back? What do they get tomorrow?'

'Georgie, we do Christmas here. This is what we do. But I don't think you're going to find starving orphans in the United States. Not yet, at least.'

They were a healthy looking bunch all right. But nobody was fat and nobody had anything extra, like good sneakers or even a backpack to put their toy in.

He went over to a clutch of pre-teens, who were huddled at the edge of the gift pile by themselves. They muttered together in the cave of their lives. In the middle grades, George had played football. A running back. He'd been a popular kid – that is, until he began to wonder about the corporate jets that passed over their schoolyard, landing and taking off from Huntley Field, a private airport down the road.

He'd ridden his bike down there, but been politely and firmly told to leave. The gleaming planes and the limousines had created in him a sort of anguish. He'd glimpsed kids his own age living in extraordinary luxury, being whisked off to camp in their family jets, and vowed that one day he would be rich, and he would never, ever be poor again.

He was not accustomed to feeling much of anything, let alone for others. But these kids, ungainly and unsure, reminded him of himself as he had been at age thirteen, angry, confused and agonizingly self-conscious.

He pulled up a chair. 'May I?'

Nobody reacted.

Finally, he sat down. One or two kids glanced his way.

'Merry Christmas,' he said.

Silence.

'You don't have any presents.'

Longer looks this time. 'They for little kids,' one of the girls muttered. 'Nothin' for us here.'

'No, I can see that.'

'Man, was I lookin' at a pair of Addys,' a boy said. There was a deep, carefully stifled crack in his voice.

'Addys, fool? That just what you deserve.'

George looked at the boy who'd just spoken. 'What would you like for Christmas?'

'Me? Addys, I guess.'

'No. What would you *really* like?'

83

'Well, I'll tell you since you ask. I would *really* like what ain't none of us trash ever gonna get. I would *really* like a ma and a pa and my own bedroom. I would really like some damn grass in my yard. I would *really* like to look at cars and think my daddy might give me one when I'm old enough.'

George could not give these kids homes, but he surprised himself very much to find that he wanted to. The impulse evoked suspicion in him. To make money and keep money, you had to be hard.

'If I could get anything I wanted,' one of the boys said, his face dreaming, 'it would be a pocket full of cash. All my life, I ain't never had more than a few bucks in my pocket. I ain't got none now.' He stuffed his hand in one of his pockets, and dug out a few coins. 'Three cents, that what I got.'

'Surely you could find some work. There must be a lot to do in an orphanage.'

'First off, it a children's shelter. We don't like "orphanage," okay?'

'Okay, sorry.'

A girl chimed in. 'We all got chores, but who pays you to do your chores? Cabrini sure don't.'

One of the boys laughed at her. 'What you gonna do with chore money, girl, load up your crack pipe?'

'I ain't got no crack pipe! I a good kid, Jerome! I got a momma, she comin' for me.'

'The great momma in the sky.' He turned to George. 'We all got somebody comin' for us.'

'She will!'

'Mister, you know who we are? Look at us. We the kids ain't gonna get fostered. Nobody want a bunch a juvies like us.' He nodded his chin toward the tree and the younger children around it. 'Them little ones, they come and go fast. They get fostered. Hell, look at those mommas an poppas, those other kids. They lookin' for cute little fosters to take home with 'em right now. You see any of 'em even look our way once? We the devil's rejects, man.'

George's hand went to his wallet, which he habitually carried in his left pants pocket. Front pocket, to keep it away from pickpockets. At the same time, he became aware of an impulse in himself so old that the feeling brought with it a nostalgia for childhood days. As a boy, he had enjoyed giving his parents gifts, had taken delight in the feeling of satisfaction that it brought.

'Look, you guys, I can't take any of you home.' A few of the faces turned his way, hard young faces. 'I can't give you sneakers. But I do have something you might like.' He slid eight one-hundred-dollar bills out of his wallet and put them in the middle of the table. 'One for each.'

They looked at the money, then back at him.

He smiled. 'Go on, it's yours. Merry Christmas.'

Perhaps, he hoped, an ugly old angel also saw those bills and thought, 'Maybe . . .'

Like ghosts or hurrying birds, the kids' hands swept out and the money was gone. Then, a glint of suspicion in an eye. Another. Was it theirs to keep? Would they be accused of something for having it?

George stood up. 'Merry Christmas!'

There was a whistle from the table, then a quiet whoop. Then a louder one.

All at once, the table came alive with whoops and hollers and claps, and then they were up and clustering around George, thanking him, their faces lit by a glory of a kind he had never before witnessed.

Flo came over and put a Santa hat on his head. 'Looks like you gettin' hooked, Daddy,' she said.

Her words scared him. Orphans would be a charitable black hole. He could throw his entire fortune their way and the money would simply drown in the need, he knew that. He was well aware that, even with eight hundred million dollars, he was a tiny drop of help in a swirling vast ocean of human misery.

Still, he pulled more cash out of his wallet. He could do better than a hundred bucks each. To squeals and shouts of delight, he peeled off more bills.

'Man, he crazy! This guy crazy!'

'You shut your mouth fool! He wanna be crazy, let it happen!'

Flo did not look as happy as the kids, not even close. 'Now, hey, wait – Mr. – I don't know your name—'

'I'm George! Merry Christmas!'

'Merry Christmas, George. Money, George – just wait – hey, kids, *wait a second*!' said Flo.

They stopped their clamoring. Their faces slammed shut.

'Hey, I've still got some left!'

'Hold it! Money around here – we're very careful about money.'

'It's Christmas,' George said.

'I know that! But, Sir, there's such a thing as throwing gasoline on a bonfire.'

His blank look must have told her that he didn't understand, because she thrust her face close to his. 'They addicts, George. These children were all either born addicts or became addicts in their homes. That's why they were removed from their parents.'

'And?'

'You don't give an addict money!' She drew him aside. 'I can't take it back, but you've really thrown us a curve, here, sir.'

'It's Christmas and they weren't given a thing.'

'The tree—'

'Flo, do you see anything under the tree for a young teenager? A dump truck? A Barbie? Come on. Take them shopping with the money. Make sure they spend it all.'

'I can't just do a shopping trip! That requires personnel. Overtime pay. Some of them have caseworkers and I'd need caseworker approval.'

'What if some citizen did it? Just took them all to the Loop on a shopping spree with their money?'

She gave him the kind of sidelong glance that says 'Yes, but I know this is a mistake.'

'Merry Christmas,' he shouted with a tip of the Santa hat. He added, 'We're going shopping, kids!' Amid whoops of joy, he pulled out his cellphone, opened it and fumbled with it for a moment as he recalled how to turn it on. Once he had a dial tone, he called the office. Three rings. Four. If she was gone, Megan had better have finished that report.

She answered. 'Moore Trading.'

'Merry Christmas, Megan!'

Silence.

'I want two stretches sent to the Clark Street Bus Depot. As directed. We'll be using them for about four hours.'

'Is this George Moore?'

'Of course! Now get me those limos.'

'Are you all right?'

'Did you hear me?'

'I heard you! It just didn't make any sense.'

'I said, get me—'

'I know what you said. They'll be there in a few minutes.'

'Megan?'

'Yes, Mr. Moore?'

'How is Charlie?'

She hung up.

He had not fully realized how much she must hate him, but when he did a dark image returned to his mind, of big, sorrowing eyes. His temple ached, and when he touched it he saw something else: a long, tapering needle.

He felt as if he was two people in the same body. One of them was giving away money, losing millions on brain-dead trades, getting drunk, hating himself. The other was – well, locked away.

Flo said, 'This is gonna be complicated. I'll go along, do my best not to let it spin outta control.'

'Let it be,' George said. 'They'll be fine.'

'Stranger things have happened, is all I gotta say.'

'Limos!' a kid shouted. 'They's limos out there!'

Some of the littler ones noticed, too, and there began a general movement toward the doors.

Mary and her husband and another woman joined George and Flo. The woman had a gray bun and the kindest, saddest eyes George thought he had ever seen. 'I'm Rebecca Freund,' she said, 'I'm the director at Cabrini.' She paused. 'We're a little more structured than this, especially with these particular clients.'

Normal George saw a way out of this expensive mess. All he had to do would be to apologize and get the hell back to real life. But Crazy George had a different idea. Crazy George was affronted. 'Assign someone to come with us. Flo, you do it! Let's give them a nice Christmas, too!'

'We really can't,' Rebecca said. 'There are procedures.'

Part of George thought, 'Good, I'm done here.' But another part of him remembered Bill Hill's warning, and all that had come after. Unless he lived out of compassion, he would— He didn't want to think about it.

Kids clustered around Rebecca and Flo. Around him. Pleading. A slow smile came into Rebecca's face. 'George, would you pay for a little overtime? So that one of our professionals can accompany the group?'

He stood there, his money in his hand.

'George?'

'Yes?'

Flo looked curiously at him. 'That hat – it fits.'

'And it stays.'

The moment the Santa hat had been put on his head, George remembered what had happened to the department store Santa. He knew that he could be taken in that same direction by those dark elfin beings.

The hat also brought other disjointed memories into focus. Going up in the air. Seeing the fragile, sinister and yet angelic being. Feeling the prick of a needle in his head, and at the same instant touching some deep, soft part of himself that he had long ago buried.

Bill Hill's warning had also become very clear, so much so that he could hear that low whisper of a voice, speaking still. 'They will walk out of your dreams, out of the air, out of the sky. Remember, George. They're your only chance. So *remember*!'

He said, 'Flo, please come with us. Make this happen.'

'I'll go. I'll be glad to.'

So he followed a screaming, laughing gaggle of excited pre-teens to the two very costly limousines that waited in the street.

On one level, George was furious with himself. He'd started throwing away money. But it was also true that he just plain liked these kids.

He got into the front limo, next to the driver. The back was filled with bouncing kids. No sane adult would even think about trying to survive in that space.

'Where to?' the driver asked.

George glanced over at him. A long faced, somber man with the edge of a smile permanently embedded in his face looked back.

'What sort of stores do fourteen-year-olds like? That are open on Christmas Eve?'

The driver looked into his mirror. 'Kids like that? A head shop, maybe? They look like a bunch of druggies to me.'

'Take us to the biggest sneaker store in town.'

This turned out to be a place called the Shoe Monster, deeper on the South Side than he liked to go, especially in a convoy of limos, and worse, on Christmas Eve when everybody who wanted something was out looking for it.

Not a single person they passed failed to lock onto the limos with a resentful gaze.

The further south they went, the worse it got.

By the time they reached the store with its wall of shoe boxes in the huge display window, George was, frankly, scared.

Kidnappers were skilled at knowing how to recognize targets, and he was as prime a target as existed.

The moment the limo stopped, the kids burst out and ran off toward the store. Before George had even opened his door, they were halfway across the parking lot, a screaming mob of shrill excitement.

'Come on,' Flo shouted. 'We're in trouble already!'

'What are you saying?'

'Don't you get it?'

'Get what?'

'This is gang turf, man. The Crystals!'

'The who?'

'This is gang territory you've brought my children to, and it's the wrong damn gang! Now you come on in here and help me before somebody gets killed!'

George, too shocked to speak, followed her into the store.

8

By the time the two adults crossed the threshold, the kids were already running wild. As they entered, Flo said, 'See that, that's a spotter.'

There was a boy wandering off across the parking lot.

'What does that mean?'

'They looking for the wrong colors.'

'What are the wrong colors?'

'I have no idea. The Crystals are green, though. That I do know. Green snake on a white background.'

'None of our kids have anything like that.'

'You ain't gonna be wearing gang clothes at Cabrini, Mister.'

The store was clanging with Christmas rock and roll and filled with kids, all of them clutching Christmas cash or gift certificates. Sneakers were scattered every-where, and the few staff members, kids also, were making little effort to keep order.

George felt a wave of helplessness. What if he lost one of these children, or if one of them was attacked by a gang member? What did gang members even look like?

'Cabrinis,' Flo shouted. 'Front and center!'

There was no reaction. George saw two of the kids moving toward a side door. 'Where are they going?'

'They gonna do a buy, they can find a dealer,' Flo said. 'Wally! Stones! Get back in here, don't you go out that door!'

The two boys sulked back into the store. George tried to help. 'Boys,' he said, 'here are some Adidas. Addys.'

The tallest of the two, Stones, met George's eyes. 'You got more cash, ain't you?'

Were they going to try to rob him? 'No,' he said, 'you got it all.'

'Yeah, you do, and you better watch out, 'cause the homes seen these limos we in. They gonna be lookin' out 'roun' here.'

Wally added, 'They gonna be lookin' out 'roun' here fo *you*.'

The boys laughed together. Stoner picked up a pair of sneakers. 'These is shit. This whole store, it shit. I gonna keep my money. I got other things I need.'

At that moment, a sneaker went flying across the barn-like room. It arced into the air, tumbled, then dropped down between two of the long rows of shelving stacked with boxes. There came with it a shriek of laughter.

The sneaker reappeared, passed overhead, and dropped down into the aisle from which it had come.

'Oh my God,' Flo said.

In seconds, there was a sneaker war under way, with shoes flying in all directions. Now the staff weren't passive. Far from it, they ran from aisle to aisle shouting and cursing. There was a scream and George saw one of them dragging a girl by her hair.

The front doors flew open and three kids in green with baseball bats swarmed in. One of the Cabrini kids went down, slammed in the side by a bat.

'Help us,' Flo screamed. Then she was hit in the back, causing her to fly forward into a row of shelves, which snaked and wobbled, then crashed into the aisle with her atop them.

A frantic George helped her up. The fight had moved to the far end of the store. But what had sparked it? Where had the gang kids come from?

'Some Christmas present,' Flo groaned.

George had his cellphone out. 'I'll get the cops.'

'The cops ain't gonna come, Mister. Not here, not now.'

'Certainly they will!'

'You ain't from the South Side. It Christmas Eve. Unless you got blood, you ain't gonna see no cops.'

'You're bleeding. Look at your hand.'

She grabbed his cellphone. 'Don't call the cops! No!'

'All right.' He didn't fully understand, but he was in way over his head as it was.

'CABRINIS! You get your asses in them limos or you goin' in, the cops is comin'!'

'I thought you said—'

'Just let me do my job, dummie! I been in this field fo' a long time.'

Like magic, the kids broke away from the fight and ran for the doors. Two of the employees tried to stop them. A third was behind the counter screaming into the phone.

'They actually manage to get some cops over here, you gonna spend the night in jail with the rest of us,' Flo hissed.

George had a personal lawyer, Malcolm Potemkin, but he probably couldn't be found on Christmas Eve. 'I thought the cops wouldn't come.'

'If the store calls, they might. You go over there and put a stop to it.'

'How?'

'Pay the man, fool!'

George really did not want to do that, but he wanted even less to spend a night in jail. Amid a hail of flying sneakers, he went to the counter. 'I need to talk to you.'

'Shut up.' The guy, a twenty-year-old, kept stabbing the dial pad.

'Our children are leaving.'

'I have a hell of a mess here. Hello! Police? This is—'

George did the only thing he knew how to do. He reached across the counter, disconnected the call, and held his wallet out in the palm of his hand. 'A grand,' he said. 'Cash. Now.'

'I got hours of work in here!'

'A buck fifty. Take it now or I'm history.'

'Let's see the cash.'

George slipped the money out of his wallet, being careful to avoid showing him how much more was there.

He took it. 'So, the cops already coming, limo. You better get on outta here fast.'

George snatched at the money, but it was too late to get it back.

The boy came around the counter and advanced on George. 'Get on outta here! Now!'

As George headed for the doors, he saw the light bars of at least two police cars approaching. He jumped into the closest limo. In it were three of the Cabrini girls and at least twenty pairs of sneakers.

The riot hadn't been about gangs. The riot had been about robbing the place. 'Take us to Cabrini,' George told the driver.

'You got an address?'

The cops were turning in the parking lot. 'Let's just move out.' He called Flo on her cellphone. 'What's the address of Cabrini?' He listened. 'Wait, let me give you to the driver.' He handed the cellphone across the front seat.

The driver was a professional, and soon had them on Lakeshore Drive, moving smoothly north in sparse traffic.

George watched the girls gloating over their stolen shoes.

'You all still have your money, don't you?'

They kept talking among themselves.

'You didn't pay for a thing. Not for a single pair.'

One of them turned on him, moving with the suddenness and speed of a striking snake. 'Shut up, old man!'

He had understood too late that these children belonged to a different, far more ruthless world even than the markets. In the markets, there were rules. With these kids, it was strictly make your own danger, and do it now. The sooner he could get them back to where they'd come from, the better.

One of the girls said, 'Thank you.'

'I thought I was supposed to shut up.'

'I didn't say for you to talk. I said "thank you". Ain't nobody ever given me no hundred bucks before.'

'Or will again,' he thought, but, of course, did not say it.

The other one laughed. 'I wish Jesus got crucified every day. Then we be rich!'

'It's his birth that's being celebrated.'

She laughed in his face. 'He got *crucified*! *That* what we celebratin'!'

George was not generally afraid of anybody. Kidnappers, perhaps, but not thirteen-year-olds sitting amid piles of stolen sneakers. He was afraid of these girls, though. He was afraid that they'd shred his face, or worse.

'You wouldn't give gifts because somebody was killed. It's because he was born. So it's believed. Born on this day two thousand years ago.'

They had turned down a dark street and were passing an elaborate crèche.

'See, that's what Christmas is about. The baby in the manger, there. The baby Jesus.'

'Yeah, we goes to mass. Father Joseph come to Cabrini.'

'She just comin' upside your head, ole man. We know what Christmas is. You got any cigarettes?'

'I'm sorry, I don't smoke.'

She lolled her tongue and gave him a cross-eyed look.

'Don't start, it's a mistake,' he said.

Another girl said, 'She starts and stops all the time. You can't smoke at Cabrini. You can't do nothin' at Cabrini.' She went back to examining shoes.

'What're you doing, if I may ask?'

'Mother Superior gonna make us take back all these sneaks. So we lookin' for the best ones we want to keep. We gonna hide those.'

The limo pulled up in front of the shelter, and the girls got out, each one taking with her a single pair of shoes. 'Security gonna come out an get the rest,' one of them said.

The other limo disgorged the rest of the children and a badly frazzled Flo. Instead of getting out himself, George called Flo's cellphone.

'I'm in here with a mountain of sneakers.'

'You sure are.'

'What're you going to do about it?'

'Not one single thing.'

'The girls said security was going to confiscate them.'

'They your problem now. I'm not goin' anywhere near that store for a good long while.'

She had a point. As soon as they realized who he was, the store would be certain to hit him with a lawsuit. Plus, there'd be juvie citations for the kids, which was going to land some of them back in state detention, and Cabrini had to be better than that.

'What would you do?' he asked the driver.

'Me?'

'Yeah. With fifty pairs of sneakers on Christmas Eve?'

The driver smiled. 'You got two more hours? On the clock?'

George was about to respond with an angry refusal, but he heard himself say instead, 'Sure, why not?'

'There are parts of this city that are a lot poorer than where we were. The Shoe Monster's in an upscale slum, brother.'

'So take me to the downscale part. It's Christmas, let's give away some sneakers.'

'This should be interesting.'

George shuddered slightly, thinking of the strange turns his life had been taking since Bill Hill had showed up. A lot had changed since then, most of it inside him.

No matter the trouble that had been caused, he was glad he'd given these kids something they enjoyed.

Tomorrow, he'd have Megan call the store and find out the damages. He'd send them a check.

As the limo slid through the streets and the sun began slanting down into the west, George became increasingly uneasy. When he saw a man pushing a huge grocery cart full of debris, he almost cried out. Maybe he was alive and maybe he was dead, but it wasn't Bill Hill.

They drove past the Shoe Monster, where a couple of police cars still stood, their flashers proclaiming his crime.

'I'm gonna send them a check for the rest of the damage,' he said into the silence.

The driver did not reply.

Soon, the neighborhood was mostly dark, the streets in poor repair, the houses low and grim. Here and there, a few Christmas decorations winked from behind closed curtains.

'We need to watch our backs,' the driver said. 'This is gang country, big time. Drive-bys are a hobby around here.'

'There's nobody out. Nobody to take the shoes.'

'Just you wait, Mister.'

'Do you even know where we are?'

'I sure do.'

'How often do you come to a neighborhood like this?'

'Every day. I live up the street.'

To George a limo driver was a uniform. But here, suddenly, was a person.

He pulled the car up to the curb. For a moment he did not move, a stillness that made George immediately uneasy.

Slowly, he turned around in his seat. He smiled. A distinct unease caused George to glance at the dark window. If he had to run from this man, where would he go?

'You saw a flash mob in the store. This time, mister, you're gonna see something else.'

Figures were coming out of houses, down the sidewalks, out from the dark between the houses. They were silent and grim and determined. They were moving slowly and carefully. Unhurried. All converging on the limo.

'They'll tear me apart!'

When the driver smiled in the thin light, his teeth gleamed.

9

When the driver pulled George's door open, he cringed away.

He laughed. 'Come on out, Mister, we don't get rid o' these shoes, you're gonna spend the night in jail. Because the cops're gonna hear about this limo bein' out here, and they're gonna show up.'

'Please, I've never done a thing to hurt anybody. Please . . .'

The driver peered in at him. 'You havin' a stroke? What's the matter with you?'

At that moment, the sweetest, the softest, the most resonant music George thought he had ever heard floated into the car. This was no Salvation Army sergeant with a boom box, this was the human voice, children's innocence mixed with adult tones of peace.

A group of carolers stood before one of the little houses. They were singing 'It Came Upon a Midnight Clear'.

The music lifted him, somehow, above himself.

Forgetting his fear for the moment, he got out of the car.

They were dressed in tattered clothes, coats even older than George's, hats that had seen better days, some boots but mostly old sneakers.

These poor people had the richest voices he had ever heard, but as he approached and they noticed him, the singing died away.

'Hey, there, Santa,' one of them said, glancing at the hat. 'You comin' this year? We been gettin' missed a lot lately.'

There was a little laughter, a silence.

Tentatively, George uttered a soft, 'Merry Christmas.'

More silence – until a tiny girl with a very big voice began singing, shaking and clapping all at once. Of all things, it was a syncopated version of 'Jingle Bells', and it was so rhythmic that it almost made him dance with the rest of the carolers, who joined her with delight.

George wanted to dance, but even when he was young, he hadn't been able to manage it.

The driver began putting pairs of sneakers onto the sidewalk. More people were appearing out of the dark.

A woman came to George. 'Where these come from? An' who you be?'

'It's Christmas,' George said, noticing that she was wearing canvas sandals. 'Take a pair. Merry Christmas!'

As she took the shoes she wanted, he experienced something very unaccustomed in his life, a sense of satisfaction that did not have anything to do with money.

The store had been looted for these shoes, true, but he was going to make that right as soon as possible.

A family of five, a mother and four children, came scampering down the sidewalk and began hunting through the shoes, speaking to one another with quiet excitement as the carolers moved to 'We Three Kings'.

It was beautiful. It was Christmas. He had done all this with his wealth, his generosity.

He saw two people lingering at the edge of the glow cast by the limo's lights, a man and a boy.

'Come one, come all,' he yelled, 'Merry Christmas to all!'

When they slipped away into the shadows, he felt anger and he shouted at them, 'Hey, it's Christmas!'

They kept walking, the man's hunched shoulders eloquently communicating his disgust.

George decided that maybe he'd been carrying too much baggage, always trying to hold onto every dollar. It was ridiculous to live that way. After all, he could give away a million dollars a day for two years and still have a couple of hundred million left to play with. So what did it matter, really? Why couldn't he open up his heart a little?

There was still cash in his wallet.

Should he?

No, it was dangerous, they'd go crazy just like the kids from Cabrini had.

He put his hand in his pocket. He closed it around the fat billfold.

The carolers was now singing 'Silent Night'. To his surprise, it touched him to the point that he was a bit choked up. The darkness of Christmas night had become deep, the few lights on this poor street swallowed by a great gloom. But wasn't that the point of this ancient winter celebration, to gather the human family against the dark?

He wanted to give. These were lovely people, they would accept his money gratefully. And he wanted that.

Excitement built in him. He pulled the wallet out. But now what? Did he walk up to people and just hand them money? What if there wasn't enough to go around?

More people took shoes, more people thanked him. The carolers began singing 'Joy to the World', and that did it for George. He threw a wad of bills into the air.

At first, nobody saw. Then they did. They stopped choosing shoes. A man looked down at a bill that had fluttered to his feet. Then he raised his eyes to George. It was almost too dark to see, but not quite. George said, 'Yes, take it. Take it!'

The man's expression tightened. He did not pick up the bill. Then a woman swooped in and grabbed it. 'Don't you let that go,' she said to him.

'I ain't gonna bow down to no white man, woman.'

'Whoa! This a C-note! Why, thank you, white man.' She chuckled and gave him a deep bow. Then she said to the man, 'Go on home, fool, I'm goin' to the store, I gonna get us a turkey! In my new shoes!'

George threw more money out. In fact, he threw money until he had just a few notes left.

People picked it up. They did it quietly. They thanked him, some of them. Others disappeared into the dark.

The carolers slipped away one by one, until there were just a couple of voices left. Somewhere in the middle of 'Oh Holy Night', they trailed off to silence, also.

'Thank you, Sir,' somebody said in the dark.

'Merry Christmas,' George shouted. 'Merry Christmas to all!'

He couldn't remember feeling like this in a very long time, not since he was a boy, in fact, and had been brimming with pleasure over his Christmas toys.

'Time for us to be movin' on,' the driver said.

'Merry Christmas!'

'We need to be goin'. Now!'

'Don't you take that tone with me.'

'Well, I'm not stayin' here with no limo to deal with. You can either get in and get back where we safe or you can take your chances on the street.'

'I'm having a nice time, and I never have a nice time and I have no intention of stopping.'

'Mister, word is passin'. Has been since the first one of these poor folk texted somebody else to tell them about the shoes. And now the cash. Mister, you show these poor people cash on Christmas Eve, you show them your blood.'

George followed him into the limo. The moment he closed his door, the driver hit the automatic locks.

The farther north they went, the more the appearance of Christmas returned to the streets. The Loop
bustled with decorations and cheerful crowds, and
George was tempted to get out and just walk among
them, to experiment with his new-found generosity.
But he didn't really trust himself, or even understand
very clearly what had changed in him.

He was just as glad when they turned onto Dearborn
and began moving through the Printer's Row
neighborhood.

'Where are you?' the driver asked. 'Not over by the
bus station?'

'Yes, just where the 205 starts.'

He didn't reply. Naturally not. Why would a man
willing to throw away money and hire limos live over
there? Printer's Row was a beautiful residential neighborhood now. Actual printers still existed in Chicago,
but not here.

'Now, you say it's near the 205.'

'Take a left next block, then another left. That's my
street.'

Silently, the driver followed his directions.

'This is fine. Stop the car.'

'Uh, there's nobody livin' over here.'

'Just do it.'

He stopped the car. George got out and without looking back let himself into his building. Let the man figure it out for himself. And as far as a tip was concerned, George had lost enough money and given away enough money in the past twenty-four hours to last him a lifetime.

He turned on the lights and climbed the stairway to his apartment. The place was absolutely silent, slightly cool, completely normal in every way.

Well, why wouldn't it be? He was fine, now. Whatever had happened to him, which he was very far from understanding, was also in the past.

The condition of his apartment, however, was not in the past. He looked across the living-dining room at the smashed monitor still lying on the floor, at the mess he'd left when he'd been sick, and the pile of unwashed dishes in the scarred old sink, and the couch cushions spread across the floor.

He liked things absolutely neat and clean.

There was no food in here and he was now very hungry.

He did something that he really hated, which was to call for a pizza. He was convinced that they were outrageously overpriced and made with dubious ingredients. Rat meat, artificial cheese, God only knew.

He telephoned the nearest place, some chain. He'd had a couple of their pies over the years. They filled your stomach, at least.

Waiting for it to come, he found himself pacing. He made sure all the lights were on in the apartment. When the door buzzer sounded, he found it difficult to go downstairs.

The stairs seemed very long, the lights dim. He kept imagining Bill Hill coming up here, pushing that basket of his.

What was the world, really? How did it actually work? Certainly not the way it appeared to.

By the time he reached the downstairs door, he had decided that he didn't want to open it to whomever was there. Instead, he pressed the intercom.

'How much do I owe you?'

'Twelve ninety-nine.'

He reached into his pocket and pulled out his now thin wallet. Well, at least he'd made some people happy. He wasn't used to doing that and, if he let himself, he could enjoy the memory.

All he had were twenties, fifties and hundreds.

He slid a twenty out through the mail slot. 'Leave my change on the box, please.'

'Sure.'

Like hell he would. George had seen the last of that money.

He waited until he heard the footsteps crunching away through the snow, then the car starting and driving away.

Unexpectedly, the correct change was indeed on top of the box along with a note: Merry Christmas!

He knew that he should have tipped, but he'd given away and lost so much lately, he felt it was time to draw a line. Still, he'd felt good earlier, giving away the shoes and then the money, watching the smiles and listening to the carols.

As he ate the pizza, he reflected on the fact that he'd done good on this day. He was amused to think that the spirit of Christmas had reached him, at least to some extent. Smiling faces, the sounds of carols, the Magdalene bells pealing, seeing Mary again, all combined in memory, leaving an unaccustomed sweetness behind. Later, midnight mass would be celebrated at St. Mary Magdalene. He wouldn't go, of course not, but he understood the appeal of the pretty fantasies.

As he chewed another bite of the cardboard pizza, he became aware of a sound in the room.

He stopped his chewing.

It was a whisper. A sort of hissing.

Was there a gas leak? Something else wrong?

It was coming from above, so it wasn't a gas leak. Could he hear words in it? His name?

No!

It was snow. Had to be. Snow on the skylight. He could see flakes flowing past the window behind the couch.

He literally leaped across the room, threw himself onto the couch and locked the window. Then he ran through the rest of the apartment, locking every window in the place.

When the stores opened again, the first thing he was going to do was to buy the most powerful gun he could legally possess. He was going to have his alarm system updated, he was going to hire a patrol service to canvas the neighborhood, he was going to get a steel door. And to hell with having a skylight, he would get it covered.

But wait a moment, here. Just a moment. Why in the world was he so afraid? It was snow falling on the skylight, and that's all it was.

As he'd jumped up, the pizza box had fallen to the floor. He gathered up the remains.

He remembered being up in the air. He remembered being in a bright room. In his mind's eye he saw a golden needle being held in long, clawed hands. He remembered whispered words of warning.

Oh, nonsense! Ridiculous!

It hadn't happened, not any of it. It was some sort of lunatic, guilt-ridden fantasy. He made money and he had a right to make money. The markets were true to themselves. If you were smart, you succeeded. If you weren't, you didn't, and there was nothing morally wrong with that at all.

He touched his left temple – and snatched his hand away. That hurt, that was sore.

He'd hit a door, or maybe he'd slept wrong.

His fingers went back, probing gently. The pain was concentrated just above and in front of his ear.

Stifling a cry, he ran into the bathroom and turned on the light.

He gasped. The face in the mirror – it was a stranger, bearded, dirty, staring. He needed a shave, he needed to comb his hair, to have a bath. He had not realized just how far he had sunk.

When he turned his head, he could see a mark very clearly. It was just where the pain was focused. There was no mistaking it. It was a puncture wound.

'Christmas past has gone, and Christmas present, too. And now there's me, come to you.'

The words had come from inside him, but from the room behind him, too.

Yes, now there was suddenly a sort of sense. Christmas past had been Bill Hill. Christmas present had started with the needle and ended with the adventure with the chauffeur.

Christmas future?

Outside the bathroom, he could see only darkness. Somebody had turned off his reading lights, his overhead lights, even the little lamp he kept in his bedroom to guide him if he awoke in the night thirsty.

The wind muttered at the windows, and there came laughter, too soft to be good.

Now the light in the bathroom dimmed, sinking away until the bulbs were red dots floating in the unknown.

Darkness enveloped him.

He felt a hand touch his hand, and it was very cold. It was very small, too, this hand. It slid around his fingers and grasped them tightly. It was also very strong.

'Let's go.'

10

He tried to pull away, but the small fingers were like steel bands.

'Don't you know me?' a child's voice asked.

When he tried to answer, he could not make his voice work; his throat had grown too dry.

'Come with me.'

'I'm not going anywhere.'

'You have to.'

Then they were in the bedroom.

'No!'

Then they were in the living room.

'Stop! This is impossible!'

Then they were outside. Snow swirled in the light at the end of the long, empty street. Full of sleet, it rattled

on the roofs of cars and sped along the shoveled naked-
ness of the sidewalk.

As they entered a pool of light on a corner that
seemed far from any street he knew, he saw that he
was being led by a little boy in a black sweater. The
boy turned to him, and smiled up at him. 'Hello Mr.
Miser.'

Yes, of course, he'd seen this child; this was Charlie,
Megan's little boy, the wretched, coughing thing with
the mental condition.

'You let me go! Leave me alone!'

Lights flashed past, streets reeled away behind them.
The Christmas flare of Printer's Row shot past, and
now they were on the deep South Side.

'Megan's fired!' said George, frightened. 'Your
mother is fired!'

'My snows have yet to fall,' said the boy. 'My gifts
yet to be given.'

Ahead he saw a dance of flashlights, then heard
voices raised in song, and he saw people there, some
thin, all poorly dressed for the cold, and yet singing,
their voices like a cascade of the Magdalene's bells.

'Now, you won't like this, but you must see. Your
soul hates itself so much that it wants to die, and this is
why.'

There was a limousine there, long and black and lustrous, pressed up against the curb like a waiting, predatory snake. In its lights, a grotesque figure capered, jumping and gesticulating, its raw, brutal laughter ripping through the music of 'It Came Upon a Midnight Clear' being sung by tattered but very skilled carolers.

He could hear in their voices the full richness of the season. The capering figure seemed almost to be mocking them.

'Why doesn't that fool just *shut up*,' he thought.

People came out of the dark, one and then another, mothers and children, men in little more than T-shirts, all of them shyly taking pairs of sneakers and then disappearing again. The figure capered and bowed – it actually bowed – and when they thanked it, the thing threw back its head and brayed in arrogant delight. On that head, the Santa hat was an ugly parody.

'Oh, God, no. Please—' Shaking his head, he turned away. 'Please, no more, I don't want to see this.'

The hand grew tighter still and colder, so cold that it trapped him in its ice. He was drawn closer, the two of them staying just outside of the light. As he knew it must, the figure saw them. It shouted 'Merry Christmas' in its sneering, insincere voice.

'Shut up, shut up, you stupid fool!'

'He won't hear.'

Jumping up, braying and shouting his cruelly false 'Merry Christmas,' he kept throwing money in the air. Now George could see the shame in people's hunched postures and in their quick, snatching gestures as they took it. A man crunched up a bill and threw it down. 'Don't you dare,' his wife cried, and bent to pick it up. But another woman dove for it and grabbed it and ran away cackling with delight. 'You a damn thief, Beryl Williams,' the first woman screamed. She ran after her, and they collided in a brutal fight.

George watched himself laughing and throwing money in the air, not seeing the discord and humiliation unfolding all around him.

The child said, 'Come on, we're done here.'

Quickly, the crowd dispersed and the limo drove away, speeding off down the empty street.

'Come on, we have to go right now.'

For what reason he could not be sure, he wanted desperately not to go down this street, not to go to the house at the end of the block, a weathered clapboard shambles of a place drunk on its foundations.

'They won't be able to see us,' Charlie whispered.

They went up onto the porch. And then they were in the front room, just like that.

'You make me sick!' shouted the woman who had retrieved the money.

George thought she was shouting at him, but a man came bursting out of the kitchen. 'That's filthy money, that man wanted you to bow, that's what it was about.'

'Well I did bow. And I'd bow again. *You* can't bring me no hundred-dollar bills, not you.'

'Black man's the last in line and you know it.'

'What do I do? We got no guv'ment check, it's gone. I got us two hundred dollars outta that fella. He was crazy, anyway, who cares what he thinks?'

'Devon Lester saw you.'

'Him in his fancy uniform! Why don't *you* drive a limo? You worthless!'

A fire came in his eye. He strode up to her. 'Don't you never call me that! Don't you *never*!'

The boy said, 'See what you did?'

'I didn't—'

'You could have handed it out. Shown respect.' He looked up into George's face. His eyes were a child's eyes, but there was an in-looking to them, though, a deepness that did not belong to a child.

'What are you?'

'I'm what hasn't happened yet.'

At that moment, there was a sharp sound, as loud as a rifle shot, and the woman lurched away from the man, lurched almost into George's arms, but never saw him or the magical child at whose feet she fell.

Charlie gazed down at her, holding out a hand as if in blessing over her hunched, weeping form.

She raised stricken eyes. Two small children had appeared from the back of the house, and stood staring in silence, tears pouring down their faces.

The man advanced again. There was something in his hand now, something gleaming.

'Stop,' George shouted, but nobody reacted.

'We can't be heard,' Charlie reminded him. 'Or seen.'

Then the man's arm went up and back, the knife gleamed, the woman looked up, the children pleading, 'Daddy, no, Daddy.'

George threw himself at them but he couldn't touch them, and the man's eyes were wild with rage over this trivial thing, but also over all the burdens of his life.

As the blade swept down and the woman cried out in her despair and her agony, George also cried out, his own voice silent.

The man stopped. Blood pulsed from the woman's neck. The knife, black with it, lay on the floor beside her.

Her eyes went to the children. Her lips formed a plea. Then something came out of her, a silver presence, glowing with love, and swept around her children again and again and again.

It stopped. It turned. This graceful presence, wrapped in dignity and radiant with a sorrow asked George, 'Why?'

'I thought you said they couldn't see us?'

'Yes but now she is out of her body she can see everything.'

She said to George, 'You're sick.' Then she swept upward and was gone in an instant.

Her husband knelt over her body weeping. Her children wailed. And George despised himself more completely and deeply than he had known was possible.

Charlie said, 'Come on.'

George gasped. He looked around himself in disbelief. But there was the pizza box, there was the broken monitor on the floor.

They were back in his living room and once more Charlie reached out to George.

Immediately, George jumped away. 'Oh, no, none of that. No more.'

The little steel hand slipped into his. Even as he tried to pull away, the grip tightened so much that he could not. He felt himself drawn away.

Lights flashing. Music blaring. Dark bodies gyrating frantically in a space that had been created by pushing desks back.

But what desks? He didn't have desks in his apartment. He stood agog, completely at a loss to explain how these people had gotten in here. And why were they dancing?

But no – those windows, those desks – this wasn't his apartment, it was an office. *His* office. They were dancing in the middle of his trading floor.

'Hey! Dancing's not allowed! Hey, stop this! Stop it!' He saw traders, support personnel, his whole staff. They were popping champagne corks, laughing, guzzling expensive Scotch, tequila, bourbon, you name it, obviously spending a fortune, and never mind the time being wasted.

Then he saw Megan. She was right in the center of the melee, dancing harder than any of them, dancing and waving a bottle of what he was sure was fabulous champagne.

Shouldering through the crowd, he went close to her. 'You're fired, and that child of yours is headed for family court. What's the matter with you, have you gone insane?'

She danced on, her eyes sparkling with happiness.

Then he saw that his own office door was wide open, and how dare they! Rushing in, he discovered a couple on the floor behind his desk, kissing with frenetic passion. 'Get out,' he shouted. 'Get out of here!'

They acted as if he didn't exist.

He kicked the disheveled young man. 'Get out, go on!'

There was not the slightest reaction.

He stared, disbelieving. Then he realized that there was sunlight pouring in his windows. Outside, the gnarled old tree that overhung the sidewalk was covered with new leaves.

'What in the name of God is going on?'

Charlie said, 'It's April 17. Next April.'

'It's not, it's Christmas Eve. Anyway, it's snowing!'

But it was not snowing. It was not even night.

'Where are we? What's going on here?'

Charlie said nothing.

11

The sun was shining, the tree was indeed leafed out, and his office was full of people, most of them complete strangers, and no matter how hard he tried, he couldn't get any reaction from anybody . . . except Charlie.

He bent down to the little boy. 'You tell me, Charlie.'

Charlie's eyes were turned in on themselves. The pain of autism.

'Charlie, please tell me, how can this be?' Then he asked the question he had been unwilling to put into words, even in thought. 'Charlie, am I dead?'

'I like calendars, I like trains, I like reliable things. Death goes after life, April 17 after 16. Want to see?'

'See? See what?'

Once again, he was in the office, but now there was no party. He was standing at the back of the trading floor. Across the room, his own office door once again stood open.

There was a feeling of quiet intensity radiating from his traders. Megan sat at her desk just outside his door. A new woman sat at Miss Jefferson's desk. Here he was in his own office looking at his own secretary, and he did not even know her name.

A voice, cruel, brutal, and ice cold came out of his office. 'How stupid are you, can you tell me that?'

There was a murmured reply, hardly audible.

'You call yourself a trader. You're a brain-dead waste of space and it's my damn space!'

Around him, the trading floor had grown quiet. Megan hunched at her desk, her ears covered with her hands. The new secretary sat rigid. His own voice was the vilest thing he'd ever heard, brutal, mean and colder than death.

'Give me back my money or get the hell out! Get the hell out! Now!'

He shamed himself to the point of agony. 'I can't bear this,' he said to Charlie.

Charlie tightened his grip on his hand. 'You asked for it.'

'I did not.'

'You're trying to save your soul, Mr. Moore.'

'People don't have souls.'

'If they don't, what did you see leave that woman's body? And where are you now?'

'In my office where I don't want to be!'

'You are in the well of the soul. You are facing your moral failure.'

Now the voice of the unseen trader rose. 'Mr. Moore, I can make it up. I've made it up before.'

'What we do here is make money. That is to say, our account balances increase. Your accounts come up even. I can't use somebody who comes up even. You're making me pay for floor space; you're getting a draw that you don't cover.'

'I cover my draw and you know it!'

'You don't make me the kind of money I want!'

'I make good money. Look at my figures.'

'I've got them right here on my screen, and it's *not enough*! So get out. *Now*!'

'Jesus, Mr. Moore, don't do this.'

'You're finished.'

He wanted to cover his ears too; it was unendurable. 'That can't be me. It's not me.'

When Charlie squeezed his hand this time, it was warm and he felt kindness. His despair increased.

His voice continued relentlessly on. 'Yeah, you're fired! Jesus God, who'd keep you on, you stupid bastard? And if you put Moore Trading on your resumé, I'll sue your ass. Damn you, *get out!*'

There was a thud followed by silence. Then the younger voice again: 'My God.' More silence. 'Hey! Hey, Mr. Moore!'

The new secretary got up from her desk and went into the office. 'Mr. Moore!' Then a shout: 'Call EMS, he's down!'

Megan ran into the office with a red box in her hand. George knew that box. It was a cardio-pulmonary resuscitation device. She'd insisted on buying it and training on it. Traders had heart attacks.

He'd thought it a waste of money, not to mention her training time that he had to pay.

Then he was in the office. On the floor lay a man in his shirtsleeves. His face was gray, his mouth gaping, his eyes blank.

Megan looked down at this man. 'Open it, get it going,' shouted George. But, of course, Megan didn't hear him.

'Okay, let's get it on him,' the new secretary said.

Megan didn't move.

'Megan!'

She got the paddles out of the box and pulled George's shirt open, then placed the paddles on his chest in the correct positions. But then nothing happened.

'Hurry, Megan, the man is dying!'

'It's out of juice.'

'Plug it in, then!'

She fumbled with it, dropped it, then found the power cord and plugged it in.

The device whined, then a recorded voice began giving instructions.

George watched his body jerk as the paddles sent jolt after jolt of electricity through his heart.

Moments later, four EMS workers burst into the room and took over. As they worked on him, he watched what appeared to be a second person come up out of his body.

This person was naked, his skin raw and fissured. With him came a stench of death, and as he shuffled to his feet, maggots dropped from the sores that covered him from head to foot.

'Who is that? What's wrong with him?'

'You said there's no such thing as the soul, so what does it matter to you?'

As the figure came closer, George had the odd impression that he was in two places at once, standing here and also walking, exhausted and sick, toward the door.

'He can't go out looking like that! He's naked!'

Now the figure was very close, and in his eyes was a hollow, empty expression.

'This isn't me!'

'On April 17, it will be.'

'But . . . what happens?'

'You'll try to find a cure for your soul.'

'There is no cure, though?'

'Physical life is where change happens, so after you die, no.'

'What about now?' He laughed a little. 'I gave away shoes. I gave away money.'

'We took a look at that. Not so good.'

The EMS men opened their gurney and lifted George onto it.

Two of the men unfolded a black rubber sheet and laid it over him up to his chest. His face was covered by an oxygen mask.

'See, I'm okay!' he said to Charlie. 'You aren't going to kill off George Moore so easily.'

But then one of them turned off the oxygen and removed the mask. The other rolled the sheet over his face.

136

Megan choked back a sound that did not sound to George like a sob.

The EMS men wheeled the gurney out of the office and across the trading floor, its wheels squeaking.

The traders watched in silence as they went out the glass doors and rolled the gurney into the elevator, which they'd kept locked open.

The doors closed.

Megan came onto the trading floor. All eyes were on her. She stood in silence. The traders watched her in silence.

She burst out laughing. First one trader smiled, then another, then they were all laughing and cheering and stomping. The place became a riot of whoops and laughter, with people slapping one another with high fives and hammering each other on the back.

The sore-covered version of himself walked slowly among them, its mouth distended in a silent scream. It tried to shake them, but it could not affect their movements. Then it saw George – or rather, he saw himself.

There was an electric vibration between them, and, horrifyingly, George could smell the stench of his own rotting soul.

He jerked away, breaking the eye contact. 'NO, NO, *NO!*'

His employees were dancing around, singing 'The wicked witch is dead,' and making plans for the party, that in Charlie's skewed version of time, had been happening when he had first brought George into the office.

'Is this real? For God's sake, Charlie, tell me!'

Charlie said, 'I'd ride the El all day if they'd let me. I know all the schedules for all the trains.'

'*Tell me!*'

'I can follow the paths that lead around time. Do you ever just suddenly want things? I do. I want a lime popsicle.'

George dropped down on one knee. He took the little boy's shoulders. 'Charlie, am I alive or dead?'

Charlie smiled. 'Now or later?'

'Do I die on April 17?'

Charlie raised his hands and held George's cheeks. He looked into his eyes. 'If you're always ready, it's always okay.'

'I demand to know!'

Charlie smiled. Furious, George strode to the kitchenette and got a glass of water from the tap and drank it down.

But there was no kitchenette in the office. Damn things were major time wasters.

So . . . he looked down at the sink.

He was back in his apartment.

'Charlie?' he whispered.

No answer.

He went into the bedroom, even looked under the bed. The closet was empty, and so was the bathroom. But little Charlie had been here. He'd been real.

Finally, he faced the fact that he would have to talk to Megan. He was feeling quite ashamed of what he had done to her, making her work through the holidays.

'Hello, Megan,' he said when she answered. 'I hope you're looking forward to a good Christmas morning.'

'What do you want?'

He said, 'I'm worried about Charlie.'

'Charlie won't affect my work.'

'I mean, is he all right?'

'Charlie is in the hospital, if you must know.'

The room seemed to close in a little tighter around him. 'Megan, I'm concerned.'

'He waited for me on a stoop for three hours in the snow. He has pneumonia.' Her voice was flat.

He wanted to say it. He had to say it. Finally forced himself. 'If there's anything I can do.'

'Is that all?'

'That's all.'

She hung up.

'Damn you!' he shouted into the silent phone, but not at Megan, at himself.

He had given Charlie pneumonia. No question, it was his fault. He was a mean, heartless, stingy bastard, that's what he was.

But what, here, was real? He'd certainly been injected in his temple. Obviously, that could mean that he'd been drugged. So how real was any of this? Had he actually gone forward in time just now and witnessed his own death, or was somebody playing with his mind?

He went on the internet, where he soon discovered that hallucinations as extreme as he was having weren't actually mentioned as symptoms of anything except the use of psychotropic drugs. Even then, they didn't have the sense of the real about them, not like his experiences.

Then he realized that he could actually test this. When the driver had taken him to see the consequences of his giving away that money, the woman had called him a name. Devon something.

Devon Lester.

He telephoned the limousine company. 'I'd like Devon Lester for an as-directed,' he said.

'Devon's off today.'

He thought fast. 'Listen, I might've left something in his car.'

'Just a minute.'

George waited through the silence as the dispatcher searched the lost and found book.

'He didn't sign anything in and the cars have been cleaned.'

Perfect. 'Maybe he's still got it. It's just a book but I need it. I wonder if you could give me his number.'

'Sure.' He gave George a cell number.

George collected himself, took a deep breath, and called it.

'George, we don't have time. We have to go to a funeral.'

Charlie was sitting at the dining table, playing a handheld video game as he talked.

George closed his phone. 'Charlie, you're in the hospital.'

'Yeah, I'm dying. That's why I can get out. I'm dying for you, George. So you can cure yourself.'

'I'm not the one who's sick, you are!'

Charlie looked up from his game. 'You're a lot sicker than I'll ever be. Pneumonia you leave behind. Your kind of sickness lasts forever.'

George went to him, pulled up a chair and sat down. He leaned forward and looked directly at the boy's face. Every detail was there, even a slight dampness under his nose. He was sitting quite calmly, looking back at George with a child's question and frankness.

George touched his cheek, which was warm. Living skin. He ran his fingers through the thatch of blond hair. A boy's head. 'You don't seem sick.'

'I left that at the hospital. You should see it though, it's all gray and covered with sweat and there must be fifty doctors in there, and my mom and dad are crying and crying. You made them pretty sad, George.'

He drew back. 'I don't see how you can be in two places at once.'

'Kids like me, we don't know we can't.' He smiled, his two missing front teeth adding to the innocent appeal. 'So we can.' He reached out his ice-cold hand. 'Now it's time,' he said.

'Time for what?'

'Come on.'

Helplessly, George followed him.

12

Sunlight flooded a trim block in a pretty suburb that George didn't recognize. It was a warm spring afternoon, with white clouds drifting off the lake. Beds of red, blue and yellow zinnias added a welcome splash of color to the small garden in front of the Vigo Funeral Home, a trim cottage with a black awning.

'Know why we're here?'

George bowed his head. He knew perfectly well. All his money, and he hadn't even left a will. He couldn't bear to give gifts, not even post-mortem. But that had to change. He had at least to leave his son something.

'Who made the arrangements?'

'My mom, who else?'

The front hall of the little place was decorated with prints of Jesus and Mary. 'I'm not a Catholic.'

'She thought you'd want the cheapest place. This is the cheapest place.'

There was only one viewing room, and in it was a simple coffin, steel gray. The front half was open and a body lay inside. When he saw it, George drew a shuddering breath.

He went closer. Looking down, he saw a fragile little figure in a cheap suit, a little bit of grayness and emptiness, really just nothing. Otherwise, the room was empty.

'So this is it?'

'This is it.'

'Your mom didn't come?'

'She's busy. Everybody's busy. We're the mourners.'

'And we can't be seen, can we?'

'No.'

There was a black curtain behind the coffin, which moved slightly. Then a voice said, 'This guy isn't getting any traffic at all.' A moment later the curtain rattled back, revealing a large, plain room with two other coffins in it. Two men came and rolled George away. 'Can you believe he's being buried sideways,' one of them said. 'He wouldn't even buy himself a decent plot.'

'That lady said he was a total shit. Said as much.'

'He's supposed to be worth a fortune.'

'So let's call the lady and save them some money. 'Cause she's not rich and this is all on her MasterCard. We don't need any funeral cars; we'll just take him over in the van.'

'Fine, you don't want that money, I don't care.'

'I just think that's a nice young woman and she's sure not rich. She had to pay for it because the stiff hasn't got a will.'

George asked Charlie, 'Is this true?'

'Mom pays for your funeral, yes. If this happens.'

'It's happening! Has happened.'

'You're being given a chance to change it, George.'

'A chance? What sort of a chance?'

'If you use your money right. Let's head on over to the graveyard.'

'No, wait, you said I had a chance.'

'Open your heart, George.'

'Who do you want me to be, Jesus Christ?'

Charlie beamed at him. Then he burst out laughing.

'I'm not a bad man. I'm not! And I'm sick of being characterized like this, it's not fair.'

'Do you want to try or not?'

Inside George, a great hurt blossomed. 'I don't want people to be happy because I died.'

Charlie took his hand again.

He was in a dingy, gray little room with a beat up couch, no carpeting and a miserable little table against the wall, at which there were two wooden chairs, one without arms, one with a broken arm. The place stank of pizza and, more distantly, vomit.

'Why are we in a slum? Where is this place?'

There was no reply.

'Charlie?'

Again, George was alone. In the next moment, he understood that this was his apartment. He was seeing it as it actually appeared, not as habit and familiarity revealed it to him.

'My God,' he muttered. 'I'm filthy.' The truth was, he lived like an animal, he dressed like a beggar and he usually stank because he economized by bathing only once a week.

Shedding clothes, he ran into the bathroom and turned on the shower. The hell with it, he would be liberal with the soap.

He raised his face into the warm stream, which seemed to open his skin in a deep, new way. Deep, deep cleansing, so pleasurable that he groaned aloud to feel it. He closed his eyes and let the water pound over him, then took the soap and lathered himself, letting the terrors of the day slide off of him and go down the drain, gray water circling and disappearing.

Then the bar of soap squeezed out of his hand and bounced into the bottom of the tub. It was as he was reaching down to retrieve it that he saw what was happening to him.

He stopped. Stared.

What was this? Was this him still?

No, it couldn't be, it was another illusion. Because he wasn't like this, not at all.

He looked down at his own abdomen, then touched the broad, gleaming scab that ran from just below his left nipple to his hip, a hard, crinkled mass of rot and blood.

He watched pus and bits of scab dropping off in the shower stream, then racing down the drain.

With shaking hands, he cradled his wounded body, hugging himself and shivering, looking down at himself.

'This is your soul you're seeing,' he told himself. 'You are looking at your truth.'

The line between his physical body and this other, hidden body had not just blurred, it had disappeared altogether.

The effect was so convincing that he attacked himself with the soap, scrubbing, making lather, dragging at the scabs, pushing the bar itself down into the open sores, screaming with the fire of it but continuing on, scrubbing and scrubbing and finally ripping at the scabs with his fingers.

'God help me,' he bellowed as he grabbed the towel and began rubbing himself with it. The mess did not rub off, though, any more than it had washed off.

'I've made mistakes,' he said as he poured rubbing alcohol over himself. 'I'm sorry, I'll do better.'

But rubbing the sores only made them stand out more clearly, puckered and angry red, dripping.

He threw himself on the floor and rolled like a man on fire, rolled and tore at himself. Then he stopped. Soap would not cleanse him. Alcohol would not cleanse him.

He went into the bedroom and dropped onto the bed. He drew his legs up and covered his head with his hands and closed his eyes. He lay there trying and failing to find prayers – any prayers – the prayers of his childhood. But all were lost.

Christmas morning was coming – had come, really, but for the dawn, and he was entirely alone. He was always alone, though. He lay imagining his son. What was Georgie doing now? Waking in the predawn, finding his Christmas stocking, eager to get to the tree?

The boy had no idea of who his real father was, and never would, George supposed. He looked to another man, and always would.

He did not want to be despised anymore. But how could he change it? Somehow, he had to find his way past the compulsive hoarding. But how? It seemed as essential as breathing.

For a long time, he lay motionless, letting the dark enclose him. There was nothing left for him. His life had been too ill-lived.

He did have one alternative. He could cheat the humiliating death that awaited him in April. He could put an end to his own misery and the misery he was causing others.

Let the State of Illinois dispose of his assets. Any bureaucrat could do a better job of it than he could, because they were not full of this grinding, clutching ugliness.

He went to one of the living room windows, unlocked it, and raised it on its creaking sash.

The seven-story drop would work, certainly. Below, he could see the back alley choked with snow, but not deep enough to break his fall. No question, it would work.

He sat on the ledge, then turned and dangled his feet out into the icy air. Just a little push, that's all that was needed. How long would it take, three seconds?

Then what?

The cold air crept around him, snow falling again, the sounds of the city grown muffled. Across the alley, the dark shapes of other buildings were etched against clouds, set aglow by the light of the Loop a mile away.

He raised his hands to the sides of the window frame. All he had to do now was lean forward. Simple.

Not simple.

Would he just cease to be . . . or did all the things that had happened to him mean that there really was some sort of reckoning?

He groaned.

Just then, the clouds parted and the moon flew clear, perfect in the dark of the sky. When men had walked there, all he'd been able to think of was the waste of money.

Was the infected horror within him really his eternal soul?

There was confession. Catholics had it. In some other denominations, public witness.

He didn't trust it, though. How could you undo an evil life with a murmured ritual? He didn't think you could, but he also couldn't jump, he just could not.

Maybe if he went up to the roof, closed his eyes and just ran, maybe that would work. Because this had to be done. He was finished here. He was hungry to embrace the consequences of his life. He'd hurt so many people, there just was no other atonement that seemed appropriate.

He turned back inside his apartment and dressed himself, putting on pants and a shirt, covering the filthy, raw sores as best he could. It was just habit to dress; it didn't really matter anymore, obviously.

He left the apartment, closed the door and took his keys out of his pocket. He looked down at the great fistful of them, each one there to lock some other part of his life away.

He inserted the apartment key and locked the master lock.

So that was his life, behind him now.

Next, the final thing. Launching himself into the void off a window sill had been beyond him; simply closing his eyes and running was something he thought he could do.

He climbed the rungs of the fire ladder that was embedded in the wall. At the top was an old skylight, which protested creakily, but eventually yielded to his efforts.

Once again, cold air gushed over him. It was very early, he knew that, but even so music was playing somewhere, perhaps the Salvation Army soldier down there in the streets, hoping for a handful of change from some early riser.

'Morning star, O cheering sight, ere thou cames't, how dark was night . . .'

Oh, 'Morning Star', he had sung that as a tiny boy at Our Lady of Grace. He had not thought of it in years.

'Morning star, my soul's true light, tarry not, dispel my night . . .'

The anguish contorted him physically, causing him to draw his fists to his chest and lower his head and screw his eyes closed.

Pushing through six inches of snow at first, it was difficult going. But toward the edge, the snow had been blown thin, and he picked up speed.

He ran into the darkness and the air.

13

The awful flow of falling would once have made him cry out, but he was so ready to die, he simply waited. Oblivion, deliverance, eternal damnation – something would come.

Groaning was what came, a chorus of it, and then strong arms stopping his fall and with them a hot reek, organic, the smell of something that lived hotter than men do.

They carried him back into the building, floating as easily as men walk, their broad faces hardly straining, their odd, insect-like eyes devoid of any expression that might have meaning to him.

He felt a kind of laughter coming from them, though, and with it a humanity that was so surprising that it brought him to the understanding that those who had plucked him out of his own suicide were, of all things, bursting with joy.

Lock or no lock, his apartment door flew open and in a moment he was standing in the middle of his living room. They surrounded him, four of them, buzzing like machines, their frog-like faces dominated by the huge mouths and the great fly-like eyes.

He blurted out the first words that came to mind, 'My God, you're hideous.'

That mirth was there though, bubbling up from beneath their physical ugliness.

'Remember,' one of them said in a rolling, buzzing voice, 'one day you'll look just like us.'

Another one said, 'We're soultechs.' Again the mirth came, bubbling up, a foam of joy. 'You need a tune-up.'

Now what? He'd just killed himself, so was this hell? Or had they saved him?

'Am I dead?'

'Call Megan. Ask after the child.'

'What child?'

'See, you do need work.'

'Oh, Charlie, of course.' He'd been so absorbed in his own problems, he'd entirely forgotten Charlie.

They left, barreling out the door and crashing away down the stairs. He didn't worry about them getting out, obviously. They went where they wanted and did what they pleased.

Charlie was not alright? But this was the twenty-first century; children didn't actually die of pneumonia.

A needle of fear pierced his spine and he grabbed the phone.

'Megan, it's George!'

'I was gonna call you, Mr. Moore, but it's so late. Look, I need the day off.'

'How is he?'

Silence like a great, dark pit.

'Megan!'

'Who is this?' It was a male voice.

'It's George Moore. Is this Frank?'

'*Bastard!*'

'No, please! Please listen!'

The line was disconnected.

He looked down at the phone. Charlie was dying, maybe already dead. 'No, please God, no . . .'

He remembered his mother's words, 'When people are in need, you just go.' Words he had always ignored.

There were no cabs around here at four o'clock on Christmas morning, that was for sure. He needed to call one, but he had no idea where his phone book was. The car service was in his cellphone, so he called them.

It rang once, twice, then again and again.

'Come on!'

Finally, there was a click. 'All of our operators are busy . . .'

'At four in the morning on Christmas Day, Jesus Christ!'

'City Limo.'

'I need a car, it's an emergency!'

'If it's an emergency call the cops.'

'No, I mean I'm in a hurry.'

'This is George Moore, am I right?'

'Yeah, but how—'

'Your cellphone, Mr. Moore. Lemme tell you something. If you think you can get a driver to come out at this hour on Christmas morning for a no-tipper like you, you need to do some rethinking.'

'I must have a car, it's urgent!'

The dispatcher hung up. When George called back, the phone wasn't picked up.

Methodist Children's Hospital was over past the Loop, about twelve miles from here. It would take hours, but maybe he'd get lucky and see a cab or find a bus. He knew nothing about buses, though.

He threw on his coat and hat, then hurried downstairs and out the front door. Predictably, there wasn't a sign of a cab, so he started slogging his way toward the hospital. Once, he would have been furious. Now, he thought that it served him right. Tips mattered to people like limousine drivers.

So he deserved this, no question there. As he walked, he clutched his cellphone. Finally, he stopped and hit Megan's speed-dial.

Frank answered. 'Mr. Moore—'

'Please, how is he?'

'He's gonna die, you scum. Now, *leave us alone.*'

He probably couldn't provide any help, but he also couldn't stop himself from going. He had to be near Charlie; Charlie was some kind of a miracle.

He strode past Taylor's, past Bickford's, under the lonely glitter of Christmas lights, the long strands strung across the street blowing in the wind.

'Hey.'

A car was gliding along beside him. A kidnapper? Robber? He increased his pace.

'Hey, crazy guy. I hear you need a ride.'

Devon Lester was hanging out the window of a rattling old jalopy.

'Excuse me?'

'You called the dispatch. You said you was havin' an emergency. So here I am.'

The filling of the heart that he experienced as he climbed into the truck was unlike any emotion he had known since childhood.

'Thank you so much. I'm trying to get to the Methodist Children's Pavilion.'

'The Children's Pavilion? That twelve mile from here.'

'I'll pay, but please—'

'No, no, I'm off duty. My time is my own. Crazy folk needs help, too.'

'I'm not crazy,' he muttered.

The driver laughed. 'You not only crazy, you famous crazy. I ax around, you got quite a rep. You a miser. Richer than God and you worryin' about every little penny all the time. So why you goin' to the Pav? They owe you money?'

'A child is ill.'

'And he owe you money?'

'It's not about money. He's – he's . . . important to me.' He paused, reflecting on the Charlie of the angels, who had wanted to save his soul. 'He means a great deal to me.'

'You feel guilty.'

George looked over at the man. 'That's very percep-tive of you.'

'Man like you ain't gonna put hisself out unless he got a real good reason. You worried the family gonna sue you?'

'I don't care.'

They rode on in silence, passing through the Loop with its riot of Christmas lights.

'Santa Claus come for you, miser?'

'Hardly.'

'Well, my little gal is gonna wake up to a brand new iPod Touch. We save for that for seven month. Fine machine, the iPod Touch.'

'I have no idea what that is.'

He chuckled. 'Me neither, Mr. Miser.'

'Don't call me that!'

'You got a name, then?'

'George.'

Soon, a large building loomed up ahead, on its marquee a sign: 'The Methodist and Stillwell Hospital Children's Pavilion.'

As George got out, he remembered the man's simple little house on that poor street. He said, 'May I offer you some compensation?'

'I won't say no. Long as you don't throw it up in the air.'

George pulled a hundred-dollar bill out of his wallet and handed it over.

The driver gave him a little, sidelong smile. 'You want change? 'Cause I only got three bucks in my pocket.'

'No change. I want to thank you.'

'Well, you're welcome. Glad I found you. You ain't gonna get a cab round there for love or money.'

'I know it.'

'You need a car, you tell 'em to send Devon. I understands you, George. You need people 'roun' you what understand.'

'What do you understand?'

Again he laughed. 'That you needed a tune-up, and at this particular hospital, you gonna get the works, ring job, new plugs.' He laughed harder. 'You gettin' the *works*!'

George was too surprised to reply. But then Devon Lester drove off down the street and was gone. Hands on hips, George looked after him.

Some people know more about the world than one might expect, and this man was one of them. Was he, also, dead and alive at the same time, like Bill Hill? Bill was serving a sort of sentence – a terrible sentence. Perhaps Devon Lester was doing the opposite, lingering among the living to give people help.

He hurried into the hospital. The lobby was cheerful and large, with an enormous Christmas tree decorated and beautifully lit. He'd always disdained the idea of dragging a tree into the house at Christmas, but he found its pine scent delicious, and the lights delightful.

'Excuse me, I'm here to see a patient, Charlie Dennis. The son of Megan and Frank Dennis.'

'Yes, Charles Dennis, he's – oh, yes. He's in the intensive care unit on Four. You can see Mr. and Mrs. Dennis if they're in the waiting area.'

'What's happening? What's the situation?'

'We don't get that information down here.'

'But you know.'

'If he's in the ICU, I'd go up there right now.'

As George waited for the lift, he considered turning around. On the way up, the desire increased. He was going to walk into a wall of hate. Worse, he knew that he deserved every bit of it and more.

The doors opened. He hesitated. What could he do here? He'd just inflame Megan and Frank.

Somewhere in his heart, he could feel Charlie calling him.

He stepped out into a wide, crowded hallway. The walls were painted with clown figures, but there was an atmosphere of intensity at the nurses' station that revealed the truth of this place. Children in an intensive care unit were fighting for their lives.

He walked up to the station's long counter. A number of nurses sat or stood behind it watching rows of life-sign monitors.

'Excuse me.'

A nurse looked up from her work. 'Yes?'

'I'm looking for Charlie Dennis. He's in the ICU.'

'ICU Three. But you can't go in.'

'I know that. Where are his parents?'

'Privacy Three. Are you a member of the family?'

'No, no, I—'

'Name, please. I'll call them.'

'No, I can just—'

'Sir, we have to let them know you're coming unless you're a family member.' Before he could stop her, she picked up a phone. 'Mr. Dennis. We have a visitor out here.' She looked at him. 'Name?'

He thought frantically. But every name of every trader he had working for him seemed to escape him at once. 'George,' he said miserably, 'George Moore.'

She spoke his name into the phone, then listened. She blinked, took the receiver away from her ear and hung it up. 'Wow. They really do not want you down there right now, Mr. Moore.'

'I want to see your superior. I want her to take them a message for me.'

'I am the head of this department, Mr. Moore, and I am not going to disturb this family any further for you.'

'No, no, of course not. Can I at least know how Charlie is?'

'We can't give out that information without parental permission, I'm sorry.' Her voice was clipped now. She turned back to her work.

'Perhaps if I could send them in a note?'

She stopped, then turned around again. 'Sir, Mr. Dennis told me that if you didn't leave, he wanted us to have you escorted out by security. Or the police, he said. I don't know who you are, but they do not want you here, and I'm sure a note would be most unwelcome.'

What could he do anyway? He wasn't a doctor. But he could afford any doctor in the world, any treatment, anything they needed. 'I can help,' he said.

'I'm sorry, but I don't see how.'

'I can help.'

'Listen, the child can't survive more than a few more hours. You need to go and leave them to their situation. Whoever you are, they really, really do not want you here.'

Sadness stooped his shoulders. But he did not move.

She stood up. 'All right, I don't want a scene. Come with me quietly right now, or I'll have the cops up here.'

'I can help.'

She picked up her phone. 'Security please.'

'No, that won't be necessary.' He turned and began walking back toward the lifts.

But leaving Charlie was just not possible for him.

He stopped.

'Sir?'

The nurse was right behind him.

'I'm sorry.' He continued on.

When he reached the elevator bank, she asked, 'Are you an estranged relative? Ex husband?'

'No. Thank you for your help.' He pressed the button that called the lift, then watched the record of its ascent, floor by floor.

The doors opened. He turned to her. 'Will you hear me out?'

'I don't understand.'

166

For a man used to being in control of every aspect of his life, his next words were almost impossible to utter. 'I can't.'

'Sir—'

'I can't leave.'

She folded her arms. 'And I can't stay here; I'm needed elsewhere, now.'

The doors slid closed. He stood facing her. 'I have to help. I can hire any doctor on earth, purchase any piece of equipment, any medication. I'll do anything!'

Her eyes grew softer. 'You're rich? How rich?'

'Ma'am, I am extremely rich.'

'Come here,' she said. She gestured toward a bench across the corridor.

He followed her. She sat down beside him. 'He has a pediatric bronchiolitis that's destroying his lungs. It's moving too fast, and he's ceased to be a candidate for a lung transplant because he's weakening too fast. The only possibility of saving him is an experimental treatment that might kill the adenovirus that's responsible and stop the advance of the disease.'

'So do it!'

'There's only a twenty percent chance it'll work, and in view of the dangers and the costs, his doctors have given it a pass.'

He knew the human mind; he beat others using his every day. He had heard that word 'costs' and knew at once to excavate around it. 'How could cost even be considered? He's a child.'

'All of our patients are children and the institution has finite resources.'

'What, exactly, does that mean?'

'Insurance doesn't cover experimental treatments, so the hospital would have to bear the expense. We've been seeking foundation partners, but that low success rate is stopping them. The truth is, we have to leave this up to Charlie, to his body. I don't want to seem hard—'

'You do. Very damn hard.'

'It's called triage, and he's not a candidate for two million dollars' worth of medical support that almost certainly will fail.'

George felt the weight of that expense, but he thought of the little slip of a child guiding him through the strange byways where his soul had been renewed. He took a deep breath. In his heart, he felt something he had never known before, even that it existed. He felt a flood of love. 'I can pay.'

'You? How?'

'They hate me because I'm her boss and—' He could not finish the sentence, he was so shamed by the words he would say: 'I'm a miser; I care only for my wealth.'

'I know who you are,' she said quietly.

'Then you know I can pay.'

She nodded. At the edges of her eyes, there appeared the gleam of tears. 'You're certain you can do this?'

'Absolutely. I can pay and I will pay.'

She turned and ran off toward the nurses' station. He heard her call out as she ran, 'I think we have an angel.'

14

George sat for a few moments on the bench, hunched, his head down.

Of course Megan and Frank hated him. How could they not? And all the money in the world was not going to change that. Maybe, if Charlie recovered, there could be some healing over time. If he did.

He wouldn't be thrown out of here, his money had ended that threat, but he knew that he still wasn't wanted. If he went into the sickroom, Megan and Frank might greet him politely, but that would be all.

He got up and once again went to the lifts.

There was a new warmth in his heart, though, so new that he didn't remember ever feeling it before, not even as a child. Riding down, little bursts of happiness kept exploding within him. He discovered, then, a secret that just a few of the rich know, that the power to give to others is among the greatest of all joys.

How strange to feel like this – to actually feel good about giving something away. But he did feel that way, and it seemed a better feeling than any he had known before.

In the lobby there was only the one clerk, now half asleep at her desk. Music played over the public address system, the carol 'Away in a Manger'.

It hit him hard, mixing the thought of Charlie up there dying and the child in the wretched manger together into one sorrow.

Then the clerk was there. He had hardly noticed her before, an elderly woman in a pink striped uniform. She smiled up at him. 'Come on, let's sit down,' she said.

He was crying. He hated it but he couldn't help it, and her little kindness brought a new wave of tears. He was too embarrassed even to look up as she guided him to a chair.

'Did you lose your patient?' she asked gently.

He shook his head. 'They don't want me near him. They hate me.' The battle to suppress the sobs made him grimace with effort.

She touched his cheek, and when she did, he felt not just the gentleness and compassion of it, but also a familiar electricity that caused him to sit up, to forget his tears and, very slowly and carefully, to turn his face toward this individual.

Out of the impossible mystery and secrecy of his inner life, the nun looked back at him. 'Christmas is a good time for us,' she said. 'The spirit of the season helps us find those who seek to be saved.'

'Who are you?'

'We're volunteers.' And so she was again an elderly woman in a pink uniform, and he wasn't certain she had ever been anything else. 'This is an old world, full of mystery,' she continued. 'Maybe your patient will have a miracle.'

That started his tears again. He fought them.

'Don't be afraid of your pain,' she said. 'Your tears honor your patient.' A phone had been ringing for some time. 'I have to get back to the desk,' she said. She laughed gently. 'I drew the short straw this year. It's a hard time in a place like this, Christmas in the early hours.'

He hoped that the call had something to do with him, maybe that they had invited him back up after all, but she put down the phone after a moment and did not look up again.

He walked out of the hospital and into the most profoundly silent hour of the year, Christmas at coming of dawn. Decorations hung slackly on lampposts, Christmas lights were out, the streets were silent pale paths in the snow.

He found himself moving aimlessly through those streets.

'Hey, again.'

The old pickup had appeared as if out of nowhere. Devon Lester was at the wheel.

'Squeeze in, Mr. Miser,' he called.

As George gratefully entered, a woman moved to the middle of the seat.

'This my wife Ella. I just pick her up from work. She on the night shift here at the Pav. We thought we'd swing by.'

'Thank you,' he said.

'Just push,' Ella said. 'We ain't shy.' Her smile gushed warmth.

'We were goin' up to look in on you,' Devon said, 'but then I see you. You don't look too good.'

George said, 'He's getting an experimental treatment. They're hopeful.'

'That little boy with pneumonia?' Ella asked.

'Yes.'

174

'I hear about that. They need a lotta money to treat that boy.'

'They have it.'

'Where they get it?' Devon asked, suspicion in his voice.

'Some guy.'

'You gave that much? *You*? Ha, I heard everything now.'

'You call him a miser, Devon, you pretty strict,' his wife said.

Silence fell, and soon they were back at George's building. He looked up at the dark old structure.

Ella said, 'This where you *live*?'

'At the moment. I'm thinking of moving to something with a little more light.'

'I should say!'

He did not want to be alone.

'Here we are,' Devon said. Then, after another pause, 'Merry Christmas.'

As he got out, he heard Ella say to Devon, 'He scared, Husband.'

Devon said, 'George?'

'Yes, Devon?'

'We gonna have Christmas with our kids now. We pray for you this mornin' at church.'

'Pray for the little boy. Charlie is his name.'

Devon laughed. 'Oh, we know Charlie very well. Sure we gonna pray for Charlie.'

As they drove away, he wondered how it would be that they knew Charlie. But as he no longer understood what the world was or how it actually worked, he took Devon's comment at face value, and did not let the mystery of it concern him.

He unlocked the front door and turned on the hall lights. As the door closed, he heard the pickup rattling away. Had George not gotten that first ride from Devon, he might still be on his way to the hospital, and by the time he got there, even the experimental treatment might have been too late to offer any chance of saving Charlie.

Going upstairs, flight by creaking flight, he remembered his suicide attempt and the soultechs rescuing him out of midair.

They had saved him, he thought, for Charlie, and for that he was more grateful to them than he could ever express, even in his own heart.

He opened his door and went in, but did not bother to lock it behind him. Why should he? Nobody who might do him harm could get in downstairs, anyway. He now understood that the apparitions had intended only the best for him. They had come not to terrorize him but to awaken him, he saw that now.

The night had exhausted him. He had done good, though, genuine good, maybe for the first time since he had slipped into the dark of his greed.

He threw off his clothes, and was just lying down on the bed when he glimpsed a shadowy form in the dresser mirror.

He was confused. That could only be one reflection: his own.

He turned on the light.

Standing naked in that mirror was the most corrupt, the most vile thing he had ever seen. He reached his hands to his cheeks, he touched the suppurating rot with shaking, wart-packed fingers.

After all he had done, *he hadn't changed.*

Filled with loathing, he flung himself away from the mirror.

Incurable.

Then, from outside, creak *thud,* creak *thud.*

Throwing on his robe, he ran into the living room. 'Bill! Bill Hill!'

'Why do you have to live at the top of all these stairs, you cheap bastard?'

'Help me, Bill!'

Bill sank down on the top step. 'Boy, I can't go another inch.'

The long, bubbling sighs of his breathing filled the silence.

'Bill, please.'

'It takes more than a big check or two, George. You have to give your life to your compassion.' His shoulders shook and he launched into a wheezing fit that George took to be laughter. 'You know what happened to my money? My wife went through it like a lawnmower on racing fuel. House in St. Tropez, can you believe. Private island in the Lesser Antilles, the whole works. She's still running through it. Probably die in a solid gold hospital bed.' Slowly he turned. 'Thousands of people didn't get what they needed because she spent it instead of used it.'

'Being rich is evil!'

'You always go overboard, George. Without the rich, the poor could not be rescued. Governments are not enough and can never be enough. Enjoy what you have, you worked for it, you have the right. But also look at the world around you. Look carefully, George. That's where salvation lies.'

Moving heavily, Bill went to his feet. Through a wheezing laugh, he continued. 'Get some sleep, buddy. You're going to need it.'

'What's going to happen to Charlie?'

'What's going to happen? Nobody knows.'

'What about the day of a person's death?'

Bill shook his head. 'You might die on April 17th, sure.'

'You know about that?'

Bill coughed. 'You're a lucky man, George. I can only wish that I'd gotten the chance you're getting.'

'Will I die on April 17th? Will they laugh?'

'You might die in two minutes or in fifty years. If the future was known, nothing would need to exist.' He sighed heavily. 'Not even me.'

He rose slowly and started down the stairs.

'Bill, wait!'

'Get some sleep.'

He disappeared below the top landing. 'Bill?'

No thuds, no shuffling, not a sound. The building was once again empty.

George went back in and threw himself down on his couch. He was frustrated, even angry and, above all, afraid for Charlie. The little boy had come to mean almost more to him than his own life. Charlie was some kind of a miracle. What he might do in this life, George could scarcely imagine. But he had to live.

179

He took out his cellphone. It was after five. Dare he call again?

He could not help himself; he did it.

'You have reached the cellphone of Megan Dennis. Please leave a message when—'

He hung up. Of course she'd turned it off. However this treatment worked, they would be doing it now.

He closed his eyes just for a moment, but the depth of his tiredness claimed him immediately to a deep sleep.

It was not until he heard the distant bells of St. Mary Magdalene and was washed by sunlight gushing through the skylight overhead that he returned to consciousness.

He sat up, but slowly. His neck was so painfully cricked that he could hardly manage to straighten out.

It was already after eight. He grabbed the cellphone. This time, though, he did not try Megan. He called the hospital instead.

'I'm inquiring after a patient, Charles Dennis.'

'Charlie, yes,' the operator said. 'Charlie is in—'

'The ICU, I know. I want to know how he is.'

'Sir, everybody here is following this case. Charlie is

undergoing hyperbaric oxygen treatment at this time. We'll know more in about two hours.'

Again, the grief overcame him, a black wave that compelled him to fight for words. 'Prognosis?'

Silence answered. Then, 'We're praying. All of us.' More silence. 'We've never lost a patient on Christmas day before.'

George had to get back over there. He had to be with Charlie. However he could, he intended to give what strength he had to Megan and Frank. They did not know it yet, but they had become part of this scrofulous old miser's family – and a very large family it was going to be.

In fact, none of them knew it yet, but they would.

He went through to the bathroom without looking in any mirrors, and dressed himself carefully. He thought maybe if he looked more presentable, it would have some sort of effect. What, he didn't know, but it was better, he felt sure, to go in a suit and tie and clean shaven, rather than a gnarly sweater and a day's old growth of beard.

When he opened the door onto the street, he encountered a cathedral silence. The snow was untouched, gleaming white in the sun. There had been a little melt, and icicles decorated the dark windows across the street.

Tolling softly, the bells of Mary Magdalene called through the city silence.

He started out for the more trafficked streets. Christmas morning was Christmas morning, but this was also Chicago, and at this hour he could expect to find a cab. If not, he would call the car service and beg. Devon, he knew, was having Christmas with his family. He was probably in church now.

The streets, however, were singularly empty. In the past, he had walked to work on Christmas just like any other day. He'd hardly noticed just how silent it could be.

He turned onto State and saw ahead a crowd. There were cars, people hurrying along the sidewalk, and the great bells of the Magdalene were echoing.

He looked at the splendid old pile, its doors hung with green boughs of fir, the white statue of Mary Magdalene that stood out front garlanded with holly. Before it there was a crèche, and he remembered how moved he had been by that carol in the lobby of the hospital, 'Away in a Manger'.

He found himself wanting to pray. But he had no idea how to do it. And dare he take a soul as ugly as his own into a church?

He knew, now, that the world was filled with spirits that had vivid life. So would not his presence in that pure place anger them?

He didn't care. He had to pray – *had to*.

He headed up the stairs.

15

Soon he was moving with the happy, converging crowd. Then he was in the doorway. Then, for the first time since he was a boy, he was inside a church.

The windows glowed with religious scenes that he could not recognize, perhaps St. Joseph and Mary, or maybe that was Adam and Eve, he wasn't sure.

Behind the great altar, though, a window shone with the fire of the morning sun, and in it stood the pale figure of the Magdalene, solemn and graceful, her robe glowing red, around her face a white mantilla that seemed to be made of light itself.

The choir sang 'The Holly and the Ivy', and his heart leaped with the leaping of the deer, and he felt in a new way the power of this extraordinary season, when the hopes of man unite with the resurrection of the earth, and the promise of new life is celebrated.

He had always scorned ritual, laughed at the waste of time.

'George Moore, Merry Christmas!'

It was Mary's husband, Jake. With him was little Georgie in a blue suit with a red buttonhole in his lapel.

'Georgie, find a place for Mr. Moore.' He winked at George. 'He's an assistant usher.'

George followed the boy down the aisle. In his life, he had always feared children, dreaded the responsibility. But now he had two, Charlie and this one, this namesake.

Solemnly, the boy conducted him to a pew. Others were kneeling, so he knelt, too. He looked up at the boy. 'Thank you.'

The child looked back at him – his own face, and, he knew, his own blood. A splendor of pain filled his heart. 'You're my family,' he muttered.

'What?'

He dared not say it again. Never again. But he had included Mary and Jake and Georgie and his sister in the great family he was creating in his mind.

The boy was waiting, a question in his face. 'Excuse me?' he said.

George responded, 'I don't know how to pray.'

The boy frowned, then gave him a quizzical, amused look. He reached into a little holder and drew out a black book.

'You can follow the mass in here,' he said. With a smile, he was gone.

George looked down at the book. Prayers. Strange, solemn entreaties.

Music came, and George found in the prayer book a folded sheet of hymns for the service. He could not sing, but he sang anyway, dirty soul and all. 'Angels recognize their lord, tho in a kine he is sleeping . . .'

He stopped. People were glancing his way. He could hear his own voice, toneless gravel in the swelling poetry of the others.

A man standing beside him leaned close. 'I can't sing either,' he said in a stage whisper. Then he raised his voice and so did George, and lifted his call from the depths of his diseased soul, perhaps somewhat farther than he imagined.

As the Christmas mass exploded in joy all around him, George knelt, his hands clutching themselves, his head bowed. Begging, pleading, he called on God, on Jesus, on Mary Magdalene, Joseph, whomever he could recall, pleading for Charlie.

When silence fell, the priest's voice rose, 'There is nothing I can give you that you have not, but there is much that you can take. No heaven can come to us unless our hearts find rest in it today. Take heaven. No peace lies in the future which is not hidden in this moment. Take peace. The gloom of the world is but a shadow. Behind it, and yet within our reach is joy. Take joy. So at this Christmastime I greet you with the prayer that for you, now and forever, the day breaks and the shadows flee away. Welcome it, grasp it, and you touch the angel's hand that brings it to you.'

The congregation then shook one another's hands, offering peace and Merry Christmas. At first, George thought of germs. He always hated missing the markets because of illness and there had been coughing and sneezing aplenty here this morning.

A hand came down on his shoulder – light and familiar.

Shocked to his core, he turned. But it wasn't the nun, it was the little ballerina he'd seen two days ago, inexplicably dancing on the snow-covered stoop of her little row house.

'Merry Christmas,' she said.

He took her hand, then the hand of her father and her mother, then of the woman beside him, and of the man who had sung with him, and as he passed the simple greeting on, a shaft of light seemed to him to enter his heart.

When the service ended, the priest came down the aisle, preceded by his altar servers. Before them all the littlest of them carried a great golden cross, and George was struck to the core of his being as if by a fire of lightning, for that boy was Charlie.

Charlie winked at him as he passed.

Immediately, George shuffled out of the pew and hurried down the aisle, a lone figure rushing after the procession. 'Excuse me, Charlie! Charlie Dennis!'

The priest turned. The little procession wavered and stopped.

The child carrying the crucifix turned, his face touched by a frown of curiosity.

It wasn't Charlie. Of course not; how could it be?

As he followed the procession down the aisle, the congregation began leaving as well, and by the time he reached the entrance, he was moving in a large and cheerful crowd.

Jake and his family were there giving out parish bulletins, and he and Mary and Georgie all wished him a Merry Christmas.

He looked out into the street, now crowded with cars. There were no taxis.

Asking for help was something he never did, not ever, and a habit he loathed in others, but he had to get to that hospital. He said, 'I've got to get to the Methodist and Stillwell Children's Pavilion.'

'Come on,' Jake said without hesitation. 'I'll take you.'

'We've got another mass in fifteen minutes,' Mary reminded him.

George followed him down to a small parking lot tucked away beside the church.

In the car, Jake said, 'You have a little one there?'

'Yes.'

'That's tough. A child in hospital over Christmas.'

George was silent. He had retreated into himself.

'What's his name? We'll remember him at nine-thirty mass.'

'Charles Dennis.'

'If I may ask, Mr. Moore, what's wrong with him?'

'He . . . may be dying.'

'On this of all days. I am so sorry.'

'I went to the church to pray for him. I really have no idea if I did it right.'

'If you tried, you did it right.'

Jake let him off and George returned to the elevator bank, this time moving with a crowd of early-morning visitors, doctors and other personnel.

This time, he didn't see the head nurse, which was a relief. He passed the nurses' station, going directly to Privacy Three.

Jubilation. People full of laughter and relief – but no sign of Megan and Frank.

'Did he make it?'

'Si! Si, lo hizo!' a woman said.

'Where's Megan?'

'Quien?'

'Megan Dennis. Frank Dennis. Where are they?'

'I no espeak – esperar.' She tugged on the shoulder of another Mexican American. 'Creo que este hombre está en el lugar equivocado. Habla con él en Inglés.'

The man turned around. 'May I help you?'

'Where are Megan and Dennis?'

'We are the family of Rosa Marindo; she has had her heart repaired.' He smiled. 'My daughter is cured, sir. Feliz Navidad!'

George all but ran out of the room. Knowing what would happen, but unable to think of anything else to do, he returned to the nurses' station. The faces were unfamiliar. The shift had changed.

'I'm trying to locate Charles Dennis,' he said to the first nurse who glanced at him.

'Are you a member of the family?'

Maybe they didn't know the truth. 'Yes, I am,' he said.

'Charlie's on Four.'

At least alive. At least that. 'How is he?'

'You'd better go up there. The stairs are that way.'

He hurried to the door marked 'Stairway,' then vaulted up and burst out onto the next floor. Once again, he went to the nurses' station. 'Charles Dennis. I'm his uncle.'

'Four twenty-two.'

It must be the longest hall in the world, he thought, as he passed what seemed to be one door after another.

Four twenty-two was closed. He rested his hand on the knob. But then he thought perhaps it would be better to call her again, at least to ask before barging in. Certainly, he had no right to be here, and he thought perhaps he couldn't justify it, either. Was his interest not first in relieving his own guilt, not in helping the boy?

He could tell himself no, but that was not true. Had his true self not been revealed to him, he would not be here. His primary concern would have been how much he could dock Megan for nonperformance, or he might even have fired her on Christmas morning. It wasn't pretty, but it was him.

He said to himself, 'This is, too,' and he pulled the door open and entered the room.

For a moment, all he saw was an absolute mass of medical equipment. Behind it, were people in greens, a whole crowd of them.

Then he saw, huddled in two chairs, Megan and Frank. They sat across a small white table, hands clutching hands.

Megan raised her eyes. 'Where have you been?'

It was as if, at that moment, she had drawn him across a great canyon of the heart. He said, 'Magdalene. I went to mass.'

She nodded toward the table. 'Come on.'

He crossed the room, and also the divide between himself and a new life. He pulled up a chair and sat down. Silently, they took his hands in theirs, and the three of them began sailing together in the dark waters of waiting.

'Let me fill you in,' Frank said. 'We're looking at oxygen exchange numbers. They've been improving for the past hour. Not as much as we'd hope, but improving.'

'If there is anything at all that you need that I can provide, it is there.'

For a moment, Megan remained with her head down and her eyes closed. There came a long sigh. Their eyes met.

He was so startled that he almost made a sound.

She blinked, and the nun was gone, returned into her.

But he'd also seen the nun in the old volunteer downstairs, in others here and there. She was not one, specific woman, then, but something like the spirit that is in them all, the dark and urgent spirit of the womb and the softness of their hearts.

One of the men in green came away from the bedside and approached the table. He drew off his surgical mask, revealing a tired, careful face. His eyes closed, then, for a moment, and the professional demeanor collapsed.

Megan's hands tightened around his and her husband's, and George knew where the iron of Charlie's grip had come from.

The doctor said, 'We've crossed the divide. The infection has receded and the lungs are intact.'

His eyes sparked, then, with what George knew was the glare of victory. He had seen it many times on the faces of great traders. Bill Hill. He had worn it, too.

Megan got to her feet. 'I want to hold him,' she said.

'Suit her and glove her,' the doctor said.

As nurses helped her, the doctor regarded George. 'You're the angel?'

'The angel is in that bed.'

'A miracle is in that bed. But you paid for it.'

'You would've found a way.'

The doctor raised his eyebrows. 'Maybe.'

Frank said, 'Thank you, George.'

He looked into Frank's eyes. 'I am very far from deserving thanks.'

Frank smiled gently, and George saw a forgiveness in the expression that told him that Frank might be the younger of the two of them, but he was the wiser. 'I'm going to start a foundation,' he stammered. 'I want you two to—' He stopped. Here he was, even at this moment, thinking of himself, attempting to gain their forgiveness. He forced himself to silence. His plans could come later.

Frank and Megan stood over the little bed, Frank's arm around her waist. She slid her hands down among the coverings. 'It's Mommy, honey. Mommy is here.'

Perhaps there was a small sound from deep within the tubes. George could not be sure.

He approached the bed. The moment he saw the insubstantial, sunken little boy, his breathing being assisted by a sighing, clicking machine, he knew that this child had never come to him as the spirit of Christmas future. No, what had come was not Charlie, but something deeper, that was perhaps part of the mysterious power of the season and the abundance of grace. What had led him home was Charlie's need.

So he had understood his spirits, in a way, although many mysteries remained. If he went up on his roof, he wondered if he would find any tracks in the snow from the run he had made?

Or did it matter? What happened finally and factually in the world was not so important as the reality of the heart. He had saved Charlie and he could save more, many more. That was all he needed to understand, was it not?

Outside, he could see that snow was falling again, slipping silently through the winter light. In the way of Chicago winters, a sunny morning had transformed into a blizzard.

Frank and Megan were now side by side, their arms around one another, looking down into the small cradling bed that held their son.

Quietly so as not to disturb them, George slipped out.

As he walked down that hall past one sickroom after another, he experienced himself in an entirely new way. A door had been opened in his heart, and each struggle that he passed moved him, and made him want to somehow help.

And he would help. He would create his foundation. He would find places in it for Megan and Frank
and Mary and Jake. He would find a place for Devon
and for Emma, and a special place for Georgie and
together they would add a new shoulder to the millions
that bear the vast need of the world.

George, as he walked out into the snows of the
midday, reflected that the giving of gifts – sometimes
scorned – is actually part of the spiritual journey of the
season, as well. To seek the dreams of others is a sacred
quest, and so it is right that Christmas also be a time
for touching dreams with gifts, even as the sun gives us
all the gift of its return, and the infant His birth.

He was thinking on these majestic realities when he
saw ahead of him on the windy street the huddled
figure of a derelict pushing a grocery cart loaded with
junk.

He stopped, instantly frightened of what that might
actually be. But no, of course not. Like the nun, like
the soultechs, like his secret Charlie, Bill Hill, also, had
been part of his moral journey. He was never an actual
man, condemned to living death. Of course not; such
things were impossible.

The man he was watching was real. He was alive. He
was cold and alone. Helping him – not just giving him

a dollar, but really, actually helping him – would not take more than an hour.

Still, they scared him. They could be violent. This one, in particular, scared him, hunching as he did, glaring at George from under his shabby hat.

Still, he went closer.

The man stopped. He stood motionless, still hunched.

'Sir? Excuse me, I can help you.'

Lowering his head, the man continued on, the squeaking of his cart the only sound but for the general sighing of the snow.

'Sir, I can get you food. I can get you clothes. If you don't want to go to the shelter, I'll put you in a hotel.'

The man stopped. His shoulders began to shake.

'It's not a joke. I'll put you in a residential hotel. I'll help you get back on your feet. We'll do it together.'

The head turned, the face reappeared from under the hat.

'We'll do it together!'

The man toppled slowly over, like a great old tree under too heavy a weight of snow.

George ran to him and bent down to him. 'Sir, let me—'

He stopped. There was nothing more to be said. This man was dead.

On his filthy old face, though, he did not see an expression of agony or even of sorrow. Not only that, he recognized the face.

No matter how impossible to explain, this man was clearly Bill Hill, and his dead face had upon it the softest, gentlest and happiest smile that George had ever seen.

George called the death in to the police, and waited for the coroner's vehicle to come. As the attendants gathered Bill's remains, he listened to their confused discussion of how a body could have remained like this on a Chicago street for so long.

'He's only been here a few minutes,' George said. 'I saw him fall.'

One of the attendants turned to him. 'Look, Mister, look at the corpse. This man has been dead for months, maybe years.'

As they bundled the remains in a bag for transport to the mortuary, George saw that there was nothing there but dust and bones, and an old, long-frozen face.

On that face was the memory of a smile.

The End

GIRL. BOY. S

GIRL. BOY. SEA.

CHRIS VICK

ZEPHYR

First published in the UK in 2019 by Zephyr,
an imprint of Head of Zeus Ltd

9 7 5 3 1 2 4 6 8

A catalogue record for this book is available from
the British Library.

ISBN (HB): 9781789541373
ISBN (E): 9781789541366

Typeset by Ed Pickford

Printed and bound in Great Britain by
CPI Group (UK) Ltd, Croydon CR0 4YY

Head of Zeus Ltd
First Floor East
5–8 Hardwick Street
London EC1R 4RG
WWW.HEADOFZEUS.COM

For a very brave lady, my mum.

Pandora

i

We were twelve nautical miles north of the Canary Islands. The sun was high and the wind was pushing the sails hard.

I loved it. Getting soaked from spray, sunburned, feeling the speed, the *force* of the yacht, screaming through the chop.

We were a crew of seven, all guys, aged fourteen to sixteen, plus first mate Dan, who was a couple of years older than us, and our captain, Jake Wilson. He was thin, ropey-strong, in charge of the boat, and of getting us in shape for the Youth Sail Challenge.

It was good. We were working together, getting a handle on what to do. I didn't feel like the seasick rooky who'd stepped off the plane days earlier. I'd even made friends, Sam and Pete.

I was told to take the wheel and keep *Pandora* steady, while Wilko answered a radio call. His head popped out of the cabin. He opened his mouth as if to speak, but took a breath and swallowed.

'Okay?' I said.

'Squall to the north. We're heading home. We need to winch up the tender.'

The crew's heads turned, like meerkats scanning the sea. The sun was dead over. I couldn't tell which way was north, but there were no clouds in any direction. The wind was strong, but not fierce.

'You sure?' I said.

'Yes! I just got off the radio. The wind's going to change too. Let's just get the tender up, yeah?'

The tender was the ship-to-shore rowing boat we were pulling. I was a novice sailor, but even I knew there was no need to winch it up. Not unless Wilko was intending to sail *Pandora* fast. I didn't question him, I did what I was told. We all did. Dan took the wheel and three of us helped Wilko with the boat. Then we took down the regular sails and put up a storm jib. In the time it took to do that, the steady southwester that had been pushing us all morning died, and a fresh wind came from the north. With the sail up, *Pandora* made a huge, arcing turn. The wind filled the sail and the yacht ran like some beast off a leash. We were riding raw power.

Someone shouted: 'Look!' The horizon behind was a blur, a thin line of night. One minute it hadn't been there, the next it was. Far away, but creeping closer.

'What now?' I said.

'Well, for a start, Bill, you can get your lifejacket on,' said Dan.

I'd taken mine off, when I'd changed my t-shirt, and hadn't put it back on. I hadn't even noticed I wasn't wearing it. I dived for the cabin, grabbed it and came back on deck.

The fun had stopped. A cold stone of fear settled in my gut. I looked at the lifejacket I was holding, *willed* my hands to move, but they were trembling. I was about to put it on when we hit a wave and I stumbled, fell and dropped the lifejacket, just dropped it, clumsily and uselessly. I watched it slip and slide off the deck and into the water.

ii

The wind began to rage. Waves heaved and pitched, as if the sea had been storm-savaged for days, not minutes. Wilko kept Dan and two others – the most competent – and told the rest of us to go to the cabin. But I stayed on deck. I had to watch, to see what was happening.

Pandora handled it at first. The sail strained and billowed, urging us forwards. But every time I turned to look, the storm seemed closer. Clouds streamed across the sky. And the wind veered this way, then that, making *Pandora* judder and stutter.

Wilko slipped and lost his grip on the wheel, leaving it spinning wildly. We went side on, with *Pandora* leaning into the sea. A crest smashed over the side, soaking me. I struggled to get upright, numbed by the force of the wave. Gasping with the shock.

There was metal sky above us now, and light ahead. It was a race to the light, but we were losing. The storm drew over us like a cloak.

Ahead was a vast mound of water, a mountain, swelling into a monster, surging and rising.

Wilko had the wheel again, spinning it hard, getting us straight on to face the wave. We went down a trough, sliding sideways as though a giant hand was pulling us.

I saw then, in the water: a shadow. For a second. Something huge, something close.

We went over the peak, tumbled down the face of a wave. The bow nosedived. The sea ate *Pandora*. The sky fell. A sky of water. We went under and there was a judder, a shock against the whole boat. I held on, battered by the rush of water.

We came up, gasping, scanning the sea for the next wave. But the one that got us had been a freak.

'Thank God,' I panted.

Wilko turned *Pandora* and barked orders. He set his jaw, his eyes dead ahead.

'That was a warning,' he said. 'There'll be others.'

I waited for *Pandora* to steady herself, to set us off, to beat the storm. But she dragged. I thought of the shadow. What had we hit? A rock? A whale?

Dan's panicked face appeared at the cabin hatch.

'Water!' he shouted.

I ran to look. Three of the lads sat at the table, watching in disbelief as seawater covered their ankles, then their shins. They drew their legs up.

Think, think, I said to myself. 'Don't panic, it's from the wave.'

But was it? The water was sloshing about so much it was hard to tell.

'Take the wheel,' I heard Wilko yell at Dan. He scrambled into the cabin.

Time slipped and rushed, quick as the wind.

Wilko panicking; fumbling, to get the electric pump working.

Wilko kicking it when it failed.

Wilko grabbing the radio mic and shouting, 'Mayday,' and the co-ordinates, over and over and over.

The radio crackling and whistling:

'We hear you *Pandora*, can you...'

And the voice drowning in a rage of howls and crashes.

The boat spinning.

Wilko getting the hand-pump working, for ten seconds, before he realised: water *was* filling the boat, really, really fast.

The boys at the table, trying to escape the rising water. Pete crying: 'Why is this happening?'

'The tender,' I said.

'No, there's a life raft,' said Wilko, 'an inflatable in the hold. The rowboat would be useless.'

He got busy hauling the raft out. We helped drag the thing on deck and unwrapped it, like a huge orange tent out of a bag. Wilko pulled a handle. The raft inflated in seconds. It was a dinghy, a solid ring of air-filled tube, with a canopy and zipped door. It had a long rope attached, which Wilko tied to the gunnels.

'Help me,' he said. Together we picked it up and hurled it onto the water. I was at the rear of the group; a huddle of scared, soaked lads. Wilko climbed over the gunnel and down the ladder.

'You can't go first!' someone shouted. But Wilko wasn't. He stood, one hand gripping the ladder, the other holding the rope and pulling the raft close.

'One at a time. Climb down and round me.'

The wind thrashed the flapping sails. *Pandora* rolled. The world was seesaw sick.

We hustled and jostled. Pete squeezing past Wilko then using the rope and flinging himself head first through the opening of the raft, vanishing into safety.

Another followed. Same procedure.

'Hurry up!' someone screamed, trying to push past the others.

The raft rose and fell. One second Wilko was waist-deep, the next clear.

We all wanted to be next, but not to look desperate. I tried not to panic; *forced* myself not to thrust my way forwards.

'Keep in a queue,' Dan said. But it sounded ridiculous.

'What about supplies?' said Sam.

'Just get in!' Wilko yelled.

Sam did as he was told. We all did.

But what Sam had said made sense. No one knew where we were. Not exactly. We could be out there for days. And there were three more in front, before it was my turn to get into the raft.

Pandora was filling with water so I had to be quick. I raced to the cabin, grabbed a hold-all bag and emptied it. The cupboard door swung open. I took tins and bottles, as much as I could carry.

Time slowed. I tried to climb the sloping deck, back to the stern. They were all on the raft. Even Dan hadn't waited. There was just Wilko, still holding the rope to the yacht, urging me to hurry. I wanted to give the bag to him, but it was awkward. He had to let go of either the rope or the ladder to get it. He chose the rope, took the bag, swinging it into waiting hands. But there was too much space between him and the raft. He swung again, teetered, and fell into the water.

Wilko vanished, appeared, vanished, appeared, held in the surging swell.

The raft ran off till the rope was taut. A chasm of churning water lay between me and it.

Somehow Wilko found the rope and pulled himself along it, till he reached the raft and they hauled him in.

They tried to pull the rope, to get the raft closer to *Pandora*, but the sea was holding it away, straining the rope hard.

I put a foot over the side, forcing steel into my gut, ready to grab the rope and let my body fall in the water. I took a breath and—

The rope snapped. Whiplashed into the sea.

The raft shot away, swallowed by waves and sheets of windblown spray.

The last I saw was their horrified faces. The last I heard was their shouts drowning in the wind.

iv

I froze. Half off the boat, clinging to the ladder for long seconds. Not believing.

But I couldn't wait, or think. I climbed back on board and rushed to the cabin. It was filling quickly. I made myself jump in, fighting panic, fighting the fear that I'd be held in there, that I'd die. I waded through. Too slow. The water nightmare thick. I grabbed a plastic bag, and filled it in a blur of action. Tins, water bottles, book and pen. My hands just grabbed stuff without thinking. I must have found the knife too, though I don't remember that.

I chucked the bag in the tender, winched it down and climbed in, cutting the rope before the sinking yacht could suck me down with it.

Like the raft, I was taken, pushed and whirled away from *Pandora* and into chaos. I kept in the centre, sitting low on the floor, gripping the sides. I went so far, so fast, I didn't even see *Pandora* go under.

I shouted: 'Wilko! Dan! Sam, Pete!'

I was thrown up and over and down valleys of water. Rain fell in sheets. The winds raged. There was no light now, I was lost.

I tried to stay in the middle, but had to move this way or that, when a wave tipped the boat sideways. More than once I thought I'd capsize.

In a moment when the storm slackened, I found the hold at the back of the boat and shoved the bag and bottles inside.

I put the oars on the floor and sat on them, to stop them going overboard.

And held onto the gunnels.

~

Grey sea and rain, rain and grey sea. The violent rollercoaster of the waves.

The storm roaring and shrieking. Endlessly furious.

I used my cap to bail. Every time I got some out I'd get hit again, or the bow would dive into a wave, and water would flood in.

I had to keep the boat upright. Shifting my weight to one side or the other wasn't enough. So I tried using the oars, to keep the boat on an even keel. But one was snatched in seconds. It vanished in the gloom.

Another wave whacked the boat.

I bailed and bailed. My muscles nagged. And the wind screamed:

You cannot carry on. I am endless.

On and on and on.

Every wave was going to be the last. The one that got me. The one that filled the tender and tossed me into the sea.

After hours of it I got kind of used to it, but more and more tired, from holding on and bailing. *Kind of* used to it. I got over and down another wave and shouted: 'To hell with you.'

Endless.

'You haven't got me!'

Another wave – *every* wave – that didn't get me was a victory.

Endless.

'I'm going to live. You hear me? I'm going to live!'

I tried to *look* brave, while my gut churned sick with fear. I know that's crazy, I was alone. But I had to look brave, I had to show it.

Hours passed. I couldn't see the waves. I couldn't see the end of the boat.

I bailed and bailed.

But I slowed too.

Muscles became dead weights.

It was winning. I was losing.

I wasn't fighting the storm any more. I was fighting my own body. Its weakness, its smallness.

I hated myself. And almost cried.

'Stop snivelling. Stop!'

I believed I was going to die.

~

At some point things changed. It let me live. That's how it felt. Whatever it was had been toying with me.

And the monster calmed. I bailed till there was only a little water in the hull, bracing myself for another storm to come out of the dark. But it never did.

I remember staring into the night, holding my cap in my hand, my head spinning.

I don't remember losing the cap. Or passing out.

The Sea

I woke.

There'd been blackness, now there was blinding light. The world had been chaos, now it was still.

The sun rose. At first I wanted the heat of it: to dry me, to warm me. But as the sun got higher it became uncomfortable, then painful. I hid under my storm-cheater for shade, and learned over minutes and hours to hate the sun. The ruler of this new world.

～

It was like that for three days. There was flat-glass-blue: north, south, east and west. No birds, no fish jumping, no wind or swell, no clouds.

I thought, over and over and wrote in my note-book:

This isn't a place. This is nowhere.

I'm alone, in a rowboat, in the Atlantic.

I'm 15. I'm not sure I'll make 16.

Pandora, Wilko, Sam, Pete, Dan and the rest of the crew. They were just memories. Mum, Dad, England. TVs, trainers, trees, butterflies. All stuff that stopped being real.

The sun, the heat. They were real.

I was terrified one minute, a hundred per cent believing I'd be found the next. I'd go from one state to the other for no reason.

I'd stand, shouting and waving my arms for help.

I'd sit, hugging my knees, rocking.

I got angry. I told myself I was an idiot for not getting on the life raft. Then I told myself I was an idiot for even agreeing to join the so-called challenge in the first place. Then I was angry with Wilko. Then I was angry with Dad.

'It'll be good for you,' he'd said. 'Always got your head in some science book, it'll make a proper change.' At the airport he'd said: 'Last summer when we messed about in a dinghy on the lake. You liked that, right? Well, this is a whole different world.' And he'd nodded and smiled as if he knew a secret and I was about to discover it.

'Is this what you had in mind?' I shouted.

When not paddling with my single oar I looked and listened for a boat or a plane.

I found a line and hook in the hold. Tried fishing, using bits of tuna or baked bean as bait. But the 'bait' turned to mush in the water.

I looked again for planes. But there was nothing. There kept being nothing, hour after hour, day after day.

~

Sea states are measured 0 to 9. 1 is ripples, 11 is the mother of all storms.

This was zero.

In the storm the sky and sea had tried to kill me. Now, I thought: *They're still trying, only more slowly.* I had this image in my head: The boat drifting ashore. A skeleton in the rags of a stupid cartoon duck t-shirt and shorts. Birds have pecked off my flesh; the sun has whitened my bones. There's no way to ID my skeleton at first, just a notebook wrapped in a plastic bag, clutched in bone fingers.

I tried not to think about that. But I couldn't help it. There was nothing to distract me. Just the sea and me, with some tins of food, three plastic bottles (two empty, one now only half full), a notebook and pen, a knife.

I made notes. I hoped I'd read them back one day. But I knew I might not. Would anyone? Some stranger who'd give the book to Mum and Dad, so they'd know what happened.

I tried writing in the notebook:

Dear Mum, Dear Dad,
If you read this then

I couldn't write any more. I wasn't ready for that. Not yet.

～

On the third day I saw a dot on the horizon. A blurred black star that faded in and out of sight. The sun hammered the water so hard it made the horizon shake. I had to squint to see the dot at all. I couldn't tell if it was even real, or my mind playing tricks.

I made my way towards it, paddling with my one oar.

What else was I going to do?

～

As I got closer it became more 'speck' than 'dot'.

The sun was a searing oven ring on max. If I reached up it would burn my fingers. It was exhausting, paddling in the heat, but if I waited till sundown – when it was cooler – I wouldn't reach it before night.

Still, I stopped every ten minutes. I huddled under my jacket, sipping water. It moistened my mouth for a second. And what had once been my lips. They'd become blisters.

ii

The thing was dark and round-ish. Jetsam. Maybe a barrel or oil drum bobbing in the water. And there was something on top of it. Some clogged-up rope or netting.

I got closer. It *was* a plastic barrel. The thing draped over the top was covered in rags.

And had two spindly legs sticking out of it.

My heart thumped. 'Hello?' I shouted. 'HEY!' My voice sounded strange in the silence.

I paddled near in the dusk.

'Oi!' I shouted. I found a euro coin in my shorts and threw it. It bounced off the rags and plopped into the water.

I sat there a while, knowing I *had* to go to the barrel, to the rags, the legs. But working up to it. Because I'd never seen a dead body before.

iii

loser, I saw a nest of black hair falling from the end of the rags and dusty feet sticking out the other. Skinny legs. Bones wrapped in skin.

I was shaking. I wanted to see. I *didn't* want to see.

I paddled up to the barrel and prodded a foot with the oar.

'Hey!' I said. Then I thought: *I'm shouting at no one. You're dead.*

I grabbed at a bit of rag and pulled the barrel closer. The rags were a blanket or cloak. I lifted it with trembling fingers. Underneath was a girl. About my age. Long thin face, closed eyes, dusk skin. She didn't seem to be breathing.

She was dead. But I had to be sure, had to *know*. I reached over the side of the boat, as much as I dared without tipping it, and got a hand under each of her armpits. I closed my eyes and turned my face away. She smelled rank. I pulled. She was skinny but a hefty weight. A dead weight. The boat rocked as I dragged and lifted, huffing and grunting, hauling her over the gunnel. She thumped on the floor like a massive landed fish.

Her eyes were closed, but her lips parted slowly, as if they'd been glued together.

Her lips closed, then opened again. Her eyes opened too. Brown and wide, rolling and spinning. Not seeing. She breathed a croaking sigh.

'Hello,' I said. I sat there like a lemon before I sussed what to do. I grabbed the water and poured a sip onto her mouth.

'Aman,' she breathed.

I gave her more water. I felt bad because it was all I had left. Then I felt bad for *feeling* bad and gave her a bit more. A bit.

She saw me then.

'Aman,' she croaked, and pointed to the sea.

'What man?' If there'd been a boat, or *anything*, I'd have seen it.

'Is that *aman*?' I said. The barrel she'd been floating on was bobbing in the water a metre or two away.

I paddled us to it. It had a short length of rope on the top end attached to a handle. I tied it to the hook on the bow.

I gave her more water. Her hand reached to grab the bottle. I pulled it away, showed her what was left, and shrugged.

'We have to save it,' I said, thinking: I *have to save it*. I had the idea that if she got hold of it she'd drink it in one go. All of it. I thought of the food in the hold, of how long we might be out here. I was glad to have found her, and at the same time, not glad. Worried.

'Aman,' she croaked, in a voice like dust.

I got a tin of peaches from the hold. I had to force myself to do it, to share. I opened it and gave her some of the juice to drink. I scooped out a piece and tried to feed her. Her hand came up and took it off me.

She struggled to get the peach in her mouth. She was so out of it. *Quarter*-alive, a *sliver*-alive. Her eyelids closed. A part-eaten chunk of peach fell from her fingers and stuck on her cheek.

I prodded her arm. She didn't move. I grabbed her shoulders and shook her. 'Wake up!' I said. And whispered: 'Please.'

I lifted her head and put my storm-cheater under her for a pillow. She opened her eyes and stared at the sky.

'You okay?' I said. 'What does aman mean? Do you speak English?'

Her eyelids flickered and closed. Her breathing steadied.

I watched her sleep. I ate the rest of the peaches. All of them.

The stars came out. Tiny specks. Thin round the

moon, thick in the blue, slowly filling the sky with a river of milky light.

It was huge and silent, beautiful and terrifying.

Everything had changed.

*

Making sure she was asleep I peed over the side. It was a dribble. I was hardly peeing at all. And when I did it was brown. I wondered how I'd manage that kind of stuff, with the girl in my boat.

I lay down, top and tail, with her feet by my head and my feet by her head. Only she was in the middle of the boat, with her cloak over her and I was squeezed to the side. And she had my storm-cheater wedged under her head.

I lay awake, getting colder and more uncomfortable by the minute. I was still pleased, *amazed*, that I'd found her, that I wasn't alone. But part of me felt grumpy. Because I couldn't sleep and she was taking all the room.

There was a more serious thought niggling at me too. The fact of so little food and so little water. And now I had to share. Which would cut the time I could survive without rescue.

I didn't want to think that. But it was a fact.

The boat seemed smaller than before. The sky and sea, bigger.

I tried to rest but couldn't sleep for thinking.
I wrote in the notebook:

I have to share. But:
   *Even if they find two skeletons, not one. In this
big nothing, that's something.*

iv

I fell into dozy sleep. But then, a gentle wind picked up and this sound started. *Sloshy – slosh.* I realised; it was coming from *inside* the barrel.

And I got it. *Ballast!* Barrels keep a raft or boat afloat, but to keep steady they are part-filled. *Pandora* was my first time on a proper yacht, so I'd read a couple of books about boats and sailing before going to the Canaries.

I looked over the side, pulled at the barrel and lifted it in. It was at least one fifth full.

'Water!'

The girl stirred and sat up, pointing at the barrel.

'Aman,' she said.

'Water?'

The top was screwed tight. I got the knife from the hold and stabbed the barrel two thirds of the way up. I sawed hard, all the way round.

The inside smelled rotten-fishy. I took the empty peach tin, reached in, scooped and sipped. It was bitter, but it was water. I filled an empty bottle.

The girl reached out.

'Aman?' I said.

'Aman.' She nodded. '*War*-ter.'

We spoke one word of each other's language.

'What's your name?' I said. But after she drank, she lay down, and was asleep in seconds.

～

I woke at dawn, sweating-hot and shivering. A fist was holding my guts and twisting them. I sat up. I couldn't feel my hands, could only see them gripping the gunnels. Pins and needles tortured my skull. Sweat rivered down my skin.

I leaned over the side and puked, then dry-retched for minutes till I collapsed, gripping my stomach.

The girl put her cloak-blanket over me and lifted my head and put the storm-cheater there for a pillow. She took the bottle, with the last of the clean water, and fed me sips.

It slipped down like liquid crystal.

～

The water cleared my head. Enough to think, and write in my notebook:

The girl's used to water that doesn't come from a bottle or tap. And I'm not.

Unless we're rescued, or it rains in the next 72 hours, I will die.

Fact.

I read what I'd written.

Then I held the pen like a knife and scribbled across the word 'fact' till I could no longer read it. So hard the pen tore the paper.

The girl raised a hand and lowered it, as though to calm me.

I searched the horizon.

Nothing. Again. Just end-of-night purple in the west. Pink – changing to blue – in the east. Another burning day coming at us.

The girl sat up. She found an empty tin, and sat with it in her hand, glaring at me.

'What are you… oh, right.' I turned away. I listened to her pee, then lean over the side and get rid of it and clean the tin, which she kept hold of.

I lay down. Right by my head was the plastic bottle. Inside was a tiny pool that the girl hadn't quite tipped down my throat. Something to save.

I checked the top with a shaking hand to make sure it was tight, so no water would escape as steam.

I watched it. I willed the bottle to be full.

Steam condensed at the top and trickled down the inside, back to the small pool at the bottom of the bottle.

I had an idea.

The barrel was at the back of the boat, in two pieces. I edged my way there, dragging my body.

The girl gestured at me to lie down. I shook my head. I took the top part of the barrel I'd cut off. I reached over the side and scooped up a few centimetres of seawater. Then I wedged the barrel top at the end of the boat. I took the peach tin and placed it in the middle of the water. Then I covered the top with my storm-cheater, and tucked it under the sides of the barrel, so the jacket was like a lid. Next, I took the knife, and placed it in the centre of the top, so the nylon lid sagged in the middle, right over the tin.

The girl watched, fascinated.

I lay down clutching my stomach. And waited.

An hour? More? Long enough for the sun to rise. But instead of hating it, I wanted it. The hotter the better: to make steam, to gather under the knife on the skin of the storm-cheater.

The first drop came slow.

Plip.

Then the next.

Plip.

It took time. But we had that. Endless loads of it. Then the drops fell, like rain we'd made.

When the base of the tin was covered I took the contraption apart. I lifted the tin and tasted. Peachy, tinny water. But clear and clean.

I worked hard not to cry I was so happy. I knew I wouldn't die. Not of thirst anyway.

I offered what was left to her.

'Water. Aman,' I said. She pressed her hands together and pointed them at me, telling me I needed to drink. I did. I was desperate.

Then I set the thing up again.

We drank water as soon as we made it. But it was slow.

I pointed at the barrel and the water in it, and then at her, suggesting maybe she could drink that, if she was okay with it. But she shook her head. She wanted the good water too. So we shared.

V

Hours came and went. We hid in pools of shade, me under my storm-cheater, her under her cloak. I wrote:

Who is she? Where has she come from? How has she survived?

She looks scraggy. A ragged sack of bones with shining teeth and mad hair. But then, how are you supposed to look when you've been clinging to a barrel for three days?

I thought about how I must look too. If my hair was bleached, if my face was burned to a beetroot.

I opened a tin of rice pudding and handed it to her, holding a finger at the middle of it, like telling her to only eat half. She shovelled it into her mouth.

'Hey, slow down!'

She did, as if she'd understood.

'D'you speak *any* English?' I said. She licked glops of pudding from her fingers.

'What kind of boat were you on, in the storm?'

She watched me, with the right side of her face turned to me. The way some people do when they're really listening.

I took the tin off her and looked inside. Had she eaten more than half? I told myself next time I'd make sure to eat my bit first.

I tried miming stuff. Like the boat sinking, to maybe get from her what happened on *her* boat. She shrank back. I'm sure I came across as a bit of a nutter, firing questions and miming.

I sat back, huffing. 'Well,' I said, 'I'm talking because you might be the last person I ever talk to. And... dunno why. It's not like you understand.'

The side of her mouth twitched. She turned away.

'Or do you?'

She was smiling. The tiniest bit. *Actually* smiling.

'You *do*, don't you?'

'Some. Oui. Un peu. Tu parles français?'

I cracked up laughing because it was so crazy.

'No, no. Not really. A bit, from school. You speak *French*! And "aman", is that Arabic?'

'I speak some words French. Little English. *Little.*' She held her hand up and pinched her fingers together. 'Mais je ne suis pas Arabe... er, I am no Arab, je suis Berbère,' she said in her soft voice. 'Je m'appelle Aya.'

'I am Bill. Your name is Aya?'

'Yes. I am Berbère. Amazigh peoples. My name is Aya.'

vi

Je m'appelle Aya is a mystery!

Do I seem as much an alien to her as she does to me?

She doesn't talk much. Sometimes her English seems pretty good, then I think maybe she's pretending not to understand, as she doesn't want to tell me stuff. Who knows. I guess I'll find out if we're stuck here together much longer.

If.

And if we are, how long can we survive for? I daren't talk about that.

If it's weeks the food rations will run out faster than if I were alone.

Except that's not right (!). Because she had the barrel. And that's the aman-/water-maker. And that's life.

And if I had to choose between water and food and being alone, versus sharing supplies and not being alone, I think I'd choose being together.

Because 3 days alone – really *alone* – *was a long time.*

We started communicating more, though it took a bit of work. She spoke some English and when she didn't know the English word she said the French. I knew some of those and wished I knew more, but I hadn't done French for a couple of years and even before that I'd focused on subjects I was good at, like maths and physics, and not bothered with French much. She flapped her hands about and mimed stuff and when I didn't get it she got frustrated with how stupid I was being, and drew in my notebook. It was a weird mix. Pictionary, charades and a language lesson all at the same time. Slow, but it worked.

'Where are… were you going?' I said.

She paused, thinking.

'Gran Canaria. Europe.'

'Where's your family?'

'Dead. No brother, no sister, only parent. They are dead.'

I took a breath. 'On the boat?'

'Oh! Non, non.' She seemed upset that I hadn't understood. 'Er, avant. Trois ans. Three year.' Heavy words. A sadness she'd lived with a while.

'How?'

'I not know word… er, like you avant.' She mimed me throwing up and shivering.

'Sick?'

'Oui.'

I wondered what kind of sickness, but it didn't feel right to ask.

She went into a trance for a while, staring at the water.

'Why didn't you speak at first?' I said.

'I not know you. This is right English? Tu comprends?'

'What happened on your boat?'

She whistled a sound of wind and moved her hand across the sea to be the waves, using her fingers as the rain.

'Storm?'

'Yes. Bad storm.'

'Were there many people?'

'No. Boat is small.'

'Sunk?'

She frowned.

'I mean, in the water. Did the other people… do you think they survived? Lived?'

'I not know. I *want* they live? It is right?'

'You *hope* they lived.'

'Yes. And you? People?'

'I don't know either. I hope they're okay too.'

'Mother, father. On boat?'

'No, they're at home. In England. Safe.'

'Ah, I think they will *think* for you. Of you? You know? I do not know the words.'

'You mean worry? Yes. They'll be worried sick. Do you have other family? Which country are you from?'

She sighed. 'Maroc. You ask many, er, thing.' She held a hand up and waved my questions away like flies.

'Okay. Sorry.'

We sat, staring at the sea.

A. Long. Time.

'I shouldn't be here,' I blurted out. I didn't mean to. I almost shouted it.

Weirdly, I'd been thinking about revision of all things.

'Je ne comprends pas,' Aya said.

'I've got work I need to do. My books were on that boat.'

'Books? You are, what word... *afraid* because you do not have books?'

'I'm not afraid! I just... I was thinking about home. What I'm doing in the next few weeks. I'm not supposed to be here.'

She looked at me, confused at first, then she laughed, a disbelieving kind of guffaw.

'It's not funny. You don't understand, it's not the same for you!' I said.

And immediately wished I hadn't. It was a dumb thing to say. I'm not sure she'd understood me, but I said: 'Sorry.'

'We live. We have food, aman, the storm is finish.'

'I should never have got on *Pandora*.'

'Pandora?'

'Yes, the boat, the yacht I was on. It was called *Pandora*.'

'Ah oui, Pandora.' She nodded, as though it meant something. And that irritated me. I don't know why.

'Does it matter what the boat was called?' I said.

'Pandora, you know…?'

'"Know *Pandora*…?" What are you talking about?'

She sighed and frowned. 'I cannot say, my English…'

'Oh, stop apologising about your flipping English! I'm not supposed to be here,' I said again. I still didn't think she knew what I meant, but the look she gave me, it was as if she *did* know. She made a 'tsch' sound between her teeth, and stared out to sea and was done talking with me for a while.

vii

DAY 5

I need to talk to Aya.

I need to do the maths. About how lost we are. About how long we can survive.

I don't know if she thinks about it like I do. She must.

?

When she dreams she murmurs and twists and turns. I whisper: 'ssshhhhh' slowly, till she settles. When I get narky, she tells me it will be okay. I don't think she's really thought this through.

'I could understand us not being found,' I said, 'if it was cloudy and a plane flew over. If the sea was so rough they couldn't see us. But not this.' I picked up the pen and book and drew the Canaries and Africa. 'But if they don't find us soon it gets harder and harder. Let me show you. I reckon they

have to pinpoint the last *known* location of *Pandora*.
Then they'd estimate how far survivors might travel,
assuming they've found the others and are looking for
me... for us. They draw a line between the two points.
Then they draw the circle, like this. This is where
they're searching.'

I drew in the notebook.

'They'd estimate how far we might travel in one
day. The radius of the circle gets longer by that amount
every day. The area of a circle is equal to the square of
its radius times pi. So if the radius doubles, say from
two to four miles, the search area will go from twelve-
ish square miles to over fifty.'

I wrote 'one day' by the first circle, drew a larger
one and wrote 'two days' by the second.

'How you know this thing?' said Aya.

'I'm working it out. It's maths. I can do maths. It
gets harder for them every hour. That's a fact. Still
I...' My voice trailed away. I looked out and around.
I knew the hard truth of it. Like Dad always said:
facts are facts, they don't care about your feelings.
So believing we were going to be found was stupid,
and getting more stupid by the hour. When I began to
think about that, about the reality of it...

'Je comprends,' Aya said. She traced the larger
circle with her finger.

'The... word you say before? *Find*? It is right? *Find*
us, oui? They will find Insh-Allah.'

She took the pen, and wrote:

إن شاء الله

'If God wills it, right? You believe that?'
'It is words we say,' she replied, not answering my question.
'Right.'

viii

Aya. Maybe she had hope. Even belief. Insh-Allah.

Me? I didn't know. I *felt* as if I had hope. Then I'd think: *Facts don't care about your feelings. They're just facts.*

I rowed early, trying to take us east. But it was a lot of energy for little distance and I worried I might be taking us *away* from the search, though it had to be better than west, which was into the Atlantic.

But I couldn't row once it was hot.

I tried fishing again. The bait just fell off, again.

I tried with no bait. That was pointless too.

'I have never felt so useless in my whole life,' I said.

'You try. We try. We must.'

So our main pastime in those hours was learning to communicate. Aya was inquisitive. She pointed: 'This is sun. Sea. Water. Thing that is make rain, what is?'

'Cloud.'

'Yes, cloud.' She made notes in my book, sometimes

in Arabic, sometimes in a strange language of circles and squares and lines, more like symbols than any writing I'd ever seen. She said this was Amazigh, her language. When we'd been through everything we had in the boat, or could see or imagine was in the water – like fish and sharks and dolphins – she started on other things. Random things, anything she could think of, or draw. She drew basic shapes and guessed at the words to describe them. The names of things from the worlds we left behind: tree, flower, car, television, camel, tent, mosque, football, mountain, cake, burger. Somehow we worked out you can eat camel burger. And the fat from the hump she told me, eaten in thick slices. Turned out she knew more English than I'd thought. She'd had to warm up to remember.

'Where you live?' she said.

'Hampshire. It's in the south of England.'

'Good life?'

'Yes.'

I found it hard to talk about. Simple things tripped me up. I wanted to remember, but it was hard to speak of those memories without getting upset. The hunger and tiredness didn't help.

I described our car. How untidy my room was. I talked about my dog, Benji.

'He's a mongrel, a scrappy little thing we got from the rescue place…' I stopped.

'You are okay?'

'I'm fine!' I couldn't say more. It wasn't homesickness. Not just that. I was thinking: *I might never see them again. That goodbye, at home, before getting in the car with Dad. Mum hugging and then another hug and too many kisses, wiped off my cheek like when I was a kid.*

'Benji will miss you,' Mum had said.

'I'll miss him.'

'Be safe!'

'I will.'

'See you in a couple of weeks.'

'Yeah. Bye.'

I didn't know it might be the last time I ever said it.

I thought all these things, but I didn't say them to Aya. I got back to sharing words. Words for food, London, countryside. But nothing too 'me'.

She learned quickly. She mimicked me, repeating each new word she learned three or four times. She taught me Berber words. But I couldn't get them out. It was all throaty and lots of 'acch' and 'szz' and Aya laughed when I tried, and couldn't get it right, even if I thought I'd said the words *exactly* as she did.

We talked, and we made aman. Every time, before we refilled it with water, we scraped salt and stored it in a tin. Aya said we would need it if we caught fish.

In the middle of the day I reached over the side to scoop up seawater and the light and angle were just right to show my warped reflection. My hair had bleached to straw. My face was berry red. There was brown-ness in the skin too. It wasn't so raw.

I woke in the night to pee.

Aya did the same after me.

A few clouds had come over us. The sky was hazy. It was still mean-hot, but a whispery breeze had picked up. There were soft greens and silvers on the sea. A gentle swell rolled the boat.

Sea state 1 to 2.

That was how it was. I noticed any little change. Every little detail.

The sea and sky were our universe, and the boat was our world. A planet that had broken gravity and left its star. Drifting in the inky blue.

ix

I didn't sleep much.

I couldn't stop thinking about that ratio of time and distance and the full horror of those facts. A horror that was real.

In the dawn light I took stock and wrote it down:

Rowboat – fibreglass hull with outer wooden shell. Pretty. But only made for ferrying to yachts or messing about near shore.
Supplies in the hold:
8 tins: tuna, baked beans, soup, peaches, rice pudding
Plastic bag of lemons and 3 bananas
I reckon we can get by on 2 tins per day between us. Not much. Just 2 days not-starving. Then one between us every day till we run out.
6 days in all.
I don't know how much longer a human can survive after that.

Equipment:
One oar
One seat, removed to give us more space
Fishing line and hook on a reel
Knife – big/sharp grabbed from Pandora.
3 x 1 litre plastic bottles, slowly filling

I tried fishing one last time. Again the bait turned to mush as soon as it hit the water.

'It's useless. It's no good,' I said.

Aya was sitting, hugging her knees and staring at me.

'The fishing?'

'That. Everything.' I looked at the hook and line in my lap. Putting it away would feel like giving up. Trying again was pointless.

'We must hope,' said Aya, softly.

'Don't you get it? No planes, no boats, that storm has put us somewhere they're not looking. We're going to die out here.'

'I do not feel this.'

'Facts don't care about your feelings.'

'Facts? What is this word?'

'Facts. What's real. The *truth*. We've got eight tins left. Six days. Maybe make it last longer, starve slower. But still starving. Get it?'

'You are angry because you are afraid.' She crossed

her legs, and sat up, her back rigid straight. 'I tell you one thing is true. We are strong.'

'Are we? Why? How?'

'We do not have a choice. We must be strong. We are not alone. We are together. There is, um, there is *truth* in this? I am not saying well.'

'A reason. You think there's a reason? There's no reason. It's just luck. We both could have drowned. We think it's a miracle we didn't die, but it's not a miracle, it's random chance. It was random chance I was on *Pandora*. At the wrong time.'

'Ah yes, Pandora, you know this story?'

I sighed heavily. Was she not hearing anything I was saying?

'Aya, what good is a story?'

'Good? I do not know. But I ask again, you know this story?'

'No. But I'm just *dying* to hear it.'

'Okay.'

'I was being sarcastic.'

'You must use word I know, Bill. I do not know this sarc—'

'Just tell it,' I snapped. 'Whatever it is. This story of Pandora, is it about a boat in a storm?'

She smiled.

'Yes, no. I say. Er, like tin but stone, shape like this.' She mimed.

'Stone tin? I dunno. Jar? Vase?'

'Say vase.'

She told me a story.

'A vase is given by the gods to the girl Pandora. She believe this vase have many treasure inside. But she does not know it is a trick.

'Pandora opens jar and inside is many djinns, and each djinn is a terrible thing. Each with a name. Hunger, sickness, death, hate. Many bad things. Pandora wants to close the vase, but she cannot. The many bad things, they are strong and they have sit in the vase so many years. All these bad things go into the world. But one thing is left. Hope.'

'That's it. *That's* the story?'

'The boat is named *Pandora*. The storm is the gods or maybe the gift of the gods. And what comes? Thirst, hunger, the hot sun. The djinns. But like Pandora we have hope.'

'The boat is like the girl? You're confusing a story with real life.'

'Yes. My uncle he say story is not true, but it has true inside, like a djinn in a vase. You understand?'

'What does your uncle know about it?'

'He is the storyteller for our village.'

'You live with him?'

'Yes and his wife. They have a daughter also, Sakkina. She is more young than me. I love her very much.'

She said it so matter of factly. She did have a family. She had a home. Like me.

'Is it important, to be the storyteller?'

'It is the most important. A story is like food or water.'

'Well, I'd swap your story about Pandora for food right now.'

'A story is important. Like food and aman also.'

'It's just a stupid story, if you ask me.'

'I did not ask you.'

~

The wind died in the heat. It was scorching, so we made aman.

But there was a problem: when I was making aman, I didn't have the storm-cheater, so I didn't have shade.

Because I'd been wearing my t-shirt, my body wasn't *that* burned, so in the worst of the heat that day, when the aman-maker was working best, I took off my t-shirt, soaked it in seawater and tied it over my head.

Aya was huddled in the bow, under her cloak.

'Tomorrow we'll have full bottles,' I said. 'Then we can start filling the barrel. Aya?'

She nodded but didn't look up.

'You all right?'

She nodded again, but she *looked* moody. I thought she was still miffed I didn't like her story, but then I got it. She wasn't meeting my eyes, she kept looking away because she was *off the scale* embarrassed about me not wearing my stupid duck cartoon t-shirt. I thought: *This boat, maybe it's two worlds. Hers and mine, and they're different.*

Her eyes glared, she breathed deeply.

It was tricky, her sitting silently, me roasting.

The heat built. After twenty minutes or so my shoulders got raw.

'Can we share shade, like we share food and water?' I pointed to the cloak, and to my shoulders. I shuffled down the boat from the aman-maker towards her. Her hands gripped the cloak and pulled it tight over her.

'Come on,' I pleaded.

'Non!' She stuck her hand into the daylight. Her palm was light. Lined like a map.

I went back to the aman-maker and sat there, stewing. I put the t-shirt back on, but my arms and neck were still exposed. Every minute the pain worsened and if I didn't cover up, the burning would get grated-skin bad. I'd had enough. I took the knife off the aman-maker, grabbed the storm-cheater and put it over my head and shoulders.

'No shade, no aman!'

Aya frowned, sucking her cheeks in. She took off her cloak and offered it to me, glaring, saying: *Either I have it, or you do.*

I took it off her. I picked the oar up off the deck too. When I sat next to her she shrank away.

'Hold this,' I said. She took the oar, reluctantly. I got her to hold it upright. I held the cloak over the side of the boat and soaked the edges so they'd be heavy. Then, using the oar as a pole, I draped the cloak over the oar and the sides of the boat at the bow.

'Voilà,' I said. 'Un tent!' I left her holding the oar, edged back up the boat and set up the aman-maker once more. Then I came back and squeezed in next to her and held the oar.

She sat, leaning against the side of the boat, as far away from me as she could get. I could *feel* how tense she was, stiff-still with her head turned away. It was as near as we'd been to each other since I'd found her and hauled her almost dead body into the boat.

I tried talking, but Aya wasn't interested. She wanted me to know she was only sitting like this because she had to.

I couldn't fully turn to look at her, but as she was turned away, I could see from the corner of my vision.

The bones below her neck, the dip in the throat below them. The shadow where her skin sank into her dress. Her crossed legs. The lightness on the sole of her foot. Her hands woven together in her lap. Bands of pale skin at the base of her fingers. One, two, three, where she had once worn rings.

After a long hazy silence she said: 'I am hot.'

I got out from under the tent. I looked over the side, into *cool* water. I stripped off my t-shirt.

It felt like standing on a cliff-edge. I was scared. *There might be sharks down there, or some other terrible thing.* But I told myself we hadn't seen a living thing the whole time. And it wasn't like we hadn't looked often enough. No, there was nothing to worry about. It was just water down there.

I dived.

The water shocked my skin, smarting cold on the burns. I opened my eyes, swam deep, then came up.

Aya's frowning face appeared over the side.

'Are you crazy?'

'Wahoo!' I cried. I swam away from the boat, all the time searching around and under, opening my eyes almost expecting to see *something*. But there was only water. Shafts of golden light danced in the shallows, waving and shaking as a gentle wind rippled the surface. Below, the light sank into a blue that seemed to go on forever.

I kept swimming. With each breath, each stroke, I felt better, stretching arms and legs that hadn't moved in days. I swam till I was calm and cool, away from the boat and down into the depths. When I turned, looking up at the floating shadow of the hull, it seemed so strange, seeing it at a distance. I suddenly felt afraid and lost and panic-swam back to the boat as fast as I could. It was not until I put my hand on its side that I felt safe.

'Come in,' I said. Aya shook her head, as if that

was the maddest idea in the world. And it *was* mad, because I'd need her to help me get back in.

I swam off again but not too far, and took the chance to pee and to put a hand into my shorts and under my armpits to scrub myself.

I swam round the boat in circles.

Then: 'Help me,' I said, holding out a hand.

She hesitated. I realised we hadn't actually touched before, only when I pulled her into the boat, and she'd been out of it then. I held my hand out, till she grabbed it and pulled, enough for me to get a grip on the gunnel and climb over.

Aya gabbled something in Berber or Arabic, all angry. The aman-maker shook. The knife fell off. I made it right again then sat in front of her, dripping and grinning.

'That's the best swim I've *ever* had. You go.'

She stared at the floor of the boat, at the sea. Anywhere but at me.

I backed away a bit.

'Go on,' I said.

'Non.'

'C'est bon. Trés, trés, bon.'

'Um… er… non.'

'Go on.'

She looked over the side, then dipped a hand in the water. She sighed.

'You,' she said, twirling a finger in the air. 'Look away.'

I did.

The boat wobbled, followed by a soft splash. Aya sliding into the water.

Why had she not wanted me to see? There was no way she was going to undress. I turned. She was swimming, her dress clinging like a second skin.

She swam further – *way further* – than I had gone.

'Hey. Not too far!' I called. When she was far from the boat I felt afraid, worried. But I didn't know what for, only that the boat was our home and we were connected to it and being a distance away – either of us – just *felt* wrong. She swam back and I helped her into the boat.

We took turns after that. We got braver; swam further and dived deeper.

I swam under the boat. I dived to where the water got colder and opened my eyes. It was fuzzy. Light blue around me, but endless dark below. I was immersed in the cool light, exploring nothing. Diving and holding my breath till my lungs ached and my ears hurt.

And saw—

I panicked, swam and surfaced, gasping.

'Help!' I shouted, grabbing her hand and tumbling in. I searched the blue.

'You see something?' said Aya.

'Yes, I saw *something*. It was big, moving...'

'Qu'as tu vu?'

'I don't know. But it was bigger than the boat!'

~~~~~~

Was it bigger than the boat? A huge fish maybe, or a dolphin? But one word, one image, swam through my mind.

Shark.

I looked over the side, wanting to see it, and not wanting to see it. To know and not know.

When the sun sank and the air cooled, we ate. One tin of tuna, one of rice pud.

It wasn't enough. It was never enough. We tortured ourselves talking about eating imaginary food. Steak and chips for me. A stew for her.

'We have one dish, it is name tagine, and it sits on the fire, like this.' Aya mimed a huge circle of a stone pot, and the lid, tapering to a chimney that sat on top of it. 'When the fire is low, the pot sits and inside tomatoes, aubergine, many spice. The smell, I wish you could smell this, it fills the tent. And we have small bread and yoghurt from the goats to eat. We all share this food, everyone. Some tagine so big it can feed ten people. More! Then, after, my uncle he tells a story.'

We tried to distract ourselves, thinking about the food. About anything other than what I'd seen in the water.

'I wish I could brush my teeth, instead of rubbing them with a finger and swilling sea water,' I said.

Aya looked over the side, then at me, then over the side again.

'What are you looking for?' I said.

'Nothing.'

'It's gone,' I said. 'Whatever I saw, it didn't hang around.'

Aya nodded, and sat, with folded arms and her legs tucked in.

'It's gone,' I said, and wished I could believe it.

It was a long time before I stopped looking.

'It's strange.'

'What?' said Aya.

'We're somewhere off the coast of Africa, the Canaries too. There are shipping lanes. There should be boats, plane trails, litter in the water. But here? There's no planes, no boats. Nothing.'

'Strange,' she said. 'Yes.'

X

A star blinked into the sky, right over the sinking sun.

'Un.' Aya raised a finger.

'One?'

She pointed. 'One other star. Three... there, four.'

It was a game: spot the next star. We reached twenty before they appeared so fast we lost count.

'I wish I had my telescope,' I said.

'What is this?'

I explained.

'You see more stars?' she said.

'Thousands more.'

'No, not thousands.'

'Yes. Lie down, look up. Stare at a patch of sky. Then you'll see more.'

She did lie down. She stared a long time.

'Yes. I see. The light of the stars.' She pointed. 'Very, veeerry far away.'

'The light of some of those stars has taken thousands

of years to get here. With some telescopes you can see stars that don't even exist any more.'

'It is impossible. If you see, then it is there.'

I tried to explain. The speed of light. The unimaginable distances. The expanding universe all coming from a single point. The Big Bang.

'Each star has a story,' she said. 'It is not told with words but light, and with your telescope you read this story.'

'Yes, I guess so.'

'The Big Bang. If this is the beginning of the story what is the end?'

'The universe expanding forever. Till there's no heat, no light, no life. That's one ending. The most likely.'

'I do not believe this story. It is not the end.'

I asked how she knew that, but she didn't explain.

When stars littered the night we drank aman.

'Water is life,' said Aya. 'Each day is one day we live. Like Shahrazad. You know?'

'Sharzad?'

'Not Shar-zad. Shah-*ra*-zad.'

'Okay. What's Shah-*ra*-zad?'

'No *what*. Who. *Everyone* know Shahrazad.'

'Not me.'

Aya rolled her eyes and laughed. 'Story you know? Story of Sind-bad, story of The Donkey?' She reeled off the titles of more stories as though I'd know what she was on about. I shrugged.

'Shahrazad tell story to make life one day more. Really, you do not know?'

'No.'

'Oh.'

I waited. I thought she'd maybe tell me one. And I wanted it to be better than the story of Pandora. But she didn't offer. So after a while I said: 'Tell me.'

'You do not like. *Just a stupid story.*' She imitated my voice. Too well.

'Sorry. I'm sorry I said that. I was... you were right, I was angry.' I didn't add: *and afraid.*

'I am no storyteller. I try but... My uncle, as I tell you, *he* is a storyteller. Everyone love him. When we live in village, in market day he tell story. Everyone sits and listen. Not only children, all peoples, I—' She caught herself, and stopped.

'Do you remember these stories?'

Aya bit her lip, thinking.

'Oui.'

'Then please,' I said, 'tell me one.'

I wanted the distraction. I needed something more than thinking about rescue, (or *not* being rescued), the endless blue desert around us. And that shadow in the water. I needed something other than heat and hunger and thirst. I could hardly bear my own thoughts any longer.

Aya chewed her lip. 'Okay. Pourquoi pas? I will try. But, my English is not...'

'Good?' I suggested.

'No, I do not mean this. Like we do not have food, you say word before?'

'We don't have *enough* food?' I said.

'Yes. I do not have *enough* English.'

'Try. Please.'

She thought about this, with my notebook open, tapping the pen on the paper.

'Please,' I said again. She put the notebook down and took herself to the aft, sitting where you would steer, above the hold. She tucked her feet beneath her, and perched, balancing, feet flat on the seat, and her knees under her chin.

She held her hands out and spread her fingers and with every sentence made a picture with gestures. She used English and French, and words I didn't know, so I had to guess what they might mean. When language stopped working she mimed. She got me to pass the notebook and drew pictures.

I had to ask her to stop and I had to think, *a lot*, to get what she meant.

It was slow. But it worked. And it was fun.

If I told it exactly how she said it, it wouldn't make much sense. Not without Aya sitting in front of you, singing the words and painting pictures with her hands.

But the next day, in my notebook, I wrote it down as well as I remembered it. This is the story. At least my version of it. It was longer. There's detail I know I'd forgotten overnight. And maybe I added stuff too. I don't know. But this is more or less what she told me.

The Tale of Shahrazad

Once, there was a wonderful country. The wheat in the fields moved like the sea in the wind, the rivers ran with crystal water. There was honey and saffron and many fine things to eat and drink. The tribes in this land were happy and at peace. Nobody was hungry. In the evening there was music and dancing and the telling of stories.

On the edge of this country there was a great desert, a place of heat and death. And beyond the desert there lived a king. He was a cruel man with a cruel army. His army took for his honour every city and land he wanted. They took diamonds, silver, crops and silks. Where this army went they left a road of bones, a path of ruins and tears. And many widows.

Yet the more the king had the more he desired.

The king heard tell of the country across the desert. His hunger grew and his greed made him brave. He travelled over the desert, though it took weeks and many of his men died. When he came to the country he put the land and the people under his sword.

The tribes fought hard for their freedom, but they were not soldiers. The king took the land, and made slaves of many people.

The king now had all he could desire but for one thing. He had no bride.

His army searched villages, hills and valleys. They looked for the most beautiful girl in the land.

One day they found her. Her smile shone more than jewels. She laughed and sang like a bird. She was joy like a spring morning. Everyone loved her.

But her beauty was the seed of her death. The king believed all men wanted her. And it is possible he was right! So each night he locked her in his room. She was only let out in the day for a few hours, and only ever with the king or his guard. And she could not speak with men, without the king's permission, nor could she look any man in the eye.

The king was not her husband, but her jailor.

Each day the light of this girl shone less, till one day she was a star that had no more light.

She hated her life. She climbed from her window. Though it was high and dangerous she escaped and ran, far and fast. But the soldiers had dogs and horses and they found her. And the king had her killed.

Aya pulled a finger across her throat, like a knife.

'Hachhhhh,' she rasped. I imagined it was *exactly* the sound of a blade sawing through flesh. I shuddered. Aya mimed the head of the girl thudding to the floor of the boat. Then picking it up.

'Thud, thud! Her head was put on a, um, long knife?'

'Spear? Spike?'

'Yes, spike. Like this.' She mimed the grisly act. 'But the king had taken *nothing* from the girl. She was already dead...' Aya's hands drew in to her chest, 'in her heart.'

I waited for the next bit. But Aya just perched there, like a massive crow.

'*That's* the story?' I said.

Aya shrugged. She had told it so well. Her eyes had flamed, her voice had filled the night. I was *there*. My mouth had watered when she described the honey and grapes. I could see the villages and fields of wheat, and the army of soldiers dressed in black, riding out of the desert, waving their curved swords, shouting war cries. I'd seen and heard it all.

'It's a pretty grim story, Aya. But... stories have happy endings, don't they? And it ended so suddenly.'

Aya's shoulders sagged.

'But... I still *liked* it,' I said. 'I liked it a *lot*.' And I had, because it had taken me away from the boat and the sea and my hunger. And the shadow beneath. 'So the bride,' I said, 'she was Shahrazad? But you said Shahrazad cheated death?'

'It is true.'

'Oh, then...'

'Yes. It is only *beginning* of the story. What could the king do now?'

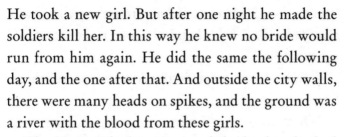

He took a new girl. But after one night he made the soldiers kill her. In this way he knew no bride would run from him again. He did the same the following day, and the one after that. And outside the city walls, there were many heads on spikes, and the ground was a river with the blood from these girls.

The king took the women of the land as he had taken cities, one by one. When soldiers came, mothers hid their daughters in barns and in wells. They sent them to forests and mountains to hide. But still the men found the girls.

Like the sun in the dawn taking the light of the stars, the king stole beauty from the land.

After three years there were not so many young women.

But there was one man, close to the king, a vizier, who had two daughters. Before the daughters had been safe, but now the king said to this courtier he must give him one daughter.

The vizier loved his daughters, Dinarzade, the beauty, and Shahrazad, the learned one. He could not refuse his king, yet how could he choose?

Dinarzade begged her father for her life. But when she saw that her sister Shahrazad was listening, she saw her tears, and was ashamed.

'Take me, Father,' said Dinarzade. 'What is the happiness of one day? All girls must be wives of the king, and all will die.'

'No,' said Shahrazad. 'I cannot bear it if you should die.' The sisters held each other and wept. 'Take me,' said Shahrazad, through her tears.

'No,' said the vizier. But his voice trembled, for he knew *one* of the girls must go to the king.

'Have you not taught me well, Father?' said Shahrazad. 'The lesson of the philosopher, the gift of song, the truth of the poet, the way of alchemy, the paths of the stars and the magic of numbers? I shall use all these, to save my own life and the life of my sister and all the girls of our land that still live.'

The soldiers came. Shahrazad went with them, and the vizier did not try to stop her.

'Where is the beauty?' said the king when Shahrazad was presented to him.

'She awaits your honour, my king,' said Shahrazad, kneeling before him. 'But wed me first, I beg.'

It was no matter to the king. He would take her sister as soon as Shahrazad was killed.

Shahrazad lay with the king. The night was hot. The king could not sleep. And Shahrazad was afraid of the morning, knowing she would face death with the rising sun. Unless she could find a way to cheat death.

With all her lessons she knew there must be *something* she had learned that could save her life.

But she could think of nothing. And as the king slept, she saw light in the east.

The king woke. He opened his mouth to call the guard.

But Shahrazad spoke then.

'Once, O great King, in a land so far away there lived…'

She wove words like thread in a cloth, one by one, making it rich and bright.

The king was amazed.

And soon it was dawn. But Shahrazad had not finished her tale. The king now had a thirst for the story like a thirst for wine, like a hunger for gold. He *begged* her to finish.

'But,' she said, 'I have no time.'

The king demanded: 'Finish the story or die.'

Shahrazad said: 'But when I have finished the story you will kill me all the same.'

So he gave her one more day.

'And *did* she finish the tale?' I said.

'Tale was *part* of a story, like a drop of aman is part of the sea. In this way Shahrazad save her life.'

'So, what was the story Shahrazad told?' I pleaded, like the king.

'Je suis fatiguée,' said Aya. 'I tell tomorrow.' She slid her knees from under her chin and, in one movement, slipped onto the deck, shoving me out of the way and lay down, using the cloak as her pillow.

'You can't end it there,' I said.

'Yes. I am like Shahrazad. Ha!'

Aya's breathing steadied and she fell asleep, leaving me alone.

When she had told the story, she'd been *alive*. She wasn't just Aya, or even Shahrazad. She was the king, clenching his fists, spitting and grimacing. She was the bride, scared and running.

We'd eaten our food and drank water and I'd listened to a story. It was as if I'd been *drunk* on those things.

I lay beside Aya, head to toe. Hunger returned and gnawed at my insides. Thirst rasped my throat. The skin on my arms stung with burning.

I tried to think about the story to distract myself. But it didn't work. All the bad things from Pandora's vase came back and sat inside me. Hateful hunger, hateful thirst and tiredness. I counted stars until I fell asleep too.

xi

Aya's cry cut through my sleep.

'Ala!'

She was asleep, but moaning.

She raised a hand and cried again: 'Ala!'

'It's okay,' I whispered.

She calmed for a while. But then: 'Ala!' as if she was in pain. She sobbed in her sleep, mumbling words I didn't understand. I grabbed her shoulders and shook her.

'Wake up.'

Her eyes shot open, seeing terrors. 'Non,' she said, 'non.'

She grabbed my arm and dug her nails in, and pulled, and grasped, as though I was a ladder she had to climb to get out of her nightmare.

'It's just a dream,' I said.

She saw me then and woke slowly. She wriggled her shoulders free of my hands.

'Are you all right?' I said.

'Oui.' She sighed. I gave her water. She pulled her cloak over her body and curled into a ball.

~

I was in a light sleep, listening to the wind. The boat rocked gently.

I heard shuffling and opened my eyes a sliver. Aya was sitting, watching me.

I kept breathing steadily so it would seem I was sleeping.

She watched me a while, then, quiet as a cat in shadows, moved to the hold.

She kept checking on me. I sneaked peeks through almost closed lids.

Aya was kneeling, gazing at something in her lap. Beads of colour lit her face like tiny torches. Sea-blue, night-purple, sun-orange.

She moved her hands and whatever she held clinked softly, white and twinkling, tiny between her finger and thumb. She held it to the moon and gazed. Then put it down and picked up another. The light shone waves of green onto her face.

Eventually she wrapped them up, putting them back in the hold and lay down.

I lay awake, watching wisps of clouds, listening to a faint, welcome wind. Thinking.

Je m'appelle Aya. A mystery, all right. A keeper of secrets too.

I woke before her. I opened my notebook, using the shimmering eastern light to see.

DAY 7

What was Aya looking at?
  What's her secret? Or does she have more than one?
  And whatever it is, what can it matter now?
  We've got a few tins left.

'You were shouting in the night,' I said when she woke. 'A nightmare.'
'Yes. I am okay. It is a new day.'
We watched stars melt in the light.
'They're like tiny diamonds,' I murmured.
We carried on watching the sky. Because that's what you do when you're at sea with hours stretching ahead. You sit, counting stars, noticing the shades of light, as if you've never seen them before. The cold night becoming ruby red in the east, then the clean, calm, sky-filling blue of the day.
'It's beautiful,' I said.

'We thank Allah for every day.'

We didn't speak for a long time then. I was lost in my thoughts, looking at the endlessness above and below. The boat felt tiny. As if it was shrinking. And us with it.

'Only the morning star now,' said Aya.

There *was* one star. Close to the rising sun. It hung stubbornly on the edge of the sky, not giving up its light.

We sat waiting for planes and boats that didn't come.

She asked me about England and my life, things she wanted to know, like how cold it got in winter.

Before it had been hard to mention those things. Now I did. Speaking made them real again.

I told her about Christmas trees. She thought it was strange. I told her every detail of a roast dinner. Sweet torture.

She asked the meaning of words. Or she described things and asked me what the English word was. She repeated them all carefully and wrote some down. Every day, every hour, her English was getting better. My Berber was still useless. She was quicker than me.

'What will you do,' I said, 'when we're rescued?' It seemed a good way to get her to tell a bit more about where she was from, what she was doing on a boat in the middle of the Atlantic. She'd never said it in so many words, but I thought she had to be a refugee.

'I do not know. Maybe...' She chewed her lip, frowning. She looked at me sharp, trying to figure out what she could say, whether she could trust me. 'Maybe I go home. I want to see Sakkina.'

'But you came from home, didn't you? Isn't that why you were on your boat?'

'Now it is *diff-er-ent*.'

'Why?'

She didn't answer.

After an hour of not-talking we got busy with our morning routine, setting up the aman-maker and the tent.

'Before, we see morning star,' she said, as she hung the cloak over the oar. 'Thief of the light. Why the morning star shines. You know?'

'Tell me.'

'Later, yes. I will tell this story.'

xii

DAY 8

4 tins.

One a day from now on.

I suppose I'd better write that letter.

Dear Mum and Dad,

This will seem crazy but the hardest thing is knowing that you are worried about me, when I'm actually okay.

Well, maybe not okay.

It's been more than a week. I know you are out there, somewhere, and I know you'll be looking. Waiting every day for news.

And I wish you knew. That I could send you some kind of message. Not even to find me, just to know I'm here.

I'm alive! Breathing, eating, drinking, burning in the sun. Thinking of you and home. Listening to Aya tell me stories. Perhaps you'll meet her one day.

I had to stop. The only way they'd meet Aya is if we were rescued. But this letter was supposed to be in case they didn't find us. Not when we were alive, anyway.

And I couldn't go on.

I closed the notebook and sat, bracing myself for the heat.

I wanted to swim. We both did. We looked for the shadow, many times.

We convinced ourselves it wasn't there, got ready to swim, then convinced ourselves it *was* there and sat, suffering, longing for the cool of the water.

But after many hours I asked myself: what *had* I seen anyway? Probably a rock, or a large fish. And it had been in the distance, I hadn't been able to make out any features.

'It could have been anything,' I said.

So I pulled myself together and went for a swim. It was precious. Moments of freedom in the quartz-clean sea.

I stayed close to the boat, treading water. I was weak. It was hard to climb back in.

Aya did the same.

When she was in the water I searched the hold, pretending I was fiddling with bottles and tins.

There was no parcel. No jewels.

Had they even been jewels? Perhaps I'd dreamed

it. Perhaps I imagined it like I'd imagined the shark. I reckoned my mind could easily be playing tricks.

No, I told myself, *I hadn't*. So where were the things I'd seen?

We ate the last of the fruit, apart from the lemons. I saw a tiny waspy thing flying about. Thin, striped black and yellow. It must have been in the fruit.

It found the top of a water bottle. It hovered, then settled on the neck.

I went to swat it. I didn't want to get stung, or have a bite that might go septic. But then I noticed it was swaying gently. The tiniest movement. It was drinking from a droplet of water.

I examined it up close, so my eye was right by it. It stayed put.

Its wings had veins. It had bug eyes and tiny feelers on its head.

It was beautiful. I didn't want to kill it.

xiii

I t was as big as the boat, winding beneath us in slow S shapes.

'What is it?' I gasped. Fear ran through my skull like an electric current.

It stopped dead still. It waited as if knowing we'd seen it. Then it moved again. The wind ruffled the sea, the shadow wobbled and stretched. It was blurred, but it was *there*.

'Shark?' I said. 'Whale?'

Whatever it was, it was big enough to smash the boat.

I picked up the oar and carefully paddled, hardly dipping the flat end into the water in case the thing rose and took it off me.

'What is?' Aya whispered.

'If it's a shark it will move further or faster,' I panted. 'If it's a whale it'll come up to breathe. All I can see is a shadow moving at the same pace as us and in the same direction…' I looked up at the sun, down to where *it* lurked, then back at the sun. I dropped the oar and sat back, laughing.

'What?' said Aya, alarmed.

'It's *our* shadow. Maybe we're in shallow water. We're spooked by our *own* shadow.'

Aya had a good long look in the water.

'Oui. Yes. Ha.'

Relief washed over me. I laughed some more, I couldn't stop. Aya joined in.

But when our laughter melted away I felt empty. Because – weirdly – I was disappointed. Even gutted. Whatever it might have been, it would have been alive. It would have been life.

'Not a shadow,' Aya shouted. 'See.'

It was rising quickly. My gut lurched. I picked up the oar and held it like a club.

It broke the surface.

Aya put her hand to her mouth and gasped. 'Hah.'

It took seconds for me to see it, to get over the shock.

A turtle, a metre long. But not as big as the boat after all.

Its dinosaur head bobbed up and down. Its beaky mouth gaped open and clacked shut. Its shell was mottled; smudged green and black. In the deep it had been a shadow. It had evolved like that. To look like the sea.

I put the oar down and we watched it swim beside

us. I hardly dared move in case it went away. After days of the blue desert, it felt like a miracle.

'It's not overtaking us,' I said. 'That means we must be drifting.'

The turtle was cruising steadily beside us. We were riding a current we hadn't known was there.

I checked the sun. Dead above.

'Well,' I said, 'wherever we're going, we've got Mr Turtle with us. Hey, Mr Turtle!' I dared put a hand out to try to touch it. But with one gentle flip it swam out of reach.

Aya watched it with beady eyes and an intense frown.

'Amazing, isn't it?' I said.

She nodded. Then she went to the hold and took out the fishing line. She got the knife off the aman-maker. She cut the hook off the line and handed it to me. I wrapped its barbed head in a rip of paper from my notebook and put it in my pocket.

'What are you doing?' I said.

'You see.'

She unreeled a good length of line from the spool, tied a loop in it, and threaded the spool through, so she had a lasso. She gave me the lasso, then tied the spool end round the oar. Then we swapped. Sitting on the bench she put her legs over the side, and slid into the water. The turtle vanished.

'You scared it,' I said. But after a few seconds it surfaced off the bow.

Aya swam to it. It dived again. Then came up on the other side of the boat.

This game went on a while, Aya trying to get close, the turtle slipping away.

'What are you *doing*?' I said. She put a finger to her lips.

It came up behind and beneath, and swam beside Aya. It was beautiful to see. Aya's arms and legs flowing, the turtle's flippers propelling it slowly along. The two of them in rhythm.

Minute by minute, Aya was gaining its trust.

'You going to catch it?' I said. She swam right beside the turtle, putting her hand ahead of it, then dashed away, yanking the loop tight. The line snagged round the turtle's head and under its flipper.

The turtle's head lurched to get free. It dived.

'Pull,' she said.

'No. It doesn't like it.' A good length of line unreeled and slipped steadily off the boat. I grabbed the oar so it wouldn't get pulled over.

Aya came to the boat and I helped her climb in, still holding the oar. The line was taut with the turtle trying to escape.

'We should let it go,' I said.

'No.'

'Why?'

She took the oar off me and pulled the line back, spun it over and over till the line was tight, then bent forward, reeled in the slack, and sat back. She did it again and again, panting.

'Why?' I said again.

'Eat.'

It took a few seconds to take in what she was saying.

'What?'

'I say eat.'

'Aya, we're not going to kill it!' I grabbed the oar, holding on so she couldn't reel in any more.

We glared at each other. Aya yanked at the oar. I pulled back. She grimaced. She was stubborn, but I was stronger. The turtle was strong too, pulling the oar to the sea. It was a three-way tug of war.

'No,' I said.

'Oui.'

Every time she pulled I gripped harder. A total standoff.

She bent down and dug her teeth into my wrist.

'Ouch!' I let go. She pulled the line in further. I picked up the knife, and got the line in my other hand.

'Ha!' I said. 'Watch this!' I pushed the blade against the line, ready to cut.

'You want to die?' she said. 'You want to die because we have no food?'

I *wanted* to cut the line. I tried to, but my hand refused to obey.

'We will eat,' she said. 'Like a goat, like a sheep.' The line was alive with the power of the turtle. It cut into my hand. I pushed the blade to the line again. It would cut easily. I just had to do it.

'We *have* food,' I said. 'A little. And we'll be rescued soon.'

'We are close to finish the food. You want to die?' she whispered.

'I am NOT. Going. To kill. A turtle and eat it raw. Do you understand? We'll be rescued soon... and...' My voice was hoarse and strained. My hands shook.

'No,' said Aya. 'No rescue. Eat or Die. Choose. Allah has given us.'

I dropped the knife and the line. I crumpled to the floor, my head in my hands, suddenly, massively exhausted.

I hated myself for dropping the knife. I hated Aya too. For being right.

～

I watched Aya struggle.

Ten minutes? Twenty? Time was nothing in that place.

If I wanted the turtle to go free all I had to do was wait. Aya didn't have enough strength. But watching her struggle felt almost as cruel as what she was doing to the turtle.

Her eyes bulged. Her arms trembled. Every inch she reeled in, she grunted and panted.

I got myself together. I took the oar from her.

She collapsed in the bow, taking huge breaths. Sweat ran off her face like rain.

I copied what Aya had done, pulling the oar tight back, then leaning over so the line slacked, and reeling the oar over and over to take up the line.

Bit by bit I brought it up, till I saw the shadow, then the turtle.

When it was next to the boat I gave the oar to Aya and leaped into the water. I got underneath it and pushed up, careful to avoid its rolling claws. Aya got a hand either side of its shell and lifted.

We huffed and grunted with the effort. The turtle landed in the boat with a thudding clunk.

Aya helped me climb back in. It was on its back with its flippers swivelling. We knelt either side of it.

It had been a curious creature. A friend, I'd thought. Now it was something else.

'I wish it was just a fish,' I said.

Aya held the blade of the knife and offered me the handle.

'I've never killed anything bigger than a fly,' I said, 'I can't do it.'

'I see goat killed,' she said. 'Many.'

She took an empty tin from the hold. She offered the edge to the turtle's mouth. It bit hard, clamping onto it. She pulled the tin so the turtle's neck stretched, then put the knife against the flesh.

I turned away. I heard a soft grating. The *exact* sound Aya made when she'd acted the execution of the bride.

I heard a *plup* in the water.

'Sorry, turtle,' I said, then retched.

I heard clunking, and Aya breathing heavily. I looked. She was balancing it on the gunnel, tipping it so blood streamed out of the carcass like a tap. It made red clouds in the water.

'Help now,' she said.

And I did.

We put offal in tins, for bait.

We put cubes of meat in tins with lemon juice.

We put meat in tins with salt.

We put thin strips on the seat to dry.

When we'd done being butchers, she cut some cloth off her cloak. I soaked it in seawater, and we set to mopping up the blood. It had got everywhere. We were murderers covering up our crime.

I didn't want to put the blood in the water. But we had no choice.

I paddled us away.

Aya took the hook back off me, rethreaded it, and using the knife – being careful not to cut herself –

folded over and scrunched up a tin lid. She tied the line round it, near the end.

'The fish will think it is another fish and will chase,' Aya said. It was a weight too.

She spooled the other end to the oar. Then took a small piece of turtle meat, and put it on the hook.

'For fish,' she said, and put it over the side.

I took the seat plank and used it as a paddle. As we moved, the tin-lid lure spun around. Slowly Aya let out the line... She pulled then released, pulled then released, doing it over and over again, so the line was never still.

We waited. But nothing happened. Eventually we let it hang in the water.

'Evening is better,' Aya said.

We used the knife to clean the shell, scraping the drying threads of turtle from it. It took a lot of effort to clean it totally, but we knew we could store water in it.

~

Evening came.

Aya went to the hold and came back with one of the tins filled with chopped up turtle, doused in lemon juice. She picked out a piece and offered it to me.

I took it. Something magic had happened. The meat was grey and brown, as if it had been cooked. Aya put a chunk in her mouth. Then another. Meaty juice trickled down her chin. She wiped it off and licked her fingers.

It *seemed* horrible. But my mouth was watering.

I ate the piece she'd given me. Tasted salt and lemon, and chewed the meat. It was like tuna and beef and veal. It was tough to bite at first, but melted quickly.

It was the most delicious thing I'd ever tasted. Iron juice squeezed from the turtle's flesh.

I sucked life out of it, into my flesh and bones.

We ate more. We ate a lot.

～

As it grew dark a fish took the bait.

We used the oar again. Working fast and pulling it up. The fish was fat and silver, longer than my foot.

When it was at the surface I leaned over with the turtle shell. Aya guided the line and the fish into the shell.

We lifted it and got the fish out. It wriggled and flapped. We wrestled with it. It kept slipping from our grasp. It took both of us to nail it to the floor, where it gasped, big and flapping.

'Give the knife,' she said.

'What will you do?'

'I put the knife here,' she pointed to the gills, 'and in head.'

'I'll do it,' I said.

And I did. I didn't feel good about it, I didn't feel bad either. It felt kind of serious. And I was grateful. The turtle and the fish were gifts.

We gutted the fish. We scaled it and salted it.

Not murderers now. Hunters.

'I didn't know I could eat raw turtle,' I said.

'Turtle, fish, meat. It is all life,' she said.

'Sure, I know. It's not that I'm a vegetarian or anything. It's just… well, it's different, isn't it?'

'You kill to live. You can. Every person can. Man, woman, child.'

'I know. I just didn't think I'd ever have to.'

'Many things you do not know. There are many things you do to live.'

'Like Shahrazad?'

'Yes.'

'Like you?'

Aya threaded more offal onto the hook, and threw the line overboard again. The lure glinted as it sank into the sea. She sat, pulling the line, releasing it, pulling, releasing.

'You haven't said much, that's all I mean. About yourself, or what happened on the boat? And before.'

Every time I thought we were getting close, every time things between us felt good, I asked this stuff. But whenever I did, we were strangers again.

'Why won't you say? Is it too hard… what?' I said

loudly, thinking: *Give me a clue,* any *clue.* 'Don't you trust me, Aya?'

'Yes, Bill. But you have to trust *me*.'

I was full of questions. But she had this way when she wanted to shut me out.

It was evening before we gave up on fishing. The food gave us life. I felt stronger, better. My mouth watered. We ate a little more. A treat.

'What was impossible this morning is normal now,' I said. 'Things change fast out here.'

~

When it was time to sleep I moved aside, expecting her to lie down. She *did*, facing away from me as usual, but with her head at *my* end of the boat.

I lay down too. I was dizzy, because she'd made north south and south north, by lying a different way.

I didn't know what this change meant or what she expected me to do. I faced her back and the thatch of hair. I reached my hand over, to hold her shoulder, maybe to hug her, but pulled back before I touched her.

I don't think she wanted us *that* close, just to be less alone.

xiv

DAY 11

End of the tinned food today.
I'll finish the letter.
Tomorrow.
Or maybe the day after.
After this tin we only have turtle and fish to eat.
It's not enough.
I don't want to die.

Hope had evaporated, beaten out of us by the sun.

It wasn't about rescue any more. It was about keeping alive. Before we'd been hungry, now we were starving.

We finished the last tin (peaches), and there's only so much turtle and raw fish you can eat. Hunger ate *me*, aching through bones and guts, making me weak and confused.

The lemon-juice-cooked and salted fish were not lasting in the heat.

I tried to get Aya to talk. About where she was from, about what happened on the boat. But she wouldn't. I thought maybe whatever it was that had happened was too fresh, too raw.

She had nightmares. Lots of them. Her back would roll against me. She'd kick out, panting. I'd sit up and wake her. She'd grab my hand and arm and hold them.

Once I tried to hug her. She started to reach up, then pushed me away, as if she'd wanted to but had changed her mind.

~

We woke before dawn, and watched the last star, before the light of the sun swallowed it.

'The morning star,' I said.

'Yes.'

'A story. You said, before.'

I hinted, reminding, hoping. I needed to escape the day, with its hunger and burning.

'Do you think you could? I mean maybe...'

'Non. Sssh.' She held up a hand, and looked at the horizon, as though the sea held her memories of this story and she was drawing them to her.

'The sun is coming. We must hide, and I will tell.'

We sat in the tent of her cloak. Aya's voice floated, painting a waking dream.

She knew most of the words she needed. She asked about some, guessed them, translated them, and weaved them together. In my memory it's a steady stream of story.

'Shahrazad live many days, she told many tales in the long hours.

'One evening the king say: "Why must dawn come? Your words are stars that vanish in the light."

'"Lord," she said. "I *tell* you why the dawn must come. And why the morning star shine."

'She told to him the tale of Lunja...'

The Thief of the Light

Once, in a city beyond the sky, there lived a thief, a girl whose name was Lunja. She had no home and no family. She slept in barns with dogs. She lived on bread she stole and scraps of meat good only for flies. She was an excellent thief and a clever one, but not too greedy! Because outside the walls of the city was the truth of greedy thieves: heads on spikes, lining the road like an avenue of trees.

Lunja owned only one thing: a ruby, big as an eye, red as fire. The stone had a name. Fire-heart.

Fire-heart hung on a chain around her neck, beneath the rags of her dress.

Like your bag of jewels, Aya? I thought. The jewels I saw. Or dreamed.

A sultan had taken the city some years before and killed its true ruler. His wife escaped the sultan's men and their daughter was never found.

The sultan grew fat from taxes. He held feasts for his court and filled the palaces beyond the sky with silks and spices and statues of gold and many other things that rich people love.

Above all he desired jewels. Diamonds, rubies, lapis lazuli and pearls.

His coffers were full. But the sultan could never have enough. Like Lunja he was a thief, but no one could take *his* head and put it on a spike.

One day he said to his people: 'I have the finest necklaces and crowns, the most dazzling jewels. No man is richer than me.'

But there was a vizier in court, who said: 'But, wise Sultan, you do not have the great ruby.'

'What ruby?' demanded the sultan.

'It is the brightest jewel in all of Allah's creation. It belonged to the wife of the old ruler.'

'Why has no one told me of this? Well, it is gone now!' the sultan said. And he tried to forget about it. But the story of the ruby was like a weed around his heart. It grew and grew until it choked him.

He dreamed of the great ruby. He tried to amuse himself by admiring the stones and cups and plates and rings of shining metal that were his and his alone. But slowly, day by day, all the sultan's treasure became like tin or painted glass in his eyes. He dreamed only of the ruby and in his dreams the stone was bigger than an eye and shone more fiercely than any fire. Almost as fiercely as the sun.

The sultan made a law. Each person must give up their jewels or face execution. In this way he planned to find the great ruby as well as claiming all the treasure in the land.

The jewellers did terrible work. Over many days they removed precious stones from thousands of necklaces and rings. Then the robe-makers made a magnificent coat, decorated with the people's jewels.

It was said he had taken the stars and the sun and moon and the light of the water, and the scales of the fish and the gold of sunset and wore the treasure of the world in one coat. The sultan wore the coat and paraded it through the streets.

It was so heavy, a dozen slaves had to carry the tail. The coat was so dazzling that the people were forced to look at the ground when he walked by. Of course he believed this was because he was a great man. And so the sultan became known as the Sun Lord.

The more the Sun Lord had, the poorer the people became. But still he was not satisfied. He desired only the ruby.

And it was Lunja, of course, who had the ruby. But now her treasure was a most dangerous thing. How could she sell the ruby? How could she show it to anyone?

Her secret became a curse.

One day, Lunja sat on a roof eating a peach, watching the fruit-seller and his friends run about like mad dogs in the street below. She watched and she laughed.

But then the Sun Lord came around the corner and the angry fruit-seller ran into him.

The Sun Lord was furious! The fruit-seller knelt before him.

'Forgive us, Lord, we are searching for a thief.'

'A thief? Well, he has not come this way.'

And someone in the crowd shouted: 'The thief is a girl!'

The soldiers laughed.

'Where is this girl?' said the Sun Lord. 'She has made a fool of you. And a girl cannot make a fool of a man.'

The man bowed ever lower.

'She is a great thief, Lord. She can steal anything. No man can find or follow her.'

Lunja loved to hear this, but she knew the man only said it so he would not seem stupid.

She leaned closer, to hear the things they said.

And in that second the light shone behind her and her shadow moved over the face of the Sun Lord. He looked up and he saw the ruby hanging around Lunja's neck.

'Bring me that girl,' he commanded, 'and the jewel she wears.'

Lunja was as good as all the stories about her. She was fast and clever, but she could not escape a hundred soldiers.

She was taken before the Sun Lord, fighting and twisting like a snake. They snatched the ruby from her and gave it to their ruler. He eyed the ruby with hunger, but he did not trust it. The jewel was beautiful, but it was not as bright as the ruby in his dreams.

'Tell me, thief,' the sultan spat, 'how do you have this jewel? Tell me, or I shall put your head on a spike!'

'I will tell you, O Sun Lord, the tale of Fire-heart.'

And there in the street, before the soldiers and shopkeepers and the sultan, Lunja told her story. And...

Aya sighed, breathing deeply. A bead of sweat ran down her forehead and dripped off her nose. 'I am weak. I cannot tell more. It is so hot.'

I didn't want her to stop. But it felt as if the boat might burst into flames. Or as if we might evaporate, becoming fainter and fainter, until there was nothing left.

'Okay,' I said. 'I'm guessing she finds a way to steal the coat. Am I right? She steals the jewels?'

'You do not want to know, Bill, before I tell.' Aya's head bowed.

I came out of the tent, into the oven of the day, and got an empty bottle, filling it with seawater. We poured it over our heads.

I checked the aman-maker. Emptied it and cleaned out the salt.

We drank a little more. It was impossible not to. My tongue was sandpaper. My limbs were lead.

Aya said we must be grateful for each day. But it wasn't as though we were staying alive. More slowly dying, and that's different.

At least we had stories. But she couldn't tell them then. It was too hot even for that.

Later, when the day was cooling, she watched me writing her story in the notebook.

'Bill, this book. If boat comes, men cannot read this. No one sees this. No one. Tell no one of me. You understand? It is important. Make swear.'

'I don't put much in there, I haven't written anything about you.' (A lie, I had.) 'It's just a record of the tins, the number of days, a rough calculation of distance we might have travelled, that sort of—'

'Swear!'

'Okay, I swear.'

'Here.' She took the knife from the aman-maker and nicked the end of her finger. A round ruby of blood sat on the tip. She pressed it to her heart. 'Like this.'

'Trust me. I won't tell anything you don't want me to.'

'You do not say. You swear!' She offered me the knife.

I thought: *Maybe if I do this, she'll trust me a bit more.* I took the knife, I was clumsy with it, there was a spike of pain and a bigger cut than I planned, and a lot of blood. I pushed it against my heart and watched it stain my t-shirt dark red.

'I swear,' I said.

'Bon.'

'But why?'

'Some peoples, I do not want them to know I am alive. If we are found because you are an English boy it will be in newspaper and television, yes? You understand?'

'Yes. I understand. But why?'

'When I go home I must be like a thief in the shadows.'

'Like Lunja?'

'Yes.'

The sky was clear and lit with stars. There was a low moaning. We listened hard. It stopped. Then it came again. Thrubbing. Ten seconds or more.

'I think it's a lighthouse foghorn,' I said. But the horizon was a crisp line of black sea against the night. And it wasn't a sound I'd ever heard.

The sound came again, becoming a groaning stretched-out cry.

It got louder still. Closer. It was no boat, no foghorn or any man-made sound. It was above us and inside us and coming from below. The groan of some unseen beast.

It was so powerful the boat trembled.

Again. Louder. Closer. I could feel it in my gut.

Aya sat up and gripped my arm.

'What is this?'

'I don't know.'

It stopped.

I saw a shadow ahead of the bow, a crooked triangle rising out of the water, sinking back in. I didn't say anything. I wanted to be sure of what I'd seen.

A *huge* shark's fin.

The sound came again. The boat shook hard as though it might rattle apart. The sound vibrated through the boat, through my skin, into my bones. Aya let go of me and curled up in the middle of the boat, hugging her knees.

'What is this?' she moaned.

I scanned the sea for that fin. Like the shadow before, I wanted to see it, and didn't want to see it at the same time.

It broke the surface.

'No!' Hot lead filled my gut.

The fin rose and rose, out of the water.

'Look, Aya, look!'

The fin was on a giant back. It *phooshed* through its blowhole, sending a plume of mist high into the air. Behind it another back soared from the sea. Like an island, it was so vast.

The thrubbing sound was joined by another, and another. And pitching and squealing. The sea, the boat, us: caught in a storm of sound.

'They're whales, Aya!' The closest arced over and dived, raising its V-shaped tail it smacked it down on the surface of the sea: *thwump*, making a wave that travelled along the water, till it hit the boat.

Aya shrieked with joy and wonder. We reached out and held each other.

A pale shape drifted through the water beneath us. Too close. I clung to Aya, she clung to me, shaking.

'I thought it was monsters, but it is... I never see this!' she whispered.

'Me neither,' I said. 'They won't hurt us.' But was that true? One nudge, one whack of a tail, is all it would take.

White skin passed beneath us again. It swam up. A

young one, smaller than the others, but still enormous next to our boat. Its head rolled over. Its giant flipper came out of the water like an arm waving. Its eye twinkled. It whistled and squeaked.

'It's talking to us,' I said. Aya just clung on, trying to steady her breathing.

A low desperate call sang out.

The young whale sank into the darkness below.

There were no more arcs or *phooshes* for a minute or so, then, when they did appear, they were further away.

'I think they're—'

The sea erupted. The whale launched like a rocket. Right in front of us, filling the sky.

It crashed, in a storm of froth, sending a tidal wave right at us.

The boat lifted, pushed back by a force so sudden and strong the aft dipped in the sea. Water smashed around us and on us, flooding in.

The boat rocked, lurching and shocked.

I grabbed the turtle shell and started bailing as quickly as I could. 'If that happens again we'll sink.'

Aya didn't budge. She scanned the horizon, breathing loudly.

I saw an arc in the distance. Heard a *phoosh*.

'I think will be okay,' Aya said.

And they were gone.

When all the water was out of the boat I put the shell down and went to her. I held her hand.

'That was amazing, wasn't it?'

Aya turned to me with eyes that took a while to see, as if she was waking from one of her nightmares.

'Are you okay?' I said.

She threw herself at me, burying her face in my neck.

I was more shocked by that than the whale breaching.

We held tight, our soaked bodies locked together.

XV

We held each other all night.
I didn't know her culture or customs.
I thought maybe even this might not be okay. But in that place, rules had no meaning.

Day 12.
  Or 13?
  14?
  I'm losing track.
  We are starving.

The sun punished us. There was no hiding, not even in the shade.

Neither of us had the strength to talk. We could barely breathe. We were like beaten dogs, bent over with hanging heads.

We made aman. We drank it. Made it. Drank it. It was never enough.

We had no fish and hadn't caught one in days.

Dots danced before my eyes. I struggled to stay awake. When I slept I had nightmares.

The sun became an evil sultan, hammering down.

'Bill... Bill!'

'What?'

'Why do you cry?'

I didn't know I was. I had been asleep. Not asleep. I didn't know which.

'There was this girl... At school. Liked her. But can't... remember her name, her face. I've tried. I keep trying. Again and again. But I can't see her face and...' I stopped. Aya's eyes closed. She wasn't listening.

I thought of school again, this girl who I couldn't remember. School, home, my books on *Pandora*, soaked in seawater, disintegrating.

'I shouldn't be here,' I whispered. 'I shouldn't be lost.' I thought back to the life of someone called Bill. I'd never been lost before, only once when I was a kid on holiday, in Italy, and how even then, I'd been safe. How I had always known what was happening, one day to the next. How my future was laid out like a carpet and all I had to do was walk along it.

And what made that carpet? Forces I couldn't control and had never even thought about. It was the same here. The storm wasn't random; some freak, chaotic spin of nature that the forecasters hadn't seen, and couldn't understand. It was something else: a demon.

And the sun was another demon.

I heard it laugh, saw it floating high above me, vague and shapeless. It was *there*. Grinning. Waiting.

All the demons had come out of the vase. But there was no hope.

I wondered which of us would die first.

~

In the middle of the day, when the sun was giving us its full fury, a shadow flicked across the hull.

I crawled from beneath the shade, on all fours. Saw nothing. Then—

'The demon. It's coming. No... a b—' The words clogged in my throat. Aya crawled out, squinting.

There it was. Flying in circles. A bird.

Aya smiled. The effort pulled her face tight; her head was a skull with paper skin stretched over it. Her eyes sank, two dark balls in her eye sockets.

I drank, just to get enough moisture to speak.

'It's coming,' I croaked.

It floated down in circles. I saw white wings and a yellow beak. A gull. It flapped and crawked, then bombed down. When it was close it veered and flew away.

It did that a few times, getting closer then flying off.

'It wants to come to us,' I said.

'Yes,' said Aya. 'It wants for us to die.'

My heart shrivelled. It was just a gull, like the ones in Brighton that steal your chips. This gull was bold like those. But we didn't have chips, we had eyes and tongues.

'It knows we're weak,' I said.

'We... can... trap,' she said. I nodded.

I wasn't sickened by the idea. It wasn't a turtle. I knew I could kill it and eat it. Easily.

'You sit. I lie,' Aya said.

I saw her plan. I hunched into the bow with my back against the hull. She undid the tent. I rolled up the blanket and held it.

Aya lay with her head at my feet.

We froze. And waited, statue-still.

I wanted to check the sky, to see where it had flown. But I couldn't move. I looked down at Aya.

One eye opened a sliver, and shut.

'Do. Not. Move,' she whispered, through barely opened lips.

I waited and waited. She seemed to have stopped breathing. I pushed the idea of death away, telling myself: *She's alive. It's just a trick.*

The bird arrived with a flap, landing on the aft.

Aya twitched a finger. A signal. I let out a long trembling sigh, keeping as still as I could.

The bird made a clumsy hop and jump onto her stomach, and turned its head.

Its cold marble eye seemed to laugh.

What do you want? I said, in my head.

Diamonds, it crawked. It lunged for Aya's eyes. She dodged its beak and grabbed its leg.

I threw the blanket over it.

We wrestled till we had it bundled and pinned and lay on top of it, panting, drained by the effort.

'Eat?' I said and mimed, my hand to my mouth. Would it taste better or worse than turtle? I didn't care.

'No,' said Aya. 'No kill.'

'Then what?'

Did she want the bird to hunt fish? How could we train it to do that? And why not kill it? We were starving.

I held it tightly. Using the blanket to protect my hands I grabbed it by the wings. Its strength almost matched mine. *That's* how weak I'd become.

Aya fetched the fishing line. She felt under the cloak for its webbed claw, tying the end of the line around it. She unreeled the other end – a good length of it – and tied it to the oar.

Aya nodded.

'One, two, three—' I flipped the cloak back. With a crawk and a fierce flurry of wings the gull pitched skyward, higher and higher, until the line pulled taut and we held it like a kite on a string.

'Why?' I asked.

It tried to fly north, pulling, failing, then circling lower with the line loose, until it turned north again, straining until the line was tight.

Aya looked to where the sky met the sea.

'The bird is high.' She pointed. 'The bird can see.'

'See what?'

She smiled.

I knew the answer.

Land

i

We followed the path of the bird. Sure as a compass.

I paddled.

Aya stood, making the boat rock.

'THERE! Regarde.'

In the distance was a hump, sticking out of the ocean like a whale's back. But it wasn't a whale. Not a cloud either. Not a trick.

We hugged and cheered and roared. We almost fell overboard dancing and jumping. Aya grinned and cried, I held her face. I kissed tears off her cheeks. I tasted the salt of them.

I paddled then, forcing myself not to use all my energy, but needing to urge myself on, afraid that my strength would run out, and we would die with the island in sight. Aya used the seat to paddle on the other side. The swell and wind had picked up, so it felt tougher.

After midday we got close enough to see the land fully. There was a lighthouse. It was in ruins, only half of it was left. The top of the tower was long gone. But it was proof: of people, of the world.

The lighthouse sat on a cliff of rock about two thirds of a mile end-to-end. As we neared the land, the purple blue became shallow turquoise. Black lava rocks jutted out of the water, jagged shapes that my tired mind formed into monstrous beasts guarding their world.

I saw a shadow. Something large and powerful, skitting between rocks, visible over patches of sand but disappearing in the deeper parts. It didn't surface, and I soon lost sight of it among the seaweed and rocks. I didn't say anything to Aya and told myself my mind was twisting what I saw. But I paddled that bit faster, even though I was exhausted.

We steered along the coast, keeping a couple of hundred metres offshore, looking for somewhere to land, a bay or even just a less-steep bit of cliff.

We came round the headland and saw the curve of the coast. Between the rocks and jagged reefs, a light blue sea made its way to a thin inlet, ending in a beach. Beyond it was a sloping hill.

We could see it clearly now: an *island*. I scanned its coast, desperate for any sign of life. It seemed to be one large barren rock, but along from where we'd land there were trees.

Life.

~

We navigated carefully to avoid the rocks. Shoals of tiny silver fish darted through the shallows. Big ones too. Purple shells and yellow coral decorated the ocean floor. Fronds of seaweed danced in the current.

'What food is down there?' I said.

'Yes, there is food. Also beauty,' said Aya hanging over the side, her jaw and eyes wide. The water was so light and clear it was like it wasn't even there, as if the fish were flying through air.

And it was beauty. After the desert of the open sea, it was heaven.

When we reached the beach we climbed out and waded, pulling the boat. We used the last of our strength to get the boat free of the water. It was heavy, but we pulled and scraped over sand and shingle to rock. Not as far as it needed, just as far as we could manage.

We lay down, panting and sighing. I grabbed a fistful of dusty sand.

'More precious than gold,' I breathed. Aya laid her head on the ground. She reached for me and we held hands. We cried tears of joy.

'Must… water,' I said.

'Yes,' she said. 'Soon… and… and…'

Her eyelids closed. I felt mine go too. A weight of weeks bore down on my head.

We fell asleep.

ii

I woke with a burning thirst.

I remembered my deck shoes in the hold. I'd taken them off on the first day after the storm and hadn't worn them since. My feet felt clumsy inside them. I grabbed an empty bottle, then started up the slope. I fell over, stood up, stumbled, fell again. My legs wouldn't work. I hadn't walked in so long.

But hope lit a fire inside me. I stood and staggered, getting used to it with every step. My head forcing my legs to do what they didn't want to.

I stumbled over sea-smoothed rock, onto dusty ground and up the hill.

At the top there was a rock about head high. I climbed onto it, and sat down, wheezing like an old man.

I looked around. The island was barren. There was no village or road. No people. Nowhere they could be. Just rock and sand. The mists had cleared in the sun. Beyond the shore there was sea in every direction. No boats, no other islands or sight of a distant shore.

I crumpled on the rock. We'd found land, but we were as alone as ever.

'There's nobody here,' I shouted to Aya.

To the east was a long spit of land and beyond that the black rock of lava reefs. At the base and highest point of the spit was the lighthouse. Birds darted and dived above it.

Along the western coast was a bay, and set back from its small beach were the trees we'd seen.

'Trees need water,' I said. I could see Aya below, leaning against the boat. Gull was crying a high-pitched ghost song, trying to get away.

'Aya!' I shouted. 'Come, follow!' She waved back.

I stumble-walked along the cliff, looking back to make sure Aya was following. I was about to start the climb down when I stopped and swivelled. I'd heard or seen something in the corner of my vision. But I couldn't say what.

'Hello?' My voice echoed.

I told myself I was imagining things.

I clambered over the lumps of warm rock down to the beach. When I hit the sand I had that same feeling. Only stronger. I spun again.

I planned to wait, but when I turned to face the trees, it was like seeing the fish in the shallows. Dazzling. I stumbled on, having to see it, to feel it. My dizzy head filled with the wonder of it.

The palms and coconut trees nearest the sea grew

straight out of the sand; giants with arms whispering in the wind. Living miracles. I put my hands on the hard bark, feeling the tree, making sure it was a real thing.

There were green coconuts in the branches. The sand was littered with dried leaves and scrubby plants. A line of ants ran up the base of a tree. A crab scuttled through the undergrowth.

I wandered through all of it, gawping.

My foot broke through twigs and squelched in black ooze. The ground became muddy and marshy.

Further back the trees ended at a steep rock face. At about double head-height, but reachable with an easy climb, was a cave. Its mouth was a couple of metres high and wide. Dark and still.

Inside it was cool and dead black. I heard the tap-tap of dripping water.

'Hello?' I called. I got onto my hands and knees and crawled inside.

The cave tapered, levelling out. My hands explored smooth rock then I fell forwards, up to my wrists in water.

'Please, God,' I murmured. 'Let it be rainwater.' I scooped some up. It was clear and clean. I drank handful after handful, then filled the bottle.

'Bill?' Aya's voice echoed. 'Are you okay?'

'Aman!' I crawled eagerly back to the entrance. Aya saw the bottle and reached for it.

She drank and drank and drank, careful at first,

then gulping, letting it wash over her face. We drank till our bellies bloated.

We waddled along the beach and climbed the rocks, drunk on water.

'What now?' I said.

'The lighthouse,' said Aya.

'Right, might make a good shelter. Then we have to think about food.'

We walked the ten minutes or so it took to cross to the southeast corner, where the lighthouse sat at the island base of the long spit.

From a distance we could see: the top was long gone, there were gaps in the stone. At the base was an old stone hut, half-ruined, but it had potential.

'You know, if we got some of those palm branches we could... Aya?'

She'd stopped dead still, watching the lighthouse like a hawk.

'What's up?' I said.

'See.' She pointed.

Logs and branches were piled against the wall of the hut. There was a fire pit too, black with ashes, surrounded by stones.

We made slow steps towards it. As we got closer I saw a tarpaulin was slung over a corner of the roof.

We stopped outside. 'Hello?' I said.

There was no answer, only a strange, quiet clinking coming from inside.

What *was* inside? Someone, no one, a skeleton?

There was no door, just a gap in the collapsed wall. I peered inside. There was a bed on the floor made of dried palm leaves and seaweed. A shelf was lined with tins filled with water. There were ashes on the floor, where there was another fire pit. A part of the roof was missing. Piles of seashells. A wind chime made of bones and feathers, tied with grass, clacked and tinkled in the breeze.

'That's what we heard,' I said.

'Is there food?' said Aya. 'Look outside.'

I went out and scoured the island for a sign of whoever lived here.

Aya searched for food but didn't find any.

Next we checked the lighthouse, all the time looking around and behind us. It felt eerie. The stone was old and weather-battered. There was a heavy door with a keyhole. I tried to budge it, but it was either stuck or locked.

I walked all the way round it. The door was the only way in.

'If there's someone here, they've got food,' I said. 'In here probably.'

'Maybe hide, when see us?' said Aya.

I didn't want to think about food. I wanted to think about rescue, and who this person was and if they had any contact with the world. But I couldn't help it. *If* someone was alive, they had food, and if they had food they could share it. My mouth watered.

'Where are they?' I said.

'Maybe not here, maybe they are dead,' said Aya.

'I don't think so… I had a strange feeling earlier, as if someone was watching us, right after we left—'

'The boat!' we shouted at the same time.

We ran, holding hands, helping each other.

I heard gull crawk. An alarm.

We reached the inlet and saw a figure in the boat, burrowing through tins and bottles from the hold.

Gull was in the air, still tied to the line, flapping and crawking.

'Hey,' I shouted, but immediately felt afraid, thinking: *They might be violent, they might not be alone.* Whoever they were, they hadn't hesitated to go through *our* stuff, on *our* boat.

Aya ran a few steps ahead, but stopped before she reached the boat.

'Hey!' I shouted.

The figure stood up. He had a dark face and burning eyes. His hair was black and wild, his body thin, like a starved wolf. He jumped over the gunnel and stood in front of us. He was wearing shorts and nothing else. He put his hand to his mouth, miming eating.

I knew things about him from one look. He was older than me, almost a man. He had been here a while. And he was desperate, even a bit mad.

He'd rifled through the hold, pulling everything out and scattering it across the hull. I saw empty tins and bottles, not our last tin of okay-to-eat turtle meat, just tins of bait. Bait we had held off eating.

'I hide turtle meat,' Aya whispered. 'And knife.'

iii

The boy-man walked up to us.

'Hello,' I said. He nodded.

We stood, staring at each other. I held a hand out and said: 'Hello,' again. I didn't know what else to do. He looked at me hard before shaking. It felt strange.

'Deutsche?' he said, in a thick accent.

'What? I don't understand.'

'German? Netherlands? England boy?'

'English.'

'Why are you here?'

'A yacht,' I said. 'The storm. We've been at sea. A lot of days.'

'More people?'

'No. Just us.'

'Tambien. Same. The storm.'

'Alone?'

'Yes.'

'Where are you from?' I asked. He didn't answer, just looked me up and down. And Aya too. She stood close behind me, holding my right arm with both hands.

'You have food?' he demanded. Aya squeezed. I wanted to say yes and tell him about the turtle; and to ask him what *he* had. But she squeezed so tightly I knew not to say anything.

'No,' I lied. 'But we have a fishing line.'

'I see the line. You have bird on line. Why?'

'The bird led us here. How have you survived?' I said, thinking: *You're thin, but you're alive. You must have eaten something.*

'Before with food from boat. Now shell animal from sea. Coconut also.'

'I'm Bill,' I said. 'This is Aya. You?'

'My name is Stephan. I am hunger-y. Tengo hambre. Entiendes. If you have food you give.' He stated it as a fact, as though he was in charge.

'We have no food,' Aya said, eyeing him warily. He smiled and gabbled a string of words at Aya, in Arabic I think. She stared at him, her eyes hard and unblinking. But she didn't answer. He fired questions at her, before changing back to English.

'Maroc? Libya? Syria?' he said to her. Aya squeezed again, harder. I didn't answer. It wasn't up to me to speak for her.

Stephan nodded and smiled. I didn't like the way he smiled.

'How did you come here?' I asked.

He turned and started walking. 'Come, you see.'

We followed, Aya and me faltering, holding each other up, because our legs were still not used to walking. And all the time we looked around us at the rocks and the few bushes and trees and the birds in the sky. Drinking it in.

We walked to the north of the island. From the cliffs we saw part of a blue fibreglass hull, upside down, trapped between rocks. It was a quarter of a boat. Less. The hull had a jagged edge, as if the rest had been bitten off.

'Fishing boat?' I said.

'Yes.'

I paused before I asked: 'The crew?'

Stephan waved an arm at the sea. 'Go in the storm. Many miles from here. I think dead.'

'That's what's happened to us too. We're survivors, aren't we? All three of us.' I nodded at Aya, thinking: *We've found another human, Aya!* She just kept an eye on the strange boy and a grip on my arm.

'Will they look for you?' I said.

'No. Not for me. Maybe for you. But if they come, I think it is before. Understand, England boy?'

'My name's Bill.'

'Okay, England boy.'

I didn't like this. We'd found someone. Someone we could work with. *Survive* with. But he hadn't welcomed us, he'd hidden from us, then ripped through our stuff, like Gull with fish guts.

'Come, you see where I live,' he said.

'We'll get our gear,' I said.

He walked off, towards the lighthouse. I turned to Aya.

'What's wrong?' I said.

'He is no fisher boy.'

'How d'you know that?'

'I see him before my boat leave. Many boats leave this place, our boat is just one. Is possible he is fisher boy, but it is possible he is one of the men making trade with people.'

'A people-smuggler?'

'Maybe. I think he works with these men.'

'Did he recognise you?'

'No.' She screwed her eyes up, chewed her cheek. 'This boy is bad.'

'How do you know?'

Aya frowned, staring hard at Stephan's back. 'I know.'

We returned to the boat to gather our things. Gull was in the middle of it, picking at a tin of bait.

'Where's the knife?' I gasped.

'I say before. I have the knife,' said Aya. 'What we do with bird?'

'Free him.'

We trapped Gull again, smothering his head so he couldn't see. Aya magicked the knife from her cloak and carefully unpicked the knot tying the line to Gull's leg.

'Shoo. You can go,' I said. But he only went to the nearest rock and sat there, twitching his head, watching.

We gathered the last bait tin and all of our stuff in Aya's cloak, using it as a sack. I put the line and hook and lure in the pocket of my storm-cheater. We left the aman-maker and the turtle shell.

'We're going to have to trust him,' I reasoned. 'Work with him. Maybe he *was* a people-smuggler, or he worked for them. But he's not now, is he? He's not anything any more. He's like us.'

~

We joined Stephan in his camp; the stone hut by the lighthouse.

We sat outside on a rock by the fire pit. There were two coconuts on the ground in front of him. I hadn't seen any when we'd first looked in the hut. I wondered where he'd got them from. He picked one up.

'Hold coconut on the ground,' he instructed. I did as I was told. He picked up a short, sharp stick, put it in one of the three eyes at the top of the nut, then picked up one of the stones from around the fire, and used it as a hammer to hit the stick into the eye. I flinched, *almost* let go of the coconut, but held it solidly. He hit it with quick, brutal force. I blinked and flinched again. Stephan smiled. He did the same with one other eye. He picked up the nut and drank. A lot. Then handed it to me. I gave it to Aya. She drank some, then it was my turn. The rich taste made my head spin. We drank until it was empty, then did the same with the other coconut. I could have drunk a dozen.

Stephan took a larger stone and handed it to me.

'Break the coconut,' he ordered.

I lined it up, raised the stone over my head and brought it down fast. The stone bounced off the side of the nut. I tried again. The coconut shot away like a rugby ball.

Stephan laughed. He picked up the coconut, and placed it between his feet, turning it over and over until he was happy with the angle. Then he raised the stone over his head and smashed it down. The coconut shattered. Pieces of its white flesh glared in the sun. He handed me a chunk, and tried to hand one to Aya, but she hesitated. He urged her to take it, using words I didn't understand.

'Why don't you speak in English?' I said.

He pushed the piece at her, barking more words.

'Hey!' I said.

'She must eat, England boy.'

'You don't have to talk to her like that.'

Aya looked at me sharply, then grudgingly took the food.

I chewed the white flesh. It was good, like the juice. When we were done, and we'd rested a while, I said: 'Now we should go fishing.'

'You don't want to rest more?' said Stephan.

'No, I'm hungry.'

I took the line and the hook wrapped in paper from my storm-cheater pocket and the last tin of bait from the cloak.

The smell of the sticky guts made me retch. It was good we hadn't been at sea longer. It was good we hadn't had to eat it.

～

Aya watched from the shore while me and Stephan took the boat. We left the barrel parts but took the turtle shell to store fish in.

We heaved the boat in, waded, and climbed aboard.

It felt strange, being back in the boat so soon. And without Aya.

I went fore and paddled. Stephan sat aft. The sea was more alive than when we'd landed. There were currents, fresh wind and waves. To get to open sea was tricky; there were big rocks and narrow spaces between them. When a wave smashed against them up ahead, it hit us hard, lifting us up and back.

'You should take the seat up and use it as an oar,' I said. 'The boat moves a lot easier if two people paddle.'

He shook his head, breathing hard. I shrugged and continued paddling, to get us to the open sea.

I was pleased to be doing something I was good at. I didn't like how Stephan acted in charge and all boss-like. The island *was* his home and he was older. But it didn't give him the right to be like he was, especially with Aya.

I kept looking back. He seemed nervous.

'You're the fisherman,' I said, 'where's the best place?'

'It is different!' he said. 'I fish in big boat. Not this.'

He was probably lying. But then, I thought, maybe he *was* a fisher boy once and worked for the people-smugglers now. It made sense for him to hide what he did. That's not the kind of thing you'd own up to. Not the kind of thing you'd want authorities knowing, if we got rescued.

We went to a place a hundred metres or so offshore. I could see the small group of trees on the coast, and Aya, sitting on the cliff watching us.

Below there were rocks and seaweed and fish, snaking and darting. *Lots* of fish. Silver and gold. Shoals of millions, whole clouds of tiny fish, and fat predators, lurking.

Stephan watched as I prepared the line, lure, hook and bait and rolled the line around the oar.

As I was busy with my hands I nodded at the water.

'See any sharks here?' I said. 'Big ones?' He put a hand on the gunnel and held it firm. He looked at the sea and shook his head.

'Do not try to scare me, England boy.'

'What country are you from?' I asked.

'Canaria.'

'Spanish? But you speak Arabic, too, or is it Berber?'

'My mother is Spanish, father Arabic. You and girl? You are England, what is the girl?'

'I don't know,' I said. That was true. I *didn't* know exactly. She'd called her tribe Amazigh as well as Berber.

'She is Berber, I think,' said Stephan. 'Life is not good for some tribes of this peoples.'

I focused on unreeling the line from the oar.

'You say name is Aya,' he said. 'Where is she from?' He wasn't giving up.

'Why do you want to know? She doesn't say much about herself, she might have reasons not to.'

'You have this girl?'

'What do you mean?'

'Do not be stupid. I see you hold hand. Many days in boat. She is yours?'

'I dunno what you mean,' I said, thinking: *You reckon Aya could be mine? You can't own someone. I don't even know what she's thinking most of the time.*

He smirked. 'Okay, England boy. Why she leave?'

I sighed and huffed. 'I don't know, right.'

Stephan looked at Aya on the island, and made a 'tsch' sound between his teeth. 'This girl is not poor. She look poor but is not.'

'How do you know?'

He tapped his head. The way he did it was odd, jabbing his finger hard on his skull. He seemed strung-out, hardly able to focus. A little crazy. Or maybe just hungry.

'Poor girl does not go to Europe,' he said. 'Muy caro.' He rubbed his fingers together. 'She *have* money.' He pointed to his eyes. 'I see. How she speak, how she *is*.'

But Aya hadn't said more than a few words to him.

I got a bite then, the tug of a strong fish. I pulled and reeled. Stephan didn't help and I didn't ask him to. The fish was broad and short, but meaty. I didn't have the knife to kill it, so once I'd unhooked it I left it flapping and gasping in the shell. It would have been better to bang its head; to smash it with the oar like Stephan had smashed the coconut. But I didn't want to do that.

That was the end of our talk. Every time I sank the line it wasn't long before we got another bite. It kept us busy. We lost a few, but got a good catch all round. I did most of the work, baiting, unreeling, pulling and teasing the line, while Stephan paddled, badly, to stop the current washing us too far along the shore.

One big fish got the hook caught far back in its

cheek. When I took the hook out, the fish struggled. It was hard to keep it steady over the shell. Ruby drops coated my hands and dripped on the deck.

'Over boat in sea!' said Stephan.

'No.'

'Why?'

'Sharks.'

That shut him up.

The blood and noise drew a small crowd of birds, swooping above.

Gull flew in and sat on the fore. He eyed the fresh fish.

'Not yet,' I said to him.

Stephan shrank from Gull, and took the seat up to shoo him away, maybe to hit him.

'No,' I said. 'Don't do that. He's our friend.'

'Bird is amigo? Tonto. Only England boy can believe this. I see the shell of turtle. It is your friend too?' He laughed.

'I don't care what you think. Don't hurt him.' I thought of when we'd caught him, how I'd have killed and eaten him without blinking. But now it was different.

~

Stephan had a fire pit in the earth floor of the hut just like the one outside. Against the wall he'd stored dried leaves and grasses. He took a large handful outside, placed them on the ground, then fetched part of an old glass bottle he told us he'd found on the shore.

When the sun showed its face from behind a cloud he used the glass to magnify the heat, directing the spotlight it made until the kindling smoked and flamed. He picked up the smoking ball and blew gently into it, and quickly carried it inside. He placed the ball in the fire pit, added more grass, then, stick by stick, turned the tongues of flame into a fire.

'I make magic,' Stephan said. His eyes glinted.

I thought about us making aman in the barrel. *Well, yeah, we can make magic too.*

We hunched around the fire. And its warmth and light *did* seem magical. We had the power to hold the night away, rather than being swallowed up by it.

We hadn't been cold on the boat much, only sometimes in the early morning. It wasn't cold in the hut either, but the wind was strong, and it was good to be sheltered and to feel the warmth from the crackling twigs and burning logs. There were enough holes in the roof for the smoke to escape.

And we had fish to cook. I wanted to use the knife to gut and clean it. But the knife was secret and had to stay that way, at least till we got to know Stephan better. So instead we went down to the rock pool by the shore and, using shells to cut open the fish, we gutted them, and took them back to the hut, spearing them on sticks.

We thrust the speared fish directly into the flames, but Aya cried: 'We must wait!'

Stephan spat words at her for daring to question him. She bowed her head. I didn't recognise this Aya. The Aya I knew had fire that flamed from her mouth when she was angry. But not with Stephan. I didn't understand why she was so wary of him.

The fish went black in the flames and smelled bad. Aya was right. After that, we built the fire slowly, till there was a bed of smouldering logs and the flames flickered. We piled stones on either side of the fire, then hung the fish skewers between them, slowly turning the catch until the skin browned and crisped and a rich smell filled the hut.

We ate from coconut shell bowls, pulling flakes of fish and devouring them. It was a hot and messy business. I burned my fingers.

We had a lot of fish. But still Aya and me ate eyes and sucked stuff out of heads. We chewed skin and spat out scales. Stephan watched, disgusted.

When we'd finished we sat with stained, sticky fingers and small piles of bones and heads in front of us. It felt so good. Not just the food, the *knowing*; that we had an endless supply of fish. Fish and water and coconuts. And who knows what else Stephan had. We could stay here, we could *live* here.

Until the boats came. Or the planes.

Stephan said something in Arabic and Aya slowly

stood and began gathering the debris of our feast, shovelling it high on her own shell-bowl.

'You don't have to do that,' I said. 'Leave it.' She shrugged and carried on.

'I take for the bird,' she said.

I meant to help her, not to let it be something she did because Stephan asked. But I didn't. I was so full and tired. Exhaustion seeped through me. And a weight had been lifted; a weight of days spent worrying about food, water, another storm. Never seeing land or rescuers, not knowing the future or if there *was* a future. Empty days of fear.

Now we had full stomachs, an island, a tomorrow.

'I didn't know what it meant to be full until I'd starved,' I said. 'Does that make sense?'

'Sound loco,' Stephan said. I laughed, and felt grateful too, not to be dizzy or delirious. I thought about what I'd be like if we *hadn't* found land. Fear, heat, hunger, exhaustion. They'd burrowed into my mind and eaten away a part of me.

I lay down.

'We haven't been on solid ground for so long,' I said. 'The earth feels strange. Still and moving at the same time.'

'*Muy* loco,' said Stephan. 'What you do, days in boat?'

'Fishing, making water, swimming.'

'The sea is a bad place.'

'Yes. A lot of the time, but…'

'But?'

'It *could* be like a monster. But it's the most beautiful thing too. In the morning it could be like milk in the mist. Under a full moon, there'd be a river of light, so strong you'd think you could walk across it.'

'So you make time with poems?' he scoffed.

'Stories, actually.'

'Story?'

'Shahrazad. Stories of thieves and sultans. Aya told them. Right, Aya?'

She carried on scraping scraps off the floor, making everything clean.

'Why don't you sit?' I said. 'Maybe you could tell us a story?' She checked Stephan's reaction.

'Story,' he said. 'You tell story?' He nodded as though this told him something he understood. 'This is for children, no?'

Aya sat beside me.

Stephan leaned over and whispered to Aya. 'Maybe I like stories. Tell me a story of your boat.' He spoke to her again, in Arabic, more softly than before. He put his hand on her knee. She drew away, saying something sharp. Stephan laughed.

'Aya, are you okay?' I asked. She nodded. 'What was he talking about?' She gave me a slight shake of her head, like saying: *Don't ask*. Then she spoke to Stephan in her language. One of them.

They got into a conversation. I listened, watching the fire. On and on it went. It seemed okay, better than before, more friendly. I was glad.

When it came to sleep, Aya curled up by herself, away from me, and on the opposite side of the fire to Stephan.

~

Day? I don't know. They're all melting into each other.

There's no need for a tally now.

We're going to live.

The world of the boat and the sun are more of a nightmare than a memory.

We have a new life on the island now, and it's a kind of paradise.

You wouldn't think that if you saw it, because there's little but a few trees, rocks and sand. At dawn the island is pink, in the day it's sandy and hot. In the sunset, the whole sky burns like it's on fire.

Offshore there is a deep blue that stretches to the horizon.

Aya hooks fish from the shallows.

Stephan has a bag of oats, though I don't know where he'd hidden it.

And he showed us where he'd found a beehive

in the trees. We lit a fire under it and smoked most of the bees out and stole their honey.

Aya and Stephan stand on the cliff-top, shouting while I climb down and pilfer eggs.

We've put weight back on. Aya's a bit rounder. Me too. Our bodies are taking all they can get and clinging to each morsel.

Her English is better too. She uses all the words she learned, apart from when she's angry, then it's short and sharp, or a babble of Berber. I learn a few words of her language that way. When we do our 'lessons', Stephan gets bored and goes off by himself. And it's just us again.

Just us is fine. There's this thing between us. I don't know what I'd call it. But it's me helping her out of her nightmares. Or her holding my head while I shook and sweated. Or feeling the song of the whale shaking the boat. I think people could live together a long time and not have our kind of sharing. Not that you'd choose to get close to someone in that way exactly. But we did. We didn't have a choice. And that time on the boat. It's in her and it's in me. And always will be.

But that last night on the boat, we fell asleep together. That doesn't happen here.

We have two major worries.

One is Stephan; how up and down he is, how he wants to be the leader. (We let him mostly.)

The second is the total lack of any plane or boat or sign.

On a clear night, back in England, if I watched long enough I'd see a satellite. But here? Not even that.

How far out of the shipping lanes or flight paths are we?

I have the feeling the storm has taken us to another world, a place that can never be reached or found. Or left.

Aya has told me about her old life. Good things, happy things. Life in the hills in summer, in the village in winter.

I've told her about walks in the New Forest, and the green of the trees and grass. About coming across a stag one day, and Benji on his lead, straining, and the stag standing, staring at us for minutes.

What are Mum and Dad doing? Are they on the Canaries, still working to find me? Or home, facing the empty chair at the table? And how do they manage to talk about anything? And do they still have hope?

I feel bad then. Sorry for what they're going through.

It's hard. And it's weird what I remember, what I say, what I feel, when Aya asks me what my life was like.

iv

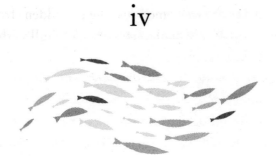

We made a giant cross using seaweed and leaves so that a plane could see. We only had enough wood to keep the fire in the hut going, not enough for a bonfire, so this was the next best thing.

To begin with we made a plan to take turns on lookout every hour, walking to the highest point near the lighthouse to scan the horizon. It was often me or Aya who got landed with this job as Stephan made excuses about needing to fetch wood or mussels.

One day the two of us were fishing at the end of the spit. I'd made a wooden float and was trying it out. I'd had no bites but I wasn't going back empty-handed. So we stayed when we should have been on watch.

Stephan came up behind us.

'Oi!'

'Shh,' I hissed, 'you'll scare the fish.'

He came and stood over us with crossed arms.

'What is it?' I said.

'Why do you not watch?'

'I lost track,' I muttered. 'Anyway, we had mussels twice yesterday. I want fish.'

'What if there is a boat?'

The float bobbed in the water. I willed it to vanish, to get a bite.

'I say,' he demanded, 'what if there is a boat?'

He gabbled at Aya. She shuffled as if to get up.

'It's my turn,' I said. 'Don't go.'

She looked at Stephan.

'We do not have to do this,' she said to him.

Stephan huffed. 'Go!' he pointed. He stamped his foot. Aya snorted, and gazed steadily at the water. Stephan glared, waiting for us to obey him. But we didn't. He was being an idiot. But weirdly, I felt sorry for him.

'What if there is a boat?' he said again.

We didn't answer. We didn't need to. We knew there wasn't any boat. So did he. He stood a while longer then walked off.

After that we looked less each day, and not in any kind of routine, just when we could be bothered. And never when Stephan said we should.

Then we hardly looked at all. We didn't talk about rescue either. We'd said everything there was to say about that.

V

He was one, we were two, and we were strong. The island wasn't his any more.

The lighthouse hut *was* his and he let us know we were lucky to sleep there. He *acted* as though he didn't want us around; he called us savages when we wolfed down mussels, and fish eyes and fish brains. But he needed us to be savages, to catch and kill and shin up trees to knock down coconuts when he didn't want to. He needed our company too. When we talked about building our own shelter, he said how difficult it would be, how we had no materials. We all knew that wasn't true.

He'd been alone for weeks. I think maybe that's what scared him more than anything. Being alone.

～

We were sitting round the outside fire talking.

'I had a good catch today,' I said. 'The float worked well.'

It was a huge fish we'd caught: a bulgy-eyed, gaping-mouthed beast, with steaky-grey meat. We celebrated catching it with sips of rum.

The rum had magically appeared, like other things, and we knew Stephan had a secret store somewhere. We wondered what else he had in it, though we didn't ask.

'We haven't caught one of these before,' I said. 'It's because I used the float and set the hook deep. What is it?'

Stephan shrugged. 'I cannot remember the name.'

'You're a fisherman and you don't know the name of a fish like this?' I scoffed. Aya glared at me.

'We never catch this one,' he said.

'Yeah?' I said. 'What *did* you catch?' The rum burned in my gut. I took another swig. 'What kind of nets did you use?'

'You ask too many questions,' Stephan said quietly. He reached and grabbed the bottle off me. And kept it.

'Why don't you just be honest?' I said.

'*Ho*-nest?' he said, frowning, as if he didn't understand the word.

'Yeah. About yourself. What's your story?'

He smiled. 'I have no story to tell. I am no storyteller. But *you*, Aya, Bill says you are a teller of stories. Why don't you tell one?' he said, trying to change the subject.

'But this is only for children,' said Aya. 'You do not want to hear a story for a child, Stephan.'

He took the sarcasm, smiling and nodding. 'Well,' he said, 'the nights are long.'

'Please,' I said to Aya. 'Why not?' It had been a long time, since the sea and the stories on the boat.

'Yes,' said Stephan. 'Tell us.'

'No,' Aya said.

But we kept on at her till she sighed and perched on a rock on the other side of the fire, with her knees under her chin, biting her cheek and frowning, thinking.

'The sun was rising,' said Aya. 'Shahrazad had not finished the story of Lunja, the thief.'

'So? How *did* Lunja save her life?' I said. 'What story did she tell the sultan?'

Stephan looked from one to the other of us, confused because we had started where we had left off, with Lunja caught with her ruby and the sultan asking her to explain how she had got it.

'Now you must listen, Bill,' Aya scolded. 'That evening Shahrazad told the king how Lunja had told the story of the great djinn to save her life, to explain how she came to own the great ruby. She tells him the story of the djinn, servant of the demon forged in the sun; servant of the Shay-ttan, who will never kneel and bow to man, who cannot be tamed. It was written that no man will defeat this djinn!

'The king say to Shahrazad: "If the djinn cannot be defeated, why does he not walk the earth?"

'"Oh, he *was* defeated," said Shahrazad.

'"But who can defeat the djinn? You said no man. A king?"

'"No."

'"A great soldier, the champion of the king?"

'"No. The Shadow Warrior was a *girl*."

'"A girl cannot defeat a djinn," said the king. "This story is stupid."

'Shahrazad say: "If you like. Believe what you will."

'"You must not speak with me this way!" say the king.

'"Why, Lord, will you have me killed?"

'The king was silent. He had much pride and did not like Shahrazad to speak to him this way. But he was… what is word, Bill? If you want to know more and more and more?'

'Curious.'

Stephan watched and listened, sipping his rum.

'Yes, the king was *curious*, like you and you!' Aya pointed at each of us. 'And he loved Shahrazad's stories. He say: "How did the girl defeat the djinn?"

'"My King," said Shahrazad. "This is the question the sultan say to Lunja. And Lunja tell him the tale of…

The Shadow Warrior

There was a time before mosques, churches and synagogues. Before writing and law. A time when demons and monsters walked the land and ruled the sea and sky like kings.

But after many years men, who had lived in fear of these demons and monsters, took control of the land. The trees of the forests were cut for wood, the plains filled with towns, the seas were sailed and mapped on charts.

The world was tamed, like a wild horse is tamed, or a djinn can be trapped and put in a vase. Men grew rich and fat. The monsters were killed or banished.

This was a golden time. But there was one djinn – the servant of he who was once an angel, banished from heaven because he would not bow to man – who could not be defeated.

He would vanish for many years. People believed

he had been sent to another world. But then, quick as a summer storm on the sea, he appeared.

He destroyed a village on the coast with a giant wave. On the plains he made a whirlwind that smashed crops and broke houses like twigs. To the city, packed with people like berries in a jar, he sent a great plague.

He killed without mercy. And wherever he went, he would leave a message, whispered in the ears of poets. In the marketplaces and courts, they spoke the words:

I am darker than the grave at midnight.

I am more powerful and terrible than fire.

I am more evil than the Shay-ttan.

There were many stories of the djinn across the land. For every fear that had a name, there was a tale:

'The djinn has many arms and claws, and feasts on the flesh of his enemies.'

'The djinn is a giant snake that breathes fire like the sun.'

'The djinn is a beautiful woman with a song that lures sailors to their death.'

'The djinn is a man, but if you fight with a sword, his body becomes a shield of steel. If you wrestle with him in water and try to drown him, he becomes like a fish.'

No one knew what the djinn looked like. Those who saw him did not live to tell the tale.

In this time a great king ruled the land. The people obeyed him in all things. But one thing they asked of him was for the djinn to be banished from the world.

So he said: 'One true champion will defeat the djinn! Any weapon, or treasure the champion asks for shall be given.'

Of course the people wanted the djinn killed, but no one wanted to fight it.

So the king said: 'Kill the djinn, and you will marry my daughter and be my son and you shall rule together when I am gone.'

Many came. The first warrior was a great archer. He believed he could kill the djinn, with one shot from far away.

He went to the mountains over many days. When he returned he had been blinded by the light of the djinn.

He cried: 'The djinn was too quick. Now I shall never lift my bow again.'

The second warrior was the greatest horseman in the land. He believed he could ride fast and cut the legs off the djinn, so he would fall like a tree. Then the warrior would put a knife in the heart of the djinn.

But he too came home after many days. A leg and an arm had been cut from his body and he had to walk with a stick.

The great horseman wailed: 'I shall never ride a horse or swing a sword again.'

The people became ever more afraid.

'What did the djinn look like? What did the djinn do?' they cried.

'I saw him from afar. A moving shadow, cutting through the trees. He surprised me. I thrashed my sword and rode away fast, but he was quicker!'

Next, the cleverest man in the land – a great philosopher – went to the mountain. He knew the djinn was strong and fast but also proud. He knew he could never defeat the djinn with a sword or with great strength, but only with his mind.

He challenged the djinn. He would say a riddle and if the djinn could not answer, the djinn would leave and be gone to the sun, the home of the Shay-ttan.

But, after many days, the man returned, ranting; his brain was as simple as a baby's.

This happened again and again. No matter what skills the warrior had, no matter how strong, how clever: the djinn defeated them all.

But one day, a girl, whose name was Thiyya, which means beauty, said she would talk to the djinn, and make him leave the kingdom.

The king laughed. 'You are a girl. You cannot ride a horse, you cannot swing a sword, you do not have the strength to pull a bow. You are too poor to be educated. You are not clever, but stupid to think you will defeat the djinn.'

Thiyya stood before the king and looked him in the eye. She spoke with a voice clear and strong: 'I am bright-eyed like a hawk. Strong, not like a mighty oak, but a young tree that bends with the wind and can live through all storms. I am clever; not like the merchant, who steals from the people, but like the thief who steals from the merchant.'

The king said: 'If you defeat the djinn, what reward shall you have? What do you wish?'

'My family, O King, are poor and starving servants, no more than slaves and I am promised to a man I would not marry. We want our freedom. My family are free people.'

The courtiers held their breath. There was a tale, a whisper, that some of the free people were worshippers of beasts and monsters and the angel who did not bow to man.

'No! I cannot give this. You may have treasure!'

'We do not want treasure. We want freedom.'

'I will not give this,' said the king.

'Then you will never defeat the djinn.'

So the king promised Thiyya. What did he have to lose? He did not believe the girl would return from the mountain. If she did, she would also be a cripple, blind, mad, or something even more terrible.

Thiyya went alone. She wandered far from village or field. She travelled where trees do not grow, high in the mountains where there is only sky and rock and snow. When she stood in a place where no man, woman or child had ever hunted, or made a fire, she stopped. Here, she knew, she would find the djinn. She knelt and faced the sun.

'Come, djinn, appear you, who...
Is darker than the grave at midnight
Is more powerful and terrible than fire
Is more evil than the Shay-ttan.'
And a voice that whispered in the ears of poets said:
I am here.
'But I cannot see you.'
Yet I am here. And I cannot be defeated.
'I know you, djinn. I know your power. I have no nightmares for you to make real. My family is starving and poor and they are slaves. My life is bound to a man I will not marry. If you kill me it will be a mercy.

'It is you who cannot defeat me. Because you feed on fear. The fear of the archer was to lose his sight, the fear of the horseman was to lose his speed, and the fear of the philosopher was to lose his mind.

'I fear nothing. I know your secret. More than this I know your *name*!'

The earth shook, the air trembled.

My name? said the djinn. And Thiyya knew she would win.

'Yes, your name. You are Nothing.

'*Nothing* is darker than the grave at midnight.

'*Nothing* is more powerful and terrible than fire.

'*Nothing* is more evil than the Shay-ttan.

'Your light burns and shines but there are places such power cannot go. And that is the shadow in my heart, which is empty because I am not afraid.'

149

The djinn had no power before Thiyya. Because she was right. She had no nightmares it could take to make itself real.

To know me is to defeat me, said the djinn, *and I will leave, but I will give you a gift.* And he gave to her a jewel.

This is Fire-heart, he said. *It burns with a fire made in the sun. Let its light fill the shadow in your heart. For it is not wise to live without fear.*

And so the djinn left and returned to its master, who burns in the sun forever. And Thiyya returned to the king, who kept his promise: Thiyya and her people were free.

Lunja bowed.

The sultan looked at the ruby. He looked very closely. But his coat was now shining so strong with the jewels he'd stolen from his people that the light was blinding. He was like the sun! And the light of this sun was *so* strong, the ruby Fire-heart seemed dull in his eyes. It was not the ruby of his dreams.

He said: 'How did you come to own this ruby?'

'Thiyya was my mother, great Sultan,' said Lunja.

Then the sultan laughed. 'It is an incredible story. But I do not believe you, thief. I think you stole this… this…' And he looked closely again. 'This piece of glass.'

'No, no, great Sultan,' Lunja said, begging. 'This is a dazzling jewel, it will be the greatest piece on your magnificent coat. Please, take it.' And she offered Fire-heart to him. He looked at her, and thought: *I do not want a girl thief to make me a fool.* So he knocked her hand and the ruby fell in the dust. And the sultan laughed, and all the men laughed.

And they walked away.

Each morning the sun takes the light of all the stars. This is the sultan taking the jewels of the land for his coat. But he cannot see the light of the morning star, though it was put before him. And he searches for it. Each day. Forever.

'And Lunja?'

'She was free.'

'But her mother was the true queen. Thiyya wasn't *really* her mother. So Lunja was the rightful ruler.'

'Yes, but it was enough that she was free. Maybe, in a different story, Lunja becomes the queen. But not in this story. It is enough that she had made a story to save her life.'

'Aya, all these Sun Lords and kings and sultans,' I said. 'Stories within stories. It's confusing. Are you making it up?'

Aya grinned. 'Some, yes, why not? But most I remember. The stories are here, this is the book.' She pointed at her head.

'Are all the heroes in your stories girls?' said Stephan, swigging rum.

'They are in the ones I've heard,' I said. 'I love the stories. Aya, did you learn them from your uncle?'

She looked at Stephan, who sat watching her, and thought before answering.

'Yes.' Her voice was soft and low. 'From Uncle. Mother too. She tells me, before I sleep. For many years.'

'You didn't have television, films?' said Stephan.

'I have seen films,' she said.

'Where?'

'It is time to sleep,' she said.

'I do not want to sleep,' Stephan said. 'What is *your* story, Aya?'

'I do not want to tell,' she said, jutting her chin.

'Why? You have a secret?'

'What about you, Stephan?' I said. 'Aya saw you, before her boat left.' I blurted it out before I could stop myself. But I was angry. I hated the way he treated her.

Stephan took a long drink, staring at Aya. And she looked back. She looked fierce and afraid at the same time.

'Don't worry,' I said. 'I won't tell. When we're rescued. But you're no fisher boy, are you?'

He put the bottle on the ground. For a second I thought he was going to hit me. But he just sighed and slumped back.

'My *father* was a fisherman,' he said. He kept on staring at Aya, as if he was seeing her for the first time. I regretted what I'd said.

'And you?' I pushed.

'I do many things. We must all eat. We do not all have a rich family and an easy road to follow, England boy. My father was a fisherman and talvez, it is possible, one day I will be a fisherman too, if I make money to buy a boat. But this job can kill, you know? You can die before you are old. You work hard for no catch and no catch is no money. You understand?'

'Yes.'

'No, you do not. And you? Do you tell us all?'

'Sure. I've got nothing to hide.'

'Then you are lucky. And?'

'And what?'

'Your life, what you are.'

'Well, I... go to school. I've got good mates. A dog. Mum and Dad... I... I'm an ordinary boy. I guess.'

'And what is that?'

'I... I don't know.'

And I thought my life maybe wasn't that ordinary, no more than Stephan's life, no more than Aya's. It just seemed normal. Or had, once.

vi

The following evening I'd been collecting firewood. It was nearly dark when I got back to the shelter.

The fire was almost out.

'How could you be so stupid?' I muttered. 'Aya, Stephan, where are you? Why'd you let it get so low?' I added a couple of logs to the embers and called again: 'Aya!'

Outside, a breeze was picking up. Clouds were streaming across the sky, burning orange in the sunset.

There was no sign of Stephan, but I found Aya on the cliff.

The wind made her hair dance around her face and shoulders.

'What are you doing?' I asked. She turned, with a strange smile on her face, and held her hand out for me to hold.

'Look!' she said.

The sea was rolling. Black waves crashed across the

reefs. The sea was coming alive again. They were the biggest waves we'd seen since arriving on the island.

'Can you see?' said Aya. 'If this will happen and we are in boat?'

I could see. I could imagine.

'We were lucky, in the storm,' I said. 'We wouldn't be so lucky again.'

'No?'

'No, not that we'll ever risk it anyway.'

'And if no boat, no plane?'

'There will be, one day.'

Aya frowned and gathered her cloak around her.

'We were lucky, Aya,' I said. 'To survive the storm, to find each other, to find the island. I say luck, it feels more like a miracle.'

'What is miracle?'

'An impossible thing. Something truly incredible.'

'Oh. You want to see a miracle?' she said, with a secretive smile.

Aya reached beneath her cloak and pulled out a small coconut bowl. Inside was a wrapped, cloth package. We sat and I watched as she so, *so* carefully opened it.

In the evening light the stones were even more brilliant than they'd been on the boat. They twinkled and shone, glinting sapphire, emerald, cobalt blue.

'I saw you with them. On the boat. I thought maybe I'd imagined it. You're rich.'

'No, I am not. This is the treasure of my village. It is easy to carry much money in jewels, easy to hide,' she said.

'How did you?'

'I will tell you. Later. My story. Mais, ils sont magnifiques, non?'

'How much are they worth?'

'I do not know. But it is much, Bill. Much. You see some men, they steal from my people. I take back. And I will go home one day, with these jewels.'

I picked up a jewel from the cloth in her hand, a small blue pebble, with a heart of fiery light. When I held it up to the dying sun, the light inside erupted.

'Wow,' I murmured. Aya did the same with a white, pearly opal.

'Yes, wow,' she said, grinning.

We were hypnotised by the jewels. We didn't hear Stephan creep up behind us.

'Ah,' he said. 'Treasure for a sultan.'

We were kids caught with our hands in the sweet jar. I dropped my jewel and scrambled in the sand and dust to find it. Aya hid the package behind her back.

We stared at him and he stared at us. No one said anything.

He stepped forward. We stepped back, closer together.

The wind rushed around us.

He took another step. We stayed where we were.

He stared, crazily, hungrily. The starved wolf, unsure if the hunt was worth the risk.

Stephan spat on the ground, turned, and walked away.

~

He didn't come to the hut that night.

We waited for him, but we didn't go looking. I reckoned he was in a proper mood; not happy about our 'secret', but we thought he'd appear sooner or later.

'I will look for him,' Aya said.

'No. Better to leave him be, for now.'

At some point I drifted off. I didn't mean to, I just did. When I woke, the fire was low, just glowing twigs.

I sat up, rubbing my eyes, and added another log.

Aya wasn't there. The wind was whistling outside. The waves a steady crash against the shore. Something didn't feel right.

'Aya, where are you?' I called. Maybe she had gone to get firewood. The moonlight was strong. Or to find Stephan.

'Aya,' I shouted again. I stood, my body feeling stiff.

This was strange. Wrong. I walked out of the hut, checking the lighthouse and all around it. Where could they be? I ran over the island, to where the boat was. I didn't get far before I heard them shouting.

They were making their way back from the boat. He had her arm. Aya was pulling, trying to get away, but he was dragging her.

'Get off her!' He let go, holding his hands up, smiling.

I ran to her but she shook me off, nostrils and eyes flaring, spitting like a snake and rubbing her arm. She backed away.

I ran at him and pushed him hard in the chest, then raised a fist, ready to hit him. He stepped back, holding his arms high, and smiling.

'Okay, England boy, okay. But you are weak. Don't do something stupid.' He was right. He was bigger and could take me in a fight easy. He could bully Aya too, if I wasn't around. But he couldn't do both at once.

'What were you doing?' I said.

'She tell you of boat? Why she is on? Why she run? She is the girl the men look for. In the port.'

'What men? What port?'

'Okay, okay. You want to know, I show.' He reached in his pocket and pulled out a large key. 'I show. You see, food, flares I have for when boat comes. Everything. Then we talk money.' He marched off, back to the lighthouse. Aya rubbed her arm.

'Did he hurt you?' I asked. She shook her head.

I shouted to his back: 'What do you mean "money"?'

'Girl has money. I knew this already. No one travels without this. Now I see the diamonds.' He stopped and turned. 'You give some to me, maybe I help her when we leave island.'

'Lea... Leave?' I couldn't believe what he was saying. 'Leave? How? And how could you help her?'

'She goes back, a girl alone? What you think happen to her? She needs me.'

I followed, tripping, confused, eager. What would he show me? How could we leave? He sounded sure it was possible, that we could return to the world.

I caught up with him as he was unlocking the lighthouse door. A breath of cold wind blew out. I wanted to see, I stepped inside.

'I can't see anything,' I said, my words echoing in the round chamber.

'I get fire,' he said, 'then you see.'

He walked off to the hut. I screwed my eyes up, trying to adjust, to see, stretching a hand into the shadow. It felt damp and cold.

'Hello?' I said. I don't know why. There was no reply, just the wind washing stale air from the chamber. I didn't move any further. I didn't trust Stephan not to lock me in.

'You coming?' I shouted.

The shove hit me hard in the back. I fell over, banging my face on the ground. The door shut and locked. Loud and final.

I was left in darkness.

I shouted 'Aya' till I was hoarse. I pushed, banged and kicked the door, till my hands and feet screamed in pain. I looked at the keyhole, it was locked with the key still in it.

Then there was silence, filled with questions and me hating myself, my own stupidity. Why had he locked me in? What did he want from Aya? What was he going to do to her? I hoped she was hiding. And if he'd found her, I hoped she was fighting. She had the knife.

And I knew, suddenly, horribly, that he could kill her, or she could kill him. Because there were no rules on the island. No laws. Not human ones, anyway.

The steps spiralling up inside the lighthouse had long gone. There were holes in the wall, old windows, but they were high. There was no way out.

I was in a chamber, a prison with a single round wall.

I shouted, and kicked the door again, knowing how much it would hurt, realising now I was stupid to think we were safe, stupid to believe that Stephan had a way off the island.

England boy. That's all I was.

I was mad. With him, with myself, with everything.

I knew I had to get out and fight him. Kill him if I had to.

'Don't think that,' I said.

My eyes adjusted to the light. I noticed more holes higher up in the tower. They might have been windows once. I knew if I could reach the first one, I could climb out. But it was many metres above me. I felt along the walls with my hands, and found rusted metal spikes jutting out horizontally. They must have held the steps once. They didn't look as though they could take much weight. But I was light. And desperate.

The first spike broke under my foot. But the second held and I quickly placed my foot on one higher and reached to grab another with my hand. I held onto the wall, scared I'd fall at any second, bearing my weight between the spike I held and the one I stood on.

They bit into my feet. It was agony, like climbing a ladder of blunt knives. But slowly, carefully, testing each spike, I heaved myself up, trembling, each step worse than the last. One metal bar was rusted and rough, cutting into my foot. Blood trickled between my toes. I climbed, I *had* to, and found the window, hauling my body through the hole, over the stone, scraping my stomach till it bled. The wall felt unstable too. I swung my body around to get my legs pointing downward. It was a long way to the ground. Sick-making. Too high. But the bricks bearing me felt as if they might give way any moment, and I had to jump. I half-fell, half-leaped, landing with a thud.

I was hurt. My ankle had twisted hard, the soles of my feet were cut, but I staggered into the dusky light.

'Aya!' I shouted. 'Aya!'

I stumbled to the beach, but as I got close I heard Gull crawking. I followed his cries.

They were north, along the eastern cliff, a spot where layers of rock made giant steps down to the sea. Gull swooped and dived, flying close to them, then veering away.

They were facing each other, shouting in Arabic. I saw Stephan lunge at her. She dodged. He sounded furious. I wondered why she wasn't running.

It was only when I got closer that I saw that Aya held the knife, brandishing it frantically to keep Stephan away. He could take her easily, if he got hold of her. But she had the knife. It glinted in the moonlight. Her eyes were wild and her teeth bared. I knew she would use it rather than lose.

'Hey!' Aya saw me. Stephan used the moment to grab her wrist. They fought. But he would win.

'Stop!' I yelled.

They wrestled and spun, in some crazy, messed up dance. Now he had *both* her wrists in his hands.

He pushed Aya towards the cliff. I saw her twisting manically in his grasp, but he was pushing her further, faster, using his strength. He wanted to force her to the edge.

She dropped the knife, right on the edge. He pushed

her away and tried leaning down to get it, holding his other hand up in case she rushed at him. He grasped clumsily for the knife, but teetered, losing his balance. And disappeared.

Aya looked down where Stephan had fallen, then ran to meet me.

We hugged. She pressed her face into my neck.

'Did he hurt you?' I said.

'Non,' she mumbled. 'I have honour.' I tore myself from her, and ran to the edge.

He'd fallen most of the way down, splayed on the reef-rock, among barnacles and seaweed. He was on his back, one arm an upside down L and one leg at a right angle. His eyes and mouth gaped open. His head hung over the edge of a pool. In the moonlight I could see the water darkening with blood.

I climbed down painfully, till I was a few metres away.

I didn't call his name or watch his lips for breathing, or check his eyelids for a flicker of life. He was dead. I knew it. I'd thought Aya might have been dead, the day I'd found her, floating on that barrel. But I saw how this was different. How certain this was.

This wasn't Stephan, it was a shell of a body.

Aya followed me down. We watched the body for a long time without speaking.

'Why?' I asked finally. 'Why were you fighting? Did he want to take our boat?'

'No. He cannot make the boat work out at sea.'

'Then why?'

The look on her face scared me. As if she'd seen a demon, as if she *was* a demon.

'He want my jewels. He say will help when we go back. But I do not give.' She spat, looking coldly at the body. Then her eyes softened, and she looked at me.

'We fight, I did not mean—'

'It's okay, it was an accident. I know. I saw.'

But everything had moved so quickly. Did I see what had really happened, or only what I wanted to see? That he had fallen…?

'He fell. It was an accident,' I said more firmly, and I was grateful that I hadn't had to fight him. Because what might have happened then? What would I have done?

A wave flooded over the rocks and into the pool, filling it, taking a wash of bloodied water to the sea.

'We can't leave him here,' I said. 'The tide's coming in.' The rocks were steep, easy to climb up or down, but not carrying a body. 'Should we have a funeral or something?' I said. 'Do you have a funeral for someone you've just ki—'

'The water will come,' Aya said. 'The sea will take.'

It was as simple as that for Aya.

We stood, watching.

I saw their shadows first. Then the fins. As the

water rose, more of the shelf was covered and the pool became part of the sea.

More of them arrived. They surfaced, diving and darting, this way and that. They weren't huge. But big enough. They searched, desperately, for the source of blood, but they couldn't reach him.

'We can't just stand here,' I said.

Aya climbed down and waded to where Stephan's body was. She edged it through the shallows, along the shelf of rock. She gave it one final push. The body tumbled into the sea.

The current took the body, a conveyor belt carrying it to open water.

The water bubbled furiously. Fins flicked the surface. Tails thrashed.

'Don't look,' I gasped. Aya didn't blink. Then the shadow came. Grey in the dark blue. It was huge. The body was pulled under. The sea erupted.

'Look away,' I said.

But Aya didn't look away. And neither did I.

~

We watched the water long after the sharks had gone.

I hadn't seen this coming. None of it. It was awful and sudden. I remembered times I'd had that same sick, punched feeling. The day Grandma told us she had cancer. The day Dad told me he'd lost his job.

The second the rope snapped and I saw Wilko and the others vanish into the waves.

'Awful things happen,' I said to Aya. 'Things that happen before you know what they really *are*.'

I felt numb. Sort of horrified. But only in a distant kind of way.

We hadn't known Stephan long. But I knew I should feel more than I did. And maybe I should have been worried about *that*. But I wasn't. I just accepted it.

I wasn't 'England boy' any more.

vii

A storm was coming. Not like the one on *Pandora*. That had come from nowhere. This was going to build. The waves steadily got bigger, and the winds stronger. We gathered as much wood for the fire as we could. I took a palm leaf from the beach and swept the floor of the hut. We carried tins to the cave and filled them with water.

We made the hut our place instead of Stephan's. I found his t-shirt in the corner. I could have worn it. Instead I got the fire stoked and used a stick to poke it into the flames till it was gone.

In the lighthouse I found a bag of oats, some more coconuts and a few tins of food. And – this made my heart sing – a jar of honey. All stuff Stephan had carried off his boat before it sank, just like I had. There were no flares. That was just one more lie.

When we were done I made porridge with oats and coconut milk and water in a tin. I used the knife blade to scoop in the dripping honey. It tasted like gold from heaven.

We ate it quickly, watching the flames and listening to the wind howling.

We had food, shelter, aman and a fire. And no Stephan to rule our lives. But there was an empty space and silence in the hut. Every time I went outside, I looked to the north and had to force myself *not* to walk up there and look, again, into the water. I told myself I wouldn't fish up there. There were sharks, and at least one was massive. Not a shadow or my mind playing tricks. We'd seen what we'd seen.

Stephan was dead. But he was everywhere and nowhere. And I felt guilty. Not even because of what had happened. But because we were gulls stealing from another bird's nest.

Gull had no such worries. He strutted round the hut, pecking in the dirt, making it his home too, before settling in the corner.

We covered the gap in the wall with the tarpaulin as best we could, wedging it into cracks and weighing it down with stones. We took the woodpiles into the hut away from the wind.

When I gathered coconuts, more fell, landing with deadening thuds. I imagined what it'd be like if one fell on my head.

We had a supply of food that would last us for days.

We double-checked the boat, dragging it to higher ground and turning it upside down.

We had been busy all day, and not just because

of the storm. We'd been busy to avoid talking about what had happened, to avoid even *thinking* about it.

Sitting quietly, waiting for the storm, we needed something to talk about, to fill the time.

'Can you tell me about your precious stones?' I asked. 'Can you tell me your story?'

And so she did.

~

'On the plains and in the towns, there is war. It is not so strange. There have been many wars, many years. There are robbers, smugglers, and sometimes war with one tribe with another. As I say, this is not new. But this war, *now*, it is bigger.

'A warlord has come with his army. He cuts through the land like a sword in wheat. They destroy so much. No one knows where they will appear, or what things they will do. There is no line between one army and another. It is a war of belief and sometimes even in one village there is this war, family against family. This army travels. They are quick. They take villages, but they can disappear too, vanish in the hills. They kill many men. They take some women for slaves. This is true for all people, but it is more true for tribes of the Amazigh. This war is like a plague that moves from town to village to field to the hills.

'My tribe is nomad. But in this time not all the year.

There is a place, a village we live, with other Amazigh tribe. But some months in year we travel. We know a place high in the desert hills. It is a place of the old life, almost forgotten, but we go there now in the time of war. There is little in this place, only rock and a few trees. They say no people can live here. But...' Aya wagged a finger in my face. 'The Amazigh, we live in this place. There are argan trees. There is food for the goats, and the nut, we use for oil. There are rabbits we hunt. We have tents, warm in the freezing night and cool in the burning day. Milk from goats. We trade meat for vegetables.

'We believe in this place we are safe. The army they can also live in the hills, but we travel high and more high until there is no road, only paths. We make a camp and we stay there some weeks.

'One day, I was with my cousin Sakkina. She is thirteen years old. We take our chickens on the hill. We love this work, we have many hours to do so little, only look after the chickens so we do not lose them and that no foxes will come. We play games for some hours, then we see the men, below in the camp. They wear black. They carry guns. They walk into our camp. Five men, maybe six. I do not know how they find us. There is no fighting, no shouting. It is like they are visitors.

'I see our men talk with them. My uncle. I see him offer they sit by fire. He offers them tea. It is our way, even for men with guns.

'But the men do not sit. I think maybe they only talk and they go, or maybe they want that we give them food. But there is much talk with my uncle and then the talk is loud. One man he takes his gun and bang, bang!' Aya acted firing a gun.

'My people are afraid. My uncle talks with the men and he is trying to make peace with them. Sakkina say, "No!" She wants to run to her father, but I hold her arms. I put my hand over her mouth because she wants to shout. She is brave, Sakkina. But these men they can do anything. I know the stories, so I am afraid for Sakkina and also for myself, my uncle and all our people.

'The men they look in our tents. But we have little. Our tribe is not so poor, but we are not rich, and we do not travel with so much. But the money we have, we hide in jewels in necklace and rings for wedding and other times.

'These men say they are holy warriors. But I think most are criminal. I think they want some food, silver or gold, our jewels.

'I hear Uncle say our money is far away with other people of our tribe, but the men put the gun in his face, and say what we have we must give. So all our men have to find the jewels. The men take. They use knife like we use shell to take mussel from shell, and they take all the jewels.

'I see all this, and Sakkina too. And we are very

angry. But we want now they will leave. But it is not only money they want. Amazigh, it means free people. I think this is what they want, our freedom. This is what they hate. We sing, we dance, we wear clothes with colour and jewels and gold, we have music. From the River Nile to the sea in the west. We do not belong to one country, we do not *live* only in one country. We also have many old beliefs and many customs. And these warriors do not like this.

'They take people like herd of goats, altogether inside a circle. I plan to hide with Sakkina. I plan that we wait, and travel after, maybe find a village. But one man hit Uncle with his gun, and Sakkina shouts and runs. Then they see us.'

Aya stopped, frowning, as though finding the words or memories was a barrier she had to break through.

'So I must follow. I must be with my people. These men have eyes empty like the sky. And I see this and I know they can kill. We can do anything or nothing and they will kill. With no reason.

'They take us down the hill, to the roads, to the plains, to the town. They say we must live in this place. It is a new life. And so many rules.

'We live this way some weeks. In this time I see two men killed. Two, before my eyes.

'Then one man comes through the town with more of this army. He is very important this man. He looks the same as others. Same eyes, same black clothes. But the men do all he say, they watch him like dogs who will do all to win the love of their master.

'He say to take some peoples. I think it is only men. But... They call all the older girls and the younger womens, and they look us like goats at market.

'They take three. One is Sakkina.

'I am afraid for her and she is young. Uncle argues but everyone is knowing you do not argue with these men. But I say to take *me*. I have no mother, no father, and she is only a child. The men laugh, they think I am not so good because sometime I do not do all they want. But the whole village is angry and, even though they are afraid, they argue with these men.

'They can do what they want but they know it will be more easy to keep peace with village if they do *not* take Sakkina. And this man look to me, and he say yes.

'This man is a leader. He is clever, he knows this is right. And so I go with them. To the sea. I do not know what plan they have. But there, there are boats and these boats go to Europe.'

'You tricked them, didn't you?' I said.

Aya's eyes flamed.

'They take from my people. I take them back. They hide us in a house. The men come and go all day. I look from the window and I see them talk with men and with boys and one is Stephan. We stay. In the evening

173

I make them food, I say I can do this. And I know one man he has the jewels. And the key for the door. I see him look at the jewels. And I serve them drink and give him more, and more. They eat a lot of food.

'When he is asleep, I am awake. I wait many hours. I try to be brave. In the night I stand, and I go to the man. I am more afraid then. If he wakes, I am dead. But I am more afraid for what will happen if I stay with these men.

'I plan to take the key. Only the key. But in his same pocket is also the jewels. And they belong to my people.

'I do not know then what is right and what is wrong.

'So I take them. They think we will not steal or run from them. If we do, they will find. But I have no fear in my heart and I take. The other women, one is awake. I wave to her, but she shakes her head. She is too afraid to run. I am too afraid to stay.

'I open the door, slow, so, so slow. Then I run! They follow, and I hide, with the rubbish. One whole day. In the evening, a woman comes. I say I will leave, but she says there is only desert and the men have been searching and there is no place to hide. If I stay they will find. If I run to the desert they will find. But she say maybe I can go on boat, if I have money. So I give her one jewel and beg she will help me. Her brother, he is taking one boat next morning. The men will not believe I will go on a boat, they believe I want to go home. So she helps me.

'With one stone I buy to go on the boat. And I go, before the men find me.

'When Stephan see the diamonds, then he knows I am this girl.'

~

The storm hit in the night. Rain, wind, lightning.

We'd been through it before; me in a rowboat, Aya clinging to an oil drum. So we could handle this, dry and warm, huddled under the cloak-blanket.

We whooped when it thundered. Aya shrieked as if she was on a rollercoaster.

Rain drummed the roof and found holes and gaps, dripping down on us. We shifted around so it hit the ground, splashing on the fire and making it sizzle.

We didn't care.

In the early hours we tried to sleep. I lay behind Aya and held the blanket over us.

The wind came in harder then, seeking gaps in the wall, kicking at the flames, whizzing sparks into the air. I couldn't sleep. I had to make sure our bed of branches and seaweed didn't catch fire. But I dozed and felt weirdly, totally calm. Safe.

~

In the early hours of the morning it started properly. Everything before that had just been a warning.

Lightning turned the room to day for flashing seconds. Thunder shook the earth. Wind buffeted the hut, blowing in shock gusts.

Aya woke.

The wind pushed the tarpaulin aside and flew in, blowing the fire across the floor. Then the tarpaulin – our door – ripped from the wall, flapping wildly. I leaped up to secure it, but it flew from my grasp and into the air.

Gull waddled out and flew off.

Sheets of white light every few seconds. Cracks in the world.

Then the water came.

I went and looked outside, the wind almost knocking me over. In a blaze of white I saw walls of water, battering the cliff and flooding over the land.

A wave rushed in; a flood. The sea was rising.

'Get the tins!' I shouted. 'Grab everything!'

We stumbled, fumbled, finding the tins and the knife and stuffing all we had into the cloak.

Outside the wind was so violent we could barely stand. We put our heads into it. I braced my legs, anchoring myself to the earth.

'Lighthouse!' Aya yelled.

'No! If the hut fills, so will the lighthouse… We have to go to the cave.'

We made our way, heads down, step by step. When

a vicious gust hit, we couldn't walk, only hold onto each other, desperately.

'The boat!' she shouted. 'We must make it safe.'

I'd thought it *was*. High and dry. But now nothing was safe.

We used the lightning to find our way. And what we saw terrified me. Great sheets of water filling the horizon. Wind tugging at the boat and scraping it along the rock to the sea. We got to it just before the sea's fingers claimed it.

We dragged and pulled, hoisting it higher and higher. When we got it as far as we could we wedged it behind a rock, turned it over and tied the bow rope to a large stone. We hid the barrel and shell under it too, groping and fumbling to secure the upturned hull, making sure the wind couldn't get under it.

Even then the wind tugged and pushed at it.

'We can't leave it!' I shouted. But as if it heard us, the wind raged. Another bolt of lightning and thunder ripped across the sky. Aya squatted low to the ground, just to stop herself being blown away.

I saw a tree flying through the sky. Flying! The storm was showing us what it could do.

'The cave!' Aya shouted. 'We must go.'

When the wind lessened a fraction, we stumbled on, each an anchor for the other.

I don't know how we found the beach, how we climbed down the rocks, how we made our way through the trees, bending and leaning in the gale, wading, ankle- then knee-deep in mud. A tree snapped clean with an almighty crack as we clambered up the rock and through the entrance to the cave. I was thankful it was so high from the ground.

We crawled in, further in, and further still. And then dropping the cloak by the pool, we lay down, our panting and sighs echoing around us. Aya whimpered with fear and shock.

To the left of the pool was a shelf of rock. I crawled up it, pulling Aya behind me. It was dry. We lay there.

'I th… thi… think maybe we… die,' Aya breathed through chattering teeth.

'Not now, not now, we're okay, we're okay.' But I was shaking too, hardly able to force words out. 'We're okay, we're okay.' And I thought: *Will the sea reach us here?* I didn't know.

Aya's dress was soaked and cold. She shivered violently.

We reached out in the dark and held each other, till we were warmer, and we slept.

viii

We woke late in the morning.

The storm had gone. The entrance to the cave was a window to a new world.

Many of the trees had broken, some had vanished; torn from the earth and sand, leaving gaping holes filled with roots.

Coconuts were scattered across the ground.

The boat had moved. From wind or water I didn't know. By some miracle, it had been dragged inland. There were cracks in the hull.

I cried and I kicked the boat. Because I didn't know how we'd fix it. Not that I was keen to go out in it, now we had seen sharks.

The hut, our home, was wrecked. The floor was a soaked mess of ash, seaweed and branches. The shelves had gone. The gap in the entrance was wider, with stones from the walls scattered in the dirt.

I walked to the spit. The tide was out and the rocks exposed. There were thousands of shells and dead fish.

Gull was down there with the other birds, stuffing themselves. How they had survived the storm I didn't know.

~

Days passed.

Life got back to normal. Our normal.

We found the tarpaulin wedged in rocks by the shore. We took leaves and branches of the fallen trees and made new beds.

We piled coconuts and wood and using sun and the broken bottle got a new fire going. We had to wait two days for enough sun for that, and had to eat raw fish.

The heat had gone, eaten up by the storm. It was still warm, but there was a gentle wind, clouds and even the occasional shower. We didn't know if this was an aftermath of the storm, or the start of a changing season.

~

A lot had changed between us too.

That night in the cave we'd been closer than ever. Because we were scared. Because we believed we could die. Maybe we'd been *too* close. Being together, holding tight, shaking as lightning broke the world. And maybe being like that wasn't right for Aya. Or

180

maybe it was what had happened with Stephan. She never said anything about it. I'd thought the night in the storm would bring us together, but the truth is we never got that close again. She wouldn't let me. She'd built new walls between us and they were stronger.

We weren't starving, but we were still hungry. We had food, but we didn't have much honey, and when the oats were gone we'd have no carbs to eat apart from mashed-up seaweed.

We'd taken the island from Stephan. We thought we'd mastered the land and the sea. We thought we could survive.

And day by day, we could.

But for how long?

ix

It was about a week after the storm that Aya said it. Something I'd thought but hadn't spoken out loud. Because it was crazy.

We were in the hut. Aya ate her supper of fish slowly.

'Are you okay?' I said. 'You've been... I dunno, kind of quiet.'

She licked her fingers clean.

'Bill, I tell you... something.'

'Go on.'

She took her time, sucking her cheek and looking at the flames.

'We must leave this place.'

'Why, because it's not safe in a storm? And go where? The cave? It's damp in there. The lighthouse has no proper roof. We can't build anything stronger than this.'

'We must leave. Go back to the world.'

I put my bowl down.

'Aya. There's been no plane, no boat. But if there are people out there... they'll come here. Eventually. Maybe Stephan's people. Maybe they use this island. Maybe that's why his boat was near here when it went down.'

'I do not believe anyone will come. We must go.'

'You saw what happened in that storm. And *that*, in a boat? I know where I'd rather be. Anyway, the boat's got cracks in it.'

'We must go.'

'It's too risky. We could die.'

'We must *try*.'

'It's safe here.'

'But it is *not* safe. We see this.'

'There's food here.'

'It is not enough. If one is ill?'

'We'll be okay. Who we gonna catch flu from?'

'No. We must go home.'

She seemed so certain. *No wonder she's been quiet*, I thought. *She's been thinking this through.*

'I want to go home. If we find people. Or if people find us. It is possible...' She sighed, struggling to find the words. She took a deep breath. 'I want to go home. With this money from jewels I will help my people. And perhaps, one day, it is possible we are together again. You and me.'

I didn't know what she meant by 'together'.

'I don't know what's possible,' I said. And I didn't.

'You and me, Aya, we're together, here, now, in *this* world, with no borders, or countries, or rules. But back there? Well, whatever happens, I'll stay with you.'

She shook her head and sighed again.

'You cannot. A lost English boy? They will put you in the newspaper. I cannot be in this as I say.' She said the words hard, with her hand open and palm up, rising and falling with every blunt word. 'Even if we are together, first. Then? After? You will go to England. I will find my people. I *will* find my people. But I must be like a secret. The men, they know I have the jewels.'

'And what will you do, Aya? How will you free your people?'

'I will be like the warrior in the shadow.'

She was serious. She meant it.

And *could* I stay with her? No, she was right. I would go home. I saw it happening. And I hated it.

'Well then, I'll come back. When you know what's happening. I'll find you.'

Aya lowered her hands, and stared at the wall. That just made me angrier.

'I will come back,' I said. 'I'll do everything I can.'

'What can you do?' she said. 'Now it is you, not me, that does not understand the world.'

I found the knife, to make the ruby blood promise. But Aya took the knife from me and put it on the ground.

'You do not know what you mean. Do not swear, because it is maybe a promise you cannot keep.'

'But I do mean it.'

We sat, listening to the crackling flames and the rustling wind.

'What happen in your life?' she said. 'In England. If we go back?'

'Next? Sixth form I guess.'

'What is this?'

'A kind of school. Then university. I want to be a scientist, a marine biologist.' And it was only when I said that out loud that I knew it wasn't true any more. That *this*, the boat and the island, had changed everything. And I didn't know what I would or could do, or be, if we made it back.

'And what will happen in your life?' I said.

'I do not know. But I know I must try to help my people. You, me, we have different journeys. But together we must leave. We must go.' She pushed her food away.

'It's a stupid conversation, Aya. We'd never make it. We're not going. We'll wait to be rescued.'

'All is possible, but you who are so good with this facts and logic, you know there is no boat. We must go home with our own strength, we must believe.'

'Even if we did go, we'd have to wait weeks. Till we had salted fish, gull eggs, till we were strong enough and had a heap of supplies.'

'We must leave now,' she said.

'Did you say now?'

Her eyes and voice were heavy with sadness. 'Yes. Very soon.'

'We're in this together, Aya, but I'm not going to let you kill us.'

'Please.' In the firelight her eyes glistened with tears.

I wanted to get out then, to escape. I didn't like seeing her like this. But... I leaned over the fire, tapping my head with my finger.

'Aya, listen to me. There's no logic in what you're saying, no sense. Facts, Aya, that's what matters. The truth. We would die.'

'I say again. You know things of this logic,' she said, her voice getting loud. 'But you do not know all. You do not know if we can go and live. A long, good life. Here is possible we die.'

'I know that. I do. I've thought about it. But out there it's one big, fat unknown. I'm *not* leaving and definitely not now. You've said yourself. What if that was the first storm? What if it's hurricane season or something?'

She folded her arms.

'All life is a "big, fat unknown". I will go myself.'

'You're *not* taking the boat! Even if we fixed it, it wouldn't last more than a day or two. You're not going alone. End of.' I picked up the knife, stabbed a mussel and ate it.

Aya mimicked me: 'Clang, clang with knife. Slurp, slurp with coconut. You eat like a goat!' She stood and walked out.

We didn't speak the following day. We avoided each other until evening. Then, the only exchange we had was short:

'We must go,' said Aya.

'We're not going, and you're not going alone.'

'We go. If not, I *am* go alone.'

'No.'

'Yes.'

'No.'

'*Yes.*'

'No!'

'YES!'

I sighed, heavily.

'Bill, I want to go home, I want to find Sakkina. Do you understand?'

I did understand. I wanted to go home, to see Mum and Dad. But I wasn't going to get killed trying.

As was our way since the storm, we slept on opposite sides of the fire.

~

In the morning I took my notebook and sat at the edge of the spit. I thought about our options and all the things that could happen to us.

Aya was certain about going. I could stop her if I wanted to. I could keep a watch on her, and make sure she didn't sneak off at dawn.

Would she do that? Would she really leave me here, alone?

I wrote down the possibilities:

1. *We stay till we're discovered. Or die.*
2. *We leave and make it back to the world.*
3. *We leave. And face sun demons and sea monsters and storms. And die.*

I made a list.

Things I have done:

Killed a turtle
Survived a storm in a rowboat
Caught and eaten raw fish
Swam in pools of seawater
Been surrounded by whales
Listened to tales of kings and demons
Sat under a million stars
Tamed a wild bird
Rescued a girl
Been rescued by a girl
Seen a dead body
Seen a shark

And I thought how I hadn't written about all those things in my notebook, but I promised myself that one day I would. Write them down, so the memories wouldn't slip away, wouldn't become not-real, the way the memories of my life before had become not-real.

And I thought about Stephan. How he had fought with Aya. And I felt awful, but told myself it had been a terrible accident.

Accident. Yes, that's right. He had pushed her away, reached for the knife, then he fell.

Or had *she* pushed *him* away? Or both of them at the same time?

Truth was, I couldn't remember for sure. It had happened so fast.

But it *was* an accident.

Then I wrote:

Things I might never do:

Go to uni
Get drunk
Marry
Have kids
Climb a mountain

Things I might never do *again*:

Eat pizza
Watch a film

Take Benji for a walk
See Mum and Dad
Have a bath
Play footy

I stopped then. Because the list would go on forever.

I looked at the three options I'd written down. They all began with 'we'.

But there was another option.

I pictured it. Aya paddling. The boat shrinking till it became a spot on the horizon, slowly vanishing.

Me eating by the fire. Waking. Alone.

I *could* stop her. I would stop her. But at the same time, I knew I didn't have the right. And the truth was I didn't need the boat for fishing.

That was a fact.

I thought of Stephan then. How he had been, when we arrived. I thought about what I might become, on the island, by myself.

As I was thinking I'd been twisting a bit of my t-shirt in my fingers. I looked at the cotton, how thin it was, at the fading ink of the duck cartoon on my chest. I looked at my chipped nails. And felt my hair, matted and thick.

I saw myself months from then, with longer, more matted hair and longer, broken nails. Clothes completely rotted away. Rambling to myself.

To Stephan's ghost.

And I knew two things.

One. If Aya wanted to go, she would go. I'd stop her, once, twice, maybe a dozen times.

But eventually…

I read what I had written in the notebook what seemed like years before.

Even if they find two skeletons, not one. In this big nothing, that's something.

And wrote:

And what about us, Aya? Even if we make it. What then?
What do you really think about all this, Aya?
You and me, flung together by the storm. Easy to be here *for each other. Okay. Not easy. We had no choice. But we are together.*
What about when we're rescued or find land? Different journeys?
Not this one. This one we'll travel together.

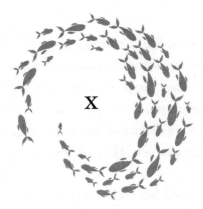

X

I found her sitting on the beach by a pile of grass and leaves. She was cutting them up with the knife and weaving them together.

'What's that?' I asked. 'A hat?'

Aya shrugged.

I stood, watching a while. She carried on as if I wasn't there.

'You're stubborn,' I said. 'You know that?'

Silence.

I picked up a pebble and chucked it so it landed in front of her. She ignored it.

'You'd really go alone?' I said.

'Yes.'

'Okay.'

Silence.

'I said okay!'

She looked up.

'We'll go. Both of us. We'll use the tarpaulin to make a sail. There's a steady wind been blowing for days now,

GIRL. BOY. SEA.

from the west. We'll make a mast with a branch from a
fallen tree. We'll glue the boat cracks together with tree
sap. We'll leave a sign saying we've been here, saying
we're sailing east. We've got coconuts and water. Give
it a day so we can catch loads of fish, smoke them to
take on the journey. Then, if the winds are still good,
we'll go.'

She stopped her work. 'Swear.'

I took the knife off her, made a small nick on my
thumb and pressed a dab of blood onto my chest. She
got up and threw herself at me so hard I almost fell over.

~

We fished all day, and smoked the catch over the fire.
Mussels and other shellfish too. We gathered coconuts. Aya finished weaving hats.

We made tiny holes in the tarpaulin and threaded
vines and string made from coconut hair into them to
use as ropes to control the angle of the tarp-sail.

We made a make-do rudder from a tree fallen in
the storm. A mast too. I tied another branch across to
hold the tarp-sail.

We took it out to test it.

We filled the hold with the tins we'd found and
coconuts and smoked fish wrapped in leaves.

I took a branch and the knife and carved a
figurehead with the face of a woman, which I stuck

193

and tied to the prow with gum from a tree and the string made from coconut hairs.

Aya said we should give the boat a name. We called it *Tanirt*, which means angel.

'Why angel?' I said.

'Because angels never die.'

Once, a few days before, a red ant had bitten me. I'd crushed it between my fingertips, which became stained. It had taken days to wash off. We made an inky paste of dead ants as their nest had been drowned in the storm. With a small stick Aya wrote *Tanirt* in Berber, with the crosses and circles and lines of her language, on the portside front of the boat, above the waterline. On the other side, I wrote *Tanirt*.

The sun was going down as we finished.

'If tomorrow is good, we go,' said Aya.

'Yes.'

The days then had been breezy but not stormy. Sometimes there was more cloud or less wind, but generally since the storm it was a steady pattern of weather. I thought maybe the weeks of heat before the storms were a seasonal thing and maybe this would hold, while we sailed *Tanirt* all the way to Africa.

We poured coconut juice and fish blood on the prow of the boat. A kind of offering.

'Keep us safe, *Tanirt*,' we said, together. 'Keep us safe.'

The Sea

i

We pushed the boat into the water and waded in till we were waist-deep. Aya climbed in first and held out her hand. I couldn't take it. My feet were glued to the rock, to the island, to safety.

'Come,' said Aya. Her eyes were bright. I took her hand and climbed aboard.

We sat in the shallows, waiting for the morning breeze. All I had to say was: 'Not today,' or: 'We don't have enough fish,' or just: 'We can't.'

But I didn't say any of those things, and all Aya said was: 'We are ready. Nous allons.'

Our world was packed into the boat: coconuts, dried seaweed, smoked fish wrapped in leaves, eggs, tins of food we'd found in the lighthouse, the knife, the fishing line, the turtle shell, the aman-maker and the half-barrel, full of water.

The sun chased the shadows away. The morning wind rippled the water and pushed at the boat, telling us it was time to go. All we had to do was lower the sail and let the breeze take us.

'Now or never,' I said.

'It is now,' said Aya. She knelt at the bow, gazing east. But her voice shook when she spoke and her hands were too tight on the gunnels.

I didn't know much about sailing. But I knew the basics. Enough to know that once we set sail, it would be hard to turn back.

'Okay,' I said, 'let's go.'

I stood and started untying the sail with hands that were heavy and numb.

Craaaawwk! Gull landed on the portside gunnel.

Yark, yark, yark. We going fishing?

'I guess you ate it all already?' I said. We'd said our goodbyes earlier and left Gull with a heap of guts and skins, to distract him. We didn't want him with us. It wouldn't be fair. We knew we had to travel east. We didn't need him to help us find our path, we just had to keep going.

'Gull, you will stay,' said Aya.

'Shoo.' I waved at him. He flapped his wings, hopping from one leg to the other. I pushed him gently off the side with the oar. He pecked at it, flapped and flew away, then came back.

'Go home!' I shouted. 'Go and fish and dive and

argue with the other birds. Go and live your gull life, because if you come with us…' I couldn't say it. That we might die. I tried to be strong but it was hard, because I was telling him to go home. And the island had been our home too. And now we were leaving.

'Shoo!' I waved the oar at him. He dodged it, opening his beak wide and crawking. I swung the oar. It hit him. He flew away, came back.

I gritted my teeth and swung the oar at him again. I hated myself, but it was the only way to make him go.

'Go!' I shouted. He flew off. Before I was tempted to follow him I unfurled the sail.

The wind tugged at it, but it flapped, uselessly.

'It's no good,' I said. 'We're too heavy. We're not going anywhere today, are we?' But as if it was answering me, the wind puffed out the cheek of the sail and the boat juddered slowly through the water.

Aya paddled, to help us along while I steered with the rudder in one hand and the sail rope in the other. Then the sail filled tightly and we were off, cutting a V, leaving a wake in the water.

There was no keel and only a make-do rudder and one sail. It was basic, we could only go where the wind wanted to take us. But it worked.

'Sit on the aft,' I told Aya. 'Now starboard… now port.' But she didn't need telling. She jumped up or sat down when she needed to, held the gunnel, leaned off the boat so far it was dangerous, moving around as though it was some kind of dance. We were harnessing the wind's power, me angling the sail with the homemade ropes so it would catch more to port or starboard as needed.

We were a few minutes offshore when the breeze and the angle of the rudder and the sail all fell into place. We cut forwards in a straight line, moving faster by the second.

'We've done it!' I cried. The island was already far away. There was no going back.

Aya didn't look back at the island, not once.

We'd set the course and been sailing ten minutes or so when she looked up, shielding her eyes with her hand.

'He is like a bad child,' she said.

Gull swooped and landed on the prow, yarking angrily.

Where are we going?

'Okay, Gull,' I said. 'You win. You're coming too.'

ii

The first days were mostly good.

I made a promise to myself not to keep a tally. Not to count the days and the food. Not to calculate or plan. But to eat as much as we needed, to sail and no more. We just needed to keep going. We'd find land or die. And if we were going to die, I didn't want a record of that. Not one Mum or Dad could ever read. I decided I wouldn't write that letter. Because that would be surrendering to death.

And that wasn't going to happen.

Sometimes it wasn't windy enough so we rested or paddled. Other times the wind was too harsh. Force 3 to 5 at a guess. That would be great in a yacht, but it was too fierce for *Tanirt*. Then the prow pushed into the sea or we lost control, spinning hard and fast.

Sometimes the boat tipped so far over, the waterline and gunnel were centimetres apart. It was dangerous, but we couldn't lose pace.

There was a lot of north in the wind and we sailed southeast, using the rudder to keep our direction true. Occasionally the wind was dead against us and we had to tack, starboard, port, starboard, port, unsure if we were even getting anywhere.

Twice we took in water and came close to capsizing. We had to bail hard.

We fished too, early morning and late evening.

We wore our ridiculous homemade hats when the sun was strong.

And all the time we looked east. Hoping.

I felt brave then because none of this had beaten us. None of it.

I said a thank you to the ocean when the fishing line pulled.

And a thank you to the sky when the wind was good.

But there were other times when the wind had a hard breath, when it howled and we thought a storm must be coming. Then I saw fear in Aya's eyes and knew I had that look too.

~

'You okay?' I asked after a long day when the wind had taken us far and fast. 'It's been hard, we've worked like dogs.'

'I am a little scared.'

'You wanted to leave,' I said. But I said it softly. We'd both chosen this.

'I am not only scared of this,' she said.

'What then?'

'Everything.'

'What do you mean?'

She didn't answer.

I was scared too. All the possible futures seemed scary.

~

In the morning light I woke to see her kneeling at the bow, hands open, palms up. She was speaking in her language. Sounds more song than words.

Prayers.

I prayed too, silently. But not to one god. I thought about all we'd been through, about how the people on Aya's boat and the crew on *Pandora* could be dead. I prayed to the sea and sky. I prayed to *Tanirt* and poured a drop of coconut juice on the deck, and spilled a drop of fish blood in the water. I felt that there were gods and demons and djinns all around us. And if we didn't respect them, they could take our lives.

These gods, these forces; they weren't good or bad. Out at sea, there's no good or evil. There is only chaos and order. Things going well or against us. I thought maybe life back in the world is like that. It just *seems* as though there's order. And then I thought, we might think we're in charge of *Tanirt* and our destiny, but we're kidding ourselves.

iii

Days passed.
Food began to run out. Aya put us on quarter-rations.

How far had we come? How far was there to go?

We knew we were heading east, to Africa. The sun told us that. But there were currents and squally winds, and they seemed like demons, playing games with us.

iv

One day the wind hit us from nowhere, stretching the sail hard. The mast creaked, groaned then cracked loudly. I leaped up and held it fast so it wouldn't break more, but the wind was so strong I had to hold onto the mast to stop it from flying into the water. A vicious gust yanked at the tarpaulin, and it tore.

I took the rig down.

The blustery wind whizzed away across the sea, like some djinn conjured from nothing that had caused its chaos and buzzed off.

I knelt with the torn tarpaulin in my hands, staring at the broken mast.

'I told you!' I shouted. 'I told you, Aya, you can't keep taking risks. Just because you've won every toss of the coin, it doesn't mean you'll keep winning. This was always going to happen. Always, Aya. Always!'

Aya huddled in the prow, crying.

I shouted to the sky: 'Why can't you give us a chance!'

We threaded coconut rope through the sail. But Aya had to put more holes in it. It was okay for gentle sailing, but weaker in a powerful wind. There was a chance it would tear even worse.

I cut a section off the line to bind the mast. The wood had dried and become brittle. That's why it had broken. I didn't know how much longer it would last.

V

'Are the sea and sky trying to kill us?' I asked one night, as we ate. 'Or giving small gifts to keep us alive?'

'I do not know,' was all Aya said.

We weren't lords of the sea any more. We were lost kids in a boat.

In the morning the winds lessened. It started getting hot again.

It was calm enough to set up the aman-maker.

When I ate some coconut and fish it was hard to bite. I felt a tooth wobble, and tasted blood. I felt my teeth with my fingers. I could move some of them.

After that I used the knife to cut up our food as small as I could.

Gull had fished before, but only for himself. Now he was weak. We would eat him when he died. But I wasn't going to kill him. I swore that to myself.

vi

Hunger ate my body and mind. It was a serpent in my head and stomach and I was disappearing into it, bit by bit.

Dreams came and went. Dreams of the boat. Dreams of the sea. The island. Where I had dreamed of a yacht called *Pandora*. There were people on it. Aliens with big heads and fat stomachs (and a captain – Wilkinson? Wilson? I couldn't remember). When I was on this *Pandora* boat I'd had a dream of the Canary Islands. And when I had been on this Canary place I had once dreamed of home.

My head was a boat that had sailed, all the way from England. And that old home was so far over the horizon that it had never been real.

I saw the sultan swooping, his great coat flying, filled with stars.

I sat up when I saw that. Called to Aya to see it too. But I had no voice. I shouted but there was no sound. The sea was frozen solid. The waves were on pause.

They were still, but the stars flowed in the sultan's cape as he rode, like specks of dust in sunlight. *Every* star was a shooting star.

By day there was a grey-green sea under a cloudy sky. Feathery waves and chop. Lively jumping fish. But when I looked at them, or started to prepare the hook and line, they disappeared.

The water held crazy patterns that looked like shark fins. One shark or many? Hundreds. I didn't know if they were real, or if I'd imagined them.

Then I saw beyond the patterns and shades a break in the water. And beyond that, in the place we were slowly drifting to, the endless, dark, deep.

And behind the last cloud, burning fierce, as if it had never left, taking off its mask...

The sun demon.

We had escaped to the island. Found a place it couldn't reach us. Got lucky. But we were only hiding, for a time. In a game of hide-and-seek. Now we were here, in its court.

It saw us and it wanted us.

vii

We scooped water with the turtle shell and tins, to wash and cool ourselves.

When evening came, we ate.

Mouthfuls. A few. No more.

We drank. But the store of water was less than the day before. And I knew, when the food ran out, we'd be drinking more than we made. Just to stay alive.

Then there'd be no aman.

No anything.

~

I saw a fin in the distance. I fixed my gaze where it had been, staring so hard that tears came to my eyes. But it was gone.

'I'm imagining things,' I whispered. 'I think I'm going mad, Aya. Do you hear?'

She looked at me as though I was a stranger, speaking in a language she didn't understand.

In the night it got cold.

In time we'd sleep. But we had hours before then. And nothing but stars to look at.

'Tell me a story,' I whispered.

'I cannot. I am tired.'

'Shahrazad had to tell stories. To stay alive. She had no choice.'

'A story will not give us food, or aman. A story will not give us home, or wind to take us there.'

I couldn't *make* her tell me a story, any more than I could have made her stay on the island. I just wanted some distraction from what we both knew in our hearts, but we didn't dare to say: our time was running out.

'How do you tell your stories?' I asked, in a scratchy voice. 'How do you learn them and remember them?'

'It is not so easy, Bill,' she said.

Even in the dark I could see the tiredness in her eyes.

She turned so she was lying on her back, gazing at the stars. Staring and staring. Without blinking, hardly breathing. A waking sleep. I nudged her. She didn't move. I nudged her again.

'Are you okay?' I said. And I was afraid then, because I thought she was slipping away.

'Some water,' I said. 'I'll get you some aman.'

'No,' she said. 'It is only a dream.' She smiled. 'Sometime it is like the stars.'

'What?'

'A story. There is this person and this thing that happen, then another thing. Each is like a star. But this is not a story. You see this.' She pointed.

'Yes, the north star.'

'No, below.'

'The frying pan, the big dipper? You take the two to the side of the pan and make a line to the north star.'

'Yes, but this is not why I say. It is a bear. This is the story.'

'What?'

'The shape of these stars is like a bear. The stars are only light in sky. It is the lines between make the story.'

'There is no line between.'

'Not line you see. You make with yourself. In here.' She tapped her head.

'I don't understand,' I said.

'Okay, this is one way. Another is like a map on the sea.'

'Chart?'

'Yes, chart. You know begin, you know the end. But you do not know the journey. This is like you and me, in *Tanirt*. And the story is like a boat on the sea. May go this place. May go that place. You do not know. Wind and sun will take the boat. We sail but we do not make a choice. Wind and sun choose.'

'You mean you tell a story but you don't know exactly what will happen?'

'Yes. And also some of the story is remember.'

'You remember the story, or *things* you remember that you put *in* a story?' I thought of us in the hut, Aya telling me about Sakkina and her uncle and the men who wore black and carried guns.

She smiled again, and seemed to have some strength left, some hidden pocket of life she was reaching into. 'I remember many stories my uncle tell. Some is short and I know every word is the same as my uncle say. Some is like how I remember the stars, but I must make the lines with words. You see? To make the bear. The sultan. The djinn.'

'You never did finish the story of Shahrazad. What happens to her? Does she tell stories forever, to stay alive?'

'You want to know?'

'Yes, like the king, or is it the sultan? The one who Shahrazad is telling the stories to?'

'Yes. King. Like him.'

'I remember it all, Aya. Thiyya has defeated the demon, and he has given her a stone, a ruby. And its name is Fire-heart. That was the story Lunja told the sultan. And Shahrazad told both these stories to the cruel king.'

'You know this well.'

'I remember.'

I could see she was pleased.

'Did he spare her life in the end?' I said.

'You want an end. You want the end to be happy, yes? It is the way of story not of life. But yes, Bill. Here you have an end.

'Shahrazad and the king have in the nights and years one child, a boy.

'Yet soon after he is born the child dies. Then Shahrazad she say to the king that she has no more tales.'

'That's it?' I say. 'That's how it ends?' My heart crashed. 'It can't be. It can't!'

Aya looked sorry and sad. I think she was weighing up, whether to say: *Yes, that's how it ends*, or if she had the strength to go on.

She turned to face me and said: 'I will tell.'

The Final Tale of Shahrazad

In the kingdom, many years ago, the woman Shahrazad had told her stories under the stars of a thousand nights. She had made her stories of sun and moon, water and earth, fire and air, of monsters and djinns that are vanished from the land, but who we still fear in our hearts. She had told many tales of treasure found, treasure lost, then found again. In her days and years with the king, the sun had set one thousand and one times and the sun had risen one thousand times.

She lay beside the king.

'Tell me a tale, Shahrazad,' said the king. 'Tell me a tale. For my heart is breaking now my son is dead. Take me from this hell. Tell me a story of our son, and let us give him a name, for we will only know that he has lived if he has a name. We shall call our son

Anamar. Tell me a tale of how Anamar is become an angel. I demand this.'

'Lord,' Shahrazad said to the king, 'I told you I have no more tales. You shall have me killed and I will die in peace. Will you make ready your executioner? And tomorrow you may take a new bride.'

'I command you.'

Shahrazad's heart was as a stone. She had no pity for him. And he saw this. He left the bed and knelt on the ground.

'Very well, I beg you,' he said.

'Then I *shall* tell you a tale, but it is not the one you wish to hear. And it shall be my final story. And then you will have me killed. Do you understand?'

The king does not answer. He only listens.

'You will like this story, O my great King, for it is a tale of endless treasure, and what is more – a great secret is shown, for this tale is true, Lord. Yes, true!'

But the king does not sit up, so eager to know, so eager to hear. When he speaks it is only a whisper: 'Will the tale mend my heart?'

'Heart! What need have *you* of a heart?' Shahrazad spits, and makes a fist, shaking it in the face of the king. 'You, who desires above all, land and gold, silks and saffron, and other fine things. Listen, now, to the tale of the greatest treasure there ever was. The chest of gold and diamonds. The trove of jewels and metals that shine like the stars, sun and sea under the moon, the most valuable treasure in all the world.'

The king stood, and his eyes opened fully, as if he had woken from a living dream.

'Yes, my King! It is a treasure blessed with magic. For the more you give to your people, the more you will have. Now I have no more of this tale to tell. Only this. Though the treasure is real, I cannot tell you where it is, my King. Only you can find where it lies. And as I say, if you find it, the more you give to your people, the more you shall have. I wish you luck, I pray you will not spend the rest of your days searching.'

The light of dawn filled the chamber. Shahrazad left her bed and went and knelt upon the ground with her head bowed: 'So, call your men. I am ready.'

The men come. They are sad to take Shahrazad for they love her and they love her stories. Many of them cry. But they know the king will not have mercy and they cannot beg for her life.

But then... *then*, the king who has been a murderer and a thief, but also a husband and a father, and who is dying with grief, he says: 'The treasure you speak of is love. It lies in our hearts with the shadow of fear. Its light will not defeat the shadow. But it may be like a fire in the night, or the moon in the sky. It will light the darkness, until the new day will come.'

And he loved his queen Shahrazad and he loved his

people. And now, after one thousand tales, he listens to this story and he promises to tell this story each day to his people, forever more, and he says to his queen, Shahrazad: '*This* is the story that will never end.'

I saw the moonlight shine in Aya's eyes.

'Why are you crying?' I said.

Aya pushed words through the tears. 'Because this story does not matter. And I will never see Sakkina again. This is the end of the story. This! Death.'

Cold empty fear pitted in my gut and spread through my whole body.

'Don't,' I said. 'Don't say that. After what we've been through we *have* to live.'

'I say we must leave the island. And I am sorry.'

viii

Water almost ran out. We made more. The sun demon was good for that.

It was slow, we made less than we drank.

We sat apart, in the shade of our hats, the cloak, the storm-cheater.

I looked for the fin. I searched and looked. But I didn't see it.

But next day:

It came behind us. The curving arc of its fin trailing in the wake of the boat. I always thought a shark had to move fast, but this monster swam slowly, almost lazily through the still blue. As it got close we saw its fin properly. White and black-edged above the water. Its body a huge, grey shadow below.

I closed my eyes.

'It's not real,' I said. 'I'm imagining things. Seeing things.'

'No, Bill. See.'

It was there, lurking and waiting.

'No, no, no. It can't *be*.'

But it was. It was real.

It followed us when we paddled. It did that for hours, till night.

I didn't sleep.

Then, in the first light, it bumped the boat. Gull crawked and flapped.

'Bill!' Aya shouted. We both sat bolt upright. I grabbed the oar. Aya found the knife and held it, ready.

I looked over the side, careful to hold steady to the gunnels with one shaking hand. The bump had been a nudge, a test. It was coming. There was no doubt. We saw it close as it swam by, a few metres off starboard side. Black eyes, white teeth. A face with no expression.

Gull watched, hopping from one leg to the other, moving around to keep an eye on it. Gull knew this thing. He knew to be wary of it.

It went away and came back, again and again. Every time we held each other with one hand, braced, with the oar and knife in our other hands. And each time I felt the same cold, sick lurch in my gut.

Then it vanished. We did nothing for hours, except watch the flat water.

In the early evening I fished. I didn't want to. I didn't want to do anything that might make it come back. But we had to find food if we could. I got a bite. The first in days. A good size fish. We reeled it in.

The shark came gliding through the water. I reeled fast. But it came and took the fish, and the hook too. I held the oar, gripped it with all I had.

'You're not having it.'

The line pinged and snapped, leaving me with nothing. I remembered the rope holding the raft to *Pandora*. How the storm had broken it.

'It is a monster,' said Aya. She had hate in her eyes. And fear and disgust like I'd seen when she looked at Stephan sometimes. She spat in the water.

'Sharks are millions of years old,' I said. 'They evolved before the dinosaurs… Not a monster. Just an animal.'

'Not animal. It *is* a monster!' she insisted.

And I thought: *She's right, it is.*

'Every shark is a copy,' I said.

'What?'

'Of one true shark,' I said. 'This one.'

'What?'

'I… I don't know. I don't know what I'm saying.' And I didn't. I could barely hold the oar, could barely see. The line of the horizon kept getting out of place, wobbling, stretching.

I felt the light of the stars and the whispers of the

sea. There's an energy in these things, strong and alive; an electric-like force that surged through my bones and across every inch of my skin. A vanishing treasure.

ix

We saw something. A dot on the horizon as the last sliver of sun was eaten by the sea. We planned to make our way to it in the morning.

We drank aman. Almost all we had.

I'd had an idea before we lost the hook. The bait we had was shrivelled and stinking, so I'd thought about cutting a chunk out of my leg and using that as bait.

That should have horrified me. Like Stephan's death should have horrified me. But the 'me' that could be horrified didn't exist any more. Cutting a piece out of my leg to use as bait seemed a sensible thing to do. But now we had no hook.

I had another thought. One that wouldn't go away.

Which one of us will die first? The other will have to eat them.

It was like a voice. Not in my head, but heard a long way off.

I forced the voice away.

I thought:

That isn't right.
None of this is right.
Stephan's death. Using flesh as bait. Cannibalism.

~

Morning.

The sea was choppy with wind and there was a swell rolling. The dot rose and fell on the waves. We kept losing sight of it. The sun kept slipping behind clouds making it hard to navigate.

It wasn't a boat. A boat would move. It was jetsam maybe, a piece of wreck, a rock, an island?

I stopped myself hoping for anything.

I paddled slowly, stopping regularly to look for the shark, hoping it would leave us alone now that it had taken our fish.

Aya slouched at the stern, huddled in the back of the boat, limp and still.

She kept rubbing her stomach with her mouth open. As if someone might feed her. Gull sat behind her, crawking gently.

~

We rested. But not for long. I was too frightened of losing the dot. My head felt light. Disconnected; struggling to get the message to my muscles.

Paddle. Paddle.

But every stroke was a world of pain.

'Tell me a story,' I croaked.

'I cannot,' said Aya. 'I am weak.'

I sat back gasping. I had no strength either.

'Please, Aya.'

'Once… there was… I can. Not.'

Her eyes were fading black stars.

When we were on the island and she swam, her dress had clung to her. She was skinny, but had girl-shape. Curves and roundness. But it had all gone. Her body was eating itself. She was a stick-girl, dressed in a rotten sack. I was a stick-boy, wearing a holey rag t-shirt and too-big shorts.

When the wind blew the sack against Aya, I saw her ribs.

'Why did we leave the island?' I said, to no one.

$$\sim$$

We got closer. But the dot was still far away.

I thought reaching it would kill me. I believed that. I collapsed.

'We're going to die,' I said.

Aya took the seat out of its place and said: 'Yes, we are going to die. When we are very old, playing with the young children of our children.' She knelt at the bow. 'Come,' she said. She helped me back to my knees. 'I will tell you a story. Once, on the great ocean, there lived a girl and a boy. Allah, in his magnificence, blessed them with a boat, full of treasure and bounty... Each day the treasure was less. But when the boat was empty, they had still one thing.'

'What?'

'Hope.'

She paddled, grimacing with the effort.

'How does the story end?' I asked, picking up the oar.

'They live.'

~

The dead whale lay on its side. Most of it was underwater but the head was above the surface. A floating island. A sick, fleshy iceberg.

Gull flew to the giant, barely able to keep above the sea. He settled where its eye had been and pecked at the hole for strings of flesh.

The whale stank, but I knew we'd soon be eating its flesh too.

The water was rising and falling and windblown. But we could see, in the fathoms, the whale's tail and most of its body eaten away, showing sections of skeleton. Clouds of fish were feeding: rays, tuna, silver-striped fish, darting yellow long fish, chubby silver scaled ones the size of my hand. Hundreds and thousands of them. And we had no hook.

Among the fish there were shadows, feeding on the water-bloated flesh of the giant. S-shaping swimmers. Sharks, sliding through the water, gathering as though the lunch bell had rung.

There were as many different sharks as there were fish: hammerheads, slick blue ones, short fat ones. They'd head in, one at a time, tearing off a bite of the carcass and thrashing their heads from side to side till they'd seized their chunk. Then they'd vanish into the blue. They took turns at the free feast, smaller fish darting and dodging out of their way.

Watching the sharks filled me with dread. The sharp fins, the beady eyes. Sharks *are* fear. That fear swam coldly round my gut.

~

Then the shadow came.

It moved among the sharks and fish and in seconds was the only thing in the water with the dead whale. Every other thing vanished.

It rose to the surface and drifted beside us.

'Jesus,' I whimpered.

'Allah protect us,' said Aya.

I grabbed the oar, ready to fight it if I had to. It turned. Only its fin broke the surface as it glided away.

'It's so... so... It's *graceful*,' I said, hardly able to breathe the words out.

I dropped the oar. We clung to each other, and sat as low in the boat as we could.

Looking over the side was impossible then. Like looking over a cliff with nothing at the bottom.

'It's okay,' I gasped. 'It doesn't want us.'

'Bill, I...'

Boom. It was an earthquake in the boat. *Everything* shuddered.

Aya screamed: 'Please, Bill, please!'

'I... I don't know...'

'Please.'

I knelt up and looked over the gunnels. But before I saw anything –

Boom.

I fell sideways. I sat up again, grabbing the oar and lifting it high.

I watched the line of its fin as it swam away. It went so far I thought it was leaving. But then it turned, 180 degrees until it faced us. And it came fast. An accelerating truck.

I looked over the bow, ready to hit it with the oar. I yelled at it.

It skimmed the boat and thrashed its tail into the bow.

The aft tipped into the water before righting, rocking and swaying.

'Bill!' Aya shouted.

'I don't... Wait, look!' Water was filling the hull. We were sitting in it.

Sinking.

I waved the oar, panting, searching. It came again. Just before it hit I punched the oar into its back. It shuddered, banging the boat, thrashing its tail, as if it had saved its energy for *this*.

I pushed Aya aside and opened the hold. It was filling with water. I grabbed the knife and the line.

'Shout at it,' I said. 'Throw something at it. Anything!'

I worked as quickly and as hard as I could. I unreeled some line, then took the knife from Aya and cut a length. Then I tore a strip from my t-shirt, and wrapped it around the knife handle and the end of the oar. I looped the line around it, tight. But my hands were trembling and everything was nightmare slow.

Boom. It hit again.

The line, the oar, the knife. I made them into a spear. And even in that frozen, panicked moment I knew: *If we lose this spear we lose everything.*

Aya thrashed the water with the seat.

When I'd made the spear, I stood, my feet wide, holding the weapon over my head.

'Where is it?' I said.

'I cannot see... there!'

It was coming at an angle. Its jaw open, teeth bared.

I lunged. It dodged, or I missed. It went off, turned and charged again. Only this time it swam deeply and then curved, coming at us from below like a heat-seeking missile. Up and up and up.

When it hit, the boat lifted as if a giant fist had struck it, then crashed down into the sea.

Water flooded in. It was up to my knees. I swung the spear, stabbing water. But it was so fast, so *clever*. It spun over, dodging the spear.

'Did you hit?' asked Aya.

'Dunno. Never mind that, we're sinking. Now bail!' I shouted. Aya grabbed the barrel lid and scooped water, swishing it over the side.

I waited. And had time to think, to see what was happening. I knew the truth. It would come again and again and again, until we were in *its* world. It might be seconds or it might be hours, but it would never stop. It would ram us until we sank. Then there'd be tugging and ripping, thrashing in the red water. Then darkness.

I knew we had a leak, that the weight of us was sinking the boat. I had no choice about what to do next.

I leaned over the bow, as far as I dared. Teetering.

'Come on!' I shouted.

It came, then, from below. I lunged.

The knife made a gash in its back. It stuck there for a second and I held the oar fast, until it wriggled free.

The shark writhed, creating a storm of white water. But it was tinged red too.

'I got it!' I shouted.

It went down, spiralling, leaving a trail of red mist.

Other sharks appeared, lured by blood. Not so scared of the white now.

Aya screamed, panicking as she bailed and bailed. But the boat was filling, we were going down. The shark turned. It was hurt but not finished, and raced up with its jaw wide.

I raised the spear and thrust it into the water. The blade stuck in the shark's head, above its eye.

It thrashed but I held the spear fast and Aya held me. I felt its raw power. I felt Aya losing her grip and then the shock of water as I fell in and went under.

I clung to the spear, could feel it shaking in my hands, and pushed. And pushed. I couldn't see the shark, only blue and white chaos. Then clouds of red. The spear was wrenched from my grip.

Thrashing my arms, swimming, panicking, spinning, needing to get to the boat but not knowing which way was up. Suddenly I was there and the water was blue.

I surfaced. Aya took my hand. She pulled hard, crying out with effort. I clambered and climbed, breaking with the strain. She pulled at my hair, my skin, my shorts, *desperate* to get me back in.

I looked over the side of the boat, to see if it was

coming again. And saw its head flailing in the red, far below. I could see it turning, getting ready for another charge, but it spasmed and lurched. The spear was near its eyehole, at the end of a long gash. Blade deep. It had no way to rid itself of the spear. It sank, drifting down in circles. Taking with it our knife and our oar and our line.

The servants turned on their master quickly, swarming to kill and eat.

We were alone.

I turned to see Aya bailing like crazy.

'I'll help,' I said, but vomited water.

Everything went blurry: the boat, the sky, Aya.

The sun beat down.

I felt Aya doing something with my foot and leg. And covering my foot with her cloak. She tore at her dress and wedged the cloth into a crack in the hull.

I wanted to help but I couldn't get up. I lay, panting and sweating. She bailed more water until we were properly afloat. Bobbing in the breeze.

'The sun,' I said. Even in my dizziness I could feel it, beating me.

'The hats are gone, in the sea. I look but I cannot see.'

'My foot,' I said. I leaned down to lift the cloak.

'No,' said Aya, 'don't.' But I brushed her hand away. I saw.

'Christ. No.' I didn't even remember it happening. I

had no idea *how* it happened. Yet it had, in the madness, in the water.

My right foot was ruined. A pulped slab of flesh, dripping blood.

Two toes were gone, others were mangled. I tried to wriggle, to move, and almost blacked out with pain.

A shark tooth was lodged in one toe, like a shard of glass.

'My foot,' I said again. Aya ripped more of her dress and tied the cloth tight around my ankle. I watched. She worked hard, but there was a lot of blood.

I passed out.

~

Fever.

Losing blood.

My throat on fire.

The sun blinding me.

Sinking.

Slipping away.

My heart beat weakly, poison crept around my body, my mind.

I woke to a sky awash with diamond stars. The lines between them formed shapes. Great tides, sweeping and shifting like sand. An archer on a horse. A dragon. A demon. The Sun Lord, parading through the sky.

Aya's soothing voice.

'Rest, sleep.'

There was no difference between dreams and waking. Sometimes there was a silent blackness and I sank into it. Wanting it, but knowing it was dangerous too.

The world of the demons.

Aya cleaning my foot. Seeing it swollen and yellow.

No reason, or sense, or rhythm to any of it.

Then:

Our holiday in Italy, when I was lost.

I'm there. I'm not six any more, I'm me now.

There are trees. I stand in the shade looking up at the branches; the wind brushing through the blossom. It falls like snow, till the sun shines through.

There are people. A young mum teaching her daughter to ride a bike. Two old men in dark suits, hunched over a chessboard on a table. Smoking, laughing, sipping coffee. I smell the coffee, I smell the cigarettes.

A white stone statue of a noble Roman emperor.

Three students reciting Latin from books as they walk.

I remember. And I live it now. Being alone, but not scared. Not worrying that I've lost my family. Because nothing really bad can happen here.

I walk out from under the shade of the tree and shield my eyes. The sun is strong and fierce.

'Why am I here?' I ask.

X

My skin is burning. Pain throbs through my leg and into my body, into my mind. Like whale song it gets into every piece of me.

Time to wake up, says the sun.

When the sun speaks, its voice is as soft as a sigh. At first. It crackles through the short-wave radio in my head, trying to make itself heard. I see Wilko slamming his fist into this radio, until it bursts with the sound of wind and waves. Wilko salutes then vanishes.

Wake up.

It swims, this voice. Coming from a long way off at first, snaking closer, until it's in my skull.

Wake up.

I try to speak but my throat is swollen closed. My eyes too, I can barely see. There's nothing *to* see. Only white light. But then, even though my throat is closed, I find I *can* speak. My voice is clear.

'Aya?' I say. But she's not there or she can't hear me. There's only the light. Glaring. And then I see. I see very clearly.

A mighty sultan. A coat of stars flowing behind him, a river of them twinkling in the sky. He has a scimitar in his hand, heavy and sharp. One swing could cut through a hundred men.

The sultan is a man but a demon too, with diamond blue eyes and a mouth that's wide and hungry, filled with tiny, sharp teeth and a tongue writhing like a snake. He laughs, because he knows he has won. That he will never bow. That he can never be defeated.

Look at me.

'Who are you?' I say. But he does not answer. 'I thought death would be dark.'

Death is dark, my friend. A night with no stars and no dawn. He is coming soon. There is time for you and him. More than you imagine. More than anyone can imagine. He will come when our talk is over.

'Who are you?'

I do not have a name. You also have no name. Not any more.

'I'm Bill. I am. You're not real… I've got septicaemia… You're poison.'

Names, words – these are nothing. This word 'Bill' is left behind. In your home country, in Canaria, on the island. Look at me.

'*Bill.*' *This word is a drop of water in a stream, then a river, running faster and faster. And now this river is running into the sea.*

Look. At. Me.

'I'll go blind.'

You are dying. You should see before you go.

'What do you want?'

I want you to know! I will never bow.

The light softens. I'm lying in the fore of the boat. My leg lies in front of me, bloated and as thick as a log. Not belonging to me any more. At the end of the leg something awful is wrapped up in the cloak. Aya is perched on the seat above the hold, watching.

'Aya?' I say.

Tears stream down her face.

'Aya?' My voice is like dry sand. I try to reach a hand up. But the light blinds and washes the vision away. The Lord is back.

Look. At. Me.

I don't feel the heat any more. I'm floating and sinking at the same time. Almost leaving. But I want him to know:

'You *do* have a name. More than one. Murder and torture and rape and slavery and hate. Many.'

Look. At. Me.

'I can't.'

You are not brave. You cannot look. No one can. Not in the end. You are a skeleton in a boat...

'Aya's seen you, hasn't she? She's looked you in the eye.'

Then I do look at it. And it doesn't blind me.

His grin drops like a stone. His burning fierceness falls into shadow. For a second I see… Is it confusion, or fear?

I feel the t-shirt ripped from my body. The sun burning my chest.

Aya's whisper: '*Tanirt* has secrets. In the hold—'

Night.

Nowhere

i

Out of darkness come shouts. Shrieks of joy.

'He's moving. Thank God!'

'Calm, darling. He has to come round in his own time.'

'Daaaad?' I slur.

'Yes, son. We're here.'

'Bill.' A woman's voice. 'I'm Dr Jones. You're in hospital, in London. You're safe. How are you feeling, Bill?'

I'm drifting. It takes a while to realise I'm floating on a soft bed, a sea of nothing. I open my eyes but see only shapes and blurs.

'Aya! Where's Aya?'

'What's Aya?' Mum says.

'Where am I?'

The doctor explains again, slowly. 'Hospital. London.'

'Where is she? Aya!' I've called her name before I think not to, before I remember my promise.

'There's no one but you, Bill,' says Dr Jones. 'You were found alone.'

I'm alive. I'm in London. Mum and Dad are here. But no Aya.

'Mum.'

'We're here, Bill.' Mum takes my hand and squeezes.

'Yes, we're here, son.' Dad holds the other hand. There are hugs and tears. Plenty.

I try to speak. We all do. But it's hard to find the words. And it's enough to hold their hands and to know they are here. Whatever happens now, they are here.

I cry. Not just because I'm back with Mum and Dad. It's not even to do with Aya. It's because I'm alive. Only…

'I can't see.' I'm alert now. The blurred vision isn't just me coming round, it's half-blindness.

'Can you see *any*thing, Bill?' says Dr Jones.

I blink and try to focus.

'A yellow blur. You're shadows behind it. I see bits in the corners…'

'The sun has damaged your eyes. We'll run tests. Your sight should return fully. But it will be days, maybe weeks.'

Then. Another realisation.

'My foot.' I can feel part of it – no – the *absence* of part of it. I try to wriggle toes that aren't there.

'You'll have to be brave, son,' Dad says, 'I'm afraid you've...' His voice breaks. 'There was nothing they could do. You've lost some of your right foot. Some toes. But they can do things with prosthetics. And... you're lucky to be alive. It's a miracle. We always believed there was a chance. Something else you should know. The boys on *Pandora*, they're all alive and well.'

'That's great,' I say. 'Were there... other boats, in the storm?'

'Yes, there was another boat. They were all rescued too, apart from one girl. She went missing, presumed drowned. But yes, the crew of *Pandora* are all alive and well.'

I picture Wilko and the others. And I think about the people on Aya's boat. I can't feel elated. I try, but I can't. Where is she?

'How long have I been here?'

'Four weeks, in an induced coma.'

'Coma!'

'Yes, but at least you get your own room,' Dad says. I laugh at that.

'It's been months all told,' Mum says. 'You're sixteen now. We'll celebrate your birthday, as soon as we get home.'

Dr Jones says I have to rest. She shoos Mum and Dad out.

Thoughts tumble. I'm told by Dr Jones that I was

found near the shore, in the boat. Alone. Was Aya
rescued? Did she swim to shore? How did she get off
the boat before I was found? Did someone take her
against her will?

There are no answers. No story I can think of that
makes any sense.

ii

Dr Jones asks a lot of questions. Her voice is posh, but warm.

Now I'm awake I've been moved onto a ward. To give me some privacy, Dr Jones pulls curtains around the bed.

'The day they brought you here, well, I've never seen anything like it. You were starved and dehydrated. Your leg was swollen, your foot was black. You've had blood poisoning, severe dehydration and skin burn. They had to hold you for *five* days in Morocco just to stabilise you before putting you on a plane. It's a miracle. How did you live, all those weeks?'

'I did what I had to. To survive.' I think about eating a turtle. The island. Stephan. Killing the shark. Aya.

'You were very brave,' Dr Jones says.

'Anyone will do what they have to do to live. It's not being brave, you don't have a choice.'

'You should tell us what happened. Everything,' Dr Jones says. 'It'll help us get you better.'

I wonder if she's thinking of my body or my mind when she says 'better'. I want to talk, but I don't want to lie.

'I had tins of food. I made an aman-maker—'

'What?'

'Water. I made a water-maker.' I change the subject. 'Who found me?'

'A fisherman.'

I wait, but Dr Jones doesn't say more.

'How? Where?' I ask.

'I don't know exactly. When you were waking you said: "Where is she?" You said: "Aya." Who is Aya?' Dr Jones is curious.

'Where is the fisherman?'

'A long way to the south of Morocco. The edge of a desert. Another country. A war zone.'

'Can I get hold of him?'

'Why?'

'I… I want to know how he found me.'

I feel Dr Jones's fingers on my arm, just below where a drip is sticking into me.

'You know you can talk to me, we have to trust each other,' she says.

I don't say more. *Can't* say more. She rubs my skin, pats my arm.

'It's okay, Bill. We have time.'

The bed is a cocoon of comfort. But it feels wrong. Soft and alien. The atmosphere is lukewarm and air-conditioned. That feels wrong too.

I remember the sea, rocking the hard bed of the boat as I drifted to sleep. I remember the cold nights and burning days. Outside I hear voices, cars, birds singing, music.

It's like that park in Italy. Civilised, but not-real.

Later there's hot soup and bread, tea, a bottle of Coke.

It all tastes new.

It will take a long time: to be well, to see, to walk, to feel normal. Or maybe there never will be 'normal'. The world of the boat and the world of after-the-boat aren't part of the same universe.

Dr Jones wants to know about my 'diet', and the weeks of sun, and survival; all the grim details of how I stayed alive, or more accurately, how I nearly died. I tell her bits, careful not to say 'we'; careful not to give too much away.

My sight comes back, more each day. Not fully. I see colours and blurred shapes. My vision is filled with the burn. Sometimes it's orange, sometimes brown. Spots of nothing swim in front of me like fish.

One thing Dr Jones doesn't ask about for a long time is my foot. Eventually we *do* talk about it, because I want to walk. I'm sick of using a bedpan and the bed is becoming a prison. So I get up and use a crutch, and walk about a bit, though it's like when we found the island, my legs don't work properly at first. They're going to stick some plastic bits on, so I have a whole foot again. I'll be able to walk on it, but it will take months for the various operations and getting used to it. For now, it's crutches.

As I hobble down the corridor Dr Jones walks besides me and says, gently: 'It might be traumatic to talk, but it might be therapeutic. Every patient is different. Do you want to tell me the story?'

I think about the shadow, the great monster shark stalking us. But I don't know what to say, where to begin with the story of how I killed it. Evidently all by myself.

'I don't think you would believe me,' I say.

'Try,' she says.

I do trust her and I want to tell it all, about Aya too, because *not* telling is like Aya not being real. I could tell our story, and the words would make the memories live. The urge to talk is a tide. But I fight it.

Mum and Dad ask if I would like an audio book, to pass the time.

I ask if they've ever heard of the tales of Shahrazad.

'Yes,' says Dad. 'More commonly known as *One Thousand and One Nights* or *The Arabian Nights*. Shahrazad is the girl who has to tell a story every evening to save her life.'

He sets up an iPad and earphones then goes online, searching. There are lots of versions. Most only cover a few examples of the stories. I want the full thing. Dad orders an audio book series. It's more than seventy hours of listening. And even *that* is a shorter version of the full thing.

It begins. It's not exactly how Aya told it, but the core is the same. The king, the executions, Shahrazad telling stories to save her sister and to cheat death.

I wait for the tale of the Sun Lord. Of the shadow, of the demon. Thiyya. Lunja. There are plenty of stories, full of magic and murder, clever thieves and brave heroes, greedy kings and cruel sultans. Djinns, demons, monsters. The stories are like the ones Aya told me in lots of ways, but they're not the same. At first I think that's because we haven't got to them yet. After all, there are a thousand and one.

But as days pass, I get the feeling that maybe they aren't in there at all.

Dad downloads some science audio books as well, popular ones about black holes, neuroscience, AI, the weird illogical quantum reality that underpins everything. I start some but can't focus. Instead I spend hours and hours listening to Shahrazad's tales.

The only one that is familiar in some way is the tale of Sind-bad the sailor, who found an island when he was shipwrecked. But when he lights a fire there, he discovers the island isn't land at all, but the back of a giant, sleeping whale.

Somehow that's like the whales we saw, and the island that was a home, but then *not* a home. Somehow it's like the whale corpse we found, eaten by sharks until it sank to the ocean floor. Somehow.

111

I have a visitor. Wilko, our captain from *Pandora*.

He tries to smile as he holds out his hand, but it seems forced. His skin is ash. He looks years older.

We shake. He doesn't let go, he keeps hold of me.

'We tried to get back to you,' he starts. 'The storm...'

I wriggle my hand out of his, because it's awkward. He sits in the chair by the bed and crumples.

'Thought you were dead,' he says.

'I thought you were. *All* of you.'

'It's good to see you. You made it.'

'Yeah.' I feel uncomfortable. I'm the one in the hospital bed, but he's the one who looks unwell.

'I searched for you,' he says. 'After we got rescued. The official effort lasted for a few weeks, but I carried on. I chartered a yacht, your parents paid. Your dad stayed in the Canaries. He wanted to come, but I told him it would slow me down.'

'You did that?'

'They didn't tell you?'

'We haven't talked much about the time I was away. Not yet.'

Wilko nods. 'I used the engine a lot because there was no wind. It was a waste of time, you must have been miles from where I looked. Can you forgive me?'

'There's nothing to forgive. You did everything you could. The storm came from nowhere. It wasn't your fault.'

'I'm not sure people saw it that way. Not the papers, anyway.'

That's why he's carrying such a weight. When a fifteen-year-old boy gets lost in the Atlantic, someone has to take the rap. They chose him.

'Well, I need to thank you,' I say.

He's confused. I smile.

'If we'd got back home, if we hadn't sunk, none of it would have happened. And I'm glad that it did.'

Now he looks at me as though I'm mad. And maybe I am.

I think about Aya afloat on the barrel, how if we'd never found each other in that desert of blue, we'd both be dead. I'm grateful for the storm, to the djinn that brought me to her and her to me.

I think of her breathing when she slept. Her voice singing and her hands painting pictures as she told her stories. Cursing me with her Berber words. Nestling with Gull in the hut. On *Tanirt*, wiping the sweat from my burning face.

Aya's alive, somewhere, now. I believe that.

'How long was it before they found *you*?' I ask.

He shifts in his chair. And I think that whatever I'm going to hear won't be easy for him to tell.

'We ran out of water quickly. We tried catching rain but it was impossible. Whenever we opened the zip door we got flooded. We were squeezed in. It was difficult to bail. *Huge* waves. We were in total darkness. And going up and down, up and down...' He stops, because he can't *not* remember, and he's living it again as he tells the story. 'Some of the lads went mad I swear. No sleep. Afraid. Waves pitching us high, then slamming us down. We got hit, thumped and dragged under more than once, never knowing if we were coming back up. Someone said at one point we were too heavy, so...' He pauses.

I know the choice they almost made. I can see it. Them grabbing one of the crew, forcing him out of the door and into the sea. How close had they been to *that*? Had Wilko stopped them? Had they stopped themselves?

He carries on. 'But we... We braved it out.' He looks straight at me, but he's talking to himself. 'Yeah, we braved it out. It was like... we came face to face with something terrible. It was like...' He sighs loudly.

'Go on,' I say.

'It was as if the storm *hated* us. The sea too. The wind was screaming. Those things were monsters. Sounds crazy, right?'

'Not to me.'

'And the sun, when that came up, it was this… *thing*. The sun, the sea, the sky. They were alive. Sometimes they were kind, sometimes cruel. You can't imagine it, it was… You don't need to imagine, do you?'

'No.'

We laugh.

'Then a helicopter saw us,' he says, 'and a boat came and got us. But we all know that story, Bill. How the hell did *you* survive? Start at the beginning. Actually… scrap that, skip to the bit about the shark!'

'How d'you know about that?'

'The nurse told me about your foot.'

But I don't know how to begin.

'I'm no hero, I had some help. A lot actually.'

'You had help killing the shark?' Wilko frowns.

I think again of the whales and the turtle we had to kill so we could live. About Gull, and the gifts of fish, coconuts and firewood. And Aya.

'Yeah, I had help all round.'

I know he can keep a secret. I don't feel I'm breaking my promise. So I tell him about Aya.

He listens, *really* listens, right to the end.

'So she's gone back, to her people, to fight this warlord?'

'I don't know. I was found alone, wasn't I? I don't know if she's even alive.'

'Do you know where her people lived, travelled, anything?'

'She didn't tell me much about herself. Only stories.'

'Stories?'

'From *The Arabian Nights*. Except they weren't, really. They were her stories.'

'You mean like fairy stories?'

I smile to myself. 'Yeah, kind of.'

'You know...' He hesitates. 'There's no island,' Wilko says, 'not on any chart I looked at.'

'Makes sense. It didn't feel like a place that could be on any chart.'

'What d'you mean?'

'Not sure I know.'

There's an awkward silence.

'So, the challenge next year?' I say.

'You're kidding, right?'

'Yes.'

We talk a bit more. He asks for details. All the messy, bloody, painful stuff. But I make excuses about not wanting to live through it again.

'I understand. I should go, leave you to rest.'

'Come again,' I say. And I mean it, and I know he knows that; that it's not just a thing to say.

A nurse comes and offers tea.

'Stay,' I say.

'Sure, and you don't have to tell me anything you don't want to.' And I see that he understands, more than Dad or Mum or Dr Jones.

The nurse gives us our tea. I sip mine.

'I think I'll always be there,' I say. 'Always on the boat. I don't know if I'd get off, even if I could.'

The nurse checks her watch.

'I think after your tea our patient might need a bit of rest.'

Wilko looks worried.

'Left part of you on that boat, right?' he says, and gently punches my shoulder. 'Leave it there, mate. It's not like you ever have to go back.'

iv

My foot has healed well enough to try water therapy.

I'm keen. Not just for my strength. Any excuse to get out of bed.

We go to a different part of the hospital. There's a room with a long pool, about a metre wide. It's got handles and a slope leading down into the water at one end.

I'm given trunks to change into and pointed to the changing room. When I emerge Dr Jones is standing with a large block in her hand like a giant TV remote.

'You get in, Bill, and walk, and we'll put the current on, so you'll be walking against a stream of water. It'll make your muscles strong again.'

I do as I'm told. The water is warm and clear.

'Stop there,' Dr Jones says, when I'm a quarter of the way along. She fiddles with the hand-held control. Bubbles froth and erupt from jets.

I breathe fast. The bubbles don't feel good. It's as if

there's something in the water. Something below the surface. I grab the rails and cling to the side.

'Okay?' asks Dr Jones.

'Yeah, it just caught me by surprise,' I mutter. Keeping hold of the rails I start to walk through the white froth. The humming is loud and getting louder. I feel hot and out of it. My breathing becomes heavy.

On the far wall there's a picture of a tropical island with perfect white sands. I focus on that, because for some reason I'm struggling to get through the water. I look at the island. It's my goal and I have to get to it. I'm finding it harder with every step, but it's not the force of the jets. My legs feel like lead. I can't see my feet.

'Out, out!' I'm scrambling, my hands on the rails, pulling myself onto the side, trying to get out as quickly as I can.

Dr Jones rushes to me. I grab her arm and use her to heave myself out, digging my fingers into her shoulder.

'Ouch! Bill. Bill! It's okay, it's okay.'

I look back into the frothing water, scanning the surface for something that's not there. I don't calm down until the machine is turned off and the water is clear.

I have a nightmare.

The body of Stephan is slipping, sliding through

the current. The shell of him, being pulled into the erupting water.

And the awful calm after he's gone. I watch it, waiting for his hand to reach out of the water. But it doesn't.

Then I wake.

It's not even a nightmare. It's a memory.

V

Two days later I'm well enough to leave hospital.

Dad wants to take me to lunch, before we drive home.

I have a shower before we leave. I look in the mirror. Even after all the vitamins and minerals they've pumped through the drips and tubes, and even with all the food I've stuffed down me, I'm still much lighter than when I flew to the Canaries.

What did I look like when they found me? That scares me.

I think back further, to who I was before the storm hit *Pandora*. But I can't recognise the 'me' that stumbled off the plane, squinting, hiding his face from the sun. There's a lot about him I don't even remember.

My skin is dirt brown. Not like a tan, more leathered. The colour of me seems more Moroccan than English. A chunk of my foot is gone. In the mirror I see it fresh for the first time. They've neatly folded the skin over where I once had toes and stitched it together. I'll get new ones soon, plastic ones. My muscles are wire-tight. I've got a patch over one eye. The other burns bright green.

I think of Thiyya and the djinn, and the champions who tried to defeat it. Like those so-called heroes, I've been half-blinded, half-crippled, driven half-mad.

～

The restaurant is nice. Polished black marble floors, white table linen and gleaming glasses.

Built into one wall is an aquarium. I recognise the fish: orange as the sun, blue as the sky. Round and round they go, in and out of a plastic reef. They move slower than in the wild. Here there's no bigger fish to chase them.

People stare at me. I stare back.

'What d'you fancy?' says Dad. 'They've got steaks, posh burgers. I bet you missed those?'

'No thanks.'

'You must be gagging for some decent grub after that hospital nosh.'

I scan the menu. 'I'll have fish. Some prawns.'

Dad tries to make conversation. But he doesn't push too hard, he's sensitive, as though I'm a bomb and he needs help to deactivate me.

A course of giant prawns arrives. Big pink beasts, grilled in oil and garlic. My mouth waters.

I grab one and twist its head off its body, then hold the neck to my mouth and suck the brains and juice out. Then I put the skull in my mouth and chew and suck, till the goodness is out of it, then put it on my plate and start on the body.

I've had two before I notice Dad is staring at me.

'You've, um...' He smiles and taps his chin and raises his eyebrows, to let me know I've got juice dribbling down my chin. Drops of oily juice have spattered over my nice new shirt.

'Oh, er, oops.'

There's a table nearby with a family of four who've been watching me stuff my face. They're halfway through their meal, but they lay their knives and forks neatly across their plates. Waiters appear and clear their food away.

I watch as a grilled fish and an unfinished lobster are dumped onto one plate so it's easy for the waiter to carry.

'Bill,' Dad whispers and prods my leg with his foot. 'You're staring.'

'They should eat that. They should finish it.'

'People eat as much or as little as they want,' he says gently. 'You do remember restaurants?' he teases me.

'Dad, I'm sorry...'

'It's okay, son, it's okay.'

'It's just.' My voice is shaking and my fingers are trembling. 'I don't belong here.' I point at the wall, with the aquarium. 'That's not real, Dad. None of this is real.' I have an urge to pick up a chair and smash it through the glass. And I don't know why. I think what a spoiled, up-himself teenager I must sound like. How mad I must seem. The family at the next table are properly staring at me now. I laugh louder; it stops the family staring too.

Dad reaches out and holds my hand.

'You don't have to apologise for *anything*. You've been through so much. I know you don't want to talk. Not to me, nor Mum, and that's okay. But you could talk to *someone*, when we get home. Er, if you want?' He winces. He's worried how I'll react to the idea.

'Sure. I should see someone. Anyone who came out of that normal would be mad, right?'

He smiles and nods. 'Okay. There's time for that. There's time for everything when you're ready. Catching up with mates. Watching TV. Walking Benji. You can have *any*thing. You can *do* anything. Anything you like...'

He carries on talking, a babble of things I can't understand.

'Bill.' Dad waves his hand in front of my face.

'Yes.'

'You've zoned out. Did you hear what I said?...
Bill?... *Bill!*'

'I can't do those things, Dad. Now I'm out there's
only one thing I'm going to do.'

'Oh, terrific! Like what?'

'I'm going back.'

'Where?'

'Where I was found. I'm going to find her.'

'Who?'

'I wasn't alone out there, Dad. There was this girl,
and if it wasn't for her, I'd be dead.'

He sits open-mouthed. I talk. He listens.

I carry on talking. I tell him everything.

There's a long pause while he absorbs what I've
said.

'You have a life, Bill. In England. I'm not sure you
can just go to Africa, looking for some girl. And this
place where you were found. It's on the edge of quite
a dangerous zone.'

'She saved me, Dad. I have to know she's all right.
I can't just... leave her.'

'But she left you, didn't she? At least that's how it
looks. You were found alone.'

'Yeah. I've thought about it. But it doesn't make
sense. She wouldn't do that.'

'Are you sure?'

I think: *Why did she leave me? Does she want me
to find her? Did we even live in the same story?*

'Yes. Yes. I'm sure,' I say. 'I have to know what happened to her. I have to find her.'

'Really?'

'Yes, really. And she's not "some girl". Her name is Aya.'

vi

'I reckon I can persuade Wilko. He's been there loads of times on surf trips. He told us, when we were on *Pandora*. He knows that part of Morocco well,' I say in the car as we drive home.

'There is no way we would let you go without one of us. We've lost you once, I'm not letting that happen again. And why am I even having this conversation? It's a crazy idea.'

'The village where I was found, I only need to go there. That's miles from any trouble.'

Is that true? I've no idea. I'm easily mixing up lies with the truth.

'And the point of that is what? She's not going to be there, is she? So the chances of you finding her are slim. Bill, it'll be like looking for a needle in a haystack. And even if I said yes, your mum's not going to let you go.'

'I won't tell her straight off, I'll wait a bit, until

I can see and walk better. Reassure her that Wilko knows the place.'

I know I have to go. I reckon Mum will listen. I'll work on it hard, and anyway, I've got my last resort well rehearsed.

I'm sixteen. You can't stop me. Not legally. I've got the money Grandma left me. I'm going.

Turns out I don't need to say those words. Mum doesn't like my plan, but she can read me. She knows me. And she sees how I've changed. Maybe before she might have persuaded me, but not now. And she knows she has to accept it. More than that, she understands, in a way that Dad never could.

I explain to her what we've already been through a dozen times. That Wilko isn't a nutter, that he did all he could to save us.

'Okay,' Mum says. 'You want to know what happened. You want to know where she is now, if she's even alive. Well, your dad would have to go with you, as well as Wilko.'

'Lucy?' Dad says. 'Are you sure?'

'He wants closure, John. Our son won't rest until he knows what's happened. I don't think it's just about the girl either, though that's important. Bill, you want to know what happened to you, don't you?'

'Yes,' I say. And it's true. From the sun demon, to waking up in the hospital. There's a blankness in my mind I want to fill.

I call Wilko. He doesn't hesitate.

'Of course, if your parents are okay with that. I know the place. I speak good French, a bit of Arabic too. But I'm sticking to you like glue! We're not losing you again.'

'Right. That's what Dad said.'

The Road of Bones

i

Wilko does know Morocco, and a large chunk of its coast, but not the place we're going to. The land that far south isn't even Morocco, not officially. It's on the edge of 'disputed territory'.

We have the name of the village where the fisherman lives and the name of the fisherman, Mohamed. But that's all.

We fly into Agadir and stay in a hotel. Wilko and Dad organise a taxi and driver. We leave first thing next morning.

Agadir is smart and modern, not what I expected Morocco to be like. It's all hotels and ice cream joints.

It doesn't seem any more real than the hospital, the restaurant, England.

But the south of the city is different. The buildings

are plain; brown and soft pink walls of concrete and breezeblocks. A lot of them are only part built. Road signs are written in Arabic and English and in Berber too.

The heat and dust get worse as the sun rises.

The taxi is an old Mercedes with leather seats and no air-con. I find I like the heat. It feels good to sweat again. We keep the windows open.

We drive through a long chain of villages. There are men in robes or jeans and caps sitting outside cafés, smoking hookah pipes and sipping tea. The villages feel peaceful, but parts of the road are hectic with revving, horn-blasting cars, a moped with a mum, dad and a kid on it, trucks loaded with fruit, even goats. Some carry gangs of women in colourful dresses. When they clock Wilko, they wave and giggle.

Then we're out of the villages and following the coast, cruising down a black tarmac road. On the left there's scrub and small fields lined by stone walls. In the distance, I can make out mountains through the haze. The heat, the dust, the sea breeze: they mix into something I can breathe.

Huge waves thump the shoreline. We pass fishing villages full of white buildings and sky-blue boats.

The road is straight and endless. Sand blows across it in wisps.

On the right is the sea, brilliant and sparkling.

'It's beautiful,' Dad says. 'How does it feel seeing it again?'

'Strange. Good, I think. It was our home.' But I think of the days of heat and thirst. And I don't know what I feel about it.

There's scrub and sand and fishing villages. For miles and hours. Then huge dunes. Hills and mountains of sand. Parts of the road are covered and the car struggles.

The tarmac ends in the afternoon and we travel on a rougher, older road.

The driver complains, but Wilko and Dad urge him to carry on.

Then we hit a roadblock. A small hut with two policemen and one army guy with a rifle hanging over his shoulder.

The driver gets out to smoke and talk with the police. He focuses on the taller one with a massive moustache. He gets lively, swinging his cigarette around and talking loudly. Dad has offered him a lot of money if he can get us to the village where the fisherman found me.

One of the policemen raises a hand and shakes his head. The driver lowers his voice and steps back.

Dad sits with me in the back, fanning his face, sighing, and shifting in his seat.

'I'll talk to him,' he says.

'No,' Wilko says. 'Better if I do. They likely won't speak much English. But they'll speak French.'

Wilko gets out to talk to the one in charge, the one with the moustache.

After a minute the other one comes to the car, takes off his cap, leans over and sticks his head inside the open window.

He wags a white-gloved finger. 'No here,' says the policeman. 'No tourist here.' He looks at my crutch and foot.

'We have to go further,' I say.

'No. It… is.' He struggles to find the words. 'Er, many problems. This.' He points south. Then: 'English?'

'English.'

The policeman grins. 'Ah, I have friend English. He live Ports-a-mouth. You haff been Ports-a-mouth?'

It seems so weird, him suddenly chatting to us like this.

'You holiday Sidi-Ifni? Agadir?'

'Yes,' Dad says.

'Why here? No tourist here. Understand?'

The other policeman walks up. They talk. They sound lively, excited. The head appears again.

'You is boy!' he squeals. 'Boy in boat?'

Wilko gets in the car.

Both of the policemen stick their white-gloved hands inside for us to shake.

'They'll take us to the village,' says Wilko.

We follow their car for an hour. We leave the main road, following tracks that criss-cross the countryside, moving away from the sea, then close, then away again, snaking a path down the coast.

I don't know why they are doing this. Wilko says he isn't paying them. But they're taking us. Out of kindness, or curiosity, for our safety, or simply so we don't get lost. Maybe all those things. All we have is the name of the village. We're lucky to have their help.

The village is a bunch of square whitewashed blocks, some with corrugated iron sheets for roofs. Plastic bags blow across the dirt track. Tins and cigarette butts are scattered over the ground.

Two skinny, barking dogs follow the car as we bump along the track.

There's a small shining mosque with elegant curved turrets and arches. A shop with a table outside it, loaded with bananas and breads. But the place is like a ghost town.

We stop when we reach the sea. There are at least a dozen boats at the shore, painted yellow and blue, stacked with piles of nets and pots. There's a natural harbour, a finger of rock that shelters the bay; the waves on the other side of it are booming. Where is everyone?

But then they appear. Men in robes. Others more western style with caps, vests and shorts. Lots of them are smoking. There's a couple of women and a gaggle of scruffy children.

The adults stare and stare. Not smiling or friendly. But the kids point and laugh, talking loudly. They ask for pens, and weirdly, because he must have known we'd be asked, Wilko has a handful of them in his bag. The kids are thrilled.

I get out of the taxi with some help and stand, leaning on my crutch.

'Salam,' I say, remembering words Aya taught me. 'Manzakine. Neck ghih Bill.'

There's a lot of talk. The villagers ask the police lots of questions.

We're beckoned to a café, and sit in the gloom at a plastic table.

Women appear with a tray of small glasses and a tall metal, curved pot. A man pours mint tea. Then he pours all the tea back into the pot. He repeats this three times before we are allowed to drink. It's hot and sweet and singing with the taste of mint.

We're given flat breads and doughnuts. We're made a fuss of by the rapidly growing crowd. Half the village seems to be in the café, the other half are standing outside. Dogs are lying in the open door.

There's a commotion outside.

A man says: 'The man who find you. He is coming.'

The crowd parts, making space, and the man who

saved my life walks through the door and to the table. He is wire-thin, creased face, crooked teeth and big, kind eyes. We shake hands. I've never met him, but of course he's met me.

I don't think I can say 'thank you' without choking up. He speaks to the police, then to me. He laughs, and all the Moroccans laugh with him. The policeman with the huge moustache translates.

'He is name Mohamed. He say is very please to see you. He say when they take you Agadir he is thinking you die! He is please when he see in news you live.'

'Can you ask him what happened?'

Mohamed sits at the table, takes a cigarette from his pocket and lights it.

The crowd leans in. This annoys the policemen who shoos them away.

One policeman, Wilko, Dad, Mohamed and me are left.

I'm hardly breathing. I'm dizzy. I want to know, but I'm scared. Because the whole drive down here I've feared the words. I've imagined them.

The girl was dead.

Mohamed talks for about a minute. Moustache-man nods, then holds a hand up to stop him.

'He saw boat near some island, but island under water, you understand? Far out many miles.'

'A reef?' Wilko offers.

'He go to see trap for lobster. He sees boat in distance. He find you and believe you dead—'

'*What* did he find?' I almost shout.

'What you mean?'

'What, *exactly*, did he find?'

The fisherman speaks directly to me. The policeman speaks.

'He find boat and he find you. Is all.'

I crash. I'm falling through the chair. I'm drowning. It's not possible.

'Did you see *anything* else, Mohamed? Out there. Anything.'

'You all right, Bill?' Dad says. He puts his arm round me, but I push it away and put my head in my hands.

They're staring at me as if I'm a freak. I've knocked my glass of tea over, spilling it across the table. A woman is mopping it up.

Wilko puts a hand on my other shoulder.

'You don't understand,' I say to Mohamed. 'Was there anything. Any*one*?'

The policeman speaks for Mohamed. 'He say you want answers. He knows this. He say he show you boat. Maybe the boat give you answer. After all...' He pauses, Mohamed speaks slowly, softly. When the policeman turns to translate, he is puzzled.

Mohamed smiles, raises his eyebrows in a tiny, quick gesture and gives me a quick nod. It's a signal, just for me.

'Mohamed, he say the angel has secrets? He say you know what this mean.'

Then Mohamed says, '*Tanirt*... hass... see-crett.'

ii

The boat is in a small shed.

Now it's Mohamed and me. Wilko and Dad stay with the police.

The boat is on its side. It's smaller somehow. No broken mast, no coconuts. It's only my writing on the side that tells me it's *Tanirt*.

I smile and say in my mind: *Thank you for getting us home.*

'I use boat. Little fishing.' Mohamed looks apologetic.

'You speak English?' I say.

'Little,' he replies.

Mohamed peers out of the door, to check we're alone. He speaks in slow and broken-up words.

'Girl. Say keep secret.'

I take a breath. 'Is she alive?'

Mohamed smiles and nods.

Waves of joy. I hug him. I feel the weight lift.

He lets out a croaky laugh and kisses both my cheeks.

'Where is she?'

He shrugs. 'Aya go. Many days.' He points outside, waving his hand.

'Far?'

'Yes.' He nods. 'Far.'

I make my way to the boat. Stripped of all we had in it, it's hard to see where a secret might be hidden. I turn to Mohamed and shrug.

He points to the hold, jabbing his finger. Whatever has passed between Mohamed and Aya, I know one thing: she trusts him.

I hobble over to the boat, climb over the gunnel and kneel – it sends an arrow of pain to my foot – and I sidle up to the aft. I take a breath and open the hold, leaning down and peering inside. It's empty.

I look at Mohamed again. He stares back at me.

I focus my attention on the hold and instead of looking I feel inside. The edges and the corners inside are smooth, but there's a line; a tiny gap between the wall and the ceiling of the small space.

'Mohamed, do you have a knife?' I mime cutting.

He finds one. The blade slips into the crack, and the wall of the hold eases open.

The notebook is there, and a wrapped package made of pages that have been torn out and written on. I carefully unfold the paper.

Inside are two tiny diamonds. Even in the thin light of the boat shed they shine like stars. Morning and evening.

And there's something else.

It's the size of a little fingernail, curved like a fin, with jagged edges, like a saw. A shark's tooth.

On the paper she has written, in curving lines and dots and sweeps of ink, her own language.

It's as if the paper is her, with me now. As if she's speaking in her own voice. But the writing is Berber and I don't know what she's telling me.

～

The police leave. The taxi too.

We stay, because I insist. We eat tagine in the café. We're given beds in Mohamed's house.

Dad thanks Mohamed and his wife for the hospitality, but all I can think about is what Aya has written.

We sit on Mohamed's terrace, overlooking the sea.

There is a plan. Mohamed speaks French. He's going to translate the Berber for Wilko, who's then going to put the words into English.

But before that, before I see her words to me, I want to know what happened. It's strange, but I have to build myself up to reading her letter. I have to put myself back in our world.

Mohamed tells Wilko in French (which he seems to speak well) and Wilko tells me.

I don't remember word for word, I make lines between the stars. But more or less, this is the story.

The Fisherman

Mohamed set off alone before the sun came up.

The boat was old. It would last weeks, but not months. He didn't have money for another one. He needed luck. He needed many fish and soon, or else the boat *must* last for months. And that was a different kind of luck.

He prayed for his nets to be full.

He knew what the sea could give, but how it could give nothing too. And how it could take. How it had taken his father, who had set off in the wind and the waves when no one else would. And not because he was brave, but because he had no choice. And his father died that day. Mohamed did not want this to be his fate too.

Mohamed thanked Allah that at least the storm had not yet started. There'd be days of waves and winds like the last one, some weeks before. Worse maybe. But not yet.

Now he had been able to set his pots, on the reef that only few fishermen visited. Many miles from the shore. If the engine failed, or the leaks got worse, it would be his end. The risk was great, but when the sea gave, it gave him a lot. And there would be no fishing when the storm came, so he had to make money now.

After some hours, when he reached the reef, he found his pots were empty. He cursed them, and himself for hoping. And thought to ask Allah, why he would tease Mohamed in this way. But he didn't. What would be the point? What could he do now? Set the traps again. Go home and return when the weather was good.

He saw the speck like a grain of sand in the distance. He thought it was probably an old barrel. He thought of going to see, but that would waste fuel. He sat a while, smoking a cigarette.

He saw a bird, high above. And frowned, because this one was alone and a long way from land.

The bird swooped and landed on the engine. The gull crawked at him.

Often birds followed him, diving for scraps and small fish thrown away. But they rarely landed on the boat. This one was brave.

'No fish today, bird. No lobster. Not for me, not for you and...'

It had something tied to its leg. A piece of cloth.

The bird flew up and away, circled and came back, and perched on the bow. It crawked again.

This was why it was on the boat. The thing couldn't fly properly with this piece of rubbish tied to it. Now it was close again he saw how scraggly the bird was, how thin.

Mohamed thought to cut it free but he knew how vicious birds could be. It would peck him if he got near. But the bird didn't fly away, and when he moved closer it stayed put. It turned its head to see him better.

He opened his bait pot and gave it a scrap. Then another. And another. He made a small pile for it on the back of the boat. As the bird ate, Mohamed – as quick as he could – grabbed its leg and nicked the cloth, freeing the bird. It pecked him, but not hard and only once, and stood with its head cocked, staring at him.

The cloth had been *tied* to the bird. Someone had done this. But why?

It was a ripped piece of a t-shirt. A European t-shirt like the surf tourists wore, with foreign writing and a cartoon of a duck.

Mohamed looked at the t-shirt and at the dot in the distance. He was such a long way offshore. The bird must have come from the dot.

Then he remembered the stories of the boats that had sunk in the storm some weeks before. A storm that had come from nowhere. A storm so sudden some had said it was the work of a demon, like the old stories.

People had talked of a missing boy. A European boy.

Perhaps this was from the wreck of one of the boats? Maybe something with value, or use…

Mohamed made a guess of the time and how far he had come. He did not know if he had enough fuel. Probably, but not definitely. And a storm was coming. It made sense to go home.

But there was the t-shirt. And the bird. And the dot like a grain of sand. He squinted. It was a long way off, hard to see, but could it even be a boat?

He started the engine. He'd go a bit further till he could see what it was, then turn around.

As he got closer he saw the dot *was* a boat. It was no fisherman's boat, it was small and modern. But it had a kind of mast and a torn sail made from tarpaulin. And as he approached, he saw; there was a small carved figurehead. And a word, painted on the side, in writing like that of a child. It was Berber writing.

Tanirt. Angel.

Again he thought about the boats that had sunk in the storm.

'Small boats do not float about on the ocean by themselves, for no reason,' he said. He called out: 'Salam. Is anyone there?' But there was no reply.

As he got near, he caught the smell. Now he was afraid of what he might find in the boat. The stench was rotten and sick. The smell of death.

He began to turn the boat. He didn't want to see. It was best to go home.

But the bird crawked and flew to the other boat and sat on the prow.

'Come, bird,' he said. 'If you do not come with me, you will have to stay, and maybe die.'

The bird crawked and stared and stared and crawked. Mohamed considered the bird a while and knew in his heart if he didn't see inside the boat he would remember the look the bird gave him forever. Which was crazy, because it was just a bird.

'Okay, bird. Okay.'

Mohamed slowly drew his boat up to the other. But before he looked, he took off his shirt to cover his mouth and nose.

The girl was not much more than bones. The boy too. And his leg, his foot. Mohamed fought the urge to be sick.

There was dried blood all over the hull. And other mess.

How long had they been dead?

But the girl opened an eye and raised a bone-hand. 'Aman,' she whispered.

Mohamed gave her water.

She took the bottle and drank a little. Then, with

an effort that seemed almost impossible, she raised herself up.

He tried to help.

'No,' she said. She knelt by the boy, she lifted his head and poured a little water into his mouth. His lips hardly parted, but his throat moved and some of the water went down.

The boy's eyes opened. But he didn't see. Mohamed gave the girl his fish and couscous. The girl ate some, chewing slowly and carefully. But she did not swallow the food. She leaned over the boy again and put her mouth to his. She held his jaw with her hand and squeezed, so the boy *had* to open his mouth. In this way she fed him, and with a little more water, he swallowed.

Mohamed was shocked to see this. A girl and a European boy. Like this!

He would never forget how the girl looked at the boy. How she had stroked her hands through his hair. And the words she whispered.

'Live. Long life. Live. Do not die. Live. I beg you.'

With her fingers she picked up more of the grains of couscous and took another mouthful, which she also fed to the boy.

Between each mouthful she put drops of water on his lips.

She fed him again and again. She did not take any food herself.

Mohamed almost cried to see this. This kiss of life. The will that made her do these things. A spirit stronger than her own body. Stronger than the boy.

But it made him sad too. Because he knew it was too late, that the boy would soon be dead.

When the food was gone, he said they should move the boy into his boat and go to land. But the girl said: 'We can't move him. And we can't leave our boat. We will not leave *Tanirt*. You must tow us.'

'You are stubborn,' he said.

But the girl wouldn't change her mind.

As they travelled, he looked behind him from time to time. The whole journey home, she cradled the boy's head, and whispered to him, and kissed his head. The bird sat on the prow.

It was slow. They made land as the gold of the day was sinking in the sea.

As they drew closer to the shore the girl said she would give Mohamed jewels, but he must not tell anyone about her. She said he had to swear it.

He did not believe her about the jewels. But she said she would show him.

When they came in, he quickly took her to the boatshed.

He had to half carry her. She stumbled and fell, all the time looking back at the boat. Then Mohamed cried and shouted for help. Men came. They carried the boy to a car. They would go to the road and the police, and then the boy would be taken to hospital. But it was many miles and Mohamed believed the boy would die before they reached a doctor. He didn't say this to the girl when he returned to the boatshed.

She gave him the jewel and thanked him and asked that he give her refuge.

He didn't know what to make of this strange girl. But she had given him a jewel worth a year of fishing. More. And she promised him another if he sheltered her.

So he hid her, in the boatshed. He brought her bread and milk. And fish for the bird.

He made sure she ate slowly. Little and often. Over the days he brought her cheese, eggs, tagine, nuts, fish. She ate it all.

The police came, and so did the newspaper and the radiomen from the city. The boy lived, and he was news. Mohamed was asked a lot of questions, and he didn't like it, and he didn't enjoy being at the centre of this whirlpool. But he was pleased about the jewel and he kept his promise to the girl.

He brought her food and clothes and every day she grew a little stronger.

She made him make more promises. He could only ever tell the boy about her if he returned. And she gave Mohamed the message.

Tanirt *has secrets.*

One morning he came with bread and eggs. The
girl and the bird were gone.

iii

'Where?' I ask.

Mohamed points to the east. He speaks in French, Wilko translates.

'Down the road of bones. To fight the Lord of the Sun.'

The warlord. Who stole the jewels. Who she stole the jewels *from*. Mohamed explains he's named after a character in some old legend.

And it makes sense. In my heart I already knew it.

'Sahit,' I say to Mohamed. Thank you.

Mohamed speaks to Wilko in French.

He says: 'Now we need to translate the words, and…' He looks out to sea.

'What?' I say.

'Well, he says he's sorry, that he and I have to read the words. He says they're private, they're meant for you.'

And what will it say? I think. *Will it tell me where you are, Aya? A map to find you?*

'It's okay,' I say. While they work I walk – hobble – to the sea, with Dad helping. The wind has died and there's a path of moonlight stretching to the horizon.

'You okay, son?'

'Yes. Because whatever is in that letter, I know she's alive. That she's out there, somewhere.'

When I get back, Wilko hands me the book, opened to where he has written the contents of the letter in English.

Dad and Wilko and Mohamed leave me alone, with a hurricane lamp to read by.

Aya speaks to me. And now I don't need to remember her stories or make my own lines between the stars because I have her words.

And before I even start to read I know I'll find her. One day.

I know that she has gone where it is impossible for me to follow and I know, as well as I know Aya, that she is going to *tell* me that it is impossible, in her own words. But I swear it to myself.

I think you will like my gifts.

One diamond is for Mohamed. One is for you. The shark tooth, also for you of course. I took it from your foot, while you lay in the boat, screaming at the sun.

You have found Tanirt, you have found this and I think you will know the story of how we came to land.

Before this was a great confusion of days. We were so near to death. Not only you, both of us. I could feel it, cold and waiting, all around us.

Many times I believed you were dead. You had spoken words of the mad, for days. And then words of things only the dying see.

And then – worse – you spoke no words at all. And though your eyes were open, you did not see.

In the end I had to fight you to even take a little water.

And I believed you were going to die. I knew it. And it broke my heart.

I knew I would follow you soon. Maybe an hour or a day but it would come. And I was more afraid then than I have ever been. Not of death. I was afraid, because I did not want to die alone. You see? I did not want to die alone.

I saw a bird, high above, and this meant that we were close to land. But still I did not hope. Until I saw the boat, and Gull, our friend, flew to the boat and Mohamed found us. Then you were taken from me. And this was hard too. Almost as hard as though death took you from me.

I know you are in England, alive. And this gives me great strength.

I must go now, down the road of bones, to fight the Lord of the Sun.

No one believes I will return. No one knows I am alive. And the Lord of the Sun, he is weak.

'A warlord, weak?' you will ask.

Yes, I will say. As the king knew only after one thousand and one nights, a man with no love in his heart is weak. I will come, a shadow in shadows. That is my story and I will write it.

And so what now? What is the end of our story? The story of the girl and the boy and the sea.

Do you think I know?

My uncle once told me that everyone who listens to a story wants answers, they want a happy end, and they want the answers to all the questions. But he told me, you must have questions. Always. With any story. I think it is true.

Not all is explained. Not everything is told.

So, you see, Bill, I do not know the end of our story. Not yet.

I know Thiyya has defeated the djinn, Lunja has tricked the sultan, Shahrazad and Dinarzade are safe. The girl and the boy have crossed the sea. The adventure is over.

But us?

I do not know if I will ever see you again. I do not know what is waiting for me along the road of bones.

I know the powers that make our worlds are strong like djinns. These same djinns also build the walls that keep us apart.

But remember when we were together, on the sea. Think of me sometimes, when you are home, in England, safe.

And this I know.

We lived in a country with no borders. We slept in a house with no walls. We said our prayers, at an altar that was not built with hands.

And I know, too, that I love you.

Aya

Acknowledgements

When I started writing, I naively believed the words on the page were the result of a gargantuan solo effort. There's a lot of work for the writer, but a book is also shaped by the wisdom and advice of others. Sometimes it takes others to see clearly what you can't see yourself.

So thanks are due to:

Catherine and the team at Felicity Bryan Associates, not only for agent-y magic, but sage advice on early drafts.

Lauren, Fiona and Alex at Zephyr, for invaluable input, wonderful editing and proper care and attention to the story.

I'm not sure you can 'thank' a place or a people, but I have to acknowledge the Amazigh and the country of Southern Morocco. I've visited many times – initially for the surf, but it was on later trips when we explored the villages north and south of Agadir, that we got to know some Amazigh, and to learn a little of their culture and history. On market day in the village of Tamraght, we saw an ancient, toothless man. He was shouting, gesticulating wildly and punctuating his speech with loud claps and a crowd quickly gathered around him. He was the storyteller. I didn't understand a word, but I sat and listened, mesmerised all the same. Storytelling is a living tradition in Morocco, and as you will have seen, its riches are a big part of Aya's story and of this book.

I'd also like to thank Isabella and our dear friends, the Norths. Bels loved an earlier book of mine, *Kook,* and tried to persuade me that I should write an alternative final chapter. I considered it, but decided I couldn't. Stories are what they are. But I *did* think: what if… And it was that idea that eventually became *Girl. Boy. Sea.*

Thanks as ever to the team at the Bath Spa MA in Writing for Young People, to the friends I made there, and to the whole community, of which I am a part.

Finally, of course, my family. I hearsay writers aren't easy to live with when they are deep into crafting a book, and I'm sure I'm no exception. So thanks for generosity with tea, love and kindness and for looking after me. Sarah, Lamorna, Toffee beast, I love you all.

Chris Vick
Wiltshire, May 2019

About the Author

Chris Vick is a graduate of the Bath Spa MA in Writing for Young People. He splits his time between writing, teaching, and working in marine conservation. He lives near Bath with his wife and daughter.